PLAGUE OF THE MANITOU

A Selection of Recent Titles by Graham Masterton available from Severn House

The Sissy Sawyer Series

TOUCHY AND FEELY
THE PAINTED MAN
THE RED HOTEL

The Jim Rook Series

DEMON'S DOOR
GARDEN OF EVIL

The Harry Erskine Series

MANITOU BLOOD
BLIND PANIC
PLAGUE OF THE MANITOU

The Night Warriors Series

THE NINTH NIGHTMARE

Anthologies

FESTIVAL OF FEAR
FIGURES OF FEAR

Novels

BASILISK
FIRE SPIRIT
PETRIFIED
COMMUNITY
FOREST GHOST
DROUGHT

PLAGUE OF THE MANITOU

Graham Masterton

Severn House Large Print
London & New York

This first large print edition published 2015
in Great Britain and the USA by
SEVERN HOUSE PUBLISHERS LTD of
19 Cedar Road, Sutton, Surrey, England, SM2 5DA.
First world regular print edition published 2015 by
Severn House Publishers Ltd., London and New York.

British Library Cataloguing in Publication Data

Masterton, Graham author.
　Plague of the Manitou.
　1. Erskine, Harry (Fictitious character)–Fiction.
　2. Fortune-tellers–Florida–Miami–Fiction. 3. Virus
　diseases–Fiction. 4. Horror tales. 5. Large type books.
　I. Title
　823.9'2-dc23

ISBN-13: 9780727870681

Severn House Publishers support the Forest Stewardship Council™
[FSC™], the leading international forest certification organisation. All
our titles that are printed on FSC certified paper carry the FSC logo.

Typeset by Palimpsest Book Production Ltd.,
Falkirk, Stirlingshire, Scotland.
Printed and bound in Great Britain by
T J International, Padstow, Cornwall.

'My convictions on this subject have been confirmed. That those tribes cannot exist surrounded by our settlements and in continual contact with our citizens is certain. They have neither the intelligence, the industry, the moral habits, nor the desire of any improvement which are essential to any favorable change in their condition. Established in the midst of another and a superior, and without appreciating the causes of their inferiority or seeking to control them, they must necessarily yield to the force of circumstances and ere long disappear.'

President Andrew Jackson, addressing Congress in 1833.

The new Bugs Without Borders Survey conducted by the National Pest Management Association (NPMA) and the University of Kentucky found that bed bug infestations in the United States continue at a high rate. The survey of US pest management professionals found that 99.6 percent of respondents encountered bed bug infestations in the past year and that infestations have increased in the majority of locations in which pest professionals typically treat for bed bugs.

Pestworld.org, 2013

One

Anna had heard men scream before, but never like this – a strangulated screech that went on and on for over ten seconds before it finally ended in a throaty gargle of despair. It sounded more like a dog being crushed inch by inch under a roadroller than a man in pain.

She lifted her head away from her Raman microscope and listened. She heard shouting and banging in the corridor outside the laboratory – then a complicated pattering of footsteps and the whirr of a gurney being propelled very fast along the polished vinyl floor.

The man screamed again as the gurney passed the laboratory door, and this time Anna could hear what he was screaming. *'Get it out of me! Get it out of me!'*

Another man's voice said, 'Jesus!'

She stood up, walked quickly across to the door and opened it. She was just in time to see the nurse and two hospital orderlies hurrying toward the elevators, rolling the gurney between them. The man who was lying on it was flailing his arms and jolting up and down as if he were being electrocuted. At the same time he was vomiting fountains of blood. It had drenched the front of his blue checkered shirt and spattered the nurse and the orderlies. It had even sprayed up the walls.

1

After they'd turned the corner at the end of the corridor, the man let out only one more scream, but Anna could hear the continuous clattering and creaking of the gurney as he kept on jolting up and down. Eventually, she heard the elevator chime, and then there was silence.

She stood in the laboratory doorway for a few moments, feeling both disturbed and puzzled. She had seen scores of patients hemorrhage before, and just as many suffering from violent seizures, but she couldn't remember seeing a patient convulsing so violently while vomiting up so much arterial blood, and screaming at the same time.

She was about to go back into her laboratory when a man suddenly appeared around the corner. He stopped and came no nearer, but stayed at the far end of the corridor, staring at her.

He had cropped gray hair and a neat gray beard. His face was ashy-pale, and his eyes were deep-sunk, with charcoal-dark circles around them. He was wearing a gray knee-length coat with a Nehru collar and buttons all the way down the front, and altogether he was so colorless that he could have stepped out of a black-and-white photograph. He continued to stare at Anna as if he were trying to commit her face to memory. At first he looked thoughtful, but then, gradually, he began to grin at her, until he was baring his teeth. His lips were moving, although he was too far away for her to be able to hear if he was actually saying anything.

By the expression on his face, however, she felt that he was mouthing something lecherous

2

like: *I could have you, lady, any time I felt like it.* As if to emphasize what she had imagined him to say, he licked his lips with the tip of his tongue.

Anna didn't recognize him as one of the Saint Louis University hospital faculty, and she was about to call out, '*Excuse me, sir!*' when he took a single step back and disappeared from sight.

She didn't go after him. Hospital security wasn't her problem, after all. But she was still standing there wondering who he might have been when her lab assistant Epiphany came click-clacking along the corridor carrying two Styrofoam cups of coffee. Epiphany was looking down with horror at the bloody footprints and wheel marks on the floor, and when she reached the doorway she said, 'Holy *moley*, Anna! What in the name of *heck* . . .?'

'I know. They just wheeled a patient past here, and he was bringing up blood by the bucketful. Convulsing, too, even worse than epilepsy. I mean, my God, he was bouncing up and down like he was on a trampoline.'

Epiphany held up the two cups of coffee. 'Here. Sorry. They didn't have no pecan sandies left. I didn't know what you'd like instead.'

'That's OK, Epiphany. I don't think I have too much of an appetite now.'

They went back into the laboratory, although Anna didn't return to her work immediately. She felt unaccountably tense, as if the blood-spattering chariot-race that had just rushed past her door was only a portent of something much worse to come. It wasn't unusual for her to feel

3

like that. It was her job to be alarmist, after all. But the way that patient had been convulsing had triggered a memory of something she'd read about unusually violent seizures a long time ago, or something that some lecturer or some specialist had told her – especially since he had been shouting: *'Get it out of me!'* It irritated her that she couldn't remember what it was.

She had also been unsettled by the man in gray who had grinned at her so suggestively. What had *he* been doing there? And why had he been looking so pleased with himself?

'Are you OK?' Epiphany asked her, looking up from her laptop. 'We have another nine batches of tests to run, don't we?'

'Sure. Yes. I don't know. No, I'm not OK. That – that's upset me.'

'Hey, come on,' said Epiphany, standing up. She came across to Anna and laid a hand on her shoulder. Both women were tall, but Epiphany was an inch or two taller, with cornrows decorated with multicolored beads. Anna had short-cropped, silver-blonde hair and high cheekbones, and she was very thin. Her mother had always said that she ought to have been a fashion model, but her father, Edward Grey, was a highly respected biochemist and she had never wanted to do anything else but follow him into medical science.

Her partner David had once told her, 'That's why I love you so much, Anna. You have Jonas Salk's brain in Heidi Klum's body.'

'I'll be fine,' she told Epiphany. 'Just give me a moment.'

'Maybe you'd feel better if you went up to

4

surgery to see how the guy's getting along,' Epiphany suggested. 'They must have been taking him into theater if he was barfing up blood like that.'

'No, no. We need to start these tests right away. We're running behind time as it is. We don't want to see any more kids going down with this bug.'

Two days ago, Anna had been sent blood samples from twenty-seven children at Meramac Elementary School in Clayton after they had been struck without warning by a devastating illness. Five- and six-year-olds had been collapsing in the classrooms and the playground with acute flu-like symptoms – weakness, shivering, projectile vomiting and explosive diarrhea. The school had temporarily been closed until Anna and her team could determine what kind of virus was causing it and come up with some effective treatment. At the moment, all of the affected children were being kept in isolation at Saint Louis Children's Hospital.

'You're *sure* you're OK?' Epiphany repeated.

'Please, Epiphany. I'm sure I'm sure. Let's just get back to this virus. The more tests I've been running, the more it looks like some kind of avian flu mutation, like H5N1, but it's much more virulent than H5N1.'

'Well, it sure *looks* like bird flu, don't it?' said Epiphany. 'It has pretty much the same symptoms as bird flu, too – even though it spreads about ten times faster and its symptoms are about ten times worse.'

Anna sipped her latte, which was still too hot,

and then nodded in agreement. 'It hasn't responded to any of the usual antivirals, either. I've tried oseltamivir and zanamivir, but neither of those could stop it from escaping from its host cell. It replicates like rabbits on fire.'

'Excuse me?' said Epiphany. '"Rabbits on fire"?'

'Well, you know what I mean. Rabbits on speed. Rabbits on Viagra. Rabbits behaving like rabbits. I'm too tired to be logical.'

She paused again. She still couldn't erase the image of that gray bearded man – the way his lubricious grin had widened slowly across his face, as if it were being spread by a warm knife. There was no question in her mind that he had said something, and she wished that she could lip-read because in her mind's eye she could still clearly see his lips moving, like watching a video loop, over and over again.

She took another sip of her latte, and then she lifted her surgical mask over her nose and mouth and sat down again in front of her microscope. When she adjusted the focus, the virus sample that had been taken from a critically ill five-year-old boy came sharply into view – clusters of bright green globules with sharp spines projecting from them, bobbing around like sea urchins.

As she started to take a series of 3-D images, her cellphone rang.

'Anna?' said a clipped voice. It was Jim Waso, the CEO. 'How's it going with the Meramac Elementary School virus samples?'

'Very slow, sir,' she told him. 'In my opinion it's almost certainly a variant of H5N1, but it's highly complex. It's *strongly* resistant to any of the antivirals I've used. I have a plan, though. I'm about to try tyranivir. I don't think tyranivir is going to destroy it, but it could make it show its hand, if you get my meaning.'

'OK,' said Jim Waso. 'But I'm sorry to tell you that I had a call five minutes ago from the Children's Hospital. A six-year-old girl passed away about a half-hour ago – Deborah-Jane Crusoe, for your records. Respiratory failure. A five-year-old boy is so critical that they don't believe he can survive the night.'

'I'm doing everything I can here, Jim, believe me. Doctor Ahmet and Doctor Kelly will both be coming in later to give me some more back-up, and the NCIRD have just sent me all the latest updates on H5N1 variants – especially that outbreak they had last month in San Bernardino.'

'Anna – I don't have to tell you how critical this is. I have to make a media statement in twenty minutes, and I need to tell them something posi-tive. We have a reputation to uphold here at SLU, and quite apart from that we don't want to kick off some kind of city-wide panic.'

'Like I say, Jim, I'm doing everything I can. By the way – before you hang up – an emergency patient was brought past my lab about ten minutes ago. He was convulsing and bringing up copious quantities of blood. Do you know anything about that?'

'Nobody's reported anything to me yet. I'll have Gerda look into it, if you like. Any special reason?'

'I'm not sure,' said Anna. 'His symptoms were

very unusual, that's all. You know me. Always on the lookout for some condition that's out of the ordinary.'

'That's almost a condition in itself, professor, if you don't mind my saying so.'

There was a pause between them before they hung up. Even though he always spoke to her so sharply, Anna had sensed for quite a few months that Jim Waso found her attractive. Maybe that was *why* he spoke to her so sharply, to conceal how he felt. She would have found *him* attractive, too, if she hadn't already been committed to David.

She heard a clatter outside in the corridor and a woman singing some Rihanna song off-key: '*You're beautiful, like diamonds in the sky . . .*' It sounded as if the cleaning crew were mopping up the blood already. She pulled up her surgical mask, ready to return to her microscope, but as she did so, she caught a flicker of movement in the corner of her eye. She turned toward the door just in time to see the gray-bearded man staring in at her through the porthole window. At once, he vanished.

Anna went across to the door and opened it. Outside, two cleaners with yellow plastic buckets and a mobile cleaning trolley were sponging off the last streaks and speckles of blood from the walls and mopping the floor with EnvirOx.

Anna looked in both directions, but the man in gray was nowhere to be seen. Either she had imagined him looking in through the window, or he was a very fast walker.

'Did either of you see a man standing here a

moment ago?' she asked one of the cleaners. 'Gray hair, gray coat, bearded?'

'Ain't seen nobody, ma'am. Sorry. Did you see somebody, Shirelle?'

'Not a soul, honey. But then I ain't got my new eyeglasses yet. I can't see squat.'

Anna slowly closed the lab door. As she crossed back to her workstation, her phone warbled again. This time it was Bernie Fishman, deputy head of surgery. His voice was a deep, rich baritone, as if at any moment he was going to start singing *Nessun Dorma*.

'Anna, I wonder if you could spare us a moment? I understand from Jim Waso that you were showing an interest in one of our latest admissions.'

'You mean the guy who was bringing up blood and convulsing?'

'That's the very one.'

'How is he? Have you managed to control his seizures? How about the hemorrhage?'

'He didn't make it, Anna. He passed away about ten minutes ago. But why don't you come take a look at him? To tell you the truth, I'd really value your opinion.'

'I'm up to my ears here, Bernie.'

'I know that. But it won't take you more than five or ten minutes. And you should see him for yourself. He's deceased, but to look at him, you'd think that he still has the Devil breathing down his neck.'

Two

Bernie Fishman was waiting for her when she stepped out of the elevator on the second floor, the emergency department. Not only did he sound like a baritone, he also looked like a baritone, with a round face and double chin and a bald suntanned crown with a halo of wild black hair around it. His chest was deep, but his legs were short, and he walked very nimbly, as if he were strutting across the stage at La Scala.

'Anna,' he greeted her. 'How are you, beautiful lady? I haven't seen you for ever.'

'You saw me last Wednesday, Bernie, at the Stroke Network fund-raiser. You bought me a glass of Prosecco.'

'Yes, *feh*! But it was much too crowded. We couldn't talk together *tête-à-tête*.'

'Bernie, your *tête* is at least six inches lower than my *tête*. We can *never* talk *tête-à-tête*.'

'God, you're so cruel to me.'

They walked along the corridor to the emergency surgery theaters. Bernie pushed open the door of Recovery Room Three and said, 'Here's our boy.'

In the center of the room stood a gurney covered with a pale-green sheet. The door swung shut behind them, and when it did the room was utterly silent, smelling faintly of disinfectant and cinnamon, like stale incense. Bernie went over

10

to the cupboards on the left-hand side and handed Anna a mask.

'The patient's name is John Patrick Bridges. He admitted himself to the ER at ten oh-five complaining of a blinding headache and nausea. He was sitting in the waiting room when without warning he started to shout and scream. He dropped on to the floor in a fit, frothing at the mouth, and then he started to hemorrhage.'

'I saw him when they wheeled him past my lab,' said Anna. 'I just couldn't believe those convulsions.'

'Well, right. Even after he was anesthetized, we had to strap him to the operating table to immobilize him, and that took three of us.'

'What about the bleeding?'

'We tried to stop it, but it was coming from everywhere, like every blood vessel in his esophagus and his stomach had burst. He was losing blood faster than we could pump it into him, and in the end he was over three liters down and there was nothing we could do to save him. We're going to carry out a full autopsy, of course, but I thought you'd be interested because he was showing symptoms of some infection. In particular, his body temperature was way up – his last anal reading before he passed away was forty point three degrees.'

'Jesus. He was practically broiling himself alive.'

Bernie circled around the gurney, took hold of the sheet and started to lift it. 'Are you ready for this?' he asked her.

Anna shrugged. 'I won't know until I've seen it.'

Bernie drew the sheet down as far as the man's bare chest. It was obvious why he had told Anna that the man looked as if the Devil was still on his tail. His brown eyes were bulging and his whole face was contorted, with his mouth dragged so far downward that it gave him the appearance of a medieval gargoyle.

Anna approached the gurney and looked at the man more closely. He was brown-haired, about thirty-five years old, with designer stubble from which all of the blood had not yet been cleaned.

From the look of his upper body, he appeared to be reasonably fit, and he had a natural tan which was beginning to fade, as if he had been on vacation for the early part of the summer, but since then had been spending his days indoors.

She pulled the sheet down further. The man had a slight paunch, which may have been the result of alcoholism, but it wasn't the grossly swollen stomach that results from ascites, when fluid is retained in the abdomen because of a terminally damaged liver.

'We gave him a preliminary once-over, after death,' said Bernie. 'There's no external trauma, not even bruising.'

'OK,' said Anna. Even when she was examining the rest of his body, she couldn't stop herself from repeatedly glancing back at his face. 'I never saw *anyone* look like that, immediately post-death,' she said. 'All our muscles *relax* when we die, before rigor sets in. How can his face have possibly stayed so rigid?'

'I have no idea,' said Bernie. 'That's one of the reasons I wanted you to come take a look at

12

him. Is there any disease which causes your facial muscles to lock up like that?'

'Well, there's Lyme disease, isn't there? That can cause psychosis as well as rigidity, which could account for him looking so scared.'

'Yes, but in Lyme disease the joints usually stiffen up, don't they, almost like arthritis, so it's unlikely that he would have been able to kick his legs and wave his arms around the way he was.'

Anna stood looking at the man's face for a long time. She had never come across anybody with such a frightened expression on their face, dead or alive. Most victims of violent killings that she had seen had nothing more on their faces than mild surprise, and people who died naturally usually looked politely bored, as if somebody were telling them a long and tedious anecdote but they didn't have the heart to interrupt them.

'No,' she said, 'I don't think it's Lyme disease. But I'd like to take a few blood samples, if that's OK, and maybe some urine and stool samples, too. What do we know about him?'

'According to the ID we found in his wallet, he works for the city as a grants administrator. Well, he *did*. The police are informing his nearest and dearest even as we speak.'

'Was he married? Single? In some kind of relationship? Where did he live?'

'He had a gold ring on the third finger of his left hand, if that means anything. These days, who knows? He lived in Maplewood, which is a pretty respectable neighborhood, but then again, who can tell?'

At that moment, the door to the recovery room opened and a gingery-haired young secretary poked her head around it. 'Doctor Fishman? There's a call for you. It's Mrs Fishman. Something about your pool filter?'

'Oh, yes,' said Bernie. 'Sorry, Anna – I really have to take this. My pool guy, he's such a *schlepper*.' He bustled out and left Anna alone with the late John Patrick Bridges.

Anna pulled out her cellphone and took six or seven photographs of his face from all angles, and then pulled the sheet down to his ankles and took some more pictures of his naked body.

She checked her watch. As fascinating as this was, she needed to get back to her laboratory. She drew the sheet back up to cover the body, but as she was about to lower it over his face a soft voice whispered, *'Save me.'*

Anna froze. She felt as if somebody were running an ice-cold fingertip all the way down her spine. She looked closely at the body's face, and she could swear that those bulging brown eyes were staring at *her* now, instead of the ceiling. The mouth was still dragged downward and there was no sign that his facial muscles had relaxed, and yet she was sure she could see something more than terror in his expression.

He looked as if he were appealing to her to save him from whatever it was that was frightening him so much. *I'm really, really scared. Save me.*

Anna slowly stood up straight, although she folded the sheet back so that it didn't drop over the body's face.

'*Save me,*' the voice repeated. She couldn't see the body's lips move, but there was no doubt in her mind now that his eyes had turned toward her. '*Get it out of me. Save me.*'

She didn't know whether to answer or not. John Patrick Bridges was dead, or at least he was supposed to be dead. If he had lost as much blood as Bernie Fishman had said he had, then he *must* be dead. If a human being lost only two-and-a-quarter liters of blood out of a total of five liters, without an immediate transfusion they would die.

As unnerved as she was, Anna thought: *If by some miracle this man is still alive, then he's going to need emergency treatment, and fast.*

Keeping her eyes fixed on his, she reached out and placed her index finger and third finger against the carotid artery in his neck. Nothing. He had already lost most of his body heat, and there was no pulse at all.

Next, she lifted his arm and felt his wrist. Again, there was nothing.

'You're dead,' she said, out loud. The recovery room was so silent that her own voice made her look around, as if the words had been spoken by a ventriloquist who was standing close behind her.

At that moment, Bernie Fishman pushed his way in through the door, shaking his head. 'What a klutz! He burned out the goddamned pump, and now it's going to cost me six hundred bucks to replace it!' He stopped, and saw the expression on Anna's face, and said, 'What? What's happened? You look like you just saw a dybbuk!'

Anna hesitated for a moment. It was more than

15

likely that she'd imagined John Patrick Bridges speaking to her. She was very tired and very stressed, after all. She had slept only two-and-a-half hours last night before coming back to the hospital early to carry out more tests on the Meramac School virus.

'It's nothing.' But then she said, 'Look at his eyes, Bernie.'

'What?'

'The deceased. Look at his eyes.'

Bernie went across and peered at the body intently. 'I don't get it,' he said. 'What about his eyes?'

'Before, he was looking straight up at the ceiling. Now he's looking over here, toward me.'

'He's dead, Anna. Maybe his muscle links are starting to tighten. Watch!' Bernie waved his hand in front of the body's face, but John Patrick Bridges didn't blink. 'He's dead, Anna. He's *nifter*. He's gone off to join *el coro invisible*.'

Anna hesitated for a long moment, and then she said, 'Bernie, he spoke to me.'

Long silence. Above his surgical mask, Bernie's eyes roamed around the room as if he had heard a blowfly buzzing around and was trying to see where it was.

'He *spoke* to you.'

'I'm sure I didn't imagine it. It was only a whisper, but I'm sure he said, "*Save me*," and then he said, "*Get it out of me*." And then he said, "*Save me*," again.'

'He's dead, Anna. He's *kaput*. You've been working too hard, that's all.'

'Bernie—'

16

'He's dead, Anna. Dead men don't speak. Sometimes they belch, for sure. Sometimes they break wind. But speak – never. They never so much as whisper.'

'Yes, well, I guess you're probably right. I should get back to my lab. Jim Waso is screaming for results.'

Bernie covered the body's face with the sheet, and then he went over to open the recovery room door. 'Come on,' he said. 'I'll buy you a coffee before you go back. You look like you could use a break.'

They sat in the hospital commissary by the window. Outside, there was a small brick-paved courtyard with bay trees in tubs, and if they craned their necks up to the sixth floor they could see a pentangle of bright blue sky, with streaky clouds in it. Anna realized that she hadn't been out in daylight for almost a week now. She had gone to work in the dark and gone home in the dark. David had been away at a business convention in Chicago for the past three days, so there had been no incentive for her to finish early in the evenings, and she hadn't been eating properly, only take-out salads at lunchtime and pizzas at night.

She didn't really feel like another coffee, but Bernie always cheered her up and she recognized that he was right: she did need a few minutes to relax and sort out her thoughts. She was constantly telling Epiphany not to get too stressed, and yet she always pushed herself right to the very limit. She could never get it out of her mind that

17

whenever she was taking time off, relaxing, some mutant virus might be silently spreading across the city and scores of people might get sick, or die. In the course of her career she had probably saved tens of thousands of lives. Her most significant success had been to find a treatment for a highly aggressive virus which had caused over two hundred fatalities last spring in Indiana and parts of Illinois. The media had called it Scalping Disease because one of its effects had been to make the sufferers' hair fall out and leave their heads raw, as if they had been scalped. After two months of painstaking research, Anna had isolated the virus and formulated a highly effective vaccine.

In spite of everything that she had achieved up to date, she still didn't believe that gave her any excuse to slacken. Even while she lay in bed asleep, viruses were changing and adapting and learning how to become more resistant to antivirals and antibiotics – a dark, heartless, nearly invisible army that *never* slept.

'You remember Bill Kober?' said Bernie, pouring four wraps of sugar into his cappuccino and noisily stirring it. 'Well, of course you remember him. Talented – *inspired*, even, almost a genius, but seriously wacky. Do you know what he did when he left here?'

'He went to India, didn't he?'

'That's right. He carried out tests on the neurotoxins given off by chemical plants and how they affected the health of the local population. He wrote a report about it for the *Journal of Medical Toxicology*, and talk about damning.'

'So what about him?'

'Well – the Indian government went ape-shit when Bill reported that hundreds of kids were being poisoned by industrial pollution. They canceled his visa and told him to take a hike. So believe it or not, he went to Haiti after that, to find out if zombies were really true.'

'You're not trying to tell me that our *nifter* upstairs is a zombie?'

Bernie said, 'No, of course not. Absolutely the opposite. When Bill looked into all the so-called evidence of zombies, he found that the prevailing wisdom was that people could be put into a death-like trance with a combination of tetrodotoxin – TTX – and datura.'

'Yes, I've heard that.'

'The thing is, Bill tested these drugs and found that this simply wouldn't happen. As you know, TTX selectively affects the sodium channels in the nerve cell membranes and the two drugs between them can give the appearance of death. But either they kill you for real or else you gradually recover and return to your normal self – or *nearly* normal, anyhow, maybe a little jingly in the brainbox for a while. Let me put it this way – what you *won't* do is to go shuffling around shopping malls looking for unsuspecting people to eat, and you won't lie on a gurney after flatlining for fifteen minutes and say, "*Save me.*"'

'All right,' said Anna. 'So you're telling me that I simply imagined him talking to me, and that I need a rest?'

'When was the last time you took a vacation?'

19

'Two years ago. Yes, that's right – we went to stay with David's parents in Boise.'

'You call that a *vacation*? Staying with anybody's parents is a punishment. Staying with their parents in Boise – that's much more than a punishment. That's a penance. It would be more fun to flagellate yourself with razor-wire.'

Anna took hold of Bernie's hand across the Formica-topped table. 'Bernie, if you weren't twenty years older and six inches shorter than me, and if you weren't married and I wasn't already spoken for, I'd marry you tomorrow.'

Bernie put on a mock-tragic face. 'That's just my luck. Born at the wrong fucking time, grew to the wrong fucking height. *Todah elohim.*'

'I'll send Epiphany up to take some samples. Thanks for the coffee, Bernie – and, you know, just thanks.'

Three

It was past eight p.m. when she eventually made it home. She parked her silver Toyota Prius in the parking structure and walked across the pedestrian bridge to the Old Post Office building where she and David shared a loft. As she opened the door, she heard thunder overhead. She hoped that it would rain tonight, to relieve some of the oppressive August heat.

The loft was spacious and modern, with high ceilings and shiny oak floors covered with red-and-black Navajo rugs. Facing each other in the center of the living area were two large white leather couches with a glass-topped coffee table in between them, on which a ceramic statuette of a harlequin was dancing next to neatly stacked copies of *Architectural Digest*. On the walls hung three large nudes by Linda LeKinff and a bright, simplistic landscape in primary colors by Eric Bodtker.

She was surprised and disappointed to find that David wasn't back yet. His convention had wrapped up last night with a final presentation and a celebratory banquet, and he had expected to be home by mid-afternoon at the latest. She had called him three times from the hospital, but every time his cellphone had been switched off, so she'd presumed that he was still in the air. She called him again, now, but his cell was still switched off.

'Where *are* you?' she said to his message service. 'If you've found yourself a go-go girl, at least have the decency to call and tell me.'

She went through to the bedroom, kicked off her shoes and sat down on the bed to tug off her skintight jeans and unbutton her blouse. Wrapping herself in her peach silk robe, she went back through to the kitchen area, opened the fridge and poured herself a glass of Zinfandel. She opened the door of the freezer and stood there with her eyes half-closed, enjoying the chill and trying to decide if she wanted a mozzarella pizza or not. In the end, she decided to wait until David came home. She was too exhausted to feel really hungry.

She sat cross-legged on one of a pair of white leather couches and switched on *The Ellen DeGeneres Show* with the sound turned right down. She couldn't stop thinking about John Patrick Bridges, the dead John Patrick Bridges, whispering, *'Save me.'*

Was it conceivable that a dead person's brain could give off a last faint telepathic message? If a person had been panicking enough before they died, could there still be a residual electrical charge left in their cerebral cortex that another, living, person could pick up? It was an interesting concept. If it *were* possible, then maybe a murder victim could tell somebody who was psychically sensitive who had killed them.

From the way that he had been screaming for help, there was no question that John Patrick Bridges had been desperate to the point of hysteria in the minutes before he had died. *'Get it out of me! Get it out of me!'*

The mystery was – what was the 'it' that he had been pleading for them to get out of him? According to Bernie Fishman, a superficial post-mortem examination had shown that he had no external trauma, so he had no bullets in him, and he hadn't been stabbed or pierced by any other kind of projectile which might have broken off inside him, like the tip of a knife-blade or an arrowhead. Maybe he had swallowed something – some caustic liquid like drain-cleaner or a fragment of broken glass. She had even heard of cases in Oregon where carpenter ants had crawled into people's mouths when they were sleeping and stung the inside of their windpipes, so that they had suffered agonizing pain and almost suffocated.

As she turned all this over in her mind, she began to recall a few fragments of that half-forgotten reference to unusually severe convulsions.

The patient is convinced that another personality is trying to force their way into their body and take possession of it – that is why they convulse with such extreme violence.

Tantalizingly, she still couldn't be sure if she had read it in a textbook or heard it in a lecture, or if somebody had been talking about it at some medical convention that she had attended.

They are not having a seizure in the normal sense of the word. They are involved in a life-or-death struggle to cling on to their very identity – to prevent themselves from being evicted from their own body.

Anna opened her laptop and Googled those few sentences, as closely as she could remember them. All that came up were the titles of several

23

fantasy novels like *Haunted Bodies* and *Possessed!* and a study of some Indonesian philosophy called *Penyewa Yang Tidak Diinginkan* (literally, *Unwanted Tenants*). This described how homeless spirits are continuously roaming the earth searching for a physical body to share, so that they can once again experience the pleasures of food, and drink, and sex.

She tried David's cellphone yet again. It was still switched off. It was past ten p.m. now, so there was no point in calling his office. She was beginning to grow anxious. Most days, David rang her so often to tell her he loved her that he was a nuisance.

She poured herself another glass of wine, took one large swallow and then went through to the bathroom to take a shower. She left her cellphone next to the washbasin in case David called back, but it stayed silent. After her shower, she combed her short wet hair straight back from her forehead, like a man. She stared at herself in the mirror and thought that she was looking too thin. Her ribs were showing, she had hardly any breasts, and she had a triangular gap between her thighs. She knew that she was working too hard and not taking care of herself, but then she had always felt driven. *What is the point of living in this world if you don't achieve anything significant while you're here?* That's what her father always told her, anyhow.

She was walking back into the living area, wrapped in a thick white towel, when the front door opened and David came in, wheeling his suitcase behind him.

24

'*David!* What happened? I've been calling you and calling you, but your cell was switched off!'

David blinked at her, as if he didn't quite know where he was, or what he was doing here. 'I don't know,' he said. 'I wasn't feeling too good this morning, and I missed my flight.'

'Sweetheart, you look *terrible*! What's wrong?' Anna went across to him and put her hands up to his face. He was two or three inches taller than she was, wide-shouldered, with curly brown hair that came over his collar at the back and a broad, Irish-looking face, which Anna had always thought was handsome with a hint of mischief. Tonight, though, his hair was uncombed and he hadn't shaved, and his pale-blue eyes were bloodshot.

He was usually such a fastidious dresser, but his fawn linen coat was badly creased, one of his shirt-tails was hanging out, and his shoes were unlaced. He was swaying as if he were drunk, although he didn't smell of alcohol. He did, however, smell of body odor and something dry and clinging and aromatic, as if he had been smoking pot.

'Come in and sit down,' she told him. She led him by the hand over to the nearest couch, and then she went back to close the front door. 'How do you feel? Feverish? Nauseous? Why didn't you *call* me?'

'I guess I forgot. I'm sorry.'

'You *forgot*? How could you forget?'

'I don't know, Anna, and that's the God's honest truth. When I woke up this morning I couldn't

25

even remember what my name was. I only remembered because Charlie Bowdre came to my room to find out why I hadn't showed up for breakfast. I told him I was sick and I was going to go home, but then I fell asleep again and I didn't wake up until the maid came in to make up my room. I guess the rest of the team must've thought I'd gone ahead of them.'

'You should have called me! Why didn't you *call* me?'

'I don't know, Anna. I just can't seem to think straight. I only remembered where I lived because it was written on my suitcase tag.'

Anna placed her hand against his forehead. 'Your temperature is way, way up,' she told him. 'Listen, why don't you get undressed and I'll run you a bath to cool you down.'

'I never felt as bad as this before, ever. I don't know what in hell's wrong with me. One minute I'm so hot that I'm sweating like a pig, the next minute I'm feeling so cold that I can't stop shaking.'

'You've picked up some infection, that's all. Your body automatically heats itself up to try to kill the hostile bacteria, and that's why you're running a fever. Just hold on a second. I'll go fetch the thermometer.'

She went into the bathroom and turned on the faucets over the bathtub. Then she took their mercury thermometer out of the medicine cabinet and came back into the living area to place it under David's tongue. She sat next to him, holding his hand.

'Apart from catching this bug, whatever it is,

26

how was the conference?' she asked him. 'Good, or just the usual waffle?'

He couldn't speak with the thermometer in his mouth so he simply nodded.

'I'm still trying to pin down this Meramac Elementary School virus,' she told him. 'I think I'm getting close to identifying what it is, and how it replicates so darn quickly, but who knows what it's going to take to control it. I've tried just about every antiviral ever invented. *Nada.*'

'*Mmmfff-mmmhh*,' said David.

Anna took out the thermometer and peered at it.

'Come on, what does it say?' David asked her. 'You're frowning already! How long have I got to live?'

'It's thirty-seven point nine. You're hyper pyretic, but you're not in the death zone yet.'

'Well, that's a relief!'

'Don't count your chickens before they're hatched. It depends how long your temperature stays up this high. If it doesn't go down in the next a day-and-a-half, I'm going to have to call Doctor DuFray. Meanwhile, you need some really aggressive cooling. Have yourself a long cold soak in the bath, drink plenty of water and try to relax. I'll bring you some ibuprofen. That should help, too. How hungry are you?'

'Something inside of me says that I'm ravenous, but I don't think I could keep anything down.'

'Maybe later, then. You get yourself out of those smelly old clothes, and I'll fetch you a glass of water.'

'Anna.'

'What?'

'I love you, Anna. But Jesus I feel rough.'

'Get undressed. The bath's almost ready.'

At midnight, she was woken up by David whispering. He was speaking so quietly that at first she couldn't be sure that it wasn't just the wind blowing west from the river along Locust Street, and she had to sit up in bed and listen hard before she realized that he was talking to himself.

'David?' she said. 'David, are you OK?'

He continued to whisper, although she couldn't make out what he was saying. It sounded like the same words over and over again.

'David?'

He still didn't answer her. She reached across the bed, but he had his back to her and he was tightly bound up in the sheet, as if he were wrapped in a shroud, so that all she could feel of him was his tangled curly hair. His scalp was sweaty, though, and the sheet was soaking, so he was clearly still running a fever.

She shook his shoulder and said, loudly, 'David, wake up! *David!*'

Their bedroom was never completely dark because the blinds were natural calico and all they did was give them privacy from the apartments on the other side of the intersection and subdue the street lighting outside. But when David didn't respond to her shaking, and continued to whisper, Anna switched on her bedside lamp.

She knelt up and tried to pull him over on to his back, but every muscle in his body was tense and he was much too heavy. She felt as if he

28

were deliberately resisting her and simply pretending to be asleep.

'David! Listen to me, darling, your temperature's still way too high. Come on, baby, you have to cool yourself down. I don't want you going into a coma!'

David abruptly stopped whispering, but when she tried again to roll him over on to his back he still wouldn't budge.

'David, please, you have to help me here. I'm not strong enough to fight you. If you won't help me, then I'll have to call for an ambulance. You feel dangerously hot.'

There was a long pause, but when David whispered next, a fire truck briefly whooped in the street below them as it crossed over Washington Avenue and she couldn't catch what he said.

'I didn't hear you,' she said.

'*I can't fight it much longer, Anna. I don't have the strength.*'

'What? What is it, darling? *What* can't you fight?'

'*I've been fighting it all day,*' he said. His voice was louder now, and hoarser. '*I can't fight it much longer. I can't.*'

There was another long pause. Anna waited with her hand resting lightly on his shoulder to see if he would say any more, but then he began to tremble, more and more violently. *That's it*, she decided. *I'm calling for the paramedics right now.*

She picked up her cellphone from her nightstand and was about to punch in 911 when David rolled over toward her. She was so shocked that

29

she dropped the phone on to the bed and jumped up on to her feet. His eyes were bulging, and his whole face was distorted. He looked as terrified as John Patrick Bridges. The only difference was that he was alive, and whatever pyrogen had invaded his body, he was still fighting it.

'*Anna,*' he whispered. '*Anna, I can't.*'

Anna scooped up her cellphone again and dialed 911.

David suddenly sat up and screamed at her, '*For God's sake, Anna! It's inside me!*'

'Nine-one-one,' said the operator. 'Where is your emergency?'

Anna was about to answer when David vomited a tide of warm blood all over the bed and into her lap. Then he pitched on to his back and started jerking and jumping and wrestling with the blood-stained sheets.

He seemed to be battling against himself, repeatedly punching his cheekbones and his chest and seizing himself around the throat. All the time he was doing this he was grunting and gargling and bringing up even more blood.

Anna said, 'The Lofts at OPOP, number thirty-seven. Ambulance, please, and fast!' Then she threw herself on top of David, slathered as he was in blood, and tried to pin him down so that he wouldn't hit himself any more. He stared up at her, his face a mask of shiny scarlet, like a demon out a medieval play.

'*I can't,*' he bubbled. '*I can't.*'

The paramedics arrived only eleven minutes later. Anna answered the door to them in nothing but her T-shirt and her thong, smeared all over with blood. Even her blonde hair was pink with blood, and stuck up like a cockerel's crest.

'Holy shit,' said the leading paramedic when she let them in.

'I'm not hurt,' Anna told her, in a shaky voice. 'It's my partner, on the bed. He's suffered a hemorrhage. He's dead.'

Four

After the paramedics had taken David away, Anna went into the bathroom to wash off his blood. She was almost reluctant to do it, because that would mean that she was washing away the very last trace of him. Some mornings, after they had made love, she had gone to work without washing so that she could smell him on her all day.

When she faced herself in the mirror she was surprised how emotionless she looked. She felt as if the ground had opened up underneath her feet, but her hazel-brown eyes were giving nothing away.

'David has just died,' she said to her reflection, but her reflection didn't answer and continued to look completely deadpan.

She took off her T-shirt and her thong and left them in the washbasin to soak. Then she took a quick shower and toweled herself, although she left her hair wet. Afterward she went into the bedroom and dressed in a plain white blouse and a gray pencil skirt, the same skirt that she had worn to her grandmother's funeral last October. She had called Laclede Cabs to pick her up and take her to the hospital because she didn't trust herself to drive. She knew what the effects of delayed emotional shock could be, and she didn't want to go driving into a storefront or three lanes of oncoming traffic just because she had lost her sense of reality.

As they drove to the hospital, the taxi-driver kept glancing at her in his rear-view mirror. After a while he said, in a clogged-up voice, 'If you don't mind me askin', something *bad* just happened?'

'You could say that.'

'Hey, if you want me to shut up, all you have to do is say so.'

It was dark, and it was still warm, but it had started raining about an hour ago and the streets were deserted and shiny with reflected light.

'That's all right,' said Anna. 'You can talk if you want to. Talking's not going to change anything.'

'That's my motto, too,' said the taxi-driver. 'Whatever you do, whatever you say, it ain't never going to make a donut's worth of difference.'

When she arrived at the hospital, she walked straight along the empty, echoing corridor to the morgue. David's body had already been wheeled in and was lying under a pale-green sheet in the corner. The room was chilly and dimly lit, with a stainless-steel autopsy table in the center. A young Asian-American doctor was standing beside David's gurney, filling out the forms which confirmed his body's time of arrival, and his condition, and that life was extinct. In the morning, when the ME turned up, his body would be examined to establish if a full autopsy was called for.

'Professor Grey, isn't it?' said the doctor, in obvious surprise. He was bald and bearded, even though he looked as if he was only in his middle twenties. 'Can I help you at all?'

'I'm here because this – this is my partner,'

33

Anna told him, trying to keep her voice steady. 'This *was* my partner.'

'You mean—?' said the doctor, pointing at the body with his ballpen. 'Oh, I'm so sorry, professor. Really. My condolences.'

'He passed away very suddenly,' said Anna. 'I need to take some samples.'

The young doctor looked dubious. 'Oh. I'm not so sure about the protocol for that, professor. Strictly according to the book, Doctor Lim should be the first to examine him.'

'I realize that. But Doctor Lim isn't here right now.'

'It's not only that, professor. If you have a personal connection to the deceased, you should not really be carrying out any medical procedure on his remains. What you do might affect Doctor Lim's assessment of the cause of his demise, and then we'd have to call in the coroner. I'm not trying to being obstructive, I promise you, but I'm sure that you're aware of the rules.'

'Of course I am. But this is the second case of hemorrhage that we've had to deal with in a matter of twelve hours, and the two cases are so similar that I think they could be connected. Catastrophic bleeding, severe convulsions. I'm concerned that this might be the beginning of something very serious. The sooner I find out *what*, the better.'

The doctor shook his head. 'I apologize, professor, but I cannot allow you to take any samples at this time. If Doctor Lim gives you his permission, of course there will be no problem. But I do not have the authority.'

'I only want to take blood and urine samples. What harm can that do?'

'I'm sorry.'

'All right. I understand. But you don't object if I sit with him for a while?'

'Not at all. Here.' The doctor carried over a blue plastic chair and positioned it next to the gurney. 'All I ask is that you please do not touch him.'

'Would you . . .?' said Anna, and gestured that she wanted the doctor to lift the sheet from David's face.

'Of course.' He folded back the sheet, and there was David. His mouth and chin were still caked with dried blood, but unlike John Patrick Bridges his eyes were closed and he looked only vaguely troubled. Anna stood beside him for a long moment. She would have done anything to be able to clean the blood away and kiss him, but she knew that already his lips would be cold.

'I can only tell you how sorry I am for your loss,' said the doctor uncomfortably.

Anna looked at him and nodded her appreciation, although she couldn't find it in herself to smile. The pain of seeing David like this was so intense that she could hardly breathe.

Somewhere outside the hospital they heard the *whip-whip-whoop* of an ambulance siren, and a few seconds later the doctor's pager buzzed.

'I have to go,' he said. 'Please – stay for as long as you like. Doctor Lim will be here at seven thirty, maybe even before that. He likes to make an early start.' He left the morgue and the heavy door closed behind him with a hiss.

35

Anna remained standing beside David's body for a while, and then sat down with her hands covering her face. She felt empty. She had witnessed so many people dying, and yet this was completely different. With every other death she had felt a strength rising within her – strength to offer sympathy and reassurance to those bereaved. But now that David was gone, she had no comfort to offer herself, no words that could help her through it. She couldn't even cry yet, although she knew without doubt that she would.

'*Anna,*' whispered a voice.

She slowly lowered her hands away from her face and lifted her head. The morgue remained utterly silent.

Not again, she thought. *This time, it* must *be my imagination. I didn't witness John Patrick Bridges dying, but David died in my arms. I saw the last breath bubble out of his mouth and burst.*

He's dead. Like Bernie Fishman told me, there is no such thing as zombies. He's dead, and dead men don't speak.

She waited. The morgue's refrigerating system suddenly clicked and whirred into life and made her start. Her presence in the room must have marginally raised the temperature. She couldn't make up her mind if she ought to stay here any longer or not. Supposing David wasn't dead? Or supposing he *was* dead, but he was still trying to communicate with her? She knew the idea was far-fetched, but right now she was still so stressed that she could have believed anything – even that David was speaking to her from that place that mediums call 'the Other Side'.

36

'*Anna*,' whispered the voice. '*Anna, help me.*'

Anna stood up. When she looked at David, her knees almost gave way, and she saw prickles of white light in front of her eyes, as if she were going to faint. His head was still in the same position, and he was still bearded with dried blood, but his eyes were open and he was staring at her.

She took two cautious steps to the side, and his eyes followed her.

'*Anna, don't leave me. Please, help me. Get it out of me.*'

The voice was louder this time, more urgent, and there was no question that it was David's.

'Are you still alive?' she asked him. 'David – listen to me, are you still alive?'

He didn't answer, but continued to stare at her, and little by little, his expression began to change. His jaw dropped down as if he were about to scream, and his eyes began to bulge. '*Anna, get it out of me!*'

Anna couldn't stop herself from shaking. Her medical training told her that she ought to check David for vital signs, feel for a pulse in his blood-encrusted neck, just as she had with John Patrick Bridges. But she knew what the result would be. He might be whispering to her, his eyes might be open, but he wasn't breathing and his heart wasn't beating, and by all of the usual clinical criteria life was extinct.

She knew that she shouldn't be afraid of him, because he was still David. He still looked like her lover and her best friend and the man she had lived with for over three years. At the same time, though, there was something inside of him that was making him plead with her to *get it out*, even though he was technically dead, and the thought of what *that* could be really frightened her. What could terrify him as much as that, even after he had breathed his last breath?

'David,' she said, but her voice was so quiet that she could scarcely hear it herself. She cleared her throat and said, '*David*,' louder this time. 'David, what is it? Don't you understand, David? I've lost you. You're gone.'

'*Anna – it hurts so much – please, Anna – I can't – I can't – Anna, I can't!*'

With that, David began to convulse – jolting up and down on the gurney more and more violently, just as John Patrick Bridges had done. Soon he was heaving himself from side to side as well. The gurney's framework crashed and clanked, and Anna was frightened that David was going to throw himself on to the floor.

She gripped his left wrist, pinning it down against the gurney's vinyl mattress, and then she reached over and took hold of his right wrist, too. She leaned across him, trying to press as much of her weight on his chest as she could, even though she weighed less than a hundred and thirty pounds.

For a few moments she had to use all of her strength to keep him flat on his back, but gradually his convulsions began to subside. He gave a few more uncontrolled twitches, and then he lay still. She lifted her head and looked at his blood-bearded face. His eyes remained open, and his jaw was still sagging in that silent scream, but now there was no sign of life at all, not even life after death.

She released her grip on his wrists and stood back. Her own heart was beating so hard and so fast that it hurt. She didn't know if she ought to go looking for the night-duty doctor or not. She didn't want to be accused of tampering with David's body, since that might compromise her chances of being allowed to take samples. And after all, if *she* couldn't understand how David had managed to throw a violent fit when he was dead, she very much doubted if *he* could.

Of course, David's expression was grotesquely different now from the placid face he had been wearing when he was first wheeled into the morgue. However, Anna guessed that it was unlikely that the night-duty doctor would come in to check him again; and when the medical examiner eventually showed up to start his post-mortem, he may well think that David's features were unnaturally rigid and distorted, but he would have no idea how much they had altered since his death.

Anna folded over the sheet to cover his face. As she did so, she said, 'May God take care of you, David, my darling,' even though she wasn't at all sure that it *was* David who was lying there. In body, perhaps, but in spirit? The morgue seemed even chillier now, and she couldn't help feeling an urge to get out of there as quickly as she could.

She was halfway to the door when another voice said, '*Anna.*'

It wasn't David's voice. It was croaky and old, but it was commanding. She stopped, with her hand raised toward the door-handle. She wanted to hear what the voice was going to say, but on the other hand she was close to panic. She had read Bible stories about people talking in tongues. It was supposed to be a sign that they were possessed. But when did dead bodies start talking in tongues?

'*Anna,*' the voice insisted, as if it expected her to stay and listen. It reminded her of Mr Burroughs, her old science teacher from the Ursuline Academy, who had probably understood her more than anybody else when she was growing up, even her father. But this voice had a threatening tone to it, too. It was as cold as a snake sliding across the tiled floor toward her.

'*Don't try to interfere, Anna. The end has been coming for a long, long time. Nothing can stop it now, especially not you.*'

'Who are you?' she retorted, even though she was so frightened that it was almost a scream.

There was no reply, so she turned around and went back to the gurney and pulled down the sheet. It was still David under there, with the same terrified expression on his face. She stood there with the corner of the sheet in one hand, breathing hard.

She was just about to drop it back when David's tongue emerged from his open mouth, pale and bluey-gray, more like a slug than a human tongue. It circled around his lips, licking off the dried blood, and then it disappeared back into his mouth again.

Anna crossed herself. She had stopped going to church long ago, but she felt that she had just seen something appear from hell, and she couldn't think what else to do for self-protection.

Five

It makes no difference how goddamn psychic you are, you can never see your own fate coming until it turns up on your doorstep with a box of moldy candies in its hand and a cheesy grin on its face. If psychics could really see the future, they wouldn't step out in front of buses without looking or contract HIV from rent boys or find themselves trapped in burning theaters halfway through their comeback performance like that famous French clairvoyant whose name escapes me (so, you know, he couldn't have been all *that* famous).

In spite of that, I should have foreseen what the consequences of my fortune-telling session with old Mrs Ratzenberger were going to be, considering her early-stage Alzheimer's and her overwhelming wealth. One day I'm going to write a book about my fortune-telling experiences in Miami, and I shall call it *The Rich And The Ga-Ga*.

Anyhow, we were sitting on the veranda of Mrs Ratzenberger's glassy and stainless-steely house on East Star Island Drive. For those of you who are not too familiar with Miami, Star Island is a man-made lozenge of land situated to the west of Miami Beach in Biscayne Bay and accessible only by a narrow causeway. If you're thinking of buying a home here, make sure you have at least seven-point-five million in your back pants' pocket. Mrs Ratzenberger's property was valued at nine.

You would have thought that life was a kind of never-ending paradise for Rosa Ratzenberger. Here we were, sitting under the crimson bougainvillea with the bay glittering all around us, drinking champagne with white strawberries bobbing around in it. You wouldn't have taken her for eighty-three, because her ash-blonde hair was immaculately bobbed and her face was as smooth and shiny as a Venetian carnival mask. She was wearing loose silky peach-colored pajamas and sandals, and her scarlet fingernails and toenails were perfectly polished. You could have opened your own jewelry store with the diamond and emerald and ruby rings that sparkled on her fingers, or at least a concession selling high-class knuckledusters.

All that gave away her age was the paper-thin skin on the back of her hands and her suntanned cleavage, which looked like one of those crinkly chicken roasting bags after two-and-a-half hours in the oven. Well – that and the fact that she was way out on the left-hand side of doolally.

As wealthy and as groomed as she was, Mrs Ratzenberger was in a state of high agitation. She was convinced that her husband Frank was having an affair with Celia Briscoe, the catering manager at Ocean Palms Golf Club, where he now spent most of his life after retiring from his bagel-bakery business in Queens. Celia Briscoe was forty-two, so she was only half Frank's age, and she was a natural blonde with blinding-white teeth and enormous *shadayim* who wiggled her ass as she walked across the restaurant. Not only that, but she was a *shiksa*. That was the way Mrs Ratzenberger described her, anyhow, which I have to confess made me pretty darn keen to meet this Celia Briscoe myself.

'Do you have any *proof* that Frank and this Celia Briscoe are playing hide the salami together?' I asked Mrs Ratzenberger. 'Have you checked his cell for any incriminating messages?'

She didn't answer at first, but watched me intently as I laid out a circle of fifteen cards on the gray oak-topped table, plus a cross of five cards in the center. This afternoon I was using a deck of eighteenth-century French cards that I had bought years ago in a magic store in Greenwich Village: the Parlor Sybil, which roughly translated means a person in your living-room who you are dumb enough to pay to tell your fortune.

'He's not *interested* in me any more,' she said at last, flapping her hand. 'He comes back home from the golf club around seven or eight, then he just sits in front of the TV and watches baseball or *Man v. Food* until it's time to go to bed. Hardly says a word, not even, "How was your day?" Monday they gave me a celebratory lunch at the Jewish Museum for all the funding I've been giving them over the years. But did Frank give a damn?'

'I don't know, Mrs Ratzenberger,' I confessed. 'Did he?'

She reached across the table and prodded my forearm with her sharp red fingernail. 'When I

43

told him all about it – the lunch, and the certificate they gave me – he said, "Oh! A certificate already! But what did they give you to *eat*?" Then before I could answer he said, "Don't tell me. Chicken-turkey soup! Chicken-turkey soup that tastes of nothing! That's all they ever serve at The Jewish Museum, chicken-turkey soup, and it tastes of nothing. Not chickens. Not turkeys. It don't even taste of water."' She threw her hands up. 'There! That's Frank for you! He's complaining about the soup, and he wasn't even *there*!'

'Um,' I said. 'Why not let me start turning these cards over and see what the future has in store for you, Mrs R?' I had been here nearly an hour already, and I was booked to give another reading at the James Hotel in two hours' time. The trouble was, most of these old biddies weren't really interested in what their cards foretold. They just wanted an afternoon's companionship from a slightly battered but reasonably good-looking reprobate like me. The rich may be richer than us, but they get just as lonely. Lonelier, even. The black American Express card may buy you anything you want, but it has never been known to whisper the words, 'I love you.'

'Even in the feathers, it's the same,' said Mrs Ratzenberger. 'Frank's rope never rises. *Never*. Not once in three years now! He's using up all his energy on that *shiksa*, that's what I think! You should see Marty! All I have to do is pop my fingers, and what do I get?'

'I don't know. What *do* you get? And who's Marty?'

'Marty's my masseur. Well, he's more of a

44

personal trainer. He comes three times a week to keep me in shape. Just because I'm eighty-three, that doesn't mean I can't stay in shape! Look at Jane Fonda! She's only eight years younger than I am, and I have a much less wrinkly neck.'

'But Marty . . .?'

'Oh, Marty! *His* rope rises! Oh, yes!' She tried to pop her fingers to demonstrate how she triggered a response from Marty, but she was wearing too many rings and it just looked as if she were desperately clawing at the air.

I didn't exactly see how Mrs Ratzenberger could give Frank a hard time for his alleged adultery with the *shiksa* if she were playing pop the *schmeckel* with Marty – especially since it was more than likely that poor old Frank couldn't get his rope to rise for *any* woman, whatever her age and whatever her religion and however impressive her *shadayim*.

But to get her off the subject I turned over the first card, and it was the nine of hearts – *Surprise* – which showed a brown-haired woman in a long red apron standing in shock in front of an empty birdcage.

'There!' I said. 'This is one of the best cards in the deck.' (It is, too, believe me. It always means good luck. You don't seriously imagine that the Incredible Erskine could ever tell anything but the truth to his gullible and highly lucrative clientele?) 'This card means that something very, very satisfying is coming your way, Mrs Ratzenberger, and it's a surprise. It may have escaped your notice but the first three letters of "surprise" can be pronounced like "sir". Then there's a "p" which may be a discreet reference to a part of this "sir's" anatomy. And then, at the end of "surprise" you get the last four letters which spell "rise"!'

'You don't mean—?' said Mrs Ratzenberger with a frown, although the frown was only in her voice. Her Botox didn't allow her actual face to frown.

'I'm only telling you what the *cards* are telling you, Mrs Ratzenberger, and you were the one who shuffled them, after all.'

It was a very warm afternoon. Even out here in the balmy breeze of Biscayne Bay it was over thirty-four degrees, and I was beginning to feel extremely sweaty and tangled-up in my ankle-length black djellaba, although I had dropped back its tall pointy hood. I had bought it online for $37 from Djellabas-R-Us because it was Moroccan and supposed to keep a man cool and comfortable in the summer heat. My current girl-friend Sandy had sewn silver stars on it in order to give me that psychic look. Actually I felt more like Mickey Mouse in *The Sorcerer's Apprentice*.

'But even if Frank *does* manage to get it up,' said Mrs Ratzenberger, 'what's going to happen then?'

'Without being crude about it, I imagine that you two will *schtup*. That's what you want, isn't it?'

'But it's not going to change anything, is it? He'll still go off playing golf every day, and he'll still come back in the evening and not say a word to me.'

'It's hard to say, if you'll excuse my *double*

46

entendre. Maybe, once his physical prowess returns to him, he'll show more interest in you. You have to take these things one *schtup* at a time. Anyhow,' I said, 'that's only the first card. We have nineteen more to go, and who knows what they're going to predict?'

'To be honest with you, Harry, I was hoping maybe for a divorce. Frank and me don't have a pre-nup, and I could easily get to keep the house and two-thirds of his money. He's worth forty-three million at least.'

'Why don't you see what the other cards have to say, before you file?'

'All right,' Mrs Ratzenberger nodded. And then, as I turned up the next card, she said, 'What surprise?'

'I'm sorry?'

'You said I was going to have a surprise. Did you say that, or was it my lawyer? I *did* talk to my lawyer, didn't I, about the divorce?'

'Mrs Ratzenberger, right now you're not filing for divorce, you're having your fate foretold in the cards.'

Mrs Ratzenberger blinked at me as if she had never seen me before. Then, suddenly, she smiled as much as her collagen-inflated lips would allow her. 'Go on, Harry,' she said, coquettishly. 'What's the next card?'

'Ah,' I said. I was almost as confused as she was. When I first came down from New York and started telling fortunes in Miami, I have to admit that I used to find these 'senior moments' pretty disconcerting. Once I visited an elderly woman in Surfside, and after I had spent

47

two-and-a-half hours reading her cards I left her house only to realize that I had left my cell behind. When I rang her doorbell to retrieve it she welcomed me inside and said, 'Come on in, Mr Erskine! I can't *wait* for you to tell me my fortune!' So – I had to read her cards twice, but at least she paid me twice.

I turned over the next card. It showed a man in a tattered yellow tailcoat sitting in a wing chair looking seriously sick. A young woman is bringing him a bowl of soup but he looks like he has no appetite. *Maladie*, Illness, the eight of spades. This card hadn't come up since the last time I read Mrs Zlotorynski's fortune and two weeks later she died of deep vein thrombosis.

'Well, *that* doesn't look too encouraging,' said Mrs Ratzenberger. She put on her upswept Cadillac-fin spectacles to peer at it more closely. 'I'm not going to get *sick*, am I? I've been very short of breath lately. My doctor says it's stress due to self-absorption, whatever that means, but I'm not so sure.'

'No . . . you won't get sick. See – the sick person in the picture, it's a man. So some man you know may contract some illness, or maybe have a seizure of some kind. When I turn up some more cards I can be more specific.'

'Maybe Frank will catch the chlamydia. Or maybe he'll have a heart attack. A heart attack, that would be simpler! A heart attack would get it all over real quick, if you know what I mean, and not nearly so embarrassing to explain to the kids how God took him.'

I turned over the next card, giving Mrs

Ratzenberger my toothiest Liberace grin as I did so. I was trying to give her the impression that I was totally upbeat about her future because totally upbeat is all that my clients ever want to hear. They don't want to face the fact that within fifteen years, tops, their relatives are going to be making an appointment for them at the Blasberg Funeral Chapel and squabbling with each other over their last will and testament.

It was the nine of spades, but there was something really weird going on here. In the Parlor Sibyl, the nine of spades is *Mort* – Death – and it shows a grim-faced skeleton in a ratty brown robe holding a half-empty hourglass in one hand and a scythe in the other. But somehow *this* nine of spades was different. It depicted a man with wild hair and a horrified look on his face sitting bolt upright in bed. He had thrown back the blanket to see that his legs had become thin and black and scaly and his feet had turned into claws, like the legs of some monstrous crow. Standing beside the bed was a smiling man with a gray beard and a long gray coat with buttons all the way down the front. Like the figure of death in the original Parlor Sibyl card, he too was holding an hourglass in one hand, although in *this* hourglass the sand had nearly all run through. In the other hand he was holding not a scythe but a charred wooden cross, from which the smoke was still rising.

The card was titled *Scourge*.

I stared at it for a long time, and I was aware that my hand was trembling as I held it, even though I felt more baffled than scared. I counted

49

the spades in the top left-hand corner of the card and there were definitely nine of them, and the nine of spades should have been the Death card, except that this wasn't. This was the Scourge card, and in two years of reading this deck I had never seen the Scourge card before, like *ever*.

'Well?' asked Mrs Ratzenberger. She was beginning to grow impatient, and she twisted around in her chair and beckoned through the window to her Chinese houseboy to bring us some more champagne. 'And more *strawberries*!' she shrieked out. Then she turned back to me and said, 'What does *that* mean? Frank's going to die of a leg infection? I mean, what's the matter with that guy? Bird flu?'

'No, no, nothing like that,' I told her, quickly improvising. 'It's, like, *symbolic*. It means that somebody is going to let you down – somebody you thought you could count on. Legs, see – they stand for *support*. They stand for *trust*. But you're going to find out that your trust in one particular person was misplaced, and that they've been two-timing you, or at the very least taking you for granted.'

'It's that Morris Dressel,' said Mrs Ratzenberger, without hesitation. 'I always thought he was a *fonfer*! He persuaded Frank to invest two-point-five million in Funeral Reef, and I'll bet you it never gets off the ground! I'll bet it never gets under the water, either!'

'Funeral Reef? What's that?'

'It's for when you pass away, God forbid. They mix your ashes into a concrete ball and drop it into the ocean, and all the balls build up to make

50

a reef for the fishes. It's supposed to be a way you keep on making a contribution to the world, even after you're dead.'

'But you get crabs on reefs, don't you, and barnacles, and shellfish aren't kosher.'

'That's exactly what I told Frank. Did he listen?'

'Well, whatever,' I told her, 'this card is definitely advising you to be cautious in your business ventures, or else you're going to get your fingers burned.'

OK . . . I admit that I was lying to her through my grinning teeth but I didn't have a clue what the Scourge card really meant any more than she did, and I was only telling her what she wanted to hear.

I hesitated before turning over the next card. It was the three of spades, which was normally titled *Pièges*, which meant Traps, and showed a poacher laying out nets to catch wild birds – probably ortolans since the Parlor Sibyl was French. At least this was a card that I recognized.

'You're going to have a disagreement with Frank,' I said. 'This card always foretells a domestic bust-up. You're going to have a fight over somebody's incompetence.'

'Morris Dressel! What did I tell you? He's going to lose all of Frank's money! We're going to have a fight and then Frank's going to have a heart attack and I'll never get his two-point-five million back!'

That's one of the things I like about my job – usually. I turn over a couple of cards and the next thing my clients are telling their own fortunes

51

for me. They know what they want to happen to them much better than I do, after all. Well, I usually like it, but this afternoon the cards were coming up with messages that I was finding both confusing and irrelevant, and I have to say scary, too.

The next card I turned over was another that I had never seen before – *Cauchemar*, which means Nightmare. It showed a skinny woman in a long white nightgown wrestling on her bed with a shapeless black figure like an octopus, except that this octopus had two red eyes like a demon. Standing at the foot of the bed watching them was the same gray-bearded man from the Scourge card, although this time he was holding a long beaded necklace in his right hand and a stick decorated with red and black feathers in his left.

On the yellow wallpaper beside the bed there was a large dark stain, or maybe it was the shadow of the woman and the demon as they struggled on the bed together. There was something about the shape of this stain or shadow that really unsettled me. I didn't know why, but it reminded me of something disturbing. It reminded me of being frightened – not just frightened, but scared shitless, like when you're a kid and it's the middle of the night and you think that the bathrobe on the back of your bedroom door has come alive. I couldn't think *when* I had been frightened as much as that, or *why*, but it was a feeling I didn't like at all – especially since I didn't have the remotest idea what this *Cauchemar* card was trying to tell me.

'Well?' asked Mrs Ratzenberger.

52

'Oh, right – this is you struggling with your conscience.'

'Conscience? What conscience?'

'You're *torn*, that's the trouble. See how this woman's nightdress is torn? The "Good You" is fighting the "Bad You". You want to give Frank a hard time for what he's been doing, but at the same time you're a very humane, tolerant woman.'

'I *am*? I mean, I am.'

'Of course you are, because you understand that husbands only stray so that they can appreciate the radiant beauty and the scintillating personality of the woman they married. After forty years of being faithful, you know – how else could they make a comparison, and fully understand how lucky they are?'

Mrs Ratzenberger seemed to be pleased enough with this interpretation. As I turned up card after card, however, each one of them proved to be stranger and grimmer and less comprehensible than the one before. It became harder and harder for me to persuade Mrs Ratzenberger that cards like *Catastrophe Tuérie, Émeute* and *Suicide* were indicators that everything in her life was coming up roses. It didn't help that the illustrations on the cards became increasingly menacing and bizarre.

Tuérie (Killing) showed a father sitting at the head of a dinner table with a carving-knife and fork clutched in his fists, smiling. On either side of him sat the five members of his family, his wife and his sons and his daughters, with their plates in front of them. They were dressed for dinner, but they had all been beheaded. Their

53

necks were nothing but bloody stumps, and their heads were lying on their plates, with perplexed expressions on their faces, as if they couldn't understand what had happened to them. Not only that, but their heads were all mixed up, so that the mother's head was lying on her daughter's plate, and so on.

The dining-room door was ajar, so that you could just see the gray-bearded man standing there, watching them, and boy did he look *smug*.

Then there was *Émeute*, which means Riot (you don't have to be too impressed with my French, I checked out all of these words with Google Translate). *Émeute* showed a whole crowd of people attacking each other in the street with knives and swords and clubs and broken bottles. Their injuries were horrific – like one woman's intestines were hanging out and trailing between her legs as she was fighting off a man with a cutlass, and a small boy had both of his legs severed below the knee. An elderly man had been impaled through his chest with an iron railing, and a young woman was having her face forcibly pressed into the red-hot coals of a brazier, and her hair was catching fire.

Fortunately for me, the Chinese houseboy arrived at the moment that I turned up that particular doozy, and Mrs Ratzenberger was distracted.

I finished the session as quickly as I could and told her that in the next few weeks of her life she was going to have more excitement than she had ever experienced before. I told her that all of her omens were amazing, and that *she* was amazing, and that the cards adored her. The stars adored her, too. She was a Gemini, and this was going to be a life-changing month for Geminis.

I deliberately omitted to remind her that just because life is going to be exciting doesn't always mean that it's going to be enjoyable. There's such a thing as too much excitement. I also didn't remind her that 'life-changing' doesn't necessarily mean a change for the better. But anyhow Mrs Ratzenberger was delighted with what I told her, and while I packed away my deck of cards and finished my champagne and threw the rest of the strawberries at the seagulls, she went into the house for a while, and when she came back she was carrying a dark-blue velvet-covered box.

'Here,' she said, handing it to me. 'Frank gave me this for our last wedding anniversary but I want you to have it as payment for today. Frank is a two-timing *noyef*, but you, Harry – you're a true *held*.'

'No, no, Mrs R,' I told her. 'I can't take your anniversary present. That wouldn't be right. Besides, I take only cash. I don't have a bank account right now and apart from that I like to make life complicated for the IRS.'

'Harry, you've done me so much good today, better than one of Marty's massages, I swear to God. Please – take it. It's only a trinket, but you could sell it for a whole lot more than four hundred dollars.'

'Actually, I didn't tell you yet, but last month I put up my fee to five. With the greatest reluctance, of course.'

'That's OK, Harry. You have to make a living.

55

But take this, please. If you don't want to sell it, give it your lady friend.'

She kept jabbing this blue velvet case at me, so in the end, very much against my will, I took it.

'*Open* it,' Mrs Ratzenberger insisted. She was so excited that she was skipping up and down like a little girl, and her flat breasts flapped up and down underneath her peach silk pajamas like two tortillas.

I opened it. Inside, nestling on cream-colored satin, was a diamond bracelet. It was plain and simple and modern and unexpectedly tasteful for the Ratzenbergers, but it was set with so many pavé diamonds that I couldn't even guess what its value could be. I wasn't a pawnbroker, but I was sure of one thing: it was worth a hell of a lot more than a measly five Benjamins,

The jeweler's name inside the box was *Van Cleef & Arpels, 9870 Collins Avenue, Bal Harbor.*

'I can't possibly accept this,' I told Mrs Ratzenberger, closing the box with a snap and holding it up to her. 'It's far too valuable. Besides, what's Frank going to say when he finds out you've given it away? He's going to go ape.'

'That's the whole darn *point,*' said Mrs Ratzenberger. 'I want to show Frank that jewelry and money don't count for *nothing*. I don't want his bracelets or his rings or his necklaces. I want him to be my *husband* again. I want him to talk to me when he comes home, and I want him to be faithful, and I want to see his rope rising because of *me*. Not *too* often, that would be a nuisance, but now and again.'

56

'I still can't take this bracelet, Mrs R. For what this is worth, I'd probably have to tell your fortune a hundred times over.' I didn't add that she would probably have checked out before I even got as far as reading number thirty-six, but then diplomacy is all part of a psychic's stock-in-trade.

'I want you to have it, Harry, and that's that,' said Mrs Ratzenberger. 'If you *won't* take it, I shall scream and scream and say that you tried to rape me.'

Now I was born and brought up in Manhattan on the Lower East Side, and believe me I've been threatened a few times in my life. But the thought of having to explain to the Miami/Dade Police that I had not attempted to have my wicked way with an eighty-three-year-old woman with a Roast-A-Bag cleavage was more than I could face.

'OK, you win,' I said. 'I'll take it.'

I was thinking to myself: next time I come here to read her fortune I'll bring it back and hide it under the bed or something, so it looks like she simply mislaid it. She probably won't even remember giving it to me.

There it was: the warning bell, *jangle-jangle-jangle*, and it didn't matter if I was genuinely psychic or not, I should have heard it ringing in my head. *She probably won't even remember giving it to me.* But I was too busy thinking what a pain in the rear end it was that I had spent two-and-a-half hours with her and I hadn't made a nickel out of it.

I stood up, lifted my djellaba and pushed the

jewelry case into the pocket of my Armani jeans. Then I gave Mrs Ratzenberger a fond embrace and kissed her porcelain cheeks. Underneath those peach silk pajamas she felt like one of those skeletons you see hanging up at the back of biology class. Her bones didn't even feel as if they were joined together.

The Chinese houseboy showed me downstairs to the front door with a scowl. I don't know why he disliked me so much. Maybe in my starry djellaba he thought I was Voldemort on vacation.

As I walked across the hot red asphalt driveway to my metallic green Mustang, Mrs Ratzenberger leaned over the rail of her veranda and called out, 'Harry! You've forgotten something!'

I stopped, squinting up at her with one eye closed against the sun. *Jesus, don't tell me she's forgotten that I've read her cards for her, and I have to go back and start over.*

'Harry, my mystic motto! You forgot my mystic motto!'

'Oh, sorry, Mrs R. So I did.' I pondered for a few moments, and then I called back, 'A diamond with a flaw is worth more than a perfect matzo ball!'

Mrs Ratzenberger silently repeated it, moving her lips as she did so. It was like watching a goldfish trying to recite the pledge of allegiance. After she had repeated it three or four times, though, she nodded.

I gave her a wave, climbed into my car, and headed back down East Star Island Drive with Mudcrutch playing *Scare Easy* on the stereo, little realizing how much trouble I was in.

58

Six

When I first came south to Miami, I was planning on staying no longer than three months. My old friend Marcos Hernandez had asked me to take care of his house in Coral Gables while he was touring Europe with the Joe Morales Mariachi Orchestra, and I looked on it like an extended vacation. It never occurred to me that I would be seduced so quickly by the sunshine and the ocean and the girls in their minuscule bikinis – not to mention the envelopes stuffed with fifties which Florida's elderly widows would press into my hands in a return for a glimpse into their very predictable futures.

It never occurred to me that I wouldn't miss for a moment the endless grumble of Manhattan's traffic and the brontosaurus honking of fire trucks and the jostling crowds on the sidewalks and my musty-smelling walk-up loft on West 13th Street. I never thought that I would have no urge whatsoever to return to those idle mornings in Think Coffee, setting the world to rights with the would-be artists and the unpublished poets and the laptop warriors, as well as the dreamy-eyed girls with their bandannas and their spiky black mascara who didn't realize that the Beatniks had died out half a century ago and still thought that Allen Ginsberg might come walking through the door at any moment.

Marcos had returned from his tour, but he had generously allowed me to stay in the dinky guest cottage at the end of his garden, which looked like Snow White used to live there, only it would have been too small to accommodate more than her and three out of the seven dwarves, tops. I had a bedroom and a living room and a shower, as well as a kitchenette that overlooked Triangle Park. It was a pretty rudimentary place to live, all rough stucco and whitewash and Mexican rugs, and Marcos and his pals kept me awake most nights playing *huapango* music and laughing and stamping on the floor. All the same, the cottage was clean and it was secluded and it was free.

I finished my day's fortune-telling at five thirty p.m. While Mrs Edwards had tutted and twitched and suspiciously sucked at her dentures, I had told her at the James Hotel that she could look forward to golden times ahead. To be fair, I knew that she was sitting on an investment portfolio worth more than three hundred million dollars, and with that kind of wealth it's pretty hard to be glum for very long. After Mrs Edwards, I had given one more reading to Mrs Bachman in Hialeah, who was lying on her sickbed with a feeding tube up her right nostril and five Persian cats on her lap who continually hissed at me as if I were the Grim Reaper come to take their meal-ticket away.

Both times I used my Tarot cards instead of the Parlor Sibyl. I didn't want any Catastrophe or Scourge or *Tuérie* cards coming up again, especially since Mrs Edwards always paid me double my normal fee and Mrs Bachman was

60

ready to snuff it at any moment, and I didn't want to be held legally responsible for scaring her to death.

I knew that I had to find out if those Parlor Sibyl cards would still be the same when I looked at them again. On my way home, however, I put off the evil moment by dropping into John Martin's Irish Pub on Miracle Mile for a pint of Guinness and a Johnny Walker chaser. OK, I admit it. I needed some Irish courage before I looked through the deck and tried to work out how some of the most optimistic of fortune-telling cards had become so threatening and so grotesque.

My old acquaintance Bridget Clearly was already at her regular table, and I went across to join her. John Martin's is oak-paneled and low-lit. Although it has a long bar, it has plenty of intimate corners, too. Bridget was enjoying her usual Johnny Walker Black. She was a chisel-faced woman in her mid-seventies, with an unkempt tangle of gingery-gray hair that was badly in need of another dye-job and protruding teeth with a gap in the middle. She was wearing a dark-green satin dress, with a silver crucifix around her neck. She looked like the Irish fairy that timelessness forgot.

'What's the story, then, Harry?' she asked me as I sat down at the table next to her. 'Holy Mother of Jesus – you're looking awful *dark* today, boy.'

I knew better than to lie to Bridget. I may have been the Incredible Erskine, Foreteller of the Future, but Bridget was the real deal. She didn't

61

need cards or a crystal ball to tell you what was going to happen to you two weeks next Tuesday. She only had to look at your aura. She only had to *smell* you. I wouldn't have let Bridget tell my fortune even if *she* had paid *me*, because I never really wanted to know my own fate.

'Hey, it's just been one of those crap days,' I told her, taking my first swallow of Guinness.

'By "crap" you mean one of those days when Mother Nature refuses to behave herself the way you expect her to, according to the rules? One of those days when a little red divil jumps up from behind you and goes *boo!* and frightens the bejesus out of you?'

'You got it,' I said with a nod. Then, 'What are you looking at me like that for?'

'You have a droopy foam moustache.' She reached across and wiped it away with her fingertip. 'It would suit you, a droopy moustache like that. Make you look like General Custer.'

'Well, I guess General Custer and I have a lot in common. We both had trouble with Native Americans.'

'There's some trouble brewing up around you right now, sure enough,' said Bridget. 'I could see it, as soon as you walked in the door.'

I looked at her narrowly. Her eyes were grayish-green, and for some reason they looked more like an animal's eyes than a woman's. A female wolf, or a mother cougar. Knowing, and understanding, but ultimately heartless. That was what always unsettled me about Bridget. She was never afraid to speak the truth, no matter how much it might hurt you.

'I read a woman's cards this morning, but the cards turned out weird,' I told her. Like I said, there was no point in trying to deceive her. She would have known straight away that I was lying.

'What do you mean, *weird*?'

'Some of the cards were totally different from the way they should have been, Different pictures on them, different names. Like Death, for example – that's the nine of spades, and it should have had a picture of Death on it. Instead it had some scared-looking guy lying in bed with his legs all scaly. And then there were six or seven cards at least that I swear to God I have never seen before, with people stabbing each other and setting light to themselves and some girl having nine-inch nails knocked into her eyes.'

Bridget was thoughtful for a moment, with her fingernail tracing an invisible pattern on the tabletop. Who knew what she was tracing – a shamrock, maybe, or a pentacle? One figure to bring luck, one figure to stir up the Devil?

'You know what's happening to you, don't you?' she said.

'No, I don't. I'm not psychic. But – you know, *hey*, don't quote me.'

'You're being *warned*, that's what it is. Whoever is warning you may be still alive, or on the other hand it's more than likely that they're dead, because they can see things that you can't see. But somebody who cares about you is trying to tell you that you could be in genuine danger.'

'Sorry, Kate. I don't agree. I'm not being warned. I'm being *threatened*. If ever I saw cards which told me to keep my *schonk* out and mind my own business or else I'm going to wind up blinded or mutilated or dead, then these are they.'

'Do you have the cards with you by any chance?'

'Unhn-hunh. They're in my car. I locked them in the glovebox in case they change into vampire bats or something and fly away.'

Bridget raised her unkempt eyebrows. 'You know what they say about books, Harry? A book is just a block of paper until you open it up. It's the same with the cards. Until you start turning them over and reading what they have to tell you, they're just a stack of pasteboard.'

'Well, that's the way they can stay for the moment, so far as I'm concerned. I've still got the heebie-jeebies about them. Right now I just want to sit here and have a drink and forget about what happened. I'll take a look at them when I get home. With any luck they'll all be back to normal, the way they should be.'

Bridget said, 'You can buy me another drink if you like. You'll be needing one yourself, too. That darkness you've got around you, that's showing no signs of fading away, so it isn't. It's as black as smoke, Harry, believe me, and in fact I'd say it's growing blacker and knottier by the minute.'

I beckoned to the waitress to bring us two more drinks. Then I leaned forward across the table and said, 'Kate . . . if those cards still look this evening the same way they did this morning, I'm going to burn them, or throw them in the bay, the entire damn deck. Whatever's going on – whether I'm being warned or threatened – I don't want to know about it.'

Bridget took hold of my hand and gently squeezed it. 'You can't ignore it, Harry. Your life is going to change so much. The wheels are already in motion. It's too late now to jump off the train.'

I loved the Irishy way she pronounced 'wheels', as if it were 'phwheelce', but it didn't make me feel any better about what she was saying. I was half-tempted to go to my car and bring back the Parlor Sibyl cards to show her, but I felt as if that would be an admission that I was genuinely frightened of them.

We drank another drink, and then we drank another drink after that, and Bridget told me about the Cóiste Bodhar, the Irish Death Coach which waits outside the house with its door open when somebody is about to die, because once it has arrived on earth it can never return to the underworld empty. That lifted my mood a whole lot, I can tell you.

Before I went, though, Bridget grasped my forearm and said, 'I'm not messing with you, Harry.' She pronounced 'with you' as 'witcha', which I thought was highly appropriate. 'You do have the shadows dancing around you, boy. You can't ignore them. So watch your step and watch your back and watch where you're going and keep any eye out for any trouble. Something dreadful is approaching, I can promise you that.'

I wasn't exactly drunk by the time I arrived back at Marco's house, but I did manage to knock over a Grecian-style concrete planter with my front bumper and tip out the yucca that was growing

65

in it, followed by a heap of potting compost. I weaved my way around the side of the house, tilting from side to side as I did so, and then I moonwalked across the back yard, and on the fifth attempt I managed to jab my key into the guest cottage door.

With exaggerated care, I placed the deck of cards in the center of the glass-topped coffee-table in the living room. Then I went through to the bedroom, slung my sweaty djellaba over the back of the wicker chair that stood in the corner, kicked off my Gucci loafers and fell backward spreadeagled on to the bed, which let out a crunchy groan of complaint.

I closed my eyes for a moment, but I didn't fall asleep. The cards from the Parlor Sibyl were whirling around in my head like some off-key carousel. *Death, Murder, Riot and Catastrophe.*

I guess you could accuse me of being a cynic, the way I tell old ladies' fortunes and charge so much for it, but I do believe in the so-called 'supernatural'. Or rather, I don't believe that there's a point where the natural ends and the supernatural begins. I've witnessed enough bizarre and inexplicable events in my lifetime to know that our whole daily existence is super-natural, from morning till night. The supernatural, in fact, is just the weirder end of natural. It's only a question of degree.

We think it's 'supernatural' that we humans have a spirit inside us which can still exist after our physical bodies have bought the farm. At the same time all of us are hurtling around in a vacuum at sixty-seven thousand miles an hour, while also rotating at more than a thousand miles an hour, with no adhesive on our feet to keep us on the ground, and yet we call that 'natural'.

If people ask me about the supernatural, I point to the moon floating unsupported in the sky and say *quod erat demonstrandum*, I rest my case. You think your grandmother's ghost appearing in your bedroom at night is more supernatural than the moon floating around unsupported? Well, not my grandmother's ghost, anyhow.

Even if spirits are real, though – which they *are* – I don't believe that we should allow them to threaten us, or harm us, or tell us how to live our lives. They're dead, right? They've had their chance. Now it's *our* turn, at least until we're buried, or cremated, or cast into concrete balls and dropped into the Atlantic for fish to fornicate on.

But despite all this, I found those Parlor Sibyl cards deeply unsettling, I have to admit. I was sure that they were threatening me, but I didn't understand why, and that's what made me feel so disturbed. It was like receiving an anonymous phone call with some whispery voice saying, *'We're coming to get you, my friend,'* and having no idea what you were supposed to have done wrong, or who you were supposed to have done it to, or what their revenge was going to be.

I opened the bathroom cabinet to see if I had any Alka-Seltzer, but the carton was empty. I remembered that I had used them up after my last evening at John Martin's, talking about horse-racing with my new friend Gus and drinking to his latest winner, and then to the winner before that, and then to his losers, and so on.

I stared at myself in the mirror for a long time. There are times when you can look at yourself and wish that you were someone else and that your life was completely different. Why are we stuck in the same body, all of our lives, from maternity ward to funeral home? I would never know what it was like to be a football star, or an African-American, or a woman.

I went through to the kitchenette to see if I had any bottled water left in the fridge, but there was nothing to drink except three bottles of Coors. Beer would have to do. I was so dehydrated that I felt as if I had been eating tablespoonfuls of dry sand all evening.

The cards were still waiting for me on the coffee table. I could see them through the half-open kitchenette door, in their pink-and-red box, emblazoned with a picture of an old French biddy in a bonnet and spectacles. I pried the top off a bottle of beer and took three long swigs before I went through to the living room and confronted them.

'OK cards,' I told them. 'Trying to put the frighteners on me, are you?' I let out an extended two-tone burp, and then I added, 'You're not dealing with any kind of greenhorn here, so be warned!'

I sat down on the worn-out saddle-leather couch and stared intently at the box of cards, willing each individual card to return to its original form before I opened it up. From the direction of Marcos' house, I could hear *huapanguera* guitars and clapping, and occasional bursts of laughter.

68

'OK, cards,' I cautioned them. I was beginning to sound like James Cagney. 'I am going to open you up now and spread you all out on the table, and you are all going to be normal. None of this *Riot* and *Scourge* and *Catastrophe* crap. You got me?'

I picked up the box, shook out the deck of cards and began to arrange them on the coffee-table in rows of seven. I used this layout for any of my clients who wanted a more detailed answer to whatever their immediate problems happened to be, rather than a long-distance prediction. It showed *specifics*, rather than themes. I was hoping that it would give me an idea of why the hell I was being threatened, and where the threat was coming from.

The first three cards were fine. *Homme de Loi*, the Lawyer. *Maison de Campagne*, A House in the Country. *Perte d'Argent*, Loss of Money. These were all cards that I had turned up for my clients time and time again.

The fourth card, however, was totally un-familiar. A pale plump woman was running naked down the aisle of some kind of cathedral, wearing a crown of thorns around her head. Her body was criss-crossed with scarlet stripes, as if she had been whipped across her breasts and her stomach and her thighs. Behind her, there was a tall stained-glass window, but there was nothing religious about it. Dark purple glass had been used to form the image of a devil, with horns and dragon-like wings and slanted red eyes.

Immediately below the stained-glass window there was an altar, and in front of the altar stood the gray-bearded man, with a Bible in one hand and a stick in the other – a stick which had hanks of hair hanging from it. In this picture the man was wearing a gray priest's biretta on his head and a surplice, although this too was gray.

The card was titled *L'Hystérie*. I hazarded a guess that this meant Hysteria.

Suddenly, I didn't feel so woozy any more. I picked up the card and examined it closely. It appeared to match the normal cards in every way, apart from its subject-matter. It was printed in the same faded colors – reds and yellows and blues – and it was just as worn from years of repeated handling. Yet I had never seen it before, and I had no idea how to interpret it. *Hysteria*? Jesus. I think I'd be hysterical if I had to run naked down the aisle of a church, covered in blood.

I cautiously laid down another card. This, again, was a regular card from the Parlor Sibyl deck – *Divertissements* – which had a picture of a young woman in a bonnet dancing with a harlequin and drinking champagne. But the card after that was *Des Ravages*, showing a small weeping child sitting on top of a huge pile of decaying bodies, which were either naked or dressed in tatters. The bodies had attracted scores of carrion crows, which were pecking out their eyes and tearing at their intestines. In the far distance rose a high, snow-capped mountain, and for some reason it seemed familiar, although I couldn't immediately think why.

I went through the whole deck, laying down the cards faster and faster until I had set out all fifty-two of them – seven rows of seven and one row of three. About two-thirds of them were unchanged from the original Parlor Sibyl, but the rest showed scenes of slaughter and plague and suicide, and some of them depicted the grisliest tortures you could ever imagine. A small boy was screaming as three mustachioed chefs were pushing him feet-first into a meat-grinder, while his mother pleaded with them to stop. A naked man had been impaled up his ass with a thick thorny branch, while two laughing girls were cramming his mouth with handfuls of turkey feathers. This card was simply called Silence. One of the weirdest cards showed a man in a long bloodstained apron sawing a boy's head in half, right the way down the center of his face, and yet the boy was still sitting up straight in a kitchen chair and smiling inanely, rather like Alfred E. Neuman on the cover of *Mad* magazine. The title of the card was *Les Deux Visages*.

Once I had laid all of the cards out, I sat back and stared at them. How the hell could this have happened? Maybe somebody I knew was playing a really obscure practical joke on me and had sneaked into the cottage when I was out and changed some of my cards. But I didn't really know too many people in Miami, and I couldn't think of anybody who would want to creep me out that much – let alone anybody who had the imagination to think of it, or the energy to carry it out. Apart from that, these new cards would have been very expensive to design and print.

Somehow, the cards must have changed spon-taneously, all by themselves. Maybe some of the original cards had been printed with an ink that disappeared at a certain level of humidity, revealing a different picture underneath. But if that were true, how come fewer than twenty cards had been altered, and how come it had never happened before? I had owned this deck for at least six years, and the humidity in New York City in the summer easily beat that of Miami Beach.

I was still sitting there, taking occasional swigs from my beer-bottle and trying to figure out where all these grisly cards had come from, when I heard a soft rattling noise coming from my bedroom. It sounded like the blind being drawn down. I sat up straight and listened, but all I could hear was Marcos and his friends playing their guitars and *zapateado* dancing, which meant that they repeatedly banged their heels on the floor.

I waited a few seconds longer. Nothing. But I had just started to pick up my cards again, one by one, when I heard another noise, a creak, as if somebody had stepped on a loose floorboard.

I put down the cards and walked across the living room to the bedroom door, which was about three or four inches ajar. Inside, it was almost completely dark, and this suggested that the blind had been closed, even though I hadn't done it myself. I usually pulled it down just before I went to bed, to block out the street lights from Triangle Park. The street lights weren't particularly bright, but they shone through the leaves of the yuccas in the park, and when the breeze blew in from the ocean they cast strange flickering shadows on the bedroom ceiling, like witches and dancing monkeys. They didn't worry me too much, to tell you the truth, but whenever Sandy stayed over she said that they scared her, like having a nightmare about *The Wizard of Oz* when she was a kid.

I thought I heard a rustling sound, so I pushed the door open a few inches further and said, 'Hey! Is there anybody there?'

I had been advised by a detective from the Miami/Dade police not to warn an intruder that I was carrying a gun, even if I was. The first thing that an armed intruder will do if he thinks you're also armed is to shoot you. Think about it – if you were an intruder, wouldn't you? So I just waited. No response. I pushed the door a little more and said, 'If there's anybody in there, you'd better come out right now. If you haven't taken anything, or done any damage, then we can just call it quits. OK?'

Still no answer. I strained my ears and thought I heard another rustle, but Marcos and his friends were making too much noise for me to be sure.

I guess the most sensible course of action would have been to shut the door and lock it and call the cops, but for starters the key was on the inside. Not only that, but any intruder would have had to climb in through the window, so they could just as easily escape the same way. On top of everything, I was feeling tired and ratty and semi-hammered and the cards had shaken me badly, so I didn't have the patience to be sensible.

I didn't give any warning. I kicked the door wide open and reached inside for the light switch.

The light went on, but almost instantly the bulb popped, and the bedroom was plunged into darkness again.

In that split-second, though, I had glimpsed who or *what* was standing in my room. It looked like a nun, in a black habit, but her face was completely covered, or else she was standing with her back to me.

I stayed where I was, in the doorway, feeling as if my skin was shrinking. The nun didn't move, or speak. She was standing right in the center of the bedroom, but it was so dark in there that I could only just make out her silhouette against the blind.

'Come on – who are you?' I said, trying to sound authoritative. In reality, I probably sounded as if I had three Johnny Walkers too many. 'What the hell are you doing in my house?'

The nun remained perfectly still and said nothing.

'Do you *want* something?' I asked her. 'Is it money you're after? What?'

No reply. My heart was beating hard, and I still felt unnerved, but I was beginning to think to myself: *Whatever she's doing here, she's only a nun, or somebody who's dressed like a nun. She's about six inches shorter than I am, and if she really is a nun then it's very unlikely that she's carrying a concealed weapon.*

'OK,' I said. 'I'm going to go over to the side of the bed and switch on the bedside lamp. I'm not going to harm you. I'm not going to call the cops. I just want to find out who you are and what you want. You understand me?'

Gingerly, I stepped into the bedroom and edged sideways toward the bed. I kept my eyes on the nun the whole time, in case she decided suddenly to rush out of the door, or attack me, but she stayed where she was.

I reached the nightstand beside the bed, groped for the lamp and knocked it over on to the bed. 'It's OK,' I said. 'That's just me being clumsy. Everything's cool.'

I picked the lamp up, found the switch-toggle and pulled it. The bedroom was all lit up now, but the nun had vanished.

Immediately, I went to the door, thinking that she must have run out of the bedroom when I was picking up the lamp. But there was no sign of her in the living room, or the bathroom, or the kitchenette, and the front door was shut, with the safety-chain still hooked up.

I went back into the bedroom and lifted up the blind. The main window was shut, and only the narrow fanlight was open, so she couldn't have escaped that way. Besides, she too would have had to lift up the blind, if she had wanted to climb out of the window. That would have let in the street light, and I would have seen her. My attention had only been distracted for milliseconds.

I went back into the living room. I opened up the large pine closet where I hung my clothes, but there was no nun crouching inside it amongst my shoes. I checked the shower-stall in the bathroom and stuck my head around the toilet door. Not a sign of her.

I unlocked the front door, went outside and

shone my flashlight around the garden. The air was warm and fragrant, and Marcos' guests were beginning to say *buenas noches*, laughing and shouting and slamming car doors. But there was no nun, anywhere.

Looking up, I saw the moon above me, hanging unsupported in the light-polluted sky, like it knew something but wasn't going to tell me. I stared up at it for a while, and then I went back into the cottage and closed the door and locked it, although I didn't know how that was going to keep out a nun who could apparently walk through solid walls.

I finished picking up the cards and sliding them back in their box. Earlier on today, I had felt like burning them or throwing them into the bay or finding some other way of disposing of them. Now, however, I put them away in one of the drawers underneath my closet and locked it. However much the cards disturbed me, maybe they were the key to what was going on. Because *something* was going on, and that was for sure. I'm not a genuine psychic, but I could feel it in the air.

I went back into the bedroom, and sniffed, and I could *smell* it, too. A flat stale cinnamon aroma. I thought to myself: *if nuns could really vanish into thin air, and leave a smell behind them, that is exactly what that smell would smell like.*

Seven

Jim Waso called her a few minutes before seven a.m. the next morning. At first she tried to ignore the call, but he kept on ringing and ringing, so she eventually picked up.

'Anna? They told me about David as soon as I came in. I'm so sorry. I really am. I don't know what else I can say to you.'

'Thanks, Jim,' she said. 'To be honest with you, I still can't believe it yet.'

She was sitting on the couch wearing one of David's stripy shirts, with her tablet open on her lap. She hadn't slept all night, and her eyes were so blurry that she could barely read the words on the screen. When she'd gotten home at about three a.m. she had called David's parents and told them what had happened – one of the most harrowing conversations she had ever had in her life. Mr and Mrs Russell had promised to come down from Boise as soon as they could. Next Anna had called her own mother, but her mother wasn't picking up so she had left a message.

Since then, she had been trying to track down any references to violent convulsions and cata-strophic hemorrhage, to pass the hours before she could go back to work. So far, though, her search had been fruitless. She had found no medical reports that exactly matched the symptoms that both David and John Patrick Bridges had exhibited before they died.

She couldn't ignore the striking similarities between their two deaths, but they were the only two cases that she could find. If a disease was rare enough, she knew that it could sometimes take only two cases for them to be officially classed by the Center for Disease Control as an 'outbreak'. So far, however, she didn't have enough information to be able to conclude that both David and John Patrick Bridges had contracted the same disease, or even if it *was* a disease that had killed them. It could have been some unusual allergic reaction, or food poisoning. Maybe their deaths weren't related at all and were simply a bizarre coincidence.

She had also been combing through more obscure websites for any recorded instances of dead people talking *post mortem*, such as *Can The Dead Communicate With Us?*, but again she had discovered nothing to match her own experiences.

She had found plenty of examples of bereaved people claiming that they had heard the voices of their deceased partners in the weeks and months after they had died. However, almost all of them had admitted that this was nothing more than their minds playing tricks on them. 'I heard my husband upstairs, calling me, but when I went to see what he wanted, of course there was nobody there.'

Not one person said that they had stood beside their partners' bodies immediately after death and heard them talk to them, out loud, as if they were still alive.

Anna was aware that she was still in shock. She was quite prepared to believe that David's death had overwhelmed her senses so much that she had imagined him talking to her. But if that were true, why hadn't he said the kind of things that he normally used to say to her, or told her that he loved her and was going to miss her now that he was dead?

Why had he warned her not to interfere and said that the end was coming? The end of what? The end of *her* life, too? The end of humanity? The end of the world?

Jim said, 'Listen, Anna, I don't expect to see you in the lab today. *Or* tomorrow, either. Take the rest of the week off. Doctor Ahmet and Epiphany can finish up all of the tests you've been running on the Meramac School virus.'

'No, Jim, really. I have to come in. I need to run my tyranivir program, and I also need to go through my results again. I'm sure that I've been missing something glaringly obvious.'

'Anna, you just lost your partner. Give yourself a break, for Christ's sake.'

'So what am I going to do? Sit at home every day for the rest of the week feeling sorry for myself? How do you think I'm going to feel if more children die and I haven't been doing anything to save them? Finishing my program will keep my mind occupied, Jim, and that's what I really, really need right now.'

'Anna, I'm the CEO. It's up to me to take care of my staff.'

'But I need to be there for David's autopsy, too. I have to know why he died.'

'You won't be permitted to participate, you know that.'

'Of course not. But I can observe, and I can check the results. And for what it's worth I can give you my opinion as to what might have caused his death.'

'Well, it's against my better judgment, but OK. But let me tell you this now – if you show any signs of distress, physical or mental, I'm sending you right back home, which is where I personally think you belong.'

'Jim – I'll send *myself* home if I think I can't cope. Believe me, I need to be thinking one hundred percent straight to get this virus nailed. *And* to find out what happened to David.'

'All right, then. Come see me when you get in. And Anna?'

'Yes, Jim?'

'I'm so sorry, Anna. You have my condolences. Really.'

She walked into the back room of her laboratory and said, 'Right. Let's see if we can nail this nasty little gremlin, shall we?'

Stacked up against the left-hand wall were thirty cages of galvanized wire, with almost every cage housing a pink-eyed albino rat. The room smelled strongly of rat urine and formaldehyde. Yesterday afternoon, she had injected each of the rats with a sample of the Meramac School virus, and she had checked them as soon as she'd come into the laboratory this morning. She'd found three of them dead and nine of them lying on their sides, trembling and gasping desperately for breath.

80

The surviving rats she was going to inject with varying doses of tyranivir, which had recently been developed to kill off the newer mutations of the H5N1 flu virus.

H5N1 caused many more fatalities than H1N1, the common swine-flu virus, but it usually spread much more gradually. In the Meramac School outbreak, however, the virus had inflamed the children's lungs with such speed and ferocity that within minutes they'd found themselves unable to breathe and had dropped on the spot.

She injected three rats, which appeared to be close to asphyxiating. They twitched as she stuck in the needle, but they didn't try to wriggle out of her hand, as healthy rats would have done. As she took out the fourth rat, she glanced back into the main laboratory and saw that Epiphany was watching her with a sad, sympathetic look in her eyes, even though her face was covered with a surgical mask. Anna turned her attention back to the rat. Right now, she didn't want sympathy. She didn't want sympathy because she wanted to concentrate on her work, and to isolate this virus, and outwit it, and destroy it. She wanted to save those children's lives and to protect any more children who might contract it.

Most of all she didn't want sympathy because if anybody gave her sympathy she would break down in tears.

It took her about forty minutes to give each rat a varying dosage of tyranivir. When she had finished, she asked Epiphany to keep her eye on them. 'I just have to go up and see Jim Waso,' she said, taking off her surgical mask and hanging

81

up her lab coat. 'I think he wants to send me home.'

'Maybe you *should* go home,' said Epiphany. 'If I was you, girl, I'd be in pieces right now.'

'I'm OK,' Anna told her. 'I won't be too long. I can give Jim a progress report.'

'Do you really think we're making any progress? This little menace seems to be able to shrug off everything we throw at it.'

'We'll get it in the end,' said Anna. 'All we have to do is out-think it.'

Jim occupied a large office on the fifth floor, with a royal-blue carpet and a huge mahogany desk and a whole wall of leather-bound medical textbooks, as well as all his medical certificates, framed. Out of the windows he had a view of the red-brick spire of the School of Medicine at the end of the street, which resembled a Gothic church, and beyond that, the hazy suburban clutter of The Gate district. Beyond The Gate lay the Mississippi.

He was talking on the phone when Anna came in, and he indicated that she should sit down. He was a neat, handsome man with short black hair that was graying at the temples. In his white short-sleeved shirt and his red-and-yellow striped necktie he looked more like a politician or a senior advertising executive.

'Anna,' he said, when his phone call was finished. She stood up, and he came across and hugged her. 'My God, what a tragic thing to happen! What a terrible, terrible shock!'

'It was very sudden,' she said. 'He had just come back from Chicago, and he complained that he was feeling shivery and feverish and that he'd been sleeping all day and missed his flight.'

'Did he have any idea where he might have picked it up? Had he eaten anything that upset him? There's been a whole rash of organophosphate poisonings this week. Three children dead in Cleveland, and six or seven more in Atlanta.'

Anna shook her head. 'If it was food poisoning, he couldn't think where he might have gotten it from. He didn't seem too bad when we went to bed, but he woke up and he was convulsing and vomiting blood and screaming, too. He kept telling me that he'd been fighting it all day but he couldn't fight it any longer.'

Jim dragged over another chair and sat down close to her. 'We'll be carrying out autopsies today on both David and the guy they brought in yesterday.'

'John Patrick Bridges.'

'Was that his name?' Jim looked surprised that Anna had remembered it. 'Well, let's hope that David and Mr John Patrick Bridges can give us some answers. I talked to Michael Lim this morning, but he said he couldn't even *guess* what the cause of death might have been, not for either of them.'

Anna was tempted to tell Jim that she had heard David and John Patrick Bridges both talking to her, after they were dead, and what they had said. But Jim was a pragmatic, professional, serious man, and she knew what his reaction would be: 'Anna, you're still in deep shock.' It was true, she was. She could hardly believe that this day was real. That David was dead, and she was sitting here talking to Jim Waso about what might have killed him. But her medical experience told her that she could cope with the symptoms of shock, and that eventually she would get over it. She needed to be here, for David's sake, and for the children at Meramac Elementary School, and the last thing she wanted was for Jim to order her to go home.

'You're absolutely sure that you can deal with this?' he asked her, laying his hand on her arm. 'If you do want to take some time off, or if there's anything you need, you only have to ask. You're the best epidemiologist we have. You're probably the best in the state of Missouri, or even the whole damned country, but you're a human being, too, Anna. I don't expect you to be a martyr.'

'Thanks, Jim,' she said. Again, she tried to smile, but she couldn't stop her mouth from puckering up with grief, and her eyes blurred with tears.

Jim went over to his desk and brought over a box of tissues. 'Peter Kelly and Rafik Ahmet are quite capable of deputizing,' he said as he watched her dabbing her cheeks. 'And Epiphany – well, I think we have a rising star in Epiphany.'

'No – no, I can manage,' said Anna. 'I have the feeling that I'm really close to nailing this Meramac School bug. Like I told you, I'm trying out tyranivir which I don't think is completely going to prevent the virus from replicating, but its reaction will show me how it mutates. No matter how it changes, I can track it down easily enough with filament-coupled antibodies, but it seems to me that it adapts very quickly to new antivirals and what I have to do is find out exactly *how*. It has eight segments to its genome like any other RNA virus, but it can shuffle them like a Reno poker player, only faster.'

'So long as you're holding up,' said Jim. 'You have my cell number, don't you? You can call me twenty-four/seven if there's anything you need, or even if you only want to talk. I'm here for you, Anna, OK?'

She nodded. She really liked Jim, in spite of his seriousness – or perhaps because of it – and she could tell that he was attracted to her. There was just something about the way he held her gaze when he spoke to her, as if his eyes were trying to give her a message that his lips weren't allowed to. At the moment, though, there was only one person she wanted to talk to, and he was lying downstairs in the Pathology Department, chilled and dead, and she didn't think that he would ever speak to her again.

Later that afternoon, Doctor Rutgers paged her and asked her to come up to pathology. By now, Doctor Ahmet had arrived and was making minute-by-minute checks on the rats that Anna had injected with tyranivir. Six or seven of the rats appeared to be a little more animated than they had been earlier, although their movements were twitchy and erratic and they seemed to be confused. They kept jumping, as if they had been given a mild electric shock.

The rest of the rats were deteriorating fast. Three of them had their pink eyes closed and were lying on their backs, their lungs clogged up, and their breathing sounded like crackling cellophane.

'Come check this out, professor,' said Doctor Ahmet, beckoning Anna over to his microscope monitor. He pointed to the green sea-urchins bobbing and circling around the screen. 'See – you were right. As soon as the virus realizes that it cannot attach itself to a host cell, because of the tyranivir, it starts to mutate almost instantly. I never saw anything like it. You would have to invent a new antiviral every day to keep up with this baby, instead of once a year. Talk about a shape-shifter.'

'We need to find a way to recode its RNA,' said Anna. 'We need to make it *think* that it's mutating into something new, when in fact it's simply repeating itself. Over and over.'

'Well, I believe I may have some ideas on that,' Doctor Ahmet told her. 'I managed a similar trick with the variola virus in Gumla in 2011. Of course variola is a DNA virus, but I don't see why we can't do pretty much the same with this one.'

'I'm relying on you, Rafik. I just have to go up to the path lab for a while. Page me if you need anything.'

'Anna, before you go—'

'What is it, Rafik?'

'I want you to know you have my greatest feeling of compassion,' he said. He took off his thick-rimmed spectacles and blinked at her with his large brown eyes. 'I realize that for you it is still very soon after the tragic event, but the day after my father died, and I was so stricken with grief, my mother said to me, "You can honor the dead by focusing on new life."' He paused, and then he said, 'That helped me very much to understand why we are here, you know, and what is the purpose of grief.'

'Thanks, Rafik,' said Anna. She leaned forward and kissed his wiry black-bearded cheek.

Upstairs in the pathology department, Doctor Rutgers was waiting for her. Henry Rutgers was tall but round-shouldered, with a shock of white hair that rose vertically from the top of his head like a cartoon of somebody who has been scared by a ghost. He had a lived-in, baggy, Walter Matthau kind of face, with hexagonal rimless spectacles that he kept perched on the very end of his bulbous nose.

John Patrick Bridges was lying naked on the autopsy table, his skin so bloodless and gray that he looked almost silver. So far Doctor Rutgers had not yet started to cut him open, but his assistant had laid out all of the required instruments: the bone-cutting forceps for splitting his sternum, the retractors for holding his chest cavity open, and all the various scalpels that he would need for taking organ and tissue samples.

'How are you, professor?' Doctor Rutgers greeted her. 'I'm so sorry for your loss.'

'Thank you, Henry. That's very kind of you.'

'Well, I know what a shock it is, and how much it hurts. You never get over it, whatever anybody says.'

Anna knew that Doctor Rutgers had lost his only son in a skiing accident last year and how deeply it had affected him. She didn't say anything, though. She didn't trust herself not to start crying again.

'I read your little paper last month in the *AJE*,'

said Doctor Rutgers. He was obviously making a deliberate effort to change the subject.

'Oh, yes?'

'I must say you have some very bold views on causal association in avian flu. That must have ruffled a few feathers, if you'll excuse the idiom.'

Anna gave him the briefest of smiles. 'Sometimes – yes – there's a very fine line between what *could* cause an epidemic and what actually *did*. Occasionally, I think we should be given the legal sanction to cross it and be a little more forensic.'

'Anyhow, talking of what *could* and what *did*,' said Doctor Rutgers, 'I carried out a very thorough examination of the skin surfaces of the gentleman we have before us and also of your late partner, Mr David Russell.'

'I thought that Doctor Lim had already done that.'

'Michael? Yes, he had indeed. But I always insist on carrying out all my own histological examinations from scratch, even if one might have been carried out by another pathologist before me. That's not to say that I mistrust the medical expertise of my colleagues. It's just that I have a very good eye for what doesn't seem quite normal. Well – you have only to look at my wife!' He paused and looked at Anna over his spectacles. 'My apologies, Anna. I'm afraid that twenty-six years of pathology have turned me into rather a second-rate comedian.'

Anna shook her head. She really didn't mind. She had worked long enough with the sick and the dying and the desperate to know that most of her profession developed a dark sense of humor in order to deal with the endless pity of it. As a rule she found that the sicker the jokes that doctors told, the more sensitive they were and the more they cared.

Doctor Rutgers beckoned her toward the autopsy table. He lifted John Patrick Bridges's right shoulder and pointed to a row of four tiny brown dots across his back. It would have been easy to mistake them for minor acne blemishes, or moles, or not to even notice them at all.

'What do these remind you of?' Doctor Rutgers asked her.

Anna frowned at them closely. 'They look as if they're punctate lesions of some kind, but quite minor ones. They could have been made by a hypodermic needle, but more likely they're insect bites.'

'Does their formation tell you anything?'

'They're almost in a straight line. Is that significant?'

Doctor Rutgers said, 'It could be. There's one insect that tends to bite its victims in straight lines instead of puncturing them here, there and everywhere, and that's *Cimex lectularius*.'

'The common bedbug?'

'That's the fellow. The same noxious little bloodsucker that infests houses, motels and hotels the length and breadth of these United States in his zillions of millions.'

'But bedbugs don't transmit disease to humans. They can be infected themselves by nearly thirty human pathogens, but they don't normally pass them *on* to us, do they? Not unless we happen to scratch their bites and break the skin and acquire an infection that way.'

'Ah, but what they *can* do is make us crazy,' said Doctor Rutgers. 'Quite a high percentage of people who have been bitten by bedbugs have developed serious psychological conditions, such as anxiety and PTSD – even a form of schizophrenia. Now, not many other bugs can do *that*, can they?'

'OK, I agree. But they still don't make us hemorrhage and have convulsions at the same time.'

Doctor Rutgers shrugged. 'Maybe they've evolved. There's been a pretty concerted nationwide effort to exterminate them. Maybe they're fighting back. If viruses can mutate in order for their species to survive, why not bedbugs?'

'Oh, come on,' said Anna. '*The Curse of the Adaptive Bedbugs*? It sounds like some really crappy horror movie.'

'Anna – your partner has similar lesions. Seven of them, to be exact.'

'*David*?' Anna suddenly felt as if her skin were shrinking. 'He had them too? I never saw them! Where?'

'Here,' said Doctor Rutgers, pointing to his own right hip. 'They're all arranged in a slightly uneven line, from his back, *here*, all the way around to his stomach.'

'Are you *sure* about that? I didn't see them.'

'I'm not surprised. You were obviously very stressed when he was taken sick, and you were concentrating on saving his life, not on giving him a histological once-over. The lesions are very faint, and the punctures themselves are microscopic. But they do look remarkably like *this* gentleman's lesions, and of course their symptoms are almost exactly similar. Which side did David usually sleep on, if you don't mind my asking?'

'His – his left,' said Anna, abstractedly. 'Why? What difference does that make?'

'Not much. Except that bedbugs usually attack exposed areas of skin while their victim is lying asleep, and these bites were on the side of his body which would have been uppermost.'

'I need to get in touch with the hotel he was staying in, when he was in Chicago, and warn them they have bedbugs.'

'Hey – *hey* – hold your horses!' said Doctor Rutgers. 'We don't even know for sure if these *are* bedbug bites yet, or, even if they are, where your David and this other guy got bitten. It *could* have been in some hotel. While you're staying in a hotel for a couple of days, bedbugs can crawl into the seams of your luggage and lay thousands of eggs, and you can take them home with you! Bedbugs can even hide inside your nice warm laptop, for Christ's sake! God alone knows how many thousands of bedbugs are circling around the world even now, courtesy of Samsonite and Apple.'

He paused, and then he said, 'Anna – all that apart, we still don't know why these two suffered such severe convulsions and such catastrophic hemorrhage. Maybe bedbug bites had nothing to do with them dying. But I did think it important that you took a look at them, in case you come

91

across any similar lesions in the next few days or weeks. It could very well be that these are two isolated cases, and that we won't see or hear of any more. I darn well hope not. But on the other hand—'

'Can I see him?' asked Anna.

'David? Oh. Maybe that's not such a good idea.'

'Why not? You can show me the bites on his hip.'

'I honestly think it would be better for you if you didn't.'

'Henry – I'm a qualified professional. This may be the man I love, but I've seen plenty of dead bodies before, and I'm not going to faint.'

'Anna . . . he suffered what I can only describe as unusual rigor mortis. For some reason his face became kind of *contorted*. We don't know what caused it, but I don't think you'd like to remember him that way.'

So, she thought, *he still looks terrified, the way he looked when I last saw him and when he was begging me to help him.* It made her wonder if he were really dead, or if he were trapped in some numbing paralysis, locked in a vice-like state of utter dread for the rest of his life, his heart arrested, his breathing stopped, but his mind still aware of everything that was going on around him and more. Because how had his tongue emerged from his mouth and licked his lips? Unless it hadn't been *his* tongue at all? When Doctor Rutgers opened him up, what would he find inside him?

Anna had been hoping that David's face would have relaxed by now and that he looked peaceful again. But Doctor Rutgers was right. She didn't want to see him that way, looking so frightened. And she didn't want to think what the results of his autopsy were going to be, either.

Doctor Rutgers laid his hand on her shoulder. 'I'll let you know as soon as I have my preliminary results,' he promised her. 'In fact, I'll tell *you* before I tell anybody else.'

'Just be careful, Henry,' she told him.

'Well, of course,' he said. It was obvious that he didn't really understand what she meant, but she wasn't going to explain herself any more than that, because she didn't really know herself. She was still in shock, after all.

She left the path lab. As the door swung shut behind her, she saw Doctor Rutgers reach across to the tray of instruments and pick up a scalpel.

Eight

As you can imagine, I didn't sleep too good that night. I kept the blind open, but when I wasn't having nightmares about faceless nuns climbing over my window sill and standing motionless at the end of my bed, I was awake and looking up at all of those witches and monkeys dancing across the ceiling.

Eventually, though, it began to grow light. The witches and monkeys faded, and I could clearly see that no diminutive nuns were creeping toward my window through the shrubbery. I rolled out of bed and padded into the kitchenette to make myself a mug of horseshoe coffee. That's what the tracklayers on the Union Pacific railroad used to call a very strong brew, because they reckoned that a horseshoe would float in it.

I seriously wondered if I ought to talk to a priest about the nun appearing in my bedroom. I'm pretty superstitious – like, I throw two pinches of salt over my left shoulder if ever I spill any, to keep the Devil off my back, and as you know I believe in the supernatural, insofar as just about *everything* in this ridiculous world is supernatural. I'm not religious, though, except in those moments when I'm so shit-scared that only God can possibly help me out. But a priest might have a better idea than most why this spooky nun had paid me a visit and what she wanted.

The only priest I knew in Miami Beach was the Reverend Father Jose Zapata (yes, really, *Zapata*, as in *Viva!*), one of the team from St Francis de Sales Church on Lenox Avenue. I knew him only because I'd bumped into him after he'd given holy communion at home to one of my clients, Mrs Nora Washburn. He was young, and skinny, and incredibly talkative, with very white teeth, so that when he opened his mouth you could almost believe that Christianity was a brand of toothpaste. He'd told me that in his opinion fortune-telling was little better than the sales department of Satanism, but in spite of that my upbeat predictions had been very beneficial for Mrs Washburn's constitution. The only reason she hadn't died yet was because she was so desperate to know what was going to happen to her next.

After two mugs of coffee and a slice of toast and boysenberry jelly, I drove up to St Francis de Sales to see if the Reverend Father Zapata was around. I had an hour to kill before my first card-reading of the day, and I didn't care too much if I was late because my client was a seventy-year-old retired house painter named Joey Vespucci and all he ever wanted to know was the next day's winners at Gulfstream Park. Fortunately, I had an old acquaintance in the thoroughbred business, Mickey 'The Stirrup' O'Brien, and it was uncanny how many of my predictions came first past the post. (Well, it seemed uncanny to Joey, who always gave me ten percent of his winnings out of gratitude.) What I didn't much like about Joey was that he was a sweaty lard-butt who never opened a window and that he repeatedly broke wind while I was laying out his cards.

I turned into the parking lot behind St Francis de Sales just as the Reverend Father Zapata came whizzing around the side of the church on his bicycle. He was wearing a gold crash helmet and mirror sunglasses and a black Lycra cycling outfit. I called out to him while he was bumping his bicycle up the church's back steps. 'Hey! Father Zapata!'

He turned and took off his sunglasses and stood up straight, as if he had been unexpectedly paged by an angel.

I went across and climbed up the steps to join him. 'I don't know if you remember me, father. Harry Erskine. We met at Mrs Washburn's.'

'Oh, yes, I recall.' He had near-together eyes and a prominent, complicated nose, like every keen cyclist I've ever met. I think those kind of noses help them to cleave their way through the air. It was already very hot, and perspiration was trickling down his cheeks like blood from the crown of thorns. 'I remember. You're the fortune-teller.'

'Predictor of personal destinies, if that's all right with you.'

'Of course,' he said, smiling. 'However we like to think of ourselves, that is what we are.' He had quite a strong Mexican accent, and he spoke rather pedantically, making a point of pronouncing the ends of his words. 'What can I do for you, Mr Erskine?'

'Is there someplace we can talk?' I asked him. 'Some really wacky stuff happened to me yesterday, and I think it may have some kind of religious connotation, although I'm damned if I can work out what it is. Well – when I say *damned*, I don't mean it literally, the way that you guys do.'

'"Wacky stuff"?' asked Father Zapata. 'What exactly do you mean by "wacky stuff"?'

'Well, *weird* rather than wacky, First of all, the pictures on some of my fortune-telling cards – they changed.'

Father Zapata blinked at me. 'What exactly do you mean, *changed*?'

'Like they *changed*, entirely by themselves. Not all of them, but some of them. I had cards that used to show scenes of people laughing and dancing and counting out their money, that kind of thing, but now they're showing people stabbing each other and cutting off their children's heads and boiling each other in oil.'

Father Zapata wiped the perspiration from his forehead with the back of his hand and stared at me with his dark, glittery eyes. 'They have changed by themselves?'

'That's right.'

'You said "first of all" the cards changed. What else has been happening?'

'Well, this is the main reason why I thought of coming to talk to you, father. The cards, OK, they could have been changed by some kind of occult aberration, some kind of seismic shift in the spirit-world, if you understand what I mean.'

'No, I don't.'

'I'm not too sure I do, either, but the point is that a nun appeared in my bedroom last night.'

'A *nun*?'

'She was all dressed in black, with her face

97

covered over. I don't know how she got into my house because only this narrow skylight was open and I didn't see her come in. When I managed to switch on a light, she vanished.'

'Had you been drinking, or taking any other stimulant?'

'Father, when I drink, or take any other stimulant, I don't see nuns, believe me. I see go-go girls. I'd had two or three whiskies at John Martin's Irish Pub, but that was all.'

'You'd better come inside,' said Father Zapata.

He wheeled his bicycle in through the open door at the back of the church and propped it up against the wall. Then he took off his golden helmet and led me along the corridor. We went into a small side room furnished with three saggy green armchairs, a side-table with a bowl of withered apples on it and a glass-fronted bookcase filled with bibles and other religious books. Jesus stared down at us sadly from his crucifix on the wall. He was the double of my bandleader friend Ramone.

'Please, sit down,' said Father Zapata. 'Can I get you a soda, maybe, or a glass of water?'

'How about a glass of communion wine? No, just kidding – I'm fine, thanks, father. I just hope I'm not wasting your time here. I mean, maybe you're right and I was just hallucinating.'

'I hope very much that you *were* hallucinating, Mr Erskine.'

'Please – call me Harry. Even people who hate my guts call me Harry.'

'Very well. But the appearance of a nun in your bedroom—' He paused for a moment, searching for the right words. 'In the Roman Catholic Church we recognize that as a very particular type of paranormal manifestation. Officially, it's called Loudun Syndrome.'

'You mean like a *ghost*?'

'In a manner of speaking, yes. But it would probably be more accurate to call it a *presence* than a ghost.'

'You've lost me.'

Father Zapata drew back his lips to reveal his gleaming white teeth, but it wasn't in a smile. It was more of a grimace of indecision, as if he couldn't make up his mind how much he ought to tell me. He knew that I wasn't a believer – not in religion, anyhow – and it was pretty obvious that he didn't want to say anything that would make me think that the church was even more dysfunctional than I thought it was already.

'Ghosts are the souls of people who have passed over,' he said. 'However, they have returned to this world for one reason or another – either because they have unfinished business or a message to impart.'

'OK, like "the stock certificates are hidden in the dog kennel" – something like that? So what's a "presence"? Is that like a spirit? I mean, I know about spirits, from experience. From bitter experience.'

'A presence may not be a spirit at all, but a sign. It may appear in many different guises and mean many different things.'

'What does it mean if it's a nun?'

Again, Father Zapata paused. Then he said, 'So far as we know, the appearance of nuns is a warning. I suppose you can compare it to the appearance of crows around a house when somebody is dying. It means that some disaster is imminent.'

'Well, that's cheered me up. What kind of disaster?'

'It generally seems to mean that the world as we know it is on the brink of being turned upside-down. It means that people we know and trust will suddenly and unexpectedly betray us. It means a devastating reversal of social and moral values.'

'OK . . .' I said, although I still didn't really understand what he meant. 'Give me a for-instance.'

'Just before the outbreak of World War One, it was reported that nuns appeared to several politicians and priests in France and Germany, and throughout history there have been many other instances. A nun was seen on the bridge of the *Titanic*, even though no nuns were listed on the passenger roster. Usually, however, the church has done its best to suppress appearances like these, for fear of being associated with such calamities, or even blamed for them.'

'But what exactly are they? Are they good, or are they evil?'

'To be honest with you, Harry, we're not at all sure. Their first recorded appearance was in Angers, in France, just before Christmas in 1658. The mayor of Angers was visited by one of them, in the middle of the night, and so were several senior clerics There were six or seven appearances altogether. About a week later, scores of townsfolk contracted some mysterious sickness and died.'

'That could have been a coincidence, couldn't it? I mean, people were always getting sick in those days, weren't they? Cholera, smallpox, typhoid. Surfeits of mussels, you name it.'

'It could have been a coincidence, I agree. But two or three months later, one of the townsfolk who had supposedly died was seen in a neighboring town, alive and well, Then more of them were recognized in other towns, further afield. It turned out that all of them had changed their names, but that somehow they had all managed to achieve prominent positions in their new locations and had become very influential. They had done this, however, by violence and extortion and were very much feared – even though in Angers, before they were supposed to have died, they had all of them been model law-abiding citizens. As I say, there were many other similar instances recorded in church annals over the years, but most of the time they were redacted.'

'OK, I get it,' I told him. 'It's like – nuns appear – people get sick and die – then the same people pop up someplace else, not dead at all, but they've changed. They used to be good guys, now they're villains.'

Father Zapata nodded. 'In essence, yes, that's right. The Congregation for the Doctrine of the Faith admit that no direct link has ever been proven between the appearance of the nuns and outbreaks of sickness that followed soon afterward, but it has happened far too frequently for us to be able to dismiss it as coincidence.'

'So what are you telling me? I'm going to get sick and then I'm going to buy the farm, but then I'm going to come back to life again as some racketeering zombie?'

'Harry – I'm only telling you what little the church has discovered about the paranormal appearance of nuns.'

'So what am I supposed to do about it? Do you rent out exorcists, here at Saint Francis de Sales? Should I get my cottage fumigated? And what about my cards? Look – I'll show them to you.'

I took out the Parlor Sibyl, moved aside the bowl of withered apples and began to lay them out on the side table. To my surprise, the face of the first card was totally black. But then I dealt out the second card and that was black, too, and so was the third. I shuffled quickly through the whole deck, and every single one of them was the same. No pictures, either happy or sad. No women in aprons or men in tailcoats or fathers beheading their families at the dining table. Solid black, every single one of them.

I sat back and stared at them. Father Zapata looked down at them too, and then at me.

'Harry – this is not some kind of a leg-pull, is it?'

'If it is, father, then I'm the one who's being suckered. When I checked these cards before I came here, they all had pictures on them. Pretty gruesome pictures, some of them, but pictures.'

'These are the cards that you use to tell the future?'

'Yes, they are. And right now I'd say that the future's looking pretty black.'

102

Father Zapata did that baring-his-teeth grimace again, and then he said, 'After the presence had vanished, Harry, did you find that anything was left behind?'

'What do you mean? Like what? I noticed a kind of an incensey smell, but that was all.'

'I think that I had better come around and take a look at your bedroom, if that's all right with you.'

'Well, sure. OK. But what do you expect to find?'

'I hope that I find nothing at all.'

'But what if you do?'

'I'm not trained in exorcism, Harry. But an exorcism may be necessary. Or at least a dismissal. A dismissal is a kind of spiritual fumigation, to cleanse your home of any malevolent influence.'

I slowly collected up my cards, shuffled them straight, and returned them to their box. 'You're taking this seriously, aren't you, father?' I asked him.

'Yes, I am. Loudun Syndrome is no joke, I can assure you. As I say, it may very well be nothing of any consequence. Paranormal manifestations can be caused by anything from static electricity to mental disorder in the people who have witnessed them.'

'Oh, thanks. Now you're telling me I'm losing my mind.'

'In some ways, Harry, that might be the preferred alternative. If you're suffering from a mental disorder, it can be treated by psycho-therapy. Disasters, on the other hand – disasters can be averted only by God, and only if he chooses to.'

Nine

I drove Father Zapata south to Coral Gables. To the east, a whole pile of dark cumulus clouds was building up over the ocean, with lightning flickering underneath it. The wind was rising, and sheets of newspaper came flying in a panic across the avenue in front of us, and dust-devils danced on the sidewalk.

'Storm's coming,' said Father Zapata, and he crossed himself. He had changed out of his cycling gear now and was wearing a blue short-sleeved shirt with a dog-collar and jeans. He had brought a purple canvas bag with him with a gold cross embroidered on it, although I had no idea what was in it.

I glanced across at him. 'You don't just mean the weather, do you?'

He didn't answer and continued to look straight ahead. He was bending forward slightly, and very tense, as if he expected somebody to come jumping out into the road in front of us.

'You're worried about this, aren't you?' I asked him as we stopped at the traffic signal at the intersection of Southwest 8th Street. 'I think you're even more worried than I am.'

'I can often sense when something bad is about to happen,' said Father Zapata. 'I've been able to do it since I was a boy. For instance, I knew about an hour before it was run over that our family cat was going to be killed.'

'Wow. You ought to be in my business; you'd clean up.'

'Psychologists say that some people's brain-waves are phased to a higher frequency, so that they have the sensitivity to detect coming events. It's a bit like hearing a train approaching long before anybody else can. My mother always used to say that I inherited it from my Great-Uncle Emiliano. On the day before he was shot he told his wife that this was his last day alive.'

'You mean Emiliano Zapata? You're actually related to him? For real?'

'He was my great-uncle, by his son by his second wife.'

'How about that? Your great-uncle was the great Mexican revolutionary. That's amazing! So how come you decided to be a priest?'

'Because I have always fervently believed what my great-uncle believed, even though I might go a different way about it. We must all stand up for what we believe in, regardless of the consequences, and that is why I chose the cloth. Emiliano Zapata said, "It is better to die on your feet than live on your knees."'

'Well, I guess so. But instead of dying on your feet, you can always run away on them.'

'What made you so cynical, Harry?'

'I don't know. Other people's gullibility, I guess. Apart from the fact that I've seen more things in heaven and earth, Horatio, than most people have ever dreamt of.'

'You're not cynical about this nun, though, are you? Otherwise you never would have come to ask for my advice.'

'No, father. I am definitely one hundred percent not cynical about this nun.'

I parked on the street because the driveway was blocked with the bright pink-and-green Ford van that the Joe Morales Mariachi Band used when they were on tour. It had tinted windows and a picture on the side panel of a high-kicking girl in a crimson dress, showing her frilly panties.

We walked around to the back yard, and I unlocked the door of my cottage.

'It's kind of bijou,' I told Father Zapata. 'At least there's no mess. There isn't any room for it.'

Father Zapata came into the living room. He dropped his purple canvas bag on to the couch, and then he looked around. He sniffed the air, and then he sniffed it again, and again. 'Camphor,' he said. 'Camphor, myrrh and agarwood. You were right about the smell of incense.'

I sniffed too, but I couldn't smell anything. Father Zapata must have had a nose for it, or maybe they have special incense-detecting training at priest school.

'You want a beer or anything?' I asked him.

'No – no thank you. It's better if we stick to the matter in hand. Do you want to show me your bedroom?'

I opened the bedroom door, and he stepped inside, ignoring my unmade bed. After last night it looked as if I had been having a wrestling match with the sheets, and in a way I had.

He pointed to the narrow fanlight at the top of the window. 'That was open?' he asked me.

'Only the same as it is now. You could hardly get your arm through there, let alone a nun.'

Father Zapata approached the window and peered out through the fanlight. 'If you were standing in the border outside, you could easily reach up high enough to throw something through it – even if you couldn't climb in.'

'Like what?' I said, looking around the bedroom. 'There's nothing here! And don't try to tell me that the nun was a blow-up doll who was kitted out in a habit, pushed through that tiny little gap up there and then self-inflated to look like the real thing. Because where did it go afterward, this blow-up doll?'

Father Zapata kept circling slowly around and around, both hands raised as if he were a conductor, quietening down his orchestra before he launched into the *Emperor* piano concerto.

'There's something here,' he said, ignoring my facetious remarks about the blow-up doll. 'It's faint, but I can definitely feel it.'

I turned around too, but I couldn't see anything out of the ordinary. On the nightstand beside the bed there was only a digital clock, a glass of stale water with bubbles in it and a paperback copy of *The Complete Idiot's Guide to Magic Tricks*, with the spine broken and the corners of the pages all turned down. I had been seriously thinking about starting an alternative career.

Underneath the wicker chair there was a rolled-up pair of dirty green socks, a single Nike sneaker with no laces and a S'mores wrapper, but that was all.

'There's something here,' Father Zapata repeated. 'As I say, it's very faint. Its power has almost completely decomposed, but I can still feel a sense of ill-will. It's like overhearing some-body whispering behind your back. You can hardly make out what they're saying, but it sounds as if they're set on getting their revenge on you and they intend to hurt you badly.'

I thought about that, and then I said, 'When you say "*you*", do you mean that generally, or do you mean me personally?'

Father Zapata stared at me with those near-together eyes. The way he looked was almost as scary as what he had just said. 'Yes, Harry, you personally. Whatever it was that visited you here in your bedroom wanted you to know that they bear you a grudge.'

'How can you know that?'

'It's not easy to explain. But all of the malice was concentrated here, in this room. I don't think there's any question that the nun appeared here as a warning – and a warning specifically directed at *you*.'

'OK,' I said. 'But if he, or she, or *it*, or what-ever it was – if they had the power to make a nun appear out of thin air, why didn't they take their revenge on me then and there? Like, the nun just *stood* there. She didn't try to stab me or strangle me or jump on top of me and suffocate me, or however it is that nuns kill people.'

'I can't answer that, Harry. I simply don't know. I can only tell you what I'm feeling, and it's only a feeling, after all.' He sniffed again. 'There *is* something here, though. Something lingering. Not only incense, although I can still smell that. You know what it reminds me of? It reminds me of the week after a funeral, when all of the flowers that the mourners have heaped on a grave begin to go rotten.'

I didn't know what to say to him. To be truthful, I was almost beginning to regret that I had gone to the church to ask him about the nun. Maybe he really *could* feel the resonance that her spooky appearance had left behind. On the other hand, he could simply be a nut job. A well-meaning nut job, for sure, and perfectly harmless – like some of those geeks who get obsessed with *The Lord of the Rings* and role-playing games and Second Life avatars, but a nut job all the same.

He got down on to his hands and knees and peered under the bed. He sniffed again, and then he reached under the bed and drew out a small bunch of dead pink roses, maybe six or seven of them, tied together with thin frayed cord.

He climbed back on to his feet and held them up in front of me. I could faintly smell them myself. He was right; they smelled rotten.

'What?' I said. I have to admit that I was baffled. 'I didn't put those there. Why would I? I never even saw them before. The last time I bought flowers was when I was taking Zoë Salinger to the high school prom.'

'Oh – I'm quite certain you didn't put them there,' said Father Zapata. 'They were probably thrown in through the fanlight and bounced underneath the bed. It was these roses that caused the nun to manifest herself here in your bedroom. It's a classic tell-tale sign of Loudun Syndrome.'

'You mentioned that before, Loudun Syndrome. What the hell is that, anyhow?'

'It's quite complex. I'll explain it to you later.

First of all we have to deal with any traces of malevolence that might still be clinging to this bouquet and purge this bedroom.'

'Yes, right,' I said. Now I seriously *was* beginning to believe that Father Zapata was several beads short of a rosary.

He went into the living room and came back with his purple canvas bag. He loosened the drawstring and reached inside, taking out a shiny silver cross, a glass bottle of water with a silver stopper, a small copper bowl and a thick, yellowish candle.

'This cross came from Rome and has been kissed by the Pope himself. The candle is beeswax and came from the Ursuline convent in Loudun, in France. Every Catholic parish possesses at least one of these candles, sometimes more, in the event that something like this occurs.'

'OK,' I said. I was growing more and more skeptical by the minute, but what would *you* have thought if some skinny young priest had found a bunch of roses under your bed and told you straight-faced that they needed to be exorcized?

Father Zapata said, 'What I'm going to do is light the candle and drip it on to the roses until they are completely encased in solidified wax This will effectively trap any remaining malice that they still contain, and I shall then be able to take them away and incinerate them according to the proper ritual. I suppose you could compare it to burning a heretic at the stake.'

'I see.'

Father Zapata took off his dog-collar and started to unbutton his shirt. 'By the time I have finished, this bedroom will be spiritually cleansed of any

110

ill will toward you. Before I leave, I will also give you a list of precautions that you can take every night to protect yourself from any future appearances. Dismissals that you can recite, herbs that you can fasten to your door, simple but effective measures like that.'

'Father—' I began. I was going to say that I didn't doubt his good intentions for a moment, but in all honesty I didn't understand what the hell he was talking about. How could a bunch of dead roses pose any kind of threat? Why didn't he simply take them away and toss them into the trash? And why was he taking off his shirt? Jesus – now he was unbuckling his belt, too, and tugging down the zipper of his pants.

He looked at me very seriously as he stepped out of his pants. He was left wearing nothing but a blue-striped pair of boxer shorts and a pair of black socks. He was cyclist-skinny, with a crucifix of black hair on his narrow chest and hairy, muscular legs.

'It's essential for this cleansing that I am completely naked, just as John the Baptist was naked in the Jordan when he baptized Christ. My nakedness shows the forces of malice that I am open and pure and that I have nothing to conceal. I am proud of myself as God made me, and nothing can shame me.'

'OK . . .' I said slowly. I was beginning to feel very dubious about this. I just hoped that my girlfriend Sandy wouldn't turn up unexpectedly to find a stark-naked priest in my bedroom. Sandy got snippy enough when she saw me lifting my eyebrow approvingly at another woman. I couldn't

111

imagine what her reaction would be to Father Zapata in the buff.

Father Zapata dropped his shorts and then sat on the unmade bed and tugged off his socks. I tried not to look at his purple curled-up penis in its rook's nest of pubic hair.

'Uh – what do you want *me* to do?' I asked him. 'Maybe I should go into the living room and leave you to it.'

'No, no! It's vital that you stay! I will be insisting that the demon leaves you alone from now on, and you must be here for it to recognize you.'

'It's a *demon*? You didn't say before that it was a demon.'

'It doesn't have horns and a tail, Harry, if that's what you're thinking. I'm only calling it a demon because I don't know how else to describe it. It's a deeply malicious presence, and so I think that "demon" is as good a way of describing it as any other.'

'Well, you're the expert. Can we get this over with? I have a whole lot of readings to do today, and I'm running late already.'

'Harry, it's more than likely that this nun appearing in your bedroom is the harbinger of some really terrible disaster. Something cataclysmic, either man-made or natural. It could be that scores of people will lose their lives. It may be even worse than that. Missing a few card-readings – by comparison, that's very small beer.'

'I just hope my Tarot deck hasn't gone all black, too, otherwise I won't be doing any readings at all.'

'Please, Harry. This is a very difficult ritual, and I need to concentrate. Why don't you sit down and witness this dismissal? That's all I'm asking you to do.'

Reluctantly, and with a creaking noise, I sat down in the wicker chair and waited to see how my bedroom was going to get exorcized.

Father Zapata sat on the edge of the bed with the copper bowl on the floor between his feet. He took a box of matches out of his bag, and with a sharp scratch he lit the candle. Then he lifted up the bunch of dead roses in front of his face and stared at it intently. I thought: *You couldn't make this up. Just wait until I tell Bridget about it in John Martin's pub. She'll kill herself laughing.*

'I adjure thee, o vile spirit, to go out,' said Father Zapata. 'God the Father, in his name leave my presence. God the Son, in his name make thy departure. God the Holy Ghost, in his name quit this place. Tremble and flee, O impious one.'

He slowly turned the bouquet so that the flowers were pointing downward, and then he lowered it into the copper bowl, with only the stalks protruding over the rim. He held the candle over the bowl, tilted at forty-five degrees, so that it quickly began to drip molten wax on to the pink, brown-tinged petals.

'For it is God who commands thee. For it is I who command thee. Yield to me, to my desire by Jesus of Nazareth who gave his soul, to my desire by sacred Virgin Mary who gave her womb. By the blessed angels from whom thou fell, I demand thee be on thy way and never return. Amen.'

'Amen,' I added, as if that might help.

'You will leave this place which you have fouled with your miasma. You will leave this place and never return to threaten this man or any of his kin or any of his loved ones.'

'And amen to that, too,' I put in.

The candle wax was now pattering rapidly on to the roses, and Father Zapata started to mutter something under his breath that sounded like 'go-and-never-go-and-never-go-and-never' without actually adding the words 'come back'.

It was then, though, that I began to sense an altered atmosphere in the bedroom. At first I put it down to being tired, but gradually it felt as though the air was growing colder, although it was just as stuffy. It's difficult to describe, but I began to feel that we had disturbed somebody. As if we had woken somebody up and they were listening to us – and weren't at all happy that we were here.

It's a deeply malevolent presence, and so I think that 'demon' is as good a way of describing it as any other.

The candle-wax ran *drip-drip-drip-drip*, and Father Zapata continued to mumble 'go-and-never-go-and-never-go-and-never', and then I heard a high-pitched scraping noise. It was like somebody who didn't know how to play the violin scraping a violin-bow – except that this went on and on without a break and grew more and more shrill with every second that passed.

I didn't like to interrupt Father Zapata in his ritual. I thought I might mess it up for him, so that he would have to start over, or maybe it

114

wouldn't work at all. I stayed where I was in my chair, although the scraping noise was growing so irritating that it set my teeth on edge.

At first Father Zapata had been leaning forward, making sure that the candle wax dripped all over the rose petals. Now, however, he slowly sat up straight, staring directly at the wall on the opposite side of the bedroom. His eyes looked glassy, as if he had been hypnotized. Maybe he was in some kind of religious trance and that was why he kept repeating 'go-and-never-go-and-never'. Years ago I tried LSD, and apparently I sang *'Good – Good – Good Vibrations!'* over and over for nearly five-and-a-half hours non-stop. You don't make a lot of friends that way, believe me.

When Father Zapata sat up straight, things started to become stranger and more disturbing, as if they weren't strange and disturbing enough already. Instead of tilting the candle at an angle, he held it so that it was upright. Because it was made of natural wax it was very fast-burning, and scalding hot droplets ran straight down the sides of it, all over his fingers. As if that wasn't hurting him enough, he lifted his left hand and held it over the candle, so that the flame was actually licking at his palm. I stared at him in horror, but he kept his hand there without flinching, and he didn't cry out.

In fact – far from distressing him – the pain of burning his own hand seemed to turn him on. His penis uncurled itself and rapidly began to rise up from between his hairy thighs, purple-headed and prong-like – so stiff that it was actually curving.

I had been a split-second away from springing

out of my chair and snatching the candle out of his hand to stop him from hurting himself any more, but the appearance of this boner made me hesitate. Maybe the hand-burning was all part of the ritual. Maybe a priest needed to experience both pain and pleasure to dismiss a demon, as well as recite his prayers. Maybe it was all about mortifying the flesh in order to get through to God. I had read about monks eating gristly bits of meat to punish their palates and flagellating themselves with barbed-wire whips. Maybe Father Zapata needed to do something like that for his dismissal to be effective. I simply didn't know. Me – I had a pretty good idea how to send a Native American demon back to the Happy Hunting Ground, but my only experience of a Roman Catholic dismissal was watching *The Exorcist* with some girl called Rona, and she had screamed in my left ear all the way through it.

I was still hesitating when Father Zapata lifted his hand from the candle flame and pinched out the wick between finger and thumb. I looked down at the roses in the copper bowl. I didn't get this at all. Hadn't he told me that he was going to seal them completely with wax from this holy candle so that none of the evil left in them could escape? So far, however, they were spattered with fewer than a dozen drips.

'Father Zapata,' I said, although I didn't think he could hear me over the continuous scraping sound, and even if he could, he chose to ignore me.

'Father Zapata? Is this, ah – is this *meant* to happen this way?'

Father Zapata still didn't respond. Instead, he leaned backward until he was lying flat on the bed, staring at the ceiling, his arms held out wide as if he were mimicking the crucifixion. When he let the candle roll off the bed on to the floor, I decided that I had nearly had enough of this, and now I stood up.

As I did so, Father Zapata lifted his legs until he was bent over double with his feet beside his ears and his scrawny backside up in the air, all rolled up like a woodlouse. I couldn't think what he was doing until I went up to the side of the bed and looked down at him. He had taken the head of his stiffened penis into his mouth, and he was staring up at me from between his thighs with an expression that I can only describe as desperate.

Afterward, I thought that I should have simply pushed him straight off the bed. But there was that frozen moment when I stood there staring down at him performing what looked like a trick from some pornographic circus, all curled up like that, fellating himself, and that frozen moment was one moment too long.

He closed his eyes, and he bit. He bit so hard that he completely took the head off his penis, and suddenly the bitten-off shaft sprang up with blood spraying everywhere. Father Zapata's face instantly became a scarlet carnival mask, and there were loops and spatters of blood all over the sheets and pillows and all over the front of my shirt.

Father Zapata didn't scream or cry out, but his legs dropped back on to the bed, and he lay flat

117

on his back in that crucifix posture, like he had been before, his arms spread out wide. He was quaking violently and snorting through his nostrils. His topless penis kept on pumping out blood, and there was only one thing that I could think of to do. I took the dead roses out of the bowl, tugged loose the fraying thread that held them together, and knotted it tightly around the shaft of Father Zapata's penis as a tourniquet. By the time I had finished doing this, my hands and arms were smothered with blood up to the elbows, and both of us looked as if we had been the victims of a pump-gun attack at close range.

I took my cell out of my blood-soaked shirt pocket and punched out 911.

'Nine-one-one,' said a woman's voice. 'What is your emergency?'

'I need an ambulance, quick, seven-seven-three Orduna Drive, Triangle Park. I'm in a cottage in back. I have a man here who's lost the top off his penis.'

'He's done *what*, sir?'

'He's suffered a serious injury to his private parts. He's bleeding really bad. I've tried to stop it, but he needs paramedics, and fast.'

'Please stay on the line, sir. We'll be sending an ambulance right away.'

There was nothing much more I could do. I stood there watching Father Zapata twitch and snort and shiver. I had managed to stop the blood from shooting out like a fire hydrant, but it was still flooding copiously all over the sheets.

It occurred to me then to look for the top of his penis that he had bitten off. Maybe the surgeons could sew it back on again. I ran my hands all over the wet bloody bed, but I couldn't find it anywhere. I looked at him. His eyes had rolled up into his head, and he was gray with shock. He certainly wasn't in any state to be able to tell me if he had swallowed it.

Minutes went past, and then at last I heard the scribbling and whooping of the ambulance siren. Father Zapata was lying still now, with his eyes closed and his mouth open, and I couldn't be sure if he was still alive.

I turned around to go to the front door, but as I did so something dark and shadowy flickered across the hallway, from the kitchen to the living room. I stopped, and called out, '*Who's that?*' It couldn't have been the paramedics because the front door was still closed.

There was silence for a long, long moment. Even that scraping noise had stopped. I waited and listened.

'Anybody there?' I called out. I thought I glimpsed another flickering shadow, in the living room. 'I said, is anybody there?'

Still silence. And then – so softly that it was barely audible – I heard a quick, urgent tapping sound. *Tap-tap-tap-tap-tap!* Then silence. Then *tap-tap-tap-tap-tap!*

Oh God, I thought. *Not that. Don't tell me it's that. It can't be.*

But then the doorbell rang, and a voice said, 'Paramedics!'

Ten

Anna was crossing the hospital reception area when a man's clear voice called out, 'Professor Grey?'

She turned, trying to focus against the dazzling evening sunlight that was reflected from the polished marble floor. It had been a long and difficult day, and she could already feel a migraine developing behind her eyes.

Early in the afternoon Jim Waso had come down to her laboratory and pleaded with her again to go home, but she had refused. Apart from the fact that she'd needed to keep working in her laboratory to keep her mind off David, she'd started to make significant progress in her understanding of how the Meramac School virus could mutate so rapidly. She was confident now that she could soon find a way to isolate it. Much of her success as an epidemiologist was that she always treated viruses as if they were sentient beings – *alien* beings, maybe, but very intelligent aliens, and very devious. As far as she was concerned, understanding viruses was an essential part of cornering them, and then destroying them. She liked to think that she worked in the same way as criminologists – painstakingly striving to unlock the minds of serial killers, and then using their own behavior patterns to outsmart them.

A broad-shouldered young man in a dark suit

120

came over to her. His face was handsome but unusual. His eyes were set wide apart, and his cheekbones were high, but his features were flat, as if he had some Native American blood in him. His glossy black hair was tied back in a ponytail. He held out his hand to her, but she didn't take it, so he lowered it again.

'Professor Grey? My name's Robert Machin. I just want to tell you that I'm very sorry for your loss.'

'Thank you,' said Anna. 'I hope you won't think I'm being rude, but do I know you? We haven't met before, have we? Were you a friend of David's?'

Robert Machin shook his head. 'We haven't met before, and I didn't know your partner personally, I'm afraid. I represent the Grandier Funeral Chapel.'

Anna swallowed hard, more to stop her throat from tightening up with emotion than because she was annoyed with him. 'You do know that my partner passed away only last night? He hasn't been dead for a full day yet.'

'Yes, I do, professor, and I hope I'm not upsetting you by approaching you so soon. All I want to tell you is that we at Grandier have only recently established ourselves in St Louis and because of that we can handle all of your funeral arrangements at a very special price, compared with other funeral directors in the area.'

'All right,' said Anna. His directness had taken her aback, but at the same time she surprised herself by feeling relieved. After she had witnessed David talking and licking his lips, when he was supposed to be dead, it would be a blessing if his body was disposed of as soon as possible. At least she could be sure then that he was at peace, and if there *was* something inside him, something that had tormented him to death, that would be disposed of, too.

She took a deep breath and said, 'I haven't seen his will yet, but he did once tell me that he wanted to be cremated.'

'Of course,' said Robert Machin. 'We can take care of absolutely everything for you. A funeral service, of any denomination. Cremation or interment, whichever you prefer. Music, live or recorded. Cars, a memorial plaque. Flowers. We fully understand what a painful time this is for you, professor, and you can trust us to give you the very best care and attention.'

'I'll have to talk to David's parents,' Anna told him. 'They live in Boise, and they may want to hold the funeral there.'

'That wouldn't be a problem,' said Robert Machin. 'We could handle all the arrangements from here and use one of our affiliated funeral directors in Boise to take care of things from that end.'

'Let me think about it,' said Anna. 'Do you have a card?'

Robert Machin took out his wallet and gave her his business card. In embossed black italics, it read: *Grandier Funeral Chapel, 1001 Gravois Road, St Louis. Service With Sympathy.* Underneath the lettering there was a miniature picture of a spray of pink roses, also embossed.

'Please, call us,' said Robert Machin with a smile. 'You won't regret it, I promise you.'

With that, he walked away, toward the elevator bank. When he reached it, he turned around to her and gave her a salute, as if she had agreed to use his company already. She didn't wave back, but watched as he stepped into one of the elevators and the door slid shut behind him. She looked at his card again. She couldn't logically think why, but she felt that if she called Robert Machin, and agreed to use Grandier Funeral Chapel, her life would take a completely new course.

She had always been intuitive. That was another reason why she was so good at hunting down viruses, even when they mutated themselves into almost unrecognizable variants. But she had never felt so strongly that a very different future could be waiting for her now, depending on what decision she made about David.

She was still standing in the middle of the reception area, looking at the card with its embossed pink roses, when she heard high-heeled footsteps click-clacking up behind her, and then Epiphany touched her on the shoulder. She knew it was Epiphany even before she turned around because she could smell the Sarah Jessica Parker perfume she always sprayed on herself after work.

'Anna?' said Epiphany anxiously. 'Are you OK?'

'Oh, what? Yes – yes, I'm fine. I was miles away there for a moment.'

'What are you doing this evening? You won't be on your own, will you?'

'I will, yes, but I want to be. I'll be fine, don't

worry. I just need to get my head around everything that's happened.'

'You're sure? You can come round to my place
if you like. It's only risotto for supper, but you're
more than welcome.'

'That's OK. I'd rather just sit on my own and
think.'

Epiphany shrugged. 'My grandma always used
to say that *thinking* was invented by the Devil.'

'Oh yes?' said Anna. She couldn't help smiling.
'And why did she think that?'

'Thinking makes you ask yourself questions
about what the Good Lord has in store for you,
and as soon as you start doing that, you're
halfway down the road to Hell already.'

'Your grandmother sounds just like mine,' said
Anna. 'Mine used to read a chapter of the Bible
every single day. She could quote Revelations
from beginning to end.' She paused and lifted
one hand like a preacher, trying to remember the
exact words. '"*And in those days men will seek
death and will not find it. They will long to die
and death flees from them.*"'

'Wow,' said Epiphany.

'Oh, don't be too impressed. That's the only
bit that I can remember.'

'All the same. Wow. I can't even remember the
Lord's Prayer.'

They went out through the revolving door into
the warm evening air and walked together toward
the parking lot. As they did so, an ambulance came
speeding in through the hospital entrance with its
lights flashing and stopped outside the emergency
room. Anna took no notice; emergency patients

124

were being brought into the hospital twenty or thirty times a day, every day. She said goodnight to Epiphany and walked toward her car, but as she opened the door her cellphone warbled.

'Anna? Are you still on site? It's Henry Rutgers.'

'I was just about to leave. What is it, Henry?'

'They brought in another one. A female sales executive from Dayton, Ohio, thirty-four years old. She's convulsing and bringing up blood.'

'Oh God.'

'There's something else, Anna. She has two very obvious patterns of bedbug bites.'

'You're sure?'

'No doubt about it, to my mind. *Cimex lectularius.*'

Anna slammed her car door shut and pressed the key-fob to lock it. 'I'm coming back up. Where are you?'

Doctor Rutgers was waiting for her in the scrub room outside the emergency operating theater, his white hair leaning to the left as if he had been out in a hurricane.

'She's critical,' he said. 'Quite honestly, I don't think she's going to make it.'

Anna peered through the oval tinted windows in the scrub room doors. She could see two surgeons and three nurses clustered around the operating table, but all she could see of the patient was a blood-drenched sheet that was violently jolting up and down, as if two dogs were fighting underneath it.

She quickly washed her hands and took a pale-blue theater gown out of the closet and pulled it on. Doctor Rutgers tied it up for her at the back.

'She's bleeding even more catastrophically than your David and that other unfortunate guy – what was his name? Bridges. It's like every gastrointestinal blood vessel has ruptured. And her convulsions are way, *way* more violent, too. At one point she was almost bouncing herself clear off the table.'

'Where are the bedbug bites?' asked Anna. She put on a flower-patterned cap and a surgical mask and tugged on a pair of latex gloves.

'The worst ones are up here,' said Doctor Rutgers, patting his left shoulder. 'There are seven on her upper arm, but a further five just above the elbow. She may have more, but the way she's jumping around I didn't get the chance to give her a full histological. I'll be running tests, of course, whether she survives or not, but I'm ninety-nine percent certain that's what they are.'

'Where was she picked up from?'

'The Gateway Inn at Union Station. All I know about her is that she was here for a convention. A work colleague came in with her, and she's waiting downstairs.'

'We need to notify the city health people. This is starting to look like an outbreak.'

'I did that already. They're sending over Phil Magruder and some bug specialist from ESSENCE.'

ESSENCE was the city's program of early notification of community-based epidemics. In the past two days, Anna had already had three visits from ESSENCE in relation to the Meramac Elementary School virus. It was the city's

126

ESSENCE team who had ordered the closure of the school until further notice and the isolation of any children with symptoms of fever.

'God knows what's going to happen if this *is* caused by bedbugs,' she said, straightening her cap in the mirror. 'They'll have to shut down half of the hotels in St Louis and have them fumigated.'

'You know something?' said Doctor Rutgers. 'This whole thing is beginning to make me feel incredibly itchy.'

They pushed their way through the swing doors into the operating theater. The woman on the table was smothered in blood. Her hair was stuck to her head like a glossy red bathing-cap and her face was streaked with scarlet. The nurses were trying to strap her down so that the surgeons could insert a gastroscope down her throat to see how extensively she was bleeding, but it was almost impossible. She was throwing herself wildly from side to side, her arms flailing, and at the same time she was violently arching her spine. With each convulsion a fresh torrent of blood spurted out of her mouth.

After the woman had brought up yet another gush of blood, she gasped for breath, as if she were desperately trying to say something. She gasped again, and again. Anna circled around the nurses to the side of the operating table and looked down into her war-painted face. Her eyes were wide with panic, and she kept opening and closing her mouth.

At last she managed to find breath enough to speak. '*Inside me!*' she bubbled. '*She's inside me!*

Please, get her out of me! Oh God! Oh God! She's inside *me!'*

One of the nurses managed to grip the sides of the woman's head, holding it steady while a second nurse wedged a contoured foam cushion underneath it and then fastened a rubber fixation strap across her temples. As soon as she had tightened up the strap, though, the woman gave a single rippling shudder, from her head to her feet, as if somebody had walked over her grave, and then she stopped convulsing altogether. A high, continuous drone from the vital signs monitor indicated that her heart had stopped.

'She's arrested!'

A nurse hurriedly wheeled over the defibrillator cart, and one of the surgeons picked up the electrode paddles and pressed them to the woman's chest. He shocked her again and again, calling out, 'Clear!' each time, but after five attempts she still showed no signs of life. One blood-streaked arm flopped down by the side of the operating table.

'She's lost far too much blood,' said Doctor Rutgers, shaking his head. 'I don't know what more we could have done.'

'Time of death nineteen-oh-three,' said the surgeon, handing the paddles to the nurse standing beside him. He came across the theater, his gown spattered in blood, peeling aside his mask. Anna knew him well. Doctor Farage was Syrian. He had a little clipped moustache, and his soulful brown eyes suited tragic occasions like this.

'I have never come across any case like this before,' he said. '*Never*, not in twenty-seven years

128

of emergency surgery. I've had bleeding from terrible internal injuries that I couldn't stop, of course. Men impaled on scaffolding poles, women nearly torn in half in auto accidents, things like that. But nothing like this; not from a virus. Not even from the worst of hemorrhagic fevers.'

'Did she speak to you at all, before I arrived?' Anna asked him.

'Two or three times, Anna, but then she started to hemorrhage so badly that she could hardly *breathe*, let alone speak. I asked her what she thought was wrong with her – maybe it was something she had eaten or drunk. But no, she kept on saying that another woman was trying to force her way into her body, whatever she meant by that.'

'Both of our other patients said something similar,' Anna told him. 'I'm not sure what it means, either, but they kept on insisting that there was somebody else inside of them, trying to force them out of their own body. They both felt as if they were being attacked from the inside out.' She didn't explain that both David and John Patrick Bridges had told her this after they were clinically dead.

Doctor Farage started to snap off his bloody latex gloves, finger by finger. 'Of course, these are just delusions. But with this woman – she was bleeding so profusely, I could almost have believed her.'

'Maybe it's some mutation of Lassa fever, or Marburg virus,' said Doctor Rutgers. 'We know that bedbugs don't normally transmit these viruses to humans. But maybe they're carrying a new variation which *can* infect us.'

Anna said, 'Henry – we still can't say for sure if this sickness *was* passed on by bedbugs. It may be a coincidence that all three of the deceased were bitten. After all, there can't be many hotels or motels across America that don't have *some* degree of infestation.'

'Now I really *do* feel itchy,' said Doctor Rutgers. 'I stayed at the Templeton Inn last night, because I finished up too late to go home.'

Anna said, 'As soon as you can provide me with a range of samples, Henry, I'll get to work on it. Meantime, I'd better go talk to this poor woman's friend and give her the sad news. Where did you say she was?'

'I didn't, but she was in the family waiting room the last time I saw her.'

Anna went over and took another long look at the dead woman lying on the operating table. She didn't have the terrified expression that she had seen on David or John Patrick Bridges, but under the smears of blood on her forehead and her cheeks she appeared to be frowning, as if she was still being troubled by something, in spite of being dead.

Doctor Rutgers came over with her notes on a clipboard. 'Mary Belling Stephens,' he told her. 'Thirty-four years old, a sales exec for Infinity Software Systems, of Dayton, Ohio.'

Anna noticed the gold wedding-band on the woman's left hand and felt a pang of sadness. Mary Belling Stephens's side of the bed would be empty tonight, and she would never again wear the clothes hanging in her closet.

She took off her theater gown and went down

in the elevator to the first floor. Seeing her reflection in the mirror at the back of the elevator car, she thought she looked pale and tired. She had always felt that when patients died, they drained something out of the soul of the doctors and nurses who had been trying so hard to save them. It wasn't surprising that hospital staff always told such cynical jokes: it was one way of protecting themselves from spiritual anemia.

The family waiting room was silent except for the soft bubbling of a tropical fish tank. Its only occupants were an anxious-looking African-American man in a blue Autotire T-shirt and a young woman with curly red hair. The young woman was wearing a pale-green business suit, but the front of her skirt was patterned like an atlas with rusty-colored bloodstains.

'You must be Mary Stephens's friend,' said Anna. 'Hi. I'm Professor Grey.'

The young woman immediately stood up. 'How is she? She's going to be all right, isn't she?'

'I think you'd better sit down,' Anna told her.

'What?' said the young woman. She remained standing and slowly lifted her hand to cover her mouth.

'I can't tell you how sorry I am,' said Anna. 'The doctors did everything they possibly could to save her.'

The young woman's eyes brimmed with tears. 'Oh, *no*,' she wailed. 'Oh, *no*. I can't believe it. Not Mary! She's always so lively! She's always laughing! Everybody loves her! Oh, what's Alex going to do? Oh God, and her children, too!'

Now she sat down, and Anna sat beside her

and held her hand. 'We're not sure yet what she was suffering from. She had some kind of convulsive fever that made her hemorrhage. She passed away from heart failure and loss of blood.'

'But it happened so *suddenly*!' the young woman sobbed. 'One minute she was *fine*, and she was holding a seminar. She was talking about gate-keeping when she stopped and coughed up blood, all down the front of her blouse. The next thing we knew she was lying on the floor kicking and shaking and bringing up even more blood.'

'We'll be running tests to find out what affected her,' said Anna. 'Meanwhile, can you please tell your colleagues that if any of them feel even slightly unwell, they should come to the ER without any delay. The city health services will be in touch with you all and tell you what to do now and what precautions you need to take. It's possible that some of you may have to go into quarantine. Can I ask you one thing? Have you been bitten at all?'

The young woman frowned at her. 'Bitten? I don't understand.'

'Do you have any insect bites anywhere on your body? Pink, inflamed and really irritating? The kind that you can't stop yourself from scratching.'

The young woman shook her head. 'No. Nothing like that. Why? Do you think Mary could have been bitten by a mosquito or something?'

'It's possible. It's too early to say. Look – if you have Mary's address and contact details, we can get in touch with her family and tell them what's happened. SLU has a wonderful support team for bereaved relatives.'

The young woman nodded. She was clearly stunned. She reached into her pocket and took out her cell. 'I have her details on here,' she said and started to prod at it. Before she had finished, though, she looked across at Anna and said, 'There was one thing. Before she went into the seminar, she did tell me that she was feeling strange.'

'Strange? Did she give you any idea what she meant by that?'

'Yes, but I couldn't really understand her. She said she felt like praying for forgiveness. That surprised me, because she wasn't at all religious. I asked her what she needed to be forgiven for, and she just laughed it off and said, "Being bad, I guess."'

Anna was about to ask the young woman if Mary Stephens had done anything that could be construed as 'bad', such as having a clandestine affair or undermining one of her colleagues at work, but then she decided that this wasn't the moment. Besides, even if she *had* done something for which she felt that she needed to pray to be forgiven, it could hardly have caused her to hemorrhage. Anna had seen patients whose guilt about some transgression had made them clinically depressed and very ill, but she had never seen it kill them.

'I'll have somebody from the relatives' support team come in to talk to you,' she said. 'They'll lend you some fresh clothes to change into, too. You must have had enough of blood for one day.'

Eleven

Anna knew she ought to go home now, take a shower and see if she could manage to eat something, and then get some sleep. But what the young woman had said about Mary Stephens had intrigued her. Why should she have felt guilty – so guilty that she needed to pray?

Anna also wanted to see for herself the bedbug lesions that Doctor Rutgers had described. Mary Stephens' body would have been taken to the morgue now and washed, so it would be possible. She might even find that she had more lesions, someplace on her body apart from her left arm.

It had also entered her mind that maybe these convulsions hadn't been caused by a virus at all. Bedbugs were rife throughout the United States, in private homes as well as hotels, so why hadn't hundreds more people contracted the same symptoms – even thousands? She remembered reading a German medical report last year about murder victims being injected with pyromellitic acid dianhydride, a chemical used in making playing cards and cigarette filters. They hadn't convulsed, but all of them had died from massive lung hemorrhage. It could be that something similar had been used on David and John Patrick Bridges and Mary Stephens. Maybe, for some reason, they had been targeted deliberately. She couldn't imagine why, or what the three of them might have conceivably had in common, but she couldn't rule it out.

She went along the corridor to the morgue. When she opened the doors she found that there was nobody there and the room was in darkness. She reached across and switched on the fluorescent lights, which flickered and loudly clicked before they came on full.

She crossed over to the nine-body refrigerator on the opposite side of the room. A handwritten card on the left-hand center drawer told her that Mary Stephens was inside. She rolled it out as far as it would go, and then she lifted the pale-green sheet that was covering Mary Stephens's body.

Mary Stephens was lying there with her eyes wide open, staring at nothing. She had been washed, so her face was no longer criss-crossed with bloody marks, but she was still frowning. The blood had been rinsed out of her hair, too, and it was still damp and straggly.

Anna folded down the sheet until her body was completely exposed. She was slim-waisted, with smallish breasts, although her hips were a little heavy.

Anna leaned over her, examining her inch by inch, sliding her fingertip along her soft, frigid skin. She located the seven bedbug lesions on her upper left arm, and the five on her forearm. She found three more behind her right knee and a further four at the side of her right ankle.

She carefully turned her on her side, and although there were no bedbug lesions on her back, there was a pattern of marks like a star-map and a tattoo between her shoulders of a crimson heart, with green leaves around it, and the letters M and A. Not 'Ma' presumably, but maybe 'Mary' and 'Alex'.

Anna lowered her on to her back again. As she did so, Mary Stephens let out a long, soft exhalation of breath. She sounded as if she were sighing impatiently, but Anna knew that it was only air that had been trapped in her lungs.

She could find no sign of any other lesions – no indications that she might have been injected with a hypodermic needle, for instance – but then Doctor Rutgers would be examining her tomorrow millimeter by millimeter, under powerful lights and high magnification, and if there were any other punctate lesions, whatever had caused them, they wouldn't escape him.

She lifted up the sheet, ready to fold it back over the body, when a voice whispered, '*Fuck you, you sniveling bitch!*'

She froze, both hands still holding up the sheet. She looked down at Mary Stephens, but Mary Stephens's expression hadn't changed at all. Her eyes were still open and staring fixedly at the ceiling. The fluorescent strip directly above her was reflected in her eyes, so that they looked more like a lizard's slitted eyes than a human's.

'*Fuck you, you fucking bitch,*' whispered the voice. '*You don't know who you're dealing with, you fucking sad excuse for a woman. You can suck my smelly cunt and then stick your tongue up my asshole and lick the tip of my shit.*'

Shocked, Anna slowly lowered the sheet over Mary Stephens's naked body, but she left her face uncovered. Mary Stephens hadn't blinked

136

once, and her lips hadn't appeared to move, either, and yet Anna had heard her quite clearly.

She stayed utterly still, barely breathing, and listening hard. The morgue was beginning to feel even colder than it was already, and she could distinctly sense a change in its atmosphere, as if the air were becoming pressurized. She could also hear a faint monotonous squeaking sound, like somebody dragging a kitchen chair along a very long corridor.

'Who are you?' she said, staring into Mary Stephens's eyes. She waved her hand backward and forward, but Mary Stephens didn't blink once.

The voice was louder, and harsher. '*If you don't know me by now, you fucking bitch, you very soon will. I'm going to fuck you and all of your fucking kind. I'm going to shove my fist up your cunt right up to the elbow, and see if that doesn't make you scream.*'

Anna backed away from the refrigerator drawer. She felt a cold sensation sliding down her back, as if ice water were being slowly poured over her neck, soaking her shirt. The whispering voice was *real*, there was no question about that. She wasn't imagining it. But Mary Stephens's lips still weren't moving, and the voice seemed to be coming from *behind* her, rather than from Mary Stephens's mouth.

'*After all this time you thought you could get away with it, you fucking whore. Well, let me tell you this: nothing costs more than what you don't pay for. I'm going to piss all over your face so that you have to drink it.*'

There was no doubt about it. The voice *was*

137

coming from behind her. Yet there was nobody else in the morgue, only three dead bodies if the labels on the drawers were anything to go by, and she hadn't heard the doors from the corridor open and close, which she would have done if anybody had come in after her.

'*Well? What do you have to say for yourself?*' whispered the voice. '*Do you want to pray for forgiveness, for what you've done? Why don't you get down on your knees, you fucking slut, and beg for absolution?*'

Anna turned around. On the opposite side of the morgue was the stainless-steel grossing station, where body parts were dissected and examined. As she turned around all of its lights flicked on, and its powerful backdraft ventilation system started up – the ventilation system that prevented laboratory assistants from breathing in fragments of human bone.

Standing right next to the grossing station was a black-draped figure that looked like a nun. She was standing completely still, although the back-draft ventilation was stirring the cloth that covered her head.

'Who are you?' Anna demanded. 'What are you doing here? This morgue is strictly off limits for visitors.'

'*Off-limits?*' said the voice harshly. Anna still couldn't be sure where it was coming from, even though this nun was standing right here in front of her. '*What do you know about off-limits, you hypocrite? You and all of your kind. You make me sick to my fucking stomach!*'

'Who the *hell* are you?' Anna retorted, although

138

she was shaking now, and she had the irrational feeling that the nun might suddenly jump on her. 'Are you a nun? Are you a *real* nun? Let me see your face!'

'*Am I a real nun? Why don't you ask Father Sooran? Ask that stupid fucker! He thought he was clever! Oh, yes! He thought he was so clever!*'

'You'd better get the hell out of here, right now,' said Anna, as assertively as she could manage. 'Get out of here, get out of this hospital, and stay out. I'm calling security so you don't have long.'

'*What are you afraid of, Anna?*' the voice whispered, and now it sounded very close to her left ear – so close that she could have sworn that she felt somebody's breath against her cheek. The nun, however, was still standing beside the grossing table, her black robes reflected in its shiny metal doors.

'*Are you afraid of having spirits inside you? Is* that *what scares you, you fucking slut? You've had enough men inside you, haven't you? What about that Jerry? He fucked you right, left and center, didn't he? Pity for you he was fucking your best friend too! And David, what you let David do to you, you fucking whore! But – ha! – he's gone off to meet his Maker, hasn't he, your David? Or has he? Souls within souls, Anna! Souls within souls within souls!*'

Anna lifted up the Rapid Reach pager that she wore around her neck, but before she could press the emergency button the morgue was instantly plunged into total darkness. At the same time, she heard a rushing, rustling sound, and the heels

139

of two bony hands pushed her backward so hard that she hit a trolley right behind her and lost her balance. She fell awkwardly on to the floor, jarring her right hip, and as she fell she was showered in surgical instruments, which jangled all around her like wind-chimes.

She tried to get on to her feet again, cutting her hands on some of the scalpels that were scattered all around her, but before she could even start to lift herself up, those bony hands pushed her back down again, so hard that the back of her head knocked against the tiles. She saw tiny white prickly stars in front of her eyes, and for a moment she felt as if she were going to lose consciousness.

As she lay there, somebody climbed on top of her, somebody skeletal, like a huge articulated spider, and sat on top of her, pinning her shoulders down with their knees. It was the nun, she was sure of it, even though the morgue was still pitch black. She could feel her habit bunched up around her hips. She could even smell its suffocating mustiness and a faint aroma of stale urine.

'*Nothing will stop us this time from getting our revenge,*' the voice whispered. '*You don't understand, do you, Anna, how much you are hated, and by how many? At last you are getting what you deserve. Now, kiss me, you fucking slut, and beg for my mercy!*'

Anna twisted her shoulders and tried to struggle out from underneath the nun's knees, but as bony as she was the nun felt impossibly heavy, and Anna couldn't shift her even an inch. She tried to wriggle herself downward, too, but the nun simply pressed down on her even harder, and Anna felt as if the nun's shins were going to snap her collarbone.

'*Kiss me, you bitch!*' the voice repeated.

With that, the nun scooped her claw-like hand under the back of Anna's head. She dug her fingernails into her scalp and forcibly lifted her head upward, so that Anna felt as if her neck could break. The nun shifted herself forward two or three inches, and Anna found her face being pressed into wet, pungent hairiness. With a surge of nausea that made her retch out loud, she realized that the nun was pressing her face between her legs.

'*Kiss me, you fucking bitch! Kiss the lips of Satan himself! Do you know who I am? Do you know who he is? Kiss his lips and beg for his forgiveness!*'

Anna closed her mouth tight and closed her eyes, too, as the nun lasciviously rubbed her face from side to side, smothering her cheeks with slippery juice. Anna could even feel the nun's stiff clitoris against her lips, and she had to suppress another retch.

At last the nun released her grip on Anna's head and let it drop back on the floor. With another rustle of musty fabric, she climbed off her, and although she couldn't see her in the darkness, Anna could sense her standing close to her.

Anna spat and wiped her face with her sleeve, She tried not to taste what was on her lips, but it was almost impossible not to. She had an overwhelming urge to get up on to her feet, but she was afraid of what the nun might do if she tried to. She groped for her pager, but she couldn't find it, or even the chain to which it was supposed to be attached. Maybe it had broken when the nun had sat astride her.

She waited, and waited, and after a short while she felt that the nun was no longer there. She hadn't heard her leave, and the doors hadn't opened, but somehow she was sure that she had gone. She stood up and blindly shuffled her way toward the light switch, holding out her hands in front of her so that she wouldn't bump into the wall.

She switched on the lights, and again they clicked and flickered. She looked quickly around the morgue, terrified that the nun might be standing right behind her, but the only other person in the room was Mary Stephens, lying in her open refrigerator drawer.

Anna went over to the grossing station. She turned on the mixer faucet and splashed her face with water as hot as she could stand it. Opening the doors underneath the sink she found a bottle of isopropyl alcohol. She diluted half a cupful in a beaker and gargled with it before she spat it out and rinsed her mouth out with water.

She stood in front of the sink for almost half a minute, her head bowed, breathing deeply, trying to understand what had just happened to her. She was sure that she wasn't losing her mind. The nun had vanished as silently and as mysteriously as she had appeared, but Anna knew that she hadn't imagined her. The surgical instruments were still scattered across the floor, and the back of her head was still sore from banging it against the tiles. She touched it cautiously and could feel a lump coming up.

She badly needed to tell somebody about this – somebody who could explain to her how she could have heard David and John Patrick Bridges talking to her when they were dead, and how she could have been attacked by a nun who seemed to be able to walk through walls. She thought at first of going to see Ken Fiedler, SLU's head of psychiatry, but she was convinced that none of these experiences were imaginary. Ken might think they were, though, and if he believed that she was psychologically unbalanced, he would be duty-bound to report it to the hospital authorities. She supposed she should have taken a sample of the vaginal fluid on her face before she had washed it off. Maybe if she had done that, and analyzed it, she would have found out what had really just happened to her.

As it was, she had been left with nothing but her bruises and a dull headache and the taste of isopropyl alcohol in her mouth, like nail-polish remover. More than that, she could still remember almost everything that the whispery voice had said to her, and she could still feel the sensation of the nun's beak-like clitoris against her lips, as if the nun had been trying to humiliate her and arouse her at the same time.

Maybe she didn't need a psychiatrist. Maybe she needed to talk to a priest, or even a medium.

She bent over and started to collect up the surgical instruments from the floor. She would have to tell Henry Rutgers that she had accidentally knocked them over and that they all needed to be sterilized again. When she had gathered them all up, she went back across the room to cover up Mary Stephens's body and slide her drawer back into the refrigerator.

Mary Stephens was still staring at the ceiling, but she was no longer frowning. Instead, her mouth was stretched wide open, and her face was distorted into a mask of absolute terror.

Anna left the morgue and went back down in the elevator to the reception area. The sun had gone down now, and it was dusk outside. She'd not only thought about talking to Ken Fiedler, she had also wondered if she ought to report what had happened to hospital security, but then she'd decided against doing that, too. How could she explain that she had been assaulted in the morgue by a woman dressed as a nun, who had appeared from nowhere and sworn obscenities at her, and then disappeared into nowhere, without even opening or closing the doors?

She decided that what she needed was to go home, calm herself down and try to work it all out rationally. There had to be some explanation for her experience, even if the nun had been some kind of psychic phenomenon.

Only last week she had been reading about research carried out at the University of Michigan which suggested that the reduction of oxygen and glucose at the moment of death stimulates brain activity and could account for people still being able to think after they were clinically dead. It was a possible explanation for NDEs – near death experiences – when people had felt themselves being drawn toward a bright light and had sometimes even seen their dead relatives waiting for them on the other side.

Once home, she opened the door of her loft and stepped inside. It was chilly and silent. No David any more, not this evening, not tomorrow, not ever. She dropped her purse and her laptop on to one of the couches and went into the kitchen to find herself a glass. She badly needed a drink.

She switched on the TV, but left it on mute. Wendy Williams was laughing with one of her show-business guests, but all Anna wanted was the flickering light of the television screen and other human faces, so that she didn't feel so alone.

She sat on the couch for a while, taking occasional sips of vodka and turning the incident in the morgue over and over in her mind, like the jerky images of an early kinetoscope. She saw the lights in the grossing station abruptly switch on, all by themselves, and the whistling sound of its extractor fans starting up. She saw the nun, standing black and motionless with her head covered. She heard the whispering voice, with its bitter obscenities. Now that she was sitting here, feeling much less agitated, she could remember almost everything, including every word that had been whispered at her, as if she had recorded it.

What disturbed her more than anything else was that the nun had known her name. *'What are you afraid of, Anna?'* And she had known details of her private life that even her best friends didn't know.

'What about that Jerry? He fucked you right, left and center, didn't he? Pity for you he was

fucking your best friend too! And David, what you let David do to you, you fucking whore!'

Six years ago she had been involved with a chiropractor called Jerry Manville. Jerry had been handsome and confident and amusing, with a sexual appetite that had led to them making love in parking lots in the back seat of his car, and even in closets at other people's dinner parties. Jerry had two-timed her with her closest friend Kay, and with several other women, too, and that had been the end of a passionate but argumentative relationship.

David had liked tying her to the bed with scarves now and again, and she had found that highly arousing. But how had the nun known about that? Was she real, or a spirit; and if she was real, was she really a nun?

'Am I a real nun? Why don't you ask Father Sooran? Ask that stupid fucker! He thinks he's so clever! Oh, yes! He thinks he's so clever.'

Father Sooran. That was the only clue to her identity that the nun had given her. But Anna only rarely attended church, and she wasn't a Catholic. She didn't know any priests, apart from Father William, who regularly visited the hospital to hear confessions from bedridden patients and to give the last rites to those who were dying.

So who was Father Sooran?

She opened her laptop and Googled the name 'Father Sooran'. Google asked her if she had really meant 'Father Horan' or 'Father Curran' or 'Father Surin'. She closed her eyes for a moment and tried to remember exactly how the nun had pronounced it. It had definitely not been

146

'Horan' or 'Curran'. If 'Surin' was a French name, then it would have sounded like 'Sooran'. She clicked on 'Father Surin'.

What came up gave her a prickly feeling of sheer disbelief. Jean-Joseph Surin had been a French Jesuit mystic, the highly respected writer of several devotional books and hundreds of letters, and an exorcist. His most celebrated exorcism had been that of Jeanne des Anges, the mother superior of the Ursuline convent in Loudun, in France, who was said to have been possessed by seven demons.

Jeanne des Anges had spoken in the foulest language, railed against God, and had lifted up her habit and openly masturbated.

Father Surin had been so shocked by her behavior that he had offered his own spirit to be possessed by the seven demons in her place. Jeanne des Anges gradually recovered, but for the rest of his life Father Surin was plagued by nightmares, as well as convulsions, paralysis and temporary bouts of insanity. He had unsuccessfully tried to kill himself by jumping out of a second-story window, and sometimes he was seen wandering through the grounds of the college in Paris where he was studying, stark naked and smeared in his own excrement.

He had been born in the year 1600 and died in 1665. He'd been sent to exorcize Jeanne des Anges in December, 1634.

'Why don't you ask Father Surin? He thinks he's so clever!' How could she ask Father Surin if Father Surin had been dead for nearly four centuries?

147

Anna closed her laptop and went over to the side table to pour herself another vodka. Her mind was churning over, and her headache was almost blinding. The nun couldn't have been imaginary, because she had mentioned Father Surin, and Anna had never heard of Father Surin before. Neither had she ever read anything about the exorcism of Jeanne des Anges, and yet the whispering voice had talked in the foulest language about demonic possession.

'Are you afraid of having spirits inside you? Is that *what scares you, you fucking slut!'*

She stared at herself in the mirror over the side table. 'There's a logical explanation for all of this,' she told herself, out loud. 'There are no such things as demons. There is no such thing as demonic possession. There are no such things as vanishing nuns, and dead people can't talk.'

She was about to tell herself something reassuring, when she thought she saw a slight movement in the mirror, and she froze. Behind her, in the shadowy corner just beside her bedroom door, in between the blinds and the door frame, she thought she saw a dark nunlike figure, standing quite still.

She turned around, dropping the vodka bottle on to the floor. It smashed, and as it smashed the mirror smashed too, as explosively as if somebody had hit it dead center with a hammer.

She stood amidst the glittering fragments of broken glass, trembling. There was no nun standing in the corner, only shadows.

Outside, a police siren suddenly shrieked.

Twelve

I had been waiting for over an hour at the headquarters of the Coral Gables Police Department before Detective Blezard came back into the interview room, accompanied by a female police officer. I badly needed a horse-shoe coffee, and my nose was feeling bunged up.

'Mr Erskine? I have some good news and some not-so-good news.'

'Oh, yes?' I didn't need a police detective to tell me my fortune. I could do that myself, although I probably wouldn't believe me.

Detective Blezard paddled his hand to indicate that I should sit down, and then he sat down himself, dropping a blue Manila folder on to the table in front of him. He was short and podgy with thinning, corrugated hair and a scarlet, corrugated forehead to go with it. He was wearing an orange shirt with dark semicircles of sweat under the armpits and khaki chinos that were two sizes too small for him.

The female police officer on the other hand was quite pretty, with blonde pixie-cut hair and a little snub nose and a very generous bosom underneath her smartly-pressed blouse. I kept my eyes on her the whole time that Detective Blezard was talking, and every now and then she glanced back at me and blushed. I really like women who

149

blush. It shows that they're thinking the same as I'm thinking.

'We've talked to Father Zapata now that he's come around after surgery.'

'How is he?'

'He's fine. He'll recover, but it's probably just as well that he's a priest, if you get my meaning.'

'OK. So what did he tell you?'

'He told us that you had invited him around in order to discuss religion. He said that during that discussion he suffered a psychiatric breakdown for which you were in no way responsible. He said that you did everything you could to prevent him self-harming, but you were unable to do so.'

'That's what he said?'

Detective Blezard opened his notebook, studied his scrawly writing for a moment, and then nodded. 'That's right. He also said that psychiatric breakdowns are not uncommon in the priesthood, on account of the demanding nature of their calling and the stress placed upon them by suppressing their natural urges and staying celebrate.'

'*Celibate*, detective.'

'What?'

'Celibate, not "celebrate". It means eschewing the wild thing in order to concentrate on serving the Lord.'

'I know what it means, Mr Erskine,' said Detective Blezard, testily. 'Anyhow, it appears that the Reverend Father Zapata's injury was self-inflicted with no assistance or encouragement from yourself. He is making no accusations of assault against you, so as far as we're concerned

150

no charges are going to be brought and the case is closed.'

'OK, great,' I said. 'I presume that's the good news. What's the not-so-good news?'

Detective Blezard picked up the blue Manila folder and produced a large black-and-white photograph. He handed it across to me and said, 'Recognize that, Mr Erskine?'

I studied it carefully, frowning as if I had never seen it before. Of course I recognized it. It was Mrs Ratzenberger's diamond bracelet, the one that despite all of my protestations she had given me for reading her cards for her. The diamond bracelet about which I had known that Frank Ratzenberger would go all colors of ape-shit if he discovered that she had given it away. 'So, what is it?' I asked Detective Blezard, handing the photograph back to him.

'You're denying you ever saw that before?'

'I'm not saying I have and I'm not saying I haven't. What's the deal?'

'This is a diamond bracelet that belongs to Mrs Rosa Ratzenberger, of East Star Island Drive. Mrs Ratzenberger is a client of yours, am I right?'

'Do I need a lawyer?' I asked him.

'It depends. Mrs Ratzenberger is claiming that after your last little fortune-telling session, she discovered that this bracelet was missing from her dressing room. Since you were the only visitor she had that day, it's not beyond the bounds of possibility that it was you who lifted it.'

I sat there for quite a while without saying anything. I looked across at the female police officer, but this time she didn't blush. Instead, she raised both finely-plucked eyebrows, as if to say, *Well, did you?* I hate fickle women. One minute you think they're going to slide all over you like warm syrup, and the next minute they're unjustly accusing you of God knows what.

Detective Blezard said, 'I'm giving you an opportunity here, Mr Erskine, to do this the easy way. If you *did* take Mrs Ratzenberger's bracelet, why don't you admit it? If you *won't* admit it, you realize that we'll have to get a warrant to search your home, and if we search your home and find it there, it's not going to look too good for you in court, now, is it?'

I still said nothing. I had to think about this very carefully. Something similar had happened to me before once, back in New York, except that time I had been accused only of purloining a fake Chinese vase with a chip in it, worth approximately zilch, not a Van Cleef & Arpels diamond bracelet that must have been valued at well over one hundred and fifty large.

'So?' asked Detective Blezard. He dragged a stringy red handkerchief out of his chino pocket, bunched it up and dabbed the perspiration from his forehead. 'What's it to be, Mr Erskine? Truth or consequences?'

'OK,' I said. 'Mrs Ratzenberger gave me the bracelet for reading her cards.'

'She gave you the bracelet just for reading her cards. Are you serious? Is that *all* you did for her?'

'Come on, detective! What are you suggesting here? I'm a well-respected predictor of personal destiny, not some bling-decorated Collins Avenue

152

gigolo. Besides, have you seen the woman? She looks like the ghost of Hannukah-Yet-To-Come.'

'That bracelet was insured for nearly a quarter of a million bucks, Mr Erskine. Apart from that, it was an anniversary gift from her husband. She told our officers that its sentimental value was beyond rubies.'

'Well, of course its value was beyond rubies, it was diamonds. I didn't want to take it, detective, believe me. But the old bat insisted. She said that she wanted to spite Mr Ratzenberger because he pretty much gave her the cold shoulder these days. According to her, he spends all day at the golf club giving the glad eye to some well-upholstered hostess, and even when he comes home he never speaks to her and he isn't exactly attentive in the bedroom. To quote her verbatim: his rope never rises.'

At this, the female police officer blushed again, but I wasn't sure that I had forgiven her yet for raising her eyebrows at me.

'Look,' I said, 'the woman is suffering from early-onset senile dementia. She's also bored, and she's lonely. Somebody like me comes along and gives her a little attention, a little flirting, and she overreacts and gives me more than I would ever ask her for.'

'You didn't make any attempt to contact her husband and tell *him* what had happened and arrange to return the bracelet, no questions asked?'

'No, I didn't. It's not my place to interfere in other people's marital spats. For all I know, he might have strangled her if he'd found out that she had given it away, and what would that have made me? Accessory to marital manslaughter?'

Detective Blezard tucked the photograph of the bracelet back into its folder. 'You still have the bracelet in your possession, Mr Erskine?'

'I'm not wearing it, if that's what you mean. It's hidden in my freezer compartment, in a bag of peas. Quite frankly I haven't had the time to think what to do with it. I've been a little distracted by some other stuff, would you believe, like priests coming around to my house and chewing off their own manhoods.'

'Well, I've been checking up on you, if you must know,' said Detective Blezard. 'Apart from this accusation of theft, I have sufficient evidence already to arrest you under Florida statute eight-one-seven-eleven.'

'Florida statute eight-one-seven-eleven? And what does *that* say, exactly? I'm not allowed to tell fortunes in all-night convenience stores?'

'Florida statute eight-one-seven-eleven says that it's a criminal offense to defraud people out of things of value by claiming to have secret, advance or inside information about persons, transactions, acts or things, when in reality you *don't* have any information about those persons, transactions, acts or things, or even if you do. I would say that fortune-telling pretty much comes under that heading, wouldn't you?'

I looked at the female police officer. Her eyes had narrowed a little, as if she were waiting for me to say something. Beg for mercy, maybe, or offer to read their cards free of charge. Whatever it was, I sensed that a deal was in the offing.

'Of course I'll give the bracelet back,' I said cautiously.

'Yes, Mr Erskine, you will. And if you do that, I won't pursue a prosecution for fraud.'

'That's very reasonable of you, detective. I'll go home and get it for you right now.'

I was about to stand up when Detective Blezard raised his hand to stop me. 'There's one more condition that I'm going to insist on, sir. Within the next twenty-four hours I expect you to leave the City of Coral Gables and never return. And by that I mean *ever.* In fact, I expect you to leave the state of Florida altogether and never return.'

I was stunned. 'Come on, detective, I don't think you can legally demand that I do that.'

'It's your choice, Mr Erskine. Either you quit this city and this state, or else I collar you for fraud. I'd rather *not* arrest you, because it would take up a whole lot of valuable time when I would rather be arresting somebody for some serious offense like drug-smuggling or pimping. It would also involve a whole mess of very tedious paperwork, and I hate paperwork. But if I have to, I will, and you can count on that.'

'Come on, detective, I have appointments to keep. What are my clients going to do if I just disappear and never come back?'

'Maybe you should read your own cards, and then you'll find out.'

I turned to the female police officer. 'Did you know about this?' I asked her.

She blushed again and nodded.

'Well, that's a very great pity,' I said. 'I was going to ask you if you wanted to come tuna fishing with me this weekend. One of my clients owns a fabulous sixty-five-foot fiberglass Viking.'

Detective Blezard stood up and said, 'Officer Kelly here will accompany you to your home, Mr Erskine, along with Officer McBride. You'll probably find you have quite a crowd of media folks waiting to talk to you. Another condition of this deal between us is that you keep your lips zippered and don't say a word to any of them.'

'How would you like a mystic motto?' I asked him. 'No charge, of course. I wouldn't like you to think that I was defrauding you under Florida statute eight-one-seven-eleven.'

'A mystic motto? What's that?'

'Just a little aphorism to keep in mind as you machete your way through the tangled jungle of your humdrum daily life.'

'Go on, then,' he said suspiciously.

'"Make sure you know which game you're playing. No matter how many sixes come up, you don't win at chess by rolling dice."'

'And what in the name of all that's holy does *that* mean?'

I tapped the side of my nose. 'You'll find out, detective. You'll find out.'

Detective Blezard was right. When we arrived at Triangle Park there were three TV vans parked outside the house and a crowd of maybe twenty or thirty reporters and cameramen and sound guys, not to mention inquisitive bystanders and stray dogs.

Officers Kelly and McBride escorted me round to my cottage. Officer Kelly may have been petite and pretty, but Officer McBride had a gray buzzcut and forearms like Virginia hams and he barged his way through the crowd as if they were skittles.

'Mr Erskine! Mr Erskine! WPLG News! Is it true that Father Zapata castrated himself with his teeth?'

'Did you actually see him do it, Mr Erskine?'

'How much did he bite off? Did he spit it out, or did he chew it and swallow it?'

'Did he scream? What did you do afterward?'

'You're a fortune-teller, Mr Erskine. Didn't you see this coming?'

I unlocked the cottage door and let the two officers inside. Even when I had shut the door behind us, the reporters kept hammering on it and knocking at the windows and shouting questions through the mail slot.

'Can we see the room where he did it, Mr Erskine?'

'How did you stop him from bleeding to death?'

'Did he pray? Or did he have his mouth full?'

I went through to the kitchenette, opened the freezer and took out the bag of Walmart Great Value frozen peas. 'Here,' I said, handing over Mrs Ratzenberger's bracelet. 'I have the case for it, too.'

Officer Kelly said, 'Thanks.' And then, 'Why did he actually do it?'

'What? Bite off the end of his thing? Don't ask me.'

'He said he came here to talk to you about religion. So why was he naked?'

'I decline to answer that question on the grounds that what happened made me sick to my stomach. All right, maybe I seem to be making a joke about it, but it was terrible and it was tragic and I'm still upset about it.'

'Father Zapata – were you and he—?'

'Having a love affair? No, Officer Kelly, we were not. I have a very lovely girlfriend here in Miami who works in a bar, and if I wanted to be unfaithful to her I certainly wouldn't go for a priest. I don't know . . . maybe if the Pope made eyes at me.'

'You're very defensive, Mr Erskine.'

'I'm being accused of something I didn't do, that's why. Apart from that, you're much too pretty to be a police officer, and I guess I'm being defensive in case you think I'm coming on to you.'

'You have a very lovely girlfriend who works in a bar, and I'm married.' She lifted up her left hand to show me her wedding band.

'Oh, well,' I said, giving her the bracelet case. 'Maybe in another life.'

'Do you believe in other lives?' she asked me. At this point Officer McBride came into the living room. He didn't look impressed. When I die, I want a headstone that looks like Officer McBride's face. He had obviously been having a sniff around my cottage to see if he could find anything interesting, like ten kilos of Peruvian coke or two naked bambuco dancers tied up underneath my bed.

'Other lives?' I told her. 'You bet I do.'

Officer McBride checked his stainless-steel

wristwatch. 'You got twenty-two hours and six minutes, Mr Erskine. In twenty-two hours and six minutes we're going to be coming back here, just to make sure that you're history.'

I went to the main house to tell Marcos that I was unexpectedly leaving and why. Marcos was short and stubby with a glossy black comb-over and a droopy black moustache and a mass of black curly chest-hair struggling to escape from the front of his splashy orange shirt. He hugged me up against his hard round belly and offered me a Corona, with a Tres Sombreros chaser, and then another Corona, with a Tres Sombreros chaser, and then another Corona, with a Tres Sombreros chaser. By early evening he was playing *Esclavo Y Amo* for me on his guitar and I had almost forgotten why I had come to see him.

'So, when did you say you had to go?' he asked me.

'Excuse me?'

'You have to leave, that's what you said. The police insist that you get out of Florida and never come back.'

'Oh, yeah, well, *that*.'

'So what are you going to do? For a living, I mean? And where will you go?'

It all began to come back to me. 'Well, I don't know, Marcos. I'll make a living like I always make a living. Telling fortunes, playing poker, working in bars. Doing whatever needs to be done.'

'Where will you stay? Do you have enough money?'

'I have a friend in New York, Rick Beamer. I've done him a few favors in the past. He'll put me up for a while, until I can find someplace permanent.'

'What about Sandy?'

'I can ask her if she wants to come with me, but I doubt she will. We were never that serious, after all. And would *you* trade Miami Beach for Manhattan, unless you really had to?'

'I guess not, *bato*.'

We sat on his veranda for a while longer. I didn't really feel like going back to my cottage, not even to pack. I kept on thinking about the nun standing in my bedroom, and about what Father Zapata had done on my bed. Like – supposing *I* got possessed in the middle of the night by some malevolent spirit and did the same thing to myself, or worse?

I kept on thinking about the tapping I had heard, too. Maybe it had been my imagination playing tricks on me, but it had sounded so much like the tapping that I'd heard from the medicine sticks of Native American shamans. It was the complicated tapping that some of them used to summon up spirits, either good or bad, and some of those Native American spirits could make Old World demons like Pazuzu and Belial seem no more scary than neighborhood kids dressed up for trick-or-treat.

Eventually, though, I had to weave my way back across the yard to my cottage, unlock the door and let myself in. I stood in the hallway for a while, listening, but all I could hear was the faint sound of traffic on the South Dixie Highway.

160

When I closed the door behind me there was total silence.

I lifted my two battered suitcases out of the closet. In spite of what had happened to Father Zapata, and in spite of the tapping noises that I'd heard, I really didn't feel like packing up and leaving Florida. Life for the most part had been pretty damn good to me here, what with the climate and the wealthy old jaybirds who had wanted me to read their cards for them. In the past couple of years I had also begun to feel relaxed, and safe, as if I had left all the weirdness of my past life behind me.

The nun appearing in my bedroom and Father Zapata's self-mutilation had been frightening and upsetting, but I couldn't see how they had anything to do with me. From my own experience with spirits, I thought it was more than likely that the nun had been nothing more than the resonance of something very nasty that had happened in my bedroom sometime in the past – probably years ago, because Marcos would have known about it otherwise. It occasionally happens that during a truly dreadful event like a rape or a murder the walls of a room can absorb extreme emotions, and these emotions can later resurface and create a ghostly action replay.

The tapping had unsettled me, but when I thought about it rationally it was probably nothing more than a woodpecker, tapping away at the bottle palm at the end of the yard.

I carried my cases through to the bedroom, opened them up and laid them on the bed. I switched on my bedside radio, and it was playing some sentimental country and western song about leaving in the morning. I went back to my closet, took out all of my shirts and pants, as well as my spare fortune-telling gown and the two creased linen coats that I hardly ever wore.

As I started to fold up my shirts and my pants I thought I heard the tapping again. I listened hard, and I was *sure* that I could hear it, complicated and urgent and quick. I went over and turned down the volume of the radio, and listened again, but all I could hear then was a tinny voice singing: '—*you're the Queen of the Go-Go Girls, you're laughin' while you work, but I don't ever seem to get the joke—*'

I listened for over half a minute, but there was still nothing. It must have been my imagination. I went through to the bathroom, opened up the cabinet and took out all of my bottles of aftershave and shower gel and crumpled tubes of toothpaste. After I had closed the cabinet door I stared at myself in the mirror, and I thought that I was looking tired and haunted and slightly out of focus, but that may have had something to do with all of those beers and tequila chasers that I had drunk with Marcos.

'*Darlin', you know I'm leavin' in the mornin','* sang the voice on the radio. '*And it's true I might not be comin' back . . .*'

After I had pretty much finished packing I tried calling Sandy, but her cell was switched off and I guessed she must have started work already. I had drunk far too much to be sitting behind the wheel of a car, but all the same I drove into

Miami Beach to see her. It was only a twenty-five minute drive, and the traffic wasn't too heavy. It was beginning to grow dark now, and the sky was turning from dusky orange into dusky purple.

Sandy worked behind the bar at the Stars-and-Bars Lounge on 14th Street, which is where I had first met her. I had walked in there one evening after reading some retired movie star's fortune at the Betsy Hotel. I badly needed a drink because the movie star had been suffering from terminal lung cancer and wanted to know if she was going to make a full recovery. You know me – I always try to make people feel better about their future, but it's not easy telling somebody an outright lie. You only had to look at this woman to tell that the Grim Reaper already had his bony arm around her and was blowing her kisses that smelled of the cemetery.

Sandy wasn't sandy but brunette, with huge brown eyes that almost made you feel like throwing her a dog-choc and a perfect squarish face that put me in my mind of Audrey Hepburn. In fact, if Audrey Hepburn had been three inches taller and worn a 38DD bra and spoken in a North Carolina twang, she and Sandy could almost have been taken for identical twins.

The Stars-and-Bars was crowded and noisy when I walked in. A DJ in a spangly shirt was playing a Wyclef Jean rap song, and the strobe lights on the ceiling were all flashing in time to the music. I saw Sandy behind the bar mixing a cocktail, and I pushed my way through the dancers and perched myself up on a stool.

'*Harry*!' squeaked Sandy. 'I was going to come

163

by when I finished work and surprise you! I got the day off tomorrow, hon . . . I thought we could maybe spend some time on the beach together. What can I get you to drink?'

'Unh-hunh, nothing to drink, thanks. I had a few too many with Marcos. Well, maybe a Coke.'

'We're real busy tonight, hon. I won't be able to talk to you much.'

'Hey, babe!' called out a shaven-headed young man with earrings and a red satin shirt. 'How's about some service here?'

'See?' said Sandy. 'I gotta go.'

'I gotta go, too. That's what I came to tell you.'

'What are you talking about?'

'I've gotten myself entangled in some stupid trouble with the cops. They're running me out of town. In fact, they're running me out of the entire state.'

'*What*? I don't believe it! *Why*? When?'

'Hey, come on, babe!' shouted the shaven-headed young man. 'We're dying of thirst here!'

'If you're coming around after work I'll fill you in then,' I told her. 'I'm so sorry, Sandy, but this detective wouldn't give me any choice. It was either go, or get busted.'

'Sandy!' said her boss, from the other end of the bar. 'There's customers waiting, for Chrissakes!'

Sandy's big brown eyes filled with tears, and her glossy pink lower lip started to pout. 'Harry, you *can't* go! What am I going to do without you?'

'Listen, sweetheart, we'll work something out. Now, you'd better serve these customers. You don't want to lose your job, do you?'

'I don't care about my job. I just care about you.' She unpinned her sparkly name badge and said, 'Look – I'll quit right now!'

'No, no, no, don't do that! Please. I don't know where I'll be going, and I don't know where I'll be living, and I can't take you with me. Let's talk it over tomorrow, but right now you have thirsty and obnoxious customers to take care of.'

'What did you call me?' said the shaven-headed man, who was now standing right next to me.

'"Obnoxious". It means "deserving of kudos and immediate service".'

The shaven-headed man gave me a long, suspicious look. He had near-together eyes like two steel nail-heads. After a moment's consideration, he said, 'OK. That's OK, then.' He probably didn't know what 'kudos' meant, either. He turned to Sandy and said, 'Two Damn-The-Weathers and one Screaming Orgasm. Thanks, doll.'

I felt even drunker when I drove back home than I had when I'd first come out, and I had to give myself a running set of instructions, out loud. 'Look, Harry, there's a red signal up ahead here. Make sure you stop. You have to take a right turn here, then a left on to the on-ramp. There's a squad car right next to you. Whatever you do, don't look at the nice policemen and give them a stupid grin.'

I managed to get home all right and park in front of the house without smashing into any plant pots. It looked like Marcos had either gone out or gone to bed early because the house was in darkness. The back yard was so dark that I had to cross it very carefully, with both hands

165

held out in front of me. I stumbled two or three times and nearly fell over, but at last I reached my front door and managed to unlock it. I cursed myself for not having left a light on.

I groped my way along the hallway. The only illumination came from the half-open door to my bedroom, where the lights from Triangle Park were shining through the blinds. I found the light-switch next to the living-room door and I clicked it. Nothing happened. The hallway remained in darkness. Goddamn bulb must have blown.

I was just feeling my way through the living-room door when I heard it.

Tap-tap-tappety-tap-tappety-tap-tap!

I froze. This time, the tapping continued, and it was coming from my bedroom, so there was no way I could kid myself that it was a woodpecker.

Tap-tap-tappety-tappety-tap!

The last time I had heard tapping like that was when I was facing the reborn spirit of Misquamacus, the Algonquin wonder-worker – Misquamacus, who had sworn eternal vengeance on white men for wiping out so many hundreds of thousands of Native Americans and destroying so much of their culture.

But it couldn't be. I had dismissed him forever. There was no possibility that he could ever come back, no matter what shape he took: man, woman, wolf or shadow.

So how could I hear his medicine sticks tapping?

I had a choice now. I could enter my bedroom and find out who or *what* was making that tapping noise . . . or I could get the hell out of that cottage and sleep on Marcos' couch tonight. That is, if Marcos was actually there. I blurrily seemed to remember him saying something about a gig at the Country Club in Hialeah. That was probably why his house was in darkness and untypically silent.

I thought: *It's a noise, that's all. What are you worried about? It could be anything. One of the blind cords, tapping in the wind.* Except, of course, that there was no wind that night, and all the windows were closed.

If I hadn't been under the influence of too many beers and too many tequila chasers, I doubt I would have dared to do what I did next. I approached the bedroom door and threw it wide open. Its handle banged against the wall, and it juddered on its hinges.

I was so shocked that I lost my balance and hit my shoulder against the door frame. There were *people* standing in my bedroom – three of them. When I saw what they were, my mouth opened and closed, but no words came out.

They were nuns, all in black, all with their heads covered, all completely motionless. At the same time, though, the tapping noise not only continued, but began to grow faster and faster and even more complicated, as if it was racing up to a climax.

Thirteen

I raised both hands protectively and started to back away. As I edged back down the hallway, I collided with the crescent-shaped side table and nearly knocked the lamp off it, but I managed to catch it before it fell to the floor.

The three nuns stayed where they were, still not moving, but the tapping was becoming more and more frantic. I reached the front door and took hold of the handle to open it, but I shouted out, 'Shit!' because it was almost red hot. I snatched my hand away, flapping my blistered fingers and blowing on them. It looked as if the nuns weren't going to allow me to get away.

'*You will come back here!*' said a harsh, accented voice. I wasn't at all sure that it was coming from any of the nuns, and I couldn't tell what accent it was, but it was loud and it sounded like it really meant business.

I tugged down my shirt cuff to cover my hand and tried again to open the front door, but the handle was not only too hot to touch, it was jammed solid.

'*Come back here!*' the voice repeated. '*We want you to know who we are!*'

'I know who you are!' I retorted. 'You're nuns!'

'*We are warnings,*' said the voice.

'Warnings? Warnings of what, for Christ's sake? I don't need warnings – I just want you to get the hell out of my house!'

'*Why do you think we are here, in your dwelling? Why do you think we have chosen to appear to* you, *of all your people?*'

I licked my fingertip and gingerly dabbed at the door-handle again, but it was still too hot to touch. I was doing my best to be defiant, but my heart was beating faster and I could feel the beginnings of panic rising up inside me, as well as alcoholic bile. I thought about dodging into the living room and climbing out of the window, but the second I thought that, *bang*, the living-room door slammed shut all by itself.

These nuns were not only inside my bedroom, but they were inside my mind too. I glanced toward the bathroom door, and that, too, slammed shut.

'OK, *why*?' I demanded, although my throat was so tight that I was finding it difficult to speak. 'What made you pick on me? I'm not even religious. Or is it *because* I'm not religious? Was it you who made Father Zapata hurt himself like that?'

'*It was a warning to the holy father not to interfere.*'

'Some warning. He could have died.'

'*It was to remind you that your people have always destroyed life and never honored it.*'

'What do you mean, "your people"?'

'*Your people always pick fruit before it ripens, and they always fell the trees before they can scatter their seeds across the earth. But the time has come at last, and we will allow nothing to stand in our way.*'

'I don't understand what you're talking about!'

169

'*You will understand when you know who we are.*'

When the voice said that, the tapping became so frenzied that I could hardly hear what it was saying. At the same time, the black veils that covered the heads of two of the nuns began to ripple and swell, almost as if they were made of boiling tar. In between the two of them, the third nun remained as she was, small and dark and motionless, and for some reason that made her all the more frightening.

The two nuns on either side of her began to grow taller and bulkier, until their heads were almost touching the bedroom ceiling. Their head-coverings took on the shape of horns, and their black habits knotted and twisted themselves into muscular bodies covered with strips of dark-brown animal furs. At the same time, I could smell incense and a strong, sour odor of charred wood. It reminded me of the time that I went up to visit my cousin in New Hampshire after a forest fire. The reek of burned pine-trees had clung to my clothes and lingered in the air for weeks, so that I could actually taste it.

'*This is who we are,*' announced the voice. '*We have returned to take back what is ours. We have learned your ways, and this time you will not defeat us.*'

'I still don't get it. What are you going to take back?'

'*Our land. Our lives.*'

I stayed where I was, in the hallway. Those two figures were enormous now, and although it was too dark to see them clearly, I could just

170

make out the glitter of their eyes, and I thought that I could see something moving on their shoulders, as if torrents of beetles were constantly running all over them.

'*We want our sky back,*' the voice continued. '*We want our clouds, and our rain, and our tornadoes. We want our sunrises, and our snow. Every river, every mountain, every lake. Every animal. Every tree, every single blade of grass. Every breath of air that we ever took, that was ours. We want it all back.*'

'Who *are* you?' I asked. All the same, I was increasingly sure that I knew *what* they were, because they had come looking for me. Purely by accident, I had become their nemesis in the past – not that I had ever wanted to, or felt that it was my duty. I had simply been protecting the people I cared about.

'*I am Matchitehew,*' said the voice. '*My brother is Megedagik. We are the sons of Misquamacus, whose spirit you condemned to the outer darkness for all time.*'

'You're his *sons*? Misquamacus died hundreds of years ago! How can you be his sons?'

'*You might have condemned his spirit to the outer darkness, but he still had the power to summon our spirits, and like him we are wonderworkers. He taught us magic in life, and we never forgot it, even after death. Now he has charged us with taking our just revenge on you and claiming back all that is rightfully ours. You might have thwarted him, but you will not thwart us.*'

'Listen,' I said. 'I know you have a genuine grievance, and I can understand it. If somebody

171

had appeared out of nowhere and massacred my people and taken all of my land, I think I'd be pissed too, and on the whole I think you Native Americans have taken it pretty well.'

'*Are you mocking us?*' asked Matchitehew, with a rasp in his voice.

'Of course I'm not mocking you. But too much time has gone by. You can't go back to the way things were before the white man showed up. It's just not possible.'

'*We can still take our revenge on you. No matter how much time has passed, why should you be allowed to go unpunished?*'

'For Pete's sake, the people around today aren't the same people who massacred your ancestors! You can't blame them for what their fathers did. Or even their fathers' fathers.'

'*They still have no title to this land. They still have no right to live here, and to eat its fruit and its fish and its animals and to profit from its riches. Our father Misquamacus was not an evil man, and he was not a vengeful man. But how could he stand by and accept the killing of thousands of his own people and the theft of the land that the Great Spirit had given us? You would have done the same, if it had happened to your people, and yet you condemned him to a fate that is worse than death itself.*'

'I know,' I said. 'And I'm sorry I had to do it. Well, I'm not sorry, really. It was either him or me.' I was trying my best to be nonchalant, but my heart was beating so hard against my ribcage that it hurt.

I thought: *These two enormous spirits are*

probably going to kill me now, in one agonizing way or another. If they hadn't forgiven white men in general for taking this country away from them, they certainly weren't going to show any mercy to the one white man who had dispatched their father to wherever it was that Native American spirits can never come back from.

But – '*You defeated our father*,' said Matchitehew. '*You showed yourself to be stronger than him. Therefore we are bound by the code of our people not to harm you.*'

'Oh, right,' I said. 'That's a relief.' All this time, though, the tapping was continuing, although I couldn't see which of the three of them was doing it. The nun remained silent and motionless, and the atmosphere in the cottage was still deeply threatening, like those few tense seconds before a thunderstorm breaks.

'*We have come to tell you that you must give a warning to your people. This time you cannot defeat us, as you defeated our father Misquamacus, because this time we have your own spirits in league with us, as our allies.*'

'You've lost me,' I told him.

'*You defeated our father in the same way that your forebears defeated us. Your forebears brought diseases to our people so that they fell like mayflies. Those diseases were unknown to us, and we were unable to protect ourselves. You defeated our father by using magic of which he knew nothing and so had no way to defend himself.*'

'Well, it wasn't really magic,' I said. 'It was what we call technology.' I still didn't really understand what he was trying to tell me.

173

'*Now we have your spirits on our side,*' said Matchitehew. '*Your spirits know your ways. They know your magic. They know what diseases can make you sick. They know how to take over your bodies and your minds. Now that we are together, you cannot defeat us. We will drive you out of this land as you once drove us. That is the warning that you must give to your people. They will leave – or they will die.*'

The tapping stopped. The bedroom was silent, all except for an endless clicking which must have been the sound of the black beetles swarming all over Matchitehew and Megedagik, because nothing else in the room was moving.

'I can *try* to give a warning to "my people", as you call them,' I told Matchitehew. 'But I don't honestly think that they'll listen. The likelihood is that they'll mark me down as a screwball.'

'*You must tell them what is going to happen to them, and why. It is important for those who are about to be punished to understand the reason for their punishment.*'

'Yes, I get that. But if I go to a local TV station and tell them that the United States is about to be attacked by the spirits of two long-dead Algonquin wonder-workers do you know what they will do?'

'*They will run to their homes to gather their families, and they will prepare to leave.*'

'No, they won't do that. They'll laugh in my face, or else they'll call for a nut doctor. Either way they won't believe me.'

'*Your people are not frightened of spirits?*'

174

'Yes, they are. Well, they are and they're not. They get scared if they see a movie with a ghost in it, or if they think that their house is haunted, like Amityville. But they don't get so scared that they'll pack everything up and leave the country.'

It was obvious that Matchitehew hadn't understood a single word of that. Although he was speaking English, and speaking it clearly, I was beginning to suspect that he was actually talking to me in his native Algonquin language, and that he had the ability to communicate with me telepathically, so that his words were translated inside of my mind. His father Misquamacus had been able to speak in English to me, even though it was highly unlikely that he had ever learned it.

My late-lamented Algonquin friend Singing Rock had told me that this was called *'nondam pawe-wa'* – literally 'hearing a dream'. The word *'pawe-wa'* means 'having a vision', and co-incidentally it also happens to mean 'shaman' or 'wonder-worker'. It's where the word 'pow-wow' comes from – sharing the things that are going on inside of your head.

'You will warn your people,' Matchitehew insisted. *'You will warn them that they will be stricken by disease against which they will have no immunity.'*

'All I can say is, I'll try. But I can't guarantee that anybody is going to take me seriously.'

'If you fail, you will suffer.'

'I thought you said you couldn't hurt me.'

'Not you, but we can hurt those closest to you. The ones you love, and your friends.'

'Hey – don't even think about it!'

175

'Then make sure that you warn your people. Warn them that a great sickness is spreading across the country, from one ocean to the other, and that the day has come for them to leave or die. That is the same choice that your people gave to our people.'

Now I was starting to feel really panicky. Matchitehew's three-hundred-year-old concept of America was obviously vastly different from the way it was today. He couldn't have any idea that the population was now more than three hundred million, and that whatever you threatened them with, three hundred million people weren't just going to pack their bags and go back to wherever they came from.

'OK,' I said. 'I'll do whatever I can. But like I say, I can't promise anything. This country is full of weirdos saying that the world is coming to an end. It won't be easy for me to make myself heard.'

'You will warn your people that they must go!'

I was about to protest to him again when the tapping started up again, but I also heard something else. A voice outside in the yard called out 'Harry! Harr-*ee!* Harry, can you switch on the light? I can't see a darned thing out here!'

It was Sandy. She must have finished early at the Stars-and-Bars. I looked at Matchitehew and Megedagik and the nun and desperately said, 'OK. Whatever you want me to do, I'll do it! I'll go out early tomorrow and start telling everybody. I promise.'

They stayed where they were, the three of them, and they were all faceless – Matchitehew and

176

Megedagik because all I could see of them were silhouettes, and the nun because she had her black cloth draped over her head.

I thought: *What happens now? Are they going to vanish, in the same way that the first nun had vanished?*

'Sandy!' I shouted out. 'Don't touch the door-handle!'

'What?'

'I said, don't touch the door-handle! Just hold on a second, stay there, the lights are all out!'

It was too late. Sandy burst in through the front door, carrying her usual cluster of shopping bags and a bag that clinked as if it had bottles in it.

'Why is it so *dark*?' she said. 'I brought you some of that steam beer you like, and I nearly dropped it!'

'Don't come in here!' I said. Frantic, I turned around to see what Matchitehew and Megedagik and the nun were doing, but the bedroom door slammed shut with such violence that I heard the frame crack, and the key dropped out of it and tinkled to the floor. Now Sandy and I were left in almost total darkness.

'What – what was that?' she said. 'Who did that? *Harry* – do you have somebody in your bedroom?'

I groped around and managed to find the table lamp. I switched it on, and to my relief it worked. Sandy was standing there with her long hair all scraped back into a ponytail, her eyes even wider than usual. She was wearing a pink T-shirt and jeans so tight it looked as if her legs had been painted dark blue.

177

'What's going *on*, Harry?' she asked me. She looked toward the bedroom door and said, 'There's somebody in there, isn't there?'

'There is and there isn't. It's hard to explain. I think we need to get out of here.'

'What do you mean, "it's hard to explain"? Is that why you told me you're leaving – because you've got yourself another woman?'

'No, Sandy, I don't.'

'Then who slammed the door just then? Don't tell me it was a man. My boss Larry said that priest thing was kind of suspicious.'

'Listen – trust me – I don't have another woman, and I'm not gay either. We need to get out of here, that's all.'

But Sandy dropped all of her shopping bags on to the floor, including the bag with the beer bottles in it. I tried to stop her, but she pushed past me and opened the bedroom door.

A cold draft rushed into the hallway, with a soft whistling sound like the wind blowing through trees. Several dark shadows danced across the walls, and then they were gone.

'What was *that*?' said Sandy. She switched on the bedroom light and looked around, and then she turned back to me and said, 'Did you feel that?'

There was nobody in the bedroom. No Matchitehew, no Megedagik, no nun. Sandy circled around the bed and even lifted the quilt and looked underneath it.

'So who slammed the door?' she asked me.

I shrugged and said, 'Maybe an earth tremor. I don't know. Maybe a ghost. These old buildings, you know.'

'Harry – you always told me you were a seller, not a buyer.'

'Just because I'm a seller doesn't mean that I don't believe in what I sell.'

Sandy crossed her arms tightly across her breasts. 'You're making me scared now.'

'Hey,' I told her. 'There's nothing to be scared of.' I went across and gave her a squeeze and two or three kisses. All the same, while I was holding her close, I was looking around the bedroom myself to make sure that my three dark visitors had really disappeared.

Later, in bed, Sandy smoothed her hand up and down my chest and my stomach, going a little further down with every stroke.

'I've decided,' she said.

I had left the blinds open, so that the witches and the monkeys were flickering across the ceiling. 'What have you decided?'

'I've decided to come with you. I don't care if you don't have much money or anyplace to stay. I have some money saved up.'

'Sandy – I can't offer you any kind of a future.'

'I thought futures was what you were good at.'

'Yeah, but imaginary futures, not real futures. You're a very pretty girl, and I really like you, but what kind of a life can I give you? You're twelve years younger than me; you should be thinking about a husband and a family and a house with a basketball hoop fixed to the garage.'

She took hold of my penis and started to squeeze it. 'Don't you want to make love to me tonight? What's wrong?'

179

I kissed her bare shoulder. 'Nothing's wrong. I'm just kind of stressed out, that's all.'

'Something's wrong, Harry. I can tell.'

I looked down to the end of the bed, and the nun was standing there. Silent, as she had been before. Not moving. Because her head was covered I had no idea if she was watching us or not.

Sandy gave me one last tug and then she said, 'OK. But I'll rape you in the morning.'

She turned over, and after a while I could hear by her steady breathing that she was asleep. Meanwhile, I lay there staring at the nun.

We are warnings.

The sky began to lighten, and as it did so the nun gradually faded. Soon she was nothing but a shadowy outline, and then she had vanished altogether.

Now we have your spirits on our side. Your spirits know your ways. They know your magic.

They know what makes you sick.

Fourteen

A shield-shaped signboard by the side of the highway announced that this was 'The Grandier Funeral Chapel'. It had a painting of a spray of pink roses underneath it, the same as Robert Machin's business card. Anna turned into the red asphalt driveway and parked next to a gleaming black Lincoln hearse. As she climbed out of her car there was a distant growl of heat-thunder from the west, over toward Sunset Hills. It had thundered like that on the evening David had died, and she was beginning to feel that she was being followed everywhere by threatening weather.

The funeral chapel was built of dark-brown brick, with a fascia like a country church, except that on its right-hand side it featured a high covered portico for hearses to draw into, so caskets could be rolled out of them in privacy. Anna walked up to the wide glass doors, and they silently slid open for her.

She found herself inside a gloomy reception area, with two potted parlor palms and two black-leather couches. It had a musty closed-in smell of oak and floor-polish. There was a desk on the right-hand side, but it was unattended. The only light came from a narrow stained-glass window, which cast a blue-and-yellow pattern across the faux-marble tiles. She could faintly hear piped

181

organ music, although it was turned down so low that it was almost inaudible.

On the left-hand side of the reception area there was a door marked 'Brian U. Grandier, Director', and as the double glass doors slid shut behind her, this door was abruptly flung open. To Anna's surprise, out stepped the gray-haired, gray-bearded man who she had seen in the hospital when John Patrick Bridges had been brought in. He was wearing the same gray double-breasted suit, and a matching bow tie which looked like a giant gray moth perched on his throat.

'Professor Grey,' he said, walking across to her with his hand held out. He looked shorter than he had in the hospital, and stockier.

Anna said sharply, 'You were at SLU. You were staring at me in the corridor, and then you peeked into my laboratory.'

Brian Grandier smiled and shrugged, as if to say: *And – so what?* 'I did, my dear, yes. I was just finding my way around. You'll probably be seeing me quite often from now on. In hospitals, people pass away, and it's my business to be there when they do.'

Although she didn't exactly know why, Anna found Brian Grandier both irritating and unpleasant. She was half-inclined to tell him that she had changed her mind about using Grandier Funeral Chapel for David's cremation, but then she had already gone to the trouble of making an early morning appointment with Brian Grandier's secretary and driving all the way out here to Gravois Road, and it seemed irrational to walk out now, just because she didn't like his

182

fastidiously trimmed beard and his supercilious smile and the way he had called her 'my dear'.

'Would you care to come into my office?' he asked her. 'I can show you our brochure, and then we can run through all of your specific requirements – number of guests, number of vehicles, music, floral tributes, all that kind of thing – and I can give you a preliminary estimate.'

As he spoke, Anna picked up the subtlest hint of an accent – probably French, considering his name. She hesitated, and then made her way directly across to his office. He followed close behind her, *too* close for her liking, with one hand raised behind her back as if he were about to lay it on her shoulder.

He pulled out a red leather armchair for her, and then sat down behind a wide mahogany desk. The wall behind him was lined with glass-fronted bookshelves, but most of them were empty. All he had on his desk was an open binder, a glossy brochure with 'Grandier Funeral Chapel' on the cover and a vase with a dozen pink roses in it. The roses were tinged with brown, and some of the petals had dropped off them.

'You'll find that our prices are highly competitive, compared with other funeral parlors,' he told her. 'In fact, because you're on the staff at SLU, and we're trying to make a good impression there, I can offer you this funeral at half what our nearest competitor would ask.'

'I see,' said Anna. 'In return for a discount, you expect me to recommend you to the relatives of any of our patients who die?'

Brian Grandier laced his fingers together and

smiled. 'Here at Grandier, we prefer not to use the "d" word. Let's just say that if any of SLU's patients failed to respond to treatment, we could give their family a very discreet and sympathetic service for a very reasonable outlay.'

Outlay, thought Anna. That's a good choice of words for a man whose profession is laying out bodies. But then she thought: *I'm being cynical here, and it's only because I'm being self-protective and trying not to think about the pain of losing David. Only a week ago the two of us were driving across the river to Chesterfield for David's favorite barbecue, laughing together like a couple of college kids, and here I am arranging his funeral.*

Brian Grandier passed her the brochure and showed her the various caskets she could choose, from traditional mahogany with gold-plated handles to eco-friendly coffins woven out of wicker, banana leaves or water hyacinths. She chose one of the simplest: pine, with pale oak veneer.

Although she instinctively disliked him, Anna couldn't fault Brian Grandier for efficiency. Quietly and quickly he noted down everything that she wanted for David's funeral service, from the single hymn that he had always liked, to the readings and the tributes and the music that would play when the drapes were drawn and David disappeared from her life forever.

When he had finished adding up the figures, he passed her his estimate without a word, although he kept his eyes on her intently, like a schoolboy submitting his homework to his teacher.

Anna read through it and nodded. 'That does seem very reasonable, Mr Grandier.'

'Good. In that case I'll get in touch with SLU and make all the necessary arrangements. Do you need any other assistance? You said that your late partner's parents were coming to St Louis from Boise. I could sort out their travel arrangements if you would like me to, and those of any other guests.'

'No – no, that will be fine, thank you,' Anna told him. As she stood up, she realized that he had taken it for granted that he would be handling the funeral, although she hadn't actually said yes, that she would accept his estimate.

Brian Grandier accompanied her through the sliding glass doors to the portico outside. The sky was charcoal gray now, and spots of rain were beginning to measle the red asphalt driveway.

'Looks like we're in for a storm,' he said, and he smiled, almost as if would relish it. As the wind rose, the trees around the parking lot started to rustle and sway, and the neatly clipped hedge that separated the chapel from the highway kept giving quick, spasmodic shivers. Brian Grandier took Anna's hand between both of his and said, 'I'll email you a PDF of the estimate later today, professor, if you would be so good as to sign it and email it back to me. I will also mail you a hard copy, of course. Please be assured of my very best attention.'

'You're French?' she asked him.

'Originally from France, yes,' he said. He sounded slightly irritated that she had been so direct. 'But, you know, that was a very long time ago, and some things we prefer to forget. *Dieu nous donne l'espoir pour l'avenir, mais le diable ne nous donne rien mais les souvenirs de nos malheurs passés.*'

Anna frowned, trying to translate what he had said. 'God gives us hope, is that it? But the devil only gives us souvenirs?'

Brian Grandier smiled that self-satisfied smile. 'God gives us hope for the future, but the devil gives us nothing but memories of our past misfortunes.'

Anna said nothing, but turned and walked back to her car. The hearse had gone now, and she could think only that somebody else had passed away, another soul had vanished, like David's had vanished, and the hearse had left to pick up their lifeless body. She had seen scores of dead people in her time at SLU, but most of them had arrived at the hospital hoping to be saved. Here, at the Grandier Funeral Chapel, they arrived already dead, and they came here only for their remains to be disposed of. This morning, as she hurried through the rain toward her car, she found that indescribably depressing.

She managed to open the door and sit behind the wheel just as there was an explosive burst of thunder right overhead, and the rain came hammering down hard on the roof of her car. She pulled down the sun visor and opened the mirror so that she could quickly comb her hair.

When she had finished, she lifted her hand to push the sun visor back into place, but as she did so she saw a flicker of lightning off to her left, and she looked out through the windshield to see if there was any sign of the storm passing over.

It was difficult to make out anything distinctly through the ribs of rain that were streaming down the glass, but she could just make out the gray-suited figure of Brian Grandier standing under the portico. She thought at first that he must be standing there to see her off, but then she realized he had his back turned toward her.

She started the Prius's engine and switched on the windshield wipers. It was then that she saw that Brian Grandier appeared to be talking to a group of maybe half-a-dozen people, who were clustered just outside the portico in the pouring rain. At first she thought they were all wearing black hooded raincoats, but after the windshield wipers had squeaked backward and forward three or four times she saw them more clearly.

Maybe their appearance here was only a co-incidence. In fact, she thought it *must* be, but all the same she felt a prickling of apprehension in her wrists and down her back.

They were nuns – and not only that, their faces were all hidden by black veils draped over their heads, exactly like the foul-mouthed nun who had materialized in the morgue when she'd gone to look at Mary Stephens' body.

Anna sat in her car staring at them for almost half a minute, but then Brian Grandier turned around and looked in her direction. He was obviously wondering why she had started up her engine but not left yet.

At the same moment, her cellphone jangled, so loudly that it startled her. She always had the ringtone set on top volume because she was in

187

the habit of leaving her cell in other rooms, both at home and at work.

It was Epiphany. 'Professor? I hope I'm not interrupting anything.'

'No, no, it's fine. I'm all through here, and I'm just about to leave.'

'It's the Meramac School virus.'

'OK . . . how is it responding to the tyranivir?'

'That's why I'm calling. Yesterday I thought we might have it licked, but all the rats we tested died overnight. I ran a couple more experiments, and the virus has mutated – now tyranivir doesn't appear to have any effect on it at all.'

'Shit,' said Anna. The rain was easing off now, and she could see Brian Grandier and the nuns entering the chapel's reception area through the sliding glass doors.

'There's one really interesting thing, though,' said Epiphany. 'I was running a comparison test, and I mixed one of the mutated Meramac School viruses with some of the viruses that I hadn't yet exposed to tyranivir . . . so they *hadn't* mutated. Guess what happened?'

'Epiphany, I'm waiting for you to tell me.' Brian Grandier and the nuns had all disappeared now, and Anna was just anxious to get back to the hospital.

'The mutated virus attacked all of the non-mutated viruses. Destroyed them, broke them all apart, completely disassembled them.'

'Now that *is* interesting,' said Anna. She checked her wristwatch. 'Listen, I'll be back in the lab in twenty-five minutes. You can give me a repeat performance then.'

188

She drove out of the funeral chapel's front entrance and headed back toward the city. As she joined Interstate 44, heading north-east, a watery sun appeared behind the clouds and the surface of the highway gleamed so brightly that she had to put on her Ray-Bans.

Back in the laboratory, Epiphany repeated her previous test, and Anna sat watching it on her microscope's display screen. She could see how much the Meramac School virus had mutated to became resistant to the antiviral drug tyranivir. In appearance, it changed from green to purple, and its burr-like surface grew scores more prickles.

She could also see that in its mutated form, it not only continued to attack the cells of its human host, but it also turned on other Meramac virus cells which had not yet been exposed to tyranivir and so hadn't mutated. It tore so many holes in their nucleotide structure that they blew apart, like bright green planets exploding in micro-miniature.

She watched the cells bursting apart again and again, and then she sat back and said, 'That's amazing. It's like a child growing up and killing its own siblings. In some ways it's like the work they've been doing at Johns Hopkins – trying to get the DNA repair enzyme to tear the HIV virus apart.'

She climbed off her stool and went across the laboratory to pick up the cup of coffee she had left on her desk. It had gone cold now, and when she sipped it she pulled a face, but she finished it off anyway. She needed the caffeine.

'Of course, the difference is that the DNA repair enzyme is completely benign – while this mutated Meramac School virus – *wow*. Just look at it. It becomes more and more aggressive with everything we throw at it. OK – it kills off all of the previous versions of itself, but what are we left with? A mutated version that's a hundred times more virulent. It's no good finding a cure if the cure is more dangerous than the sickness it's supposed to be curing.'

She watched more viruses exploding, and then she said, 'It's pretty damned obvious, isn't it? What we have to do now is find a mutated form of this virus that can destroy *this* mutated form, but which in turn isn't harmful to humans.'

'Maybe that's too much to ask,' said Epiphany.

'Come on, Epiphany, you know my motto. "If you can imagine it, you can make it happen."'

'I don't know. I'm not so sure that's true. I used to imagine that Jason Derulo knocked on my door, saying that he wanted to take me out on a date.'

Anna shook her head. 'I'm sorry. I don't know who that is.'

'He's a singer. He's so cute. And he can dance! He can stand on his head without supporting himself with his hands.'

'Sometimes I feel like I'm doing that all day, every day.'

That afternoon Henry Rutgers came down to Anna's laboratory with a Styrofoam tray of samples and a thick blue plastic folder.

'I've run preliminary tests on all three deceased,'

190

he told her, lifting out their individual files one by one. 'John Patrick Bridges, Mary Stephens and – here, last but not least – your David.'

'So, did you found anything?'

'Oh, I found something all right. All three of them were infected by what looks like a retrovirus.'

'But?' said Anna. 'I definitely sense a "but".'

'You certainly do. Quite frankly, it's like no virus I've ever come across before. In fact, if my readings are correct, its behavior is quite bizarre. That's why I've brought down these samples. I'd like *you* to run some tests on it, too – see if you agree with me.'

'In what way "bizarre"?' Anna asked him. She was beginning to feel deeply tired now. Arranging David's funeral had emotionally drained her much more than she had expected. She had hoped that doing something practical about his death would help her to come to terms with losing him so suddenly, and to deal with the symptoms of shock, but she had hardly been able to think about anything else all day. She kept visualizing the Grandier Funeral Chapel, with its dark-brown brick, and Brian Grandier standing outside talking to those nuns, and the rain streaming down her windshield as if it were trying to hide them from sight.

She had the feeling that something strange and threatening was happening in her life, but she couldn't work out what it was. When she was a child she had seen demons' faces in her bedroom wallpaper, but when she looked at the wallpaper more closely the faces had been nothing but rose-petals. The events of the past two days had given her the same kind of uncertainty. Maybe the artist who'd designed the wallpaper had deliberately hidden the demons' faces in the flowers, just like the nuns were giving her a message that she couldn't yet decipher.

'I'll tell you what's so goddamned bizarre about it,' said Doctor Rutgers. 'It's *picky*.'

'"Picky"?' What do you mean by that?'

'Most viruses will invade any host cell, regardless of who the host is, and I'm talking about ethnic origin here. Viruses don't usually care if you're black, white, Chinese or whatever. But not this little piggy. Oh, no. I carried out a series of control tests on host cells of five different ethnic origins, and it simply ignored the cells of anyone who was anything other than white, although it did infect a small percentage of Hispanics.'

'That *is* bizarre.'

'Wait, there's more. Not only did this virus ignore the cells of every other ethnic type apart from white or Hispanic, it ignored a high percentage of *those*, too, and I have absolutely no idea why. There doesn't seem to be any biological reason for it being so choosy about who it infects – none that *I've* been able to find, anyhow. But here we have a virus that will kill *some* people, but shows absolutely no interest in infecting any others.'

Anna took the samples and the folder of printouts. 'I won't be able to go through these all today, Henry. I have to get myself something to eat and a few hours' sleep. But I'll have Rafik look them over when he comes in.'

192

'Thanks, I appreciate it,' said Doctor Rutgers. He paused by the door for a moment, and then he said, 'I know this sounds fanciful, but do you know what this virus reminds me of? The Carlson Coombs killings.'

Anna looked up at him. The Carson Coombs killings had happened late last year, when a deeply resentful employee of Carson Coombs Insurance in St Louis had turned up at the company's offices one morning, after years of being bullied and mocked by other staff, and had shot twenty-three of them. However, he had done this very selectively, shooting only those who had been making his life unbearable. He had shown no interest in killing anybody else, even though there were more than two hundred employees in the offices at the time and he could have shot far more.

'Henry,' said Anna, 'what you're talking about is *revenge*. Viruses don't infect people out of revenge. It'll be some aberration in its protease, that's all.'

'I know,' said Doctor Rutgers. 'I don't know why it made me think of Carson Coombs, but it just did. I've probably been working too hard.'

When she returned home that evening, Anna carried all of her shopping bags into the kitchen and then went back out into the living room. The smashed mirror was still hanging on the wall, and when she stood in front of it, it was like looking at herself through a kaleidoscope. Fifty fragments of Anna, all seen from different angles.

She walked around the loft, switching on lights

and drawing down the blinds. Although there were no nunlike shadows lurking in any of the corners, she still felt uneasy, and she opened all of her mirrored closet doors just to make sure there was nobody hiding inside.

'Anna – you're being ridiculous,' she told herself. 'You're suffering from stress, that's all.'

But something had been niggling her ever since Henry Rutgers had brought his samples down to her laboratory. What was it about the virus that had made him think about the Carson Coombs killings? Those murders had been a classic case of revenge, the bullied underdog finally getting his own back. And what had that nun said to her, in the morgue, where the bodies of John Patrick Bridges and Mary Stephens and David had been lying? *'Nothing will stop us this time from getting our revenge.'*

She made herself a bagel with lox and cream cheese and ate it standing up in the kitchen. Then she tidied up, showered and went to bed. Tonight the bed seemed even wider and emptier than ever. She dressed in David's blue-striped pajamas, but they felt tangled and hot and uncomfortable, and after a half-hour she climbed out of bed again and took them off. It was no good trying to bring him back by wearing his clothes. He was gone.

That night she had a nightmare about nuns. The bedroom window was slightly open at the top, and nuns were silently pouring in through the gap, a whole black flock of them, scores of them, like bats.

Soon they were covering the entire ceiling,

194

hanging upside-down, rustling and whispering and climbing all over each other. Their whispering sounded like prayers, or perhaps it was nothing but malicious gossip.

She sat up, clutching the sheet against her breasts, straining her eyes in the shadows to see what had woken her. She could hear traffic noises from the street outside, but was she awake, or was she simply dreaming that she was awake?

She glanced upward. There were no nuns clustering on the ceiling so she must be awake.

She reached across for the glass of water on the nightstand next to her. She had just picked it up when she heard a sharp slithering sound which seemed to be coming from down on the floor, right underneath her. She paused and listened. Seconds went past, and all she could hear was an occasional car, and then the mournful, echoing hoot of a ship on the river.

She raised the glass to her lips, but as she did so she heard that slithering sound again, as if something was being dragged across the bedroom carpet. A black shape suddenly slid out from the narrow gap from underneath the bed and sat up next to her. It was a nun, all draped in black, with her face covered like the nun in the morgue.

Anna didn't cry out, but she was so shocked and frightened that she dropped her glass of water on to the floor. With two pale hands the nun drew back the veil that covered her face and her face was pale too, deathly pale, with shadowy smudges around her eyes and dragged-down lips.

The nun opened her mouth wide and screamed at her. Her scream was so shrill and so penetrating that Anna rolled herself away from her and scrambled wildly across the bed. The sheets wound themselves around her legs as if they were trying to stop her, and for a few seconds she was trapped, but then she managed to twist and kick herself free and tumble off the opposite side of the bed on to the carpet.

The nun rose up to her full height and threw herself after her, but as she launched herself over the bed she vanished, vaporized, as if she had been nothing more than a cloud of black smoke.

Anna knelt by the bed, shaking. She looked around the room, and then up at the ceiling, but there was no sign of any nuns anywhere. *Nightmare*, she thought, *it must have been a nightmare*. But if it had been a nightmare, she must have been asleep when she sat up and reached for her glass of water, and asleep when she dropped it on to the floor. She must have still been asleep when she rolled across the bed to get away from the nun, because there was no nun here now.

She switched on the bedside lamp. She quickly glanced left and right, but there was nobody else in the room. Not only that, the gap between the bed and the carpet was less than three inches high, so nobody could have been hiding underneath it.

She stood up and circled around the end of the bed to the bathroom. She hesitated for a moment, and then she threw open the door and checked inside. There was nobody in there, either.

Come on, Anna, she told herself. *Don't let this get to you. You have an important job to do, so*

you can't let David's death mess up your mind.
People are depending on you to save their lives.

In spite of that, she got dressed in jeans and a pink sleeveless T-shirt and spent the rest of the night on one of the couches in the living-room, with the lights on. She slept only fitfully, and at five a.m. she got up and went into the kitchen to make herself a mug of coffee.

Fifteen

It didn't take long for me to pack, because I had given away almost everything I owned before I left New York and came down to sunny Miami. I used to have leather armchairs and card tables and a bookcase full of books, including bound copies of *Playboy*. I used to have a vacuum cleaner and cutlery and most of a Willow Pattern dinner-service with only a few side-plates missing. I used to have a large framed picture of Vermont in the fall, with the trees turning crimson and yellow. I don't know why: I had never been to Vermont, and I had never had the slightest intention of going there, either.

All I owned now was my clothes, and a few CDs, and three sets of fortune-telling cards – and I hadn't looked at the Parlor Sibyl deck since they had all turned black. My Mustang I was going to leave here with Marcos, who could either use it himself, or sell it for me. There was no point in owning a car in Manhattan.

Sandy had gone home to pack, too, although I had tried to persuade her to let me find someplace for us to stay before she joined me. I really liked her, but right at this juncture in my life I didn't want to be responsible for her, especially since Matchitehew and Megedagik and the nun had threatened to hurt my friends and loved ones if I didn't warn the world that they were going to spread some terrible sickness.

As I packed I was so jittery that I was right on the point of panic, and every time I heard a noise in the yard outside I couldn't stop myself from peering out of the windows to see what it was. I kept trying to convince myself that I had been hallucinating last night, and that the appearance of the nun and the two sons of Misquamacus had been caused by nothing more than stress and exhaustion and too much alcohol. But I had been there before. I had seen the enormous power of Native American magic, and I knew how devastating it could be. It comes from the ground right underneath our feet, because after all this was *their* ground, not ours.

What was scaring me so much was that I couldn't think how I was possibly going to do what they had ordered me to do. Who could I warn that some disease was going to spread across the United States – some disease against which we had no immunity? The emergency services wouldn't listen to me. They would probably think that I was simply trying to find a way to stay in Florida – either that, or I was cracked. The media would probably think the same.

But like I say, I had seen for myself how devastating the forces of Native American shamanism could be. What would happen to me if an epidemic *did* break out and millions of people died because they had no resistance to it? I would probably get the blame for being some kind of terrorist and having started it myself.

All I could think of doing was getting the hell

out of Florida and never coming back. Misquamacus had been the most terrifying spiritual apparition that I had ever come across, and if Matchitehew and Megedagik had only *half* his vengefulness between the two of them then we were heading for disaster, on a scale that I couldn't even begin to imagine. And what about that nun? If any occult appearance had ever given me the shivering cold creeps then it was her.

When I was almost finished packing I called my old friend Rick Beamer's number in Brooklyn. I had rescued Rick from some sticky situations more than once, mostly from what you might call 'relationship misunderstandings' with women, and two or three times I had let him stay in my spare bedroom – once for almost four months. Rick was a good-looking guy in a thin, sharp, Clint Eastwoody way, with a high gray pompadour and a permanently self-satisfied smirk on his face. Women always fell for him, but not for long, because he couldn't stay faithful. He shuffled go-go girls and waitresses and pole dancers as fast as I shuffled Tarot cards.

A hoarse-voiced woman answered the phone. 'Yes?' she said. Then, *'Billy* – take your dirty sneakers off of that chair!'

'Is Rick there, by any chance?'

'Rick? No. Nobody of that name here.'

'Rick Beamer. Skinny guy, gray hair.'

'Oh, *him*. Sure. I always knew him as Sharky.'

'That's right. Sharky. Is he there? I really need to speak to him.'

'No, he's not. *Billy* – how many goddamned times do I have to tell you?'

'Oh,' I said. 'Will he be back later?'

'Who?'

'Sharky. Could you ask him to give me a call?'

'Sorry, I can't do that.'

'All you have to do is leave him a note. I'll give you my cell number, and he can call me any time.'

'He went to LA. That was maybe six or seven months ago. I don't think he'll be coming back, ever.'

'Oh, OK. You don't have a number for him, by any chance?'

'No, I don't. *Billy*! This is the last time I'm going to tell you! If you don't take your sneakers off of that table I'm going to break your goddamned legs in three places, and *then* see how you like it!'

'Thanks, anyhow,' I said to the woman.

'What for?' she asked me. But just as I was about to hang up, she said, 'Hey – wait up a second. Sharky did say that he was going to start his own business in LA. Maybe you can find him in the *Yellow Pages*.'

'What kind of business?'

'Exterminator. He was going to call it something like Beamer's Bug Blitzers. I told him what a crappy name that was.'

'Yes,' I said. 'That sounds like him. He did that kind of work before.'

'Well, I hope you find him,' the woman told me. 'If you do, tell him that Lauretta still thinks of him.'

'Lauretta? OK.'

'Tell him he's a pig and if I ever meet him

again I'll spit in his eye. Tell him I'll spit in both of his eyes. Tell him I'll spit up his nose.'

'Oh. OK. Thanks, Lauretta.'

It took me another couple of calls before I located Rick. I found the number of Beamer's Bug & Termite Blitzers through 411-NDA, but Rick wasn't in his office when I called. Some grindingly slow-voiced Hispanic guy took about five minutes to write down my name and number, and he promised to have Rick call me back, but then he told me that he was probably at the Tiki-Ti tropical cocktail bar on Sunset with his girlfriend Dazey.

'Thanks,' I said. 'Why didn't you tell me that in the first place?'

'Because . . . you don't ask me in the first place.'

I called the Tiki-Ti, and the bartender answered. 'You have a customer called Rick Beamer with you?' I asked. 'Sometimes known as Sharky.'

'Sharky? Sure. Who shall I say is calling?'

'Tell him it's the Wizard.'

'Sharky! It's the Wizard!'

I could Rick over the hubbub of customers. 'You're kidding me! The Wizard? I haven't heard from that sumbitch in years! Thanks, Michael!'

I waited for a few seconds, listening to the laughing and chattering in the Tiki-Ti bar, and then Rick picked up the phone. 'Harry Erskine, by all that's unholy! How'd you track me down here, man?'

'Lauretta put me on to you. She says hi, by the way.'

202

'Lauretta, that ratchet pussy.'

'Rick, every woman you're no longer involved with is a ratchet pussy. You know that. But you're still with Dazey?'

'Dazey appreciates my noo-ances. Always has. Besides, she has the greatest gazongas of any woman I ever dated. What do you want, Wizard? Haven't just called me to pass the time of day, have you?'

'No, Rick. I'm in Coral Gables in Florida right now, and among some other stuff I've gotten myself into some minor tangle with the law. They're insisting that I vacate the state, and I was hoping that I could crash with you for a day or two.'

'They want you to leave the entire *state*? Jesus! What have you *done*, man? I always thought you were one of life's saints. Telling old ladies all that optimistic shit about their futures and everything, just to make them feel happy. That's almost a public service!'

'I'll tell you when I get there – that's if it's OK for me to stay with you for a while.'

'Sure. Of course it is. You and me, Wizard, shit, we go way back. Just so long as you don't mind sharing a room with Dazey's sister Mazey.'

'*Mazey*? Are you pulling my chain?'

'No way. Dazey has a sister called Mazey. Blame their parents, not me. Mazey's a beautician. You'll like her. I mean, you always went for really stupid women, didn't you, Wizard?'

'Stupid women don't hurt you, that's why.' I was thinking of Amelia Crusoe. Unlike me, Amelia Crusoe was a genuine clairvoyant. I had

203

always hankered after Amelia, not only because of her fortune-telling abilities, but because she was so pretty that she practically gave men an ischemic stroke whenever she walked into a room, *and* she had brains. But it had been one of those relationships that for one reason or another had never worked out. And it had hurt.

But – 'Here's the problem, Rick,' I told him. 'My current girlfriend Sandy wants to come with me.'

'Sorry, Wizard. There just won't be the room.'

'OK, Rick. I guess I'll just have to put her off.'

'I'm sorry, man.'

'That's all right,' I told him, but to tell you the truth I was relieved. It gave me a legitimate excuse to put Sandy off from coming with me.

'OK, Wizard . . . here's my address . . . four-eight-eight-one Ambrose Avenue, Hollywood. If there's nobody home when you arrive you'll find a spare key under the concrete statue of an under-dressed woman beside the front door.'

'Thanks, Sharky. I'll see you later.'

'Hey, Wizard – before you go, you got me one of your mystic mottoes?'

'Sure, Sharky. "No matter how much caviar you pile on a baked potato, it will never turn into a seagull."'

I booked a seat on American Airlines leaving Miami for Los Angeles at 18:10 that evening. I didn't call all of my clients to tell them that I would probably never see them again, but that would have taken time and money and I didn't have much of either, and for all I knew it might have given some of them a cardiac arrest. Some of them seemed to be under the impression that if they couldn't find out what their future was going to be, it was because they didn't have one.

I closed the door of my cottage behind me for the last time, and I can't say that I didn't feel bitter about it. Up until yesterday, I had enjoyed every day I'd spent in Miami Beach. At the same time, though, I couldn't help picturing how those three nuns had materialized in my bedroom, and two of them had risen right up to the ceiling and turned into Matchitehew and Megedagik, with their horns and the beetles that swarmed all over their shoulders. I didn't ever want to come face-to-face with those three again. Like, *ever*.

The taxi that I had called was waiting for me in the street outside. When I climbed in, I asked the taxi driver to take me to Coral Gables Hospital on Douglas Street. It was still too early for my flight, and I had a critical call to make before I went to the airport.

Outside the front doors of Coral Gables Hospital there is a resident black cat, which always rubs itself up against visitors' legs. I had been there a few times before to visit friends who were either giving birth to triplets or who had gotten their noses broken in bar fights, and I always used to think that the black cat rubbing itself up against me was a sign of good luck. This afternoon I wasn't so sure. I lugged my two battered old suitcases into the lobby, and a cute African-American receptionist with big hoop earrings allowed me to leave them behind her desk. She was not just cute, she was *very* cute, but I couldn't ask her if she'd like to go marlin fishing with me on my friend's sixty-five foot fiberglass Viking. By early evening, Pacific Time, I'd be touching down in LA.

Father Zapata was asleep when I entered his room. He was so ashy that he looked as if he was dead and they had already made a start on cremating him. There were charcoal-black circles around his eyes, his cheeks were sunken and his white teeth were bared in a skull-like snarl. He was breathing, though, whistling through one nostril, and he wasn't on any kind of a drip, so presumably the deep dorsal artery in his penis had stopped bleeding. I sat next to his bed for a while, watching his silent TV and eating his grapes. After about ten minutes there was a clatter outside the door as a nurse dropped a tray, and he opened his eyes and stared at me.

'*Harry,*' he croaked.

'Hi, father. Just dropped by to see how you were doing.'

'I'm dying for a drink of water. My throat's so dry, I could strike a match on it.'

I passed him a plastic mug of water, and he lifted up his head from the pillow and drank it all down in five noisy gulps.

'You want some more?' I asked him.

'No, no, that's fine,' he said, handing back the empty mug. He looked me up and down, and then he said, 'You're all dressed up. Going someplace special?'

'I'm leaving for LA in about two hours. Permanently, and for ever.' I told him all about Detective Blezard running me out of Florida.

However, I didn't mention that three more nuns had appeared in my bedroom, or how two of them had turned themselves into Matchitehew and Megedagik, the sons of Misquamacus. I thought he'd probably had enough of supernatural manifestations for one lifetime, especially nuns who made you bite your own dick off.

'So – what do the doctors say?' I asked him. I nodded toward the hump under his blanket – the supporting cage which protected his nether regions while his sutures healed.

'Oh – they said that normal functions wouldn't be impaired. If I was planning on starting a sexual relationship, though, I might like to consider an extension. John Wayne Bobbitt did it, after all, and he went on to be a porn star.'

'*Jesus*, father!'

'No, no, of course I'm not thinking of copying John Wayne Bobbitt!' said Father Zapata, coughing so hoarsely that he had to stop for a moment and gasp for breath. 'I just consider myself lucky to be alive, and it's thanks to you that I didn't bleed to death. What happened to me – that proved beyond question that I need to return to the ministry as soon as I can and devote myself with even greater fervor to the struggle against Satan.'

'To be honest with you, father, I don't really understand what *did* happen to you. I mean, what made you bite yourself like that? Do you even know?'

Father Zapata looked at me with those glittery, near-together eyes. 'Harry – would you believe me if I told you that it was a demon?'

'Father, you know what I do for a living. I'm a fortune-teller, even though I don't know how it's possible to predict what's going to happen to us in the next five minutes, let alone the next five days. Well, *I* can't, anyhow. I know at least one person who's pretty good at it, but me – I can only make educated guesses. But – listen – if you say that it was a demon that made you do it, then I believe you.'

'You do?'

'Sure I do. I know for a fact that there are other forces in this world, not just us. We can't always see them, and I don't think we'll ever understand what they actually are, but I *do* know from my own experience that they exist.'

'Really? That's almost a relief to hear you say that.'

'Oh, for sure. I've come up against them more than once, and it wasn't any fun, I'm telling you. Whatever they are – spirits, ghosts, presences – sometimes they want to help us, yes. But most times they want to drive us out of our minds or rip us into pieces or bury us alive.'

'It *was* a demon, Harry, I swear on the Bible. I felt it inside me.'

'Do you have any idea which demon it was, or where it came from, or why it wanted you to bite yourself like that? Was that a punishment, because you were trying to exorcize that nun? Some kind of a warning? What?'

Father Zapata nodded. 'I'm almost sure I know which demon it was, and why it forced me to mutilate myself like that. I think I mentioned to you when you first came to see me that I thought the nun's appearance was an example of what the church calls Loudun Syndrome.'

'That's right. You didn't really finish telling me what it was.'

'Well – in 1632, in Loudun, in France, the nuns in the Ursuline convent came to believe that they had been possessed. They claimed they had been taken over by a whole swarm of different demons, including Astaroth, Celsus, Uriel and Cham.'

'OK,' I said. 'Did they know *why* these demons had chosen to possess them?'

'Not entirely. A nearby parish priest was arrested and found guilty of having initiated their possession. He was said to have done it partly in defiance against the local church hierarchy, and partly for his own sexual pleasure. They tried to make him confess by breaking his legs, among other hideous tortures, and then he was burned alive at the stake. The nuns themselves had their demons driven out of them by two expert exorcists.

'Even after this, however, the mother superior Jeanne des Anges claimed that she was *still* possessed – not just by one but by seven different demons – so the church authorities sent a Jesuit preacher called Jean-Joseph Surin to carry out a special exorcism on *her*.'

'I see,' I said, although I didn't. How could some religious mumbo-jumbo that had taken place in France in the seventeenth century have any relevance to *me*, or my life, or the people I was fond of?

Father Zapata coughed and cleared his throat, and then he said, 'One of the demons that

209

possessed Jeanne des Anges was a demon who had never shown himself to humans before, ever, and was previously unknown in the hierarchy of hell. Because of that, Surin had absolutely no idea what ritual was needed to exorcize him.

'This demon was by far the most powerful of all the presences inside her. Years later he was identified as Gressil, the demon of impurity and infection, third in the line of thrones. But at the time Surin could think of no other way to exorcize him but to invite him into his own body – like Father Karras does with Pazuzu, in *The Exorcist*. I suppose that's where the author got the idea from. So – although Surin saved the mother superior, he spent the next twenty-five years in a state of sickness and psychosis, and tried to kill himself more than once.'

'So what exactly *is* "Loudun Syndrome"?' I asked him.

'Please, be patient, I'm trying to explain it to you,' said Father Zapata. 'The demonic possessions in Loudun between 1632 and 1637 were very well documented. This was because the exorcisms were carried out in public, in front of seven thousand people. The life that Jean-Joseph Surin lived afterward – that's very well documented, too. For more than twenty years after he exorcized Jeanne des Anges, his behavior was violent and irrational. One of his closest colleagues, Père Jacques Nau, wrote that Surin frequently lashed out with his fists, trampled on the sacraments, and walked around naked, filthy and covered with sores, screaming at people.

'In the summer of 1658, though, the church

authorities called on him and ordered him to go back to the convent at Loudun. A young nun called Sister Marysia had become pregnant, and the mother superior was convinced that only a demon could have impregnated her, since the convent was so secure. She wanted Surin to carry out an exorcism as soon as the child was born, because it was the child of unholy seed. She trusted nobody else but Surin to do it, and according to church records, he did. We don't know what happened to the child, although we know that it was a boy, but it is recorded that Sister Marysia herself died shortly after giving birth.

'It was only a few months later that the first mysterious nun appeared to the mayor of Angers, as I described to you before. Then more nuns appeared to other townspeople, and soon afterward those people who had seen them began to get acutely sick and die. The rumor was that these nuns came from the convent in Loudun and were all carrying some virulent infection, such as bubonic plague, although nobody could ever find any evidence of this. So – even today, if nuns inexplicably appear before the outbreak of any major epidemic, or indeed any other disaster, the church still calls it "Loudun Syndrome".'

'But where did the nuns get this sickness from?' I asked him. 'I don't see the connection between this child being exorcized and the nuns getting infected.'

Father Zapata said, 'So far as the Vatican researchers have ever been able to find out; there is no written record of this. After the child was exorcized, however, it *is* on record that Jean-Joseph Surin's behavior returned almost to normal. He recovered his self-control and wrote many books and inspirational letters, although he never prayed again or went to Mass. His later writings are still revered today.'

'I still don't get it.'

Father Zapata said, 'Some members of the Congregation for the Doctrine of the Faith have suggested that the child was not a demon's child at all. Some have said that it could simply have been the illegitimate offspring of some local boy, which is not at all unlikely. If Sarin realized this – which he would have done – he could well have taken the opportunity to coax the demon Gressil out of himself and transfer him into the newborn baby. The demon would have been very tempted by such an innocent, spotless soul, after all. Gressil was the source of filth and disease, and in the first few months of the baby's life, the nuns took care of him – suckling him even, those who could – and *that* could have been how nearly all of them became infected.'

'That's all pretty circumstantial,' I told him. 'Like – there's no documentary proof of that, is there?' *But I've seen the nuns for myself,* I thought. *I've seen them turn into Matchitehew and Megedagik, too, and they warned me that a dreadful sickness is going to spread among us, just like it happened in the seventeenth century. Maybe the idea of a 'Loudun Syndrome' is not so far-fetched as it sounds.*

I was so close to telling Father Zapata about the nuns and the two sons of Misquamacus, but he was coughing and heaving for breath, and I didn't want to make him any worse than he already was. Not only that – I wasn't at all sure that I wanted to hear what his explanation might be.

Then he said something that convinced me that it really was time for me to go – to get the hell out of Florida, and as soon as American Airlines could take me.

'The young nun who gave birth . . . Sister Marysia, she swore on her deathbed to a Capuchin confessor, Father Tranquille, that she had never had sexual relations with anybody, neither human nor demon, neither asleep nor awake. Father Tranquille wrote this in his memoirs. He also wrote that the birth itself was highly unusual.'

I didn't say anything, but waited for Father Zapata to continue.

'The child was not carried in her womb, apparently, as any normal child might have been.'

Father Zapata's breathing became even more labored, and he was having difficulty in getting his words out. He tried to lift his head from the pillow, but then he had to let it drop down again. He beckoned me to come closer, so that I could hear what he wanted to tell me.

I leaned over the bed. His breath had that metallic smell of chicken when it has just started to turn bad.

'She *carried* her baby, according to Father Tranquille—'

He clutched my shirt collar with his bony hand, trying to pull me down even closer. As he did so, a runnel of blood slid out of the left-hand-corner of his mouth and on to the pillow.

213

'Father – you're bleeding! I need to call for the nurse.' I tried to lift up my head, but his grip on my shirt-collar was relentless. It was like being gripped by some huge rancid-smelling bird of prey.

'She *carried* it—'

He coughed again, and this time he sprayed out blood. I felt warm wet droplets spatter against my the side of my face, and Father Zapata had scarlet bubbles of blood clustered between his lips.

This time I managed to wrench myself away from him, ripping two buttons off my shirt. I picked up the emergency call button that was dangling beside his bed and pressed it. As soon as I had done that, I went to the door of his room, flung it open and shouted out, 'Nurse! I need a nurse here! Emergency! I need a nurse here *now*!'

I went back to Father Zapata's bedside. He was shaking now, and the front of his hospital gown was covered by a dark-red bib of blood.

He was staring at me, one hand still lifted, as if he was still desperate to finish telling me what he had started to say.

'*Harry.* . . .' he whispered.

He convulsed again and brought up even more blood. I could hear soft-soled nurses' sneakers pattering down the corridor, and a woman's voice calling out, 'Sister!'

I said, 'Just keep still, father,' but again he tried to lift his head off the pillow.

'Her back,' he whispered.

'What?'

'Her *back*, Harry. Not in her womb. She carried the baby on her *back*.'

Sixteen

I waited for another two-and-a-half hours at the hospital, standing outside the front doors with that black cat continually rubbing up against my legs and purring like a death-rattle. At a quarter after four I knew that I would have to go or I would miss my flight. I couldn't afford to forfeit the fare – or get arrested and charged with fraud, for that matter.

While I was waiting several clergy arrived in shiny black limos and taxis and went bustling into the building grim-faced, including the Reverend Deacon Jose Valdes from St Francis de Sales. None of them knew me so they didn't acknowledge me, and in any case I must have looked pretty dubious hanging around outside a hospital where a priest was suffering from demonic possession with a black cat smooching around my ankles. Just as well I wasn't wearing my black djellaba with the silver stars on it.

Eventually, I went inside to collect my suitcases from the receptionist. 'Could you call upstairs and ask how Father Zapata is doing?' I asked her. 'I'd like to stay longer, but I have a plane to catch.'

She picked up the phone and talked for a moment to one of the nurses on the third floor. Then she said, 'I'm so sorry, sir. Father Zapata passed about ten minutes ago.'

215

'Oh, shoot. That's terrible. Did they say how?'

'Are you a relative, sir? If you're not a relative, all I can tell you is that he passed.'

I didn't know what to say. I stood in the hospital's reception area with my suitcases, feeling almost as if I was personally responsible for Father Zapata's death. I shouldn't have asked him for help and advice about that nun. I should have relied on my own experience of supernatural appearances and quit the cottage then and there and not mentioned the nun to a soul. Supernatural appearances are nothing like the ghosts you read about in ghost stories. Even the scariest ghost stories don't come close. More often than not, they have some grisly and complicated agenda that is impossible for us to understand. They have no sympathy for us whatsoever, and they don't give a rat's ass how much they hurt us. Either they were once human, and now that they're dead, they're jealous of us because we're still alive, or else they were *never* human: they were demons, or spirits, or loogaroos, or manitous, and they have no feelings for us at all. Do you expect a shark to go into mourning if it bites you in half? Do you expect a rock to feel sorry if it topples down a cliff and crushes you? Do you think a lake is going to cry if you drown in it?

I hailed a taxi and asked the driver to take me to the airport.

He checked me suspiciously in the rear-view mirror as we drove east on SW 22nd Street.

'You know you got blood on you?' he asked me. 'I ain't makin' a mistake, am I? That *is* blood?'

216

'Yes, it is,' I said. I lifted my hands and turned them this way and that. I had blood on my hands, too, in every sense.

'Are you hurt? You want me to take you back to the hospital?'

'No, I'm fine. Honestly. This isn't my blood.'

The driver passed me a pack of wet-wipes. 'Here, one of these should clean it off.'

'Thanks,' I said, although I was thinking: *Nothing will ever clean away this stain, ever.* And as we turned northward toward the airport on SW 27th Avenue, I was thinking about the last words that Father Zapata had spoken to me: *She carried the baby on her back. Not in the womb, as any normal child might have been. On her back.*

What he had said had chilled me right down to the soles of my feet, because I had come across this before, more than once, and each time scores of people had been killed or injured so badly that they had never fully recovered.

Sometime in the seventeenth century, the Algonquin wonder-worker Misquamacus had committed suicide by drinking blazing oil. This was part of a magic ritual which he had carried out for the express purpose of being reborn hundreds of years later. He had believed that when he reappeared, he would be able to take his revenge on the colonists who had already slaughtered so many of his people and stolen so much of their land. I had confronted Misquamacus several times and managed to defeat him – but only by a combination of luck and modern technology. Mostly modern technology: in the

217

centuries that had rolled by while Misquamacus had been waiting to be reborn, science had developed to the point where we could pretty much hold our own against ancient Native American magic, as powerful as it was. I don't think I could ever have beaten him otherwise.

I'm still not sure why, but Misquamacus had chosen a young New York woman named Karen Tandy to act as the host for his reincarnation. He may have selected her at random, or maybe he consulted some kind of Algonquin star chart, or tapped some magic bones together, who could tell. As his fetus had grown larger, though, he had not only fed himself on her blood and her bones but also her spinal fluid, so that he could leech out her intellect as well as her physical strength. That was why he had implanted himself on the back of her neck, and not in her womb.

Now Father Zapata had told me that Sister Marysia from Loudun convent had also carried a fetus on her back. OK – it could be nothing more than some freaky coincidence. But it was a possibility that Karen and Sister Marysia had *both* been chosen as surrogate mothers by sorcerers trying to be reincarnated – one Algonquin and one European. Maybe the magic ritual is essentially the same, whichever part of the world you came from.

On the face of it, Karen and Sister Marysia seemed to have nothing in common. They came from totally different cultures and religions and totally different ethnic backgrounds. They had lived not just thousands of miles apart from each other, but *centuries* apart, too. Yet they had both carried parasitical babies on their backs, and they both shared one more thing. In different ways, no matter how distantly, they had both become connected to *me*.

The flight to Los Angeles was bumpy and uncomfortable. I was sitting next to a nervous woman who kept twisting her scarf around and around and saying, '*Oh! – oh my God! – ohhh!*' whenever the plane dipped or jolted, which was every two or three minutes.

Myself, I've never been frightened of flying, but it didn't help that when I went to the galley at the back of the plane to get myself another Jack Daniel's, I passed by a nun sitting in one of the aisle seats with a silky black veil draped over her head.

The sight of her seriously gave me what Louisiana people call 'the freesons'. Not only that, but as I passed her the plane suddenly dropped and I was flung sideways toward her so that I bumped against her shoulder. When I did that, however, she lifted up her veil to reveal a pink, plump face with bulging blue eyes and ginger freckles across her nose.

'Sorry,' I said. 'Turbulence.'

'Oh, don't you fret, boy,' she said, in a strong Irish accent, patting my arm. 'If the Good Lord had really wanted us to fly, he would have given us propellers.'

A second nun was sitting three rows behind her in a window seat, with her blind drawn tightly down and a veil covering her head, too. I just had to assume that she was normal under that shiny black silk and not another 'appearance'.

219

As I passed the end of the row in which she was sitting, I glanced sideways and noticed that her hand was lying on the armrest of her seat, and that she was wearing gray suede gloves. I didn't know if that signified anything. Maybe she suffered from poor circulation, that was all.

I saw this nun again while I was waiting for my suitcases at the baggage carousel. She was standing alone on the opposite side of the baggage hall, her head still covered. I couldn't work out if she was waiting for her luggage to appear; or if she was lost; or if she was specifically standing there to remind me that I was supposed to be warning my fellow Americans about the plague that was soon going to strike us all down, unless we upped sticks and all went back to Lithuania, or Nigeria, or wherever the hell we'd come from. Maybe she was here to do all three, or maybe none of the above.

My own suitcases appeared, and I was just heaving them off the carousel when I saw a gray-bearded man in a high-collared gray suit weave his way through the crowds in the baggage hall and walk directly up to the nun. I could see that he was saying something to her, and he raised his arm as if to guide her out of there, although he didn't actually touch her. She didn't move at first, didn't even nod her head as if she was talking to him. But she must have said something, because he turned around and looked in my direction – or what I thought was my direction.

I humped my two cases on to a baggage cart and made my way toward the exit, although I couldn't stop myself from looking back to see what the nun and the gray-bearded man were doing. She was probably a bona fide nun, and he was probably a priest who had come to collect her, and it was more than likely that they hadn't even noticed me. Most likely I was suffering from nun-o-phobia, whatever the technical name for that is.

As I pushed my way through the door, though, I saw them cross over to the information desk in the very far corner of the baggage hall. Already gathered around this desk were six or seven more nuns, also with their heads covered. As soon as they were joined by the gray-bearded man and the second nun that I had seen on the plane, they all hurried off together, as if somebody had clapped their hands to shoo away a flock of crows.

I stood by the curb for a while with the sun in my eyes, wondering if I ought to forget about LA and book a flight straight to New York. At least I knew more people there. Maybe I could persuade Amelia to put me up a few days, if her husband didn't object too vociferously. Amelia's husband didn't trust me with her, and frankly I don't blame him.

On the other hand, I was here now, and I was dog tired, and I wasn't sure that my credit card could stretch to it. I also reasoned that if nuns were appearing in Coral Gables and nuns were appearing in Los Angeles, then it was perfectly possible that nuns were appearing in Manhattan, too. Maybe there was no getting away from them.

Ambrose Avenue is three blocks north of Hollywood Boulevard, and Rick Beamer's single-story house was on the right-hand side of North Edgemont Street, where the avenue starts to twist its way uphill.

Chez Beamer was a shabby-looking building with loose shingles on the roof and a dilapidated porch. The faded gray paint on the clapboard was flaking, and the window frames were rotten. The front yard was overgrown and weedy, but the van that was parked on the sharply sloping driveway was immaculate, with shiny alloy wheels. It was a late-model Ford Transit painted metallic silver with pictures of hundreds of assorted bugs running up the sides – cockroaches and termites and wasps and fleas and bedbugs. In black lettering it announced 'Beamer's Bug & Termite Blitzers'. So it looked like the exterminator was at home.

As soon as I climbed the creaking front steps to the porch, two dogs started furiously barking somewhere inside. A few seconds later the screen door opened and Rick appeared, with a Labrador Retriever and a German Shepherd both straining at their leashes. Rick was skinny as ever, although he looked much older and more wizened than when I had last seen him. As always, he was dressed in a skinny-fitting black shirt and spindly black jeans, with lots of silver junk around his neck, on chains.

'Hey, Wizard, it's you, man!' he said, and then, to the dogs, *'On jest przyjacielem! Przestan' robic' ten głupi hałas!'*

The dogs immediately stopped yapping and sat down beside him, their tongues hanging out like red flannel facecloths.

I lugged my suitcases on to the porch.

'Great-looking dogs, Rick. What did you just say to them?'

'I told them to shut the fuck up. I bought them from this Polish guy. He trained them fantastic. They can sniff out anything. You could fart in a Tupperware box in Eureka and they'd smell it in San Diego. They cost me hardly nothing, but that was because he trained them in Polish, and I had to learn Polish dog commands. *Przestan' szczeka!* That means, "Stop barking!"'

'You haven't changed, have you?' I told him, patting the dogs on the top of their heads and tugging their ears. 'Always find the most incredible bargains, don't you, but there's always some ridiculous snag. Remember those sneakers?'

'Good to see you, too, Wizard, Don't remind me of that, if you don't mind. That was a freak of nature. Nobody could have foreseen that, not even you and your Tarot cards.' He pronounced 'Tarot' to rhyme with 'carrot'.

Rick had bought into a scam whereby several thousand right-footed sneakers were imported from the Far East into New York, while their left-footed counterparts were imported into New Orleans. Both shipments had remained unclaimed until US Customs sold them off at auction, and Rick had bought them dirt cheap and without paying import taxes because none of them ostensibly made up a pair. The idea was to match them together and sell them at their usual retail price. That was the idea, anyhow, except that Hurricane Katrina had hit New Orleans and the container with all the left-footed sneakers had been washed out to sea, never to be seen again.

'I got in touch with the Veteran's Hospital, to see if they needed right-footed sneakers for guys who had lost their left leg in Afghanistan. They took two.'

Rick helped me to carry my suitcases inside. The living room was small and cramped, with a sagging brown couch that looked like a half-starved donkey and five ill-assorted plastic chairs that had probably been expropriated from various diners and college classrooms. The olive-green carpet was threadbare although it was partially covered by a rumpled red Navajo rug. Two framed posters hung on the walls – one for the Grateful Dead and another for Ronald Reagan's 1984 election campaign.

What hit me most of all, though, was the pungent smell of skunk and the woman who was sitting with her bare feet up on the couch smoking a joint. She was bleached-blonde and pretty in a strangely dated, puffy-faced way, like a 1960s' movie starlet. Her enormous breasts were crowded into a tight red satin vest, and she was also wearing the shortest red-and-white striped shorts that I had ever seen.

As I followed Rick into the living room she gave me a smile and wiggled her fingers and said, '*Hi*! You must be the Wizard! Welcome to LA, Wizard! I'm Dazey!'

I went across to shake her hand, but she took hold of my sleeve and pulled me down toward her and gave me three lipsticky kisses, one on each cheek and then one on the mouth.

'Are you going to tell my fortune for me?' she asked, breathing marijuana breath right into my face. I could have gotten stoned just talking to her. 'Rick says you can read Tarot cards. That is *so* cool.'

'For sure, yes, I'll tell your fortune for you, Dazey. Just give me a little time to settle in.'

Rick showed me through to the room that I would be sharing with Dazey's sister, Mazey. There was barely enough room for the two single beds, closet and dressing table underneath the window. The dressing table was cluttered with nail polish and powder compacts and jars of foundation and half-squeezed tubes of depilatory cream. One of the beds was unmade, with its pillow punched in and its sheet twisted, while the other was heaped with skirts and jeans and T-shirts and black lacy underwear.

'Don't take any notice of the mess!' called Dazey. 'Mazey had to go out in a hurry this morning. I'll help her to tidy up when she gets back.'

'She doesn't mind me sharing with her?' I called back.

'So long as you don't snore!'

'No, I don't snore. Leastways, I don't think I do. Nobody has ever complained.'

Rick lifted his skinny tattooed wrist and checked his heavy stainless-steel watch. 'Listen, Wizard, you only just caught me. I have an appointment at eight. Why don't you stay here and make yourself at home, and we can catch up when I get back. I'm checking out the Elite Suites just off of Franklin. It's not too far away, so I won't be long.'

We went back into the living room, and the

225

two dogs immediately came up to him, their tails wagging, panting with anticipation.

'OK, Bobik – OK, Kleks! Let's go sniff out those nasty bugs, shall we?'

'I thought you had to talk to them in Polish,' I said.

'It works both ways. They've learned the word "bug".' Rick picked up a gray taffeta windbreaker from the back of one of the chairs. It had the silhouette of a giant cockroach on the back and the white letters 'BBTB'. On his way out of the front door, with the dogs almost tripping him up, he lifted a gray baseball cap off the peg and pulled it down over his wiry gray pompadour.

I looked around. Dazey was taking another deep drag on her joint, with her eyes half-closed.

'Hey, Rick, why don't I come with you?' I said. 'I'd like to see you in action.'

'Sure. I thought you'd be too tired, is all.'

He opened the back doors of his van so that Bobik and Kleks could jump inside, and then we climbed in, too.

'I was going to get a night porter's job at the Magnolia Hotel,' Rick told me as we backed down his driveway and turned down North Edgemont. 'I was early for the interview, so I went down the alley at the side for a smoke. These two exterminators had their van parked out back, and I got talking to them – me being in the bug business once upon a time. They said that the Magnolia had called them in because of bedbugs.'

'*Bedbugs*? I thought the Magnolia was pretty upscale.'

226

'It is. But bedbugs don't make no social distinctions. So long as they can find a nice cozy box mattress to make their home in, they don't care if it's in some doss-house for down-and-outs or the Hotel Bel-Air. There's no reverse snobbery in bedbug world.'

'I guess not. But you don't expect a hotel like the Magnolia to be riddled with bedbugs.'

'Hey – like I say, there's a *plague* of bedbugs sweeping across the country. They're getting in everywhere you can think of – hotels, bed-and-breakfasts, people's private homes. They don't get put off by class.'

'Jesus. So that's why you decided to go back into the extermination business?'

'Well, not really. It was the dogs, more than anything else. Those two guys at the Magnolia showed me their sniffer dogs and explained how brilliant they were at locating bedbug infestations. They said that they were making a *fortune* out of these dogs because they could sniff out any kind of bug you could think of, from roaches to termites to wood-boring beetles, and yet the only wages they ever needed were a pat on the snout and a daily can of Blue Buffalo.'

He paused for a moment, screwing his head around almost 180 degrees so that he could follow a girl in a tight pair of white jeans cycling out of Sun Cleaners.

Then he said, 'I didn't think nothing of it until about three weeks later when I was sitting in a bar on Sunset and this Polish guy comes in and asks the barkeep if he knows anybody who wants a couple of dogs. He has to go back to Poland

227

because his mom's sick or something, and he needs to find a home for them quick. We got talking, and it turns out his dogs were sniffer dogs – specifically trained to smell out unwelcome bugs. I said, "Bedbugs?" and he said, "Sure," so I gave him a hundred bucks for the two of them, then and there. And that's how I started BBTB.'

'I still can't believe you're using *dogs* to smell out bedbugs.'

'Come on, Wizard, they use dogs to check for drugs and explosives at airports, don't they? Sniffer dogs can follow somebody's trail for miles, just because they left a sock behind and the dogs can identify the scent. You can find bedbugs with high-speed gas chromatography, but the quickest and the cheapest and the most efficient way is still dogs. Dogs can smell a hundred thousand times better than we can, man. We only have about five million smell receptors, but dogs have anything up to two hundred fifty million. A dog can smell a human fingerprint that's a week old.'

'So, how's business?'

'Not too bad. Not terrific, not yet. But it's getting better all the time. My problem now is that I need to expand. Right now, I'm getting a whole lot of inquiries, but I have to turn them down. I need more staff, at least two more vehicles, and most of all I need some serious investment.'

'Don't look at me,' I told him. 'I could barely rake enough money together to get here.'

We turned off Franklin Avenue into North

228

Wilton Place, a quiet street of small hotels and private houses. When we reached the Elite Eco-Suites, Rick called the front desk on his cellphone and they opened up the automatic gate of the underground parking facility.

'That's the first lesson: be discreet,' said Rick as we drove down into the neon-lit gloom. 'The last thing any hotel wants is to have an exterminator's van standing outside.' He parked, and then he said, 'Why don't you come upstairs with me – see me and the dogs at work? Maybe I can rope you into help. You know, like instead of rent.'

'Did I ever charge *you* rent?' I retorted. 'Did I ever make you tell old ladies' fortunes to pay for all those pizzas and beer you went through?'

'Hey, Wizard, I'm only kidding. But come up, anyhow. What are you going to do – sit here playing Super Mario Brothers for the next half-hour?'

We went up to the reception area in the elevator, with the dogs' tails beating against our shins. We were greeted at the desk by a short tubby man with slicked-back black hair and a sweeping-brush moustache. He looked around furtively to make sure that there were no guests within sight, and then he beckoned us over to the elevator.

'One of our guests came down this morning and complained that he got bit all over,' he said. 'He went to the pharmacy for something to stop the itching, and when he came back he said that the pharmacist had told him he had bedbug bites.' As we reached the second floor, and the elevator doors opened, he threw up his hands and said,

'Bedbugs! Here! I can't believe it. We've never had bedbugs before. Roaches, sure. Everyone gets roaches. But bedbugs! We're going to be ruined if this gets out.'

He bustled along the corridor ahead of us and led us to a room at the back of the building. He unlocked the door and said, 'Here – help yourself. I can't go in there. Bedbugs! It makes me shudder just to think of them!'

Rick let the dogs off the leash and said, '*Hajda! Znalez´c´ kilka owadów dla taty!*'

The Labrador turned around and stared at him, as if it didn't understand what he meant.

'*Bugs*, you dumb dog!' he snapped. 'Go find daddy some bugs!'

Both dogs immediately trotted off in the direction of the bedroom.

Rick said, 'It's my crappy Polack accent. Maybe I should go to night school, but I don't think they run any courses in Polish Canine Conversation.'

While the dogs were sniffing around, I took a look at the apartment. It was a typical Hollywood self-catering suite, with a living room, a kitchen, a bedroom and a bathroom, and a balcony over-looking the lamplit back yard. It was designed to be eco-friendly, so it had bamboo towels and organic bath oils and a sound machine that made whale noises. It smelled of bamboo and incense, and to tell you the truth it may have been preten-tious, but it was very peaceful, very Zen. It would have been ideal for me, if I had been able to afford $165 a night, every night.

The dogs started barking in the bedroom, so

we followed them in there. They were snuffling around the end of the king-sized bed.

'Good boys,' said Rick. '*Dobrzy chłopcy!*'

I looked at the woven bamboo-green bedcover. 'I don't see anything.'

Rick lifted the bedcover and tugged out the sheet underneath it, exposing the cream-colored mattress. At one end, it was speckled with dozens of minuscule brown dots. 'There you are – bedbug shit. And if we dig a little further . . .'

He lifted the seam of the mattress with his thumb, and I saw that seven or eight tiny bedbugs were scurrying along it.

'It don't look like this particular infestation has been here too long,' Rick remarked. 'You can *smell* 'em, though, can't you, now that you're close? Bedbugs always smell like rotten raspberries, except when they've really taken a hold for a while, and then they smell like old men's piss.' He reached into the pocket of his jeans and took out a clasp knife. Sticking the point into the seam of the mattress, about halfway along, he made a deep cut all the way back to the corner. Bobik and Kleks grew even more excited, and Kleks began to jump up and down.

'They love their bugs, these two boys,' said Rick. 'They know that if they find bugs, they're going to get a dog choc.' He opened up the incision he had made in the mattress and held it apart as wide as he could. Inside, it was teeming with hundreds of bedbugs, maybe even thousands. They swarmed all over each other, trying desperately to escape from the light and to bury themselves in the depths of the fluffy kapok stuffing.

231

'Shee-it,' said Rick. 'This is a whole lot more than I thought we'd find. One heck of a whole lot more.'

'What now?' I asked him.

He let the mattress drop back down. 'Cypermethrin. It's a pretty standard neurotoxin, kills most bugs, and it'll kill off these little bastards. But we also need to fumigate the rest of this apartment, not just the bedroom. Whoever brought these in here, they could have dropped their eggs just about anyplace. Out of their clothes, out of their luggage. We'll have to check the other apartments, too, on either side.'

He went back out into the corridor. The manager was still standing there, looking anxious. 'Well?' he said. 'Do we have them, or don't we?'

'Oh, you got them, sir,' Rick told him. 'You got them in spades.'

'But I don't understand. Where did they come from? Our guests are always very clean, very respectable. We never allow no vagrants in here.'

'That makes no difference,' said Rick. 'Your common bedbug will hitch a ride on anyone and anything. I once found bedbugs in a Louis Vuitton keepall, which probably cost more than two-and-a-half thousand bucks. Tell me, sir – did you receive any complaints about this suite *before* this last guest?'

'No, never. None at all.'

'I guess you have a record, though, of everybody who stayed here? The point is, if we're aware that somebody is likely to be carrying bedbugs on their person, we have an obligation to notify the LA Department of Public Health.'

The manager looked uneasy. 'I don't see how it's possible.'

'I told you,' said Rick. 'Anybody can carry bedbugs on them, adult bedbugs or eggs. The President could be carrying bedbugs; he sleeps in enough different hotels. The pop star Miley Cyrus could be carrying bedbugs, although God knows where.'

'We never had Miley Cyrus stay here,' said the manager.

'I know you didn't. But who was the previous guest, before the guy who got bit?'

'Like I told you, it's not possible. You couldn't have gotten more respectable than these two. They were nuns.'

Seventeen

It was another hot, thunder-grumbly morning when Anna arrived with Jim Waso for David's funeral service. Toward the east, storm clouds were hanging over the city, thick and gray and ragged, but the Gateway Arch and the downtown skyscrapers were all picked out by a few stray rays of sunlight, like shining memorials.

Outside the Grandier Funeral Chapel, the parking lot was crowded. David's family had all arrived from Iowa, as well as his colleagues from St Louis Design Solutions and twenty or thirty college friends. As Anna walked toward the entrance, the hearse arrived outside, speckled with raindrops from the storm that hadn't reached here yet. She stood with Jim Waso by her side as the casket was rolled out and on to a gurney, and then lifted by the pall-bearers and carried inside. The casket was heaped with white lilies, and also carried a message that Anna had written. *Too Soon, My Darling.*

Inside the chapel's reception area, Brian Grandier was waiting to meet her, his hands clasped piously together. He was dressed in the same gray suit as before, although now he was wearing a black armband. 'A sad day, Professor Grey,' he told her. 'You have my deepest sympathies.'

Anna nodded, but said nothing. There was still something about him which made her feel irritated and unsettled. Maybe it was the way that the look in his eyes appeared to be so much at odds with the words that came out of his mouth. She had seen men look at her like that before: men who thought that they could have her, in spite of her standing in the medical profession. *So she's a professor? She's still a woman and I'm still a man and I could make her scream for more.*

Inside the chapel, David's casket had been placed on a catafalque, with a framed photograph of him standing beside it. The sound system was playing the soothing second movement from Beethoven's Emperor Concerto. Anna walked to the front of the chapel to take her seat. The piano music was punctuated by occasional sobs.

She was barely aware of the service passing, or the tributes that David's family and friends paid to him. She stood to sing the hymn, but the words in the order of service were too blurred for her to be able to read them. She couldn't keep her eyes off the casket, and she couldn't stop herself from thinking that David was inside it, her David. He was lying there so close to her, and yet he was dead.

At the end of the service, Brian Grandier had told her that the catafalque would slowly roll back, and that heavy blue velvet drapes would be drawn across, like the end of a theatrical performance. 'It represents the end of the drama that was somebody's life.' However, she had asked him to give her a few moments beside the casket before this happened, so that she could say a last goodbye.

Organ music played softly in the background as she stood up and walked across to the casket, her heels clicking on the chapel floor. David's face was smiling at her from the framed photograph that stood beside it. She could even remember the morning when that photograph was taken.

'I'm going to miss you so much,' she said, laying her hand on top of the casket, among the lilies. 'What am I going to do without you?' Her eyes filled up with tears, but she did nothing to stop them sliding down her cheeks. Her throat was clenched so tightly that she could barely speak. 'We were going to be married. We were going to have children. We were going to do so much together. All those days of dancing and laughing . . . they're gone now, all of them, but they never even arrived.' She closed her eyes. She couldn't think of anything more to say to him, except goodbye.

As she stood there, she heard a sharp rapping sound. Two knocks, then a single knock, then another three knocks. The last three sounded almost frantic.

She opened her eyes and looked around. There was nobody standing within twenty feet of her. But then she heard the rapping sound again – *knock, knock – knock – knock, knock, knock!*

Surely, she thought, *surely it can't be coming from the casket.*

She looked across at Brian Grandier. He was standing beside the lectern from which David's relatives had been reading from the Bible and paying their personal tributes. He had the same expression on his face. *You may think you know something, lady, but you know nothing at all.*

She opened and closed her mouth. She was about to call him over and ask him if he could hear the rapping sound, when there was another flurry of knocks.

Then, faintly but distinctly, she heard David's voice. It sent a cold crawling sensation all the way up her back.

'*Get it out of me! Please, I can't stand it! Get it out of me!*'

Anna turned back to Brian Grandier, aghast. 'He's alive!' she said.

'*Anna! Get it out of me! Please!*'

'He's alive!' screamed Anna. 'He's still alive!'

She swept her arm across the top of the casket so that all the lilies were scattered across the floor. She gripped the edge of the lid and tried to lift it up, but it was firmly screwed down.

'David! *David!*' she cried. 'It's all right, darling, I can hear you! I can hear you!' Then – to Brian Grandier, 'Open this casket! Get it open, quick! *He's still alive!*'

The chapel echoed with gasps and chairs shuffling and mourners saying, 'What? What's happening?' Brian Grandier came stalking across from the lectern, while David's father and mother left their seats and came up to the catafalque, too. David's mother Jean put her arm around Anna and said, 'You *heard* him? I can't believe it! You actually *heard* him?'

'He was *knocking*!' sobbed Anna. 'He was knocking! He knocked again and again, and then he called out to me! Quick! Open it up! Open it

237

up. He's still alive in there, and he could be suffocating!'

Brian Grandier said, 'My dear professor – please – I can assure you one hundred percent that he has passed! I oversaw the preparation for his cremation myself. There is absolutely no question that he can still be alive.'

'*I heard him!*' Anna screeched at him. 'I heard him! He's alive! Open this casket now!'

Brian Grandier turned to David's father. 'Sir – I appeal to you. This is most distressing, but your son is dead. Professor Grey saw him herself in the morgue at SLU, and she knows that there has been a full post-mortem. It is impossible that he is alive.'

'Oh, so I'm going mad, am I?' Anna demanded. 'I was hearing things, just now? I imagined I heard knocking inside of that casket, did I? I imagined I heard David calling out to me?'

Brian Grandier said nothing, but he shrugged as if to say, *Well – you said it.*

Anna's face was blotched with tears and mascara, and she was shaking. 'I insist you open the casket. Jean – will you support me on this? I swear to God I heard him, and if you send that casket to be cremated without checking to make sure that he is really dead then you will be guilty of murder.'

'Professor, a certificate of death has been issued, and anyhow it is illegal to open a casket once it has arrived at the crematorium.'

Anna, still shaking, took her cellphone out of her shiny black crocodile purse, which she had bought especially for David's funeral. She held it up in front of Brian Grandier and said, 'If you

238

don't open up this casket now I'm going to call the state police and have them force you to open it, and *that* won't do your business a whole lot of good, will it – if people believe that you sometimes cremate their relatives without making sure that they're deceased? Or don't you care about burning people alive?'

When she said that, Brian Grandier's face emptied of color. He opened and closed his mouth, and clenched his fists, and then he looked to the right, and then to the left. His chest rose and fell, as if he were finding it difficult to breathe. It was the kind of reaction that Anna would have expected if she had hit him very hard in the testicles.

'Open it,' he said, without looking at anybody in particular.

One of his assistants took a step forward – a big bald-headed young man in a funeral suit that was two sizes too tight for him. 'What did you say, sir?'

'I said, open it! Take the lid off! Show her!'

'But, Mr Grandier, sir, with all due respect—'

'Open it, Kellerman. Open it now.'

'Yes, sir.'

While his assistant went off to find a screwdriver, Brian Grandier walked back to the lectern and picked up the microphone.

'Ladies and gentlemen, that concludes this funeral service. There has been a slight technical problem, I regret to say, but we are dealing with it promptly. If you would be kind enough to leave the chapel now, it will enable us to do so in privacy. Thank you.'

The funeral guests began to file out. Above their heads, there was a rumble of thunder, and rain began to spatter against the chapel windows. Brian Grandier's assistant returned with a screwdriver, accompanied by two of the pall-bearers.

'Will you *hurry*?' said Anna. 'He won't be able to breathe in there!'

The bald-headed assistant looked across at Brian Grandier, as if he was questioning Anna's sanity, but all the same he started to unscrew the lid of David's casket. David's mother kept a tight grip on Anna's hand as he came to the last screw. Then he and the pall-bearers carefully took hold of the lid and lifted it off.

Anna took a step toward it, and then stopped. She could tell from the smell that David was really dead. His eyes were open, but the pupils were milky, and his face was still stretched into that last death-mask of absolute terror. His mother said, 'Oh . . . oh my God,' and promptly collapsed.

'Put it back on!' ordered David's father. 'Put it back on!'

Anna was already kneeling beside David's mother, holding her head, but now his father knelt down, too, and said, sharply, 'It's all right, Anna! I can take care of her. I think you've caused quite enough mischief for one day.'

'I heard him, Mr Russell,' Anna insisted. 'I distinctly heard him. Why would I make that up?'

'I have no idea!' said David's father. 'Maybe you just wanted to be the center of attention, even at our son's funeral. David always said that you were never happy unless all eyes were on you.'

'Mr Russell – I'm really, really sorry. I didn't want to distress you. I truly believed that I heard him knocking and calling out to me.'

'You're a psycho, lady, that's what you are. Now leave us alone, will you? You think David's mother is ever going to forget this, for the rest of her life? You think *I* will?'

Anna stood up and took a few steps back.

Brian Grandier said, 'I only did what you asked me to do, professor. I'm deeply sorry that it turned out like this.'

'Well, no, it wasn't your fault,' said Anna. 'Maybe I need to take some time off.'

Jim Waso came up to her and put his arm around her. 'Jesus,' he said. 'Are you OK?'

'I'm kind of shaken. Do you think you can take me home?'

'There's supposed to be a big get-together now, isn't there, at Bixby's?'

Anna shook her head. 'I don't think I'll be very welcome, for some reason.'

'OK then, I'll take you home. But I'll take you for a drink first. You look like you could use one.'

He ushered her outside. It was raining hard, but as they hurried across the parking lot to his car, several of David's friends and relatives stopped and turned to stare at her.

On their way back toward the city center, with the windshield wipers thwacking wildly from side to side, Anna said, 'I'm not going crazy, Jim. I know I'm not. I heard him.'

'Well, maybe people *do* speak to us after they're dead. You should find yourself a medium.'

'You're not laughing at me, are you?'

241

'You think I'm in the mood for laughing, after seeing your David like that? Holy Christ, Anna, what makes somebody die with a look like *that* on their face?'

Jim took her to the Morgan Street Brewery at Laclede's Landing, and they sat outside under umbrellas while the rain continued to hammer down all around them.

'So, how do you feel now?' Jim asked her. There was a strong smell of electricity in the air, and behind him Anna could see mist rising from the river. Now and then, lighting flickered in the distance, but the storm was gradually beginning to pass.

'I don't know,' said Anna. 'I think I'm losing my sanity. I keep hearing dead people talk. I keep seeing people who can't possibly be there.'

Jim reached across the table and held her wrist. 'Go on,' he said. 'Tell me about it. I promise I'm not going to laugh at you.'

She took two swallows of her vodka-tonic. Then, haltingly, she began to describe her experiences in the morgue, when she had heard John Patrick Bridges and David talking to her, and how she had seen their expressions change. She told him how she had gone to look at Mary Stephens, and how the nun had appeared, apparently from nowhere.

She was reluctant at first to tell him what the nun had said, or what she had made her do, but it was such a relief to talk to somebody who was prepared to listen to her with such sympathy that she told him everything.

When she had finished, he was silent for a while, looking down into his beer glass, but then he looked up at her and said, 'Did you call security?'

'Jim – they wouldn't have believed me. I don't even know if I believe it myself.'

'We can't really tell for sure. Not yet, anyhow. Henry Rutgers reported to me that all three victims exhibited signs of severe facial contortions after death. I saw your David today for myself. All I can say is that he looked scared out of his wits. I think if I had realized how severe those contortions were, I would have ordered him to carry out some further tests.'

'Facial expressions, Jim, that's one thing – that could have been nothing more than extreme rigor mortis. I heard them *speak*.'

'OK . . . maybe this particular strain of virus has the effect of shutting down brain functions one after the other, so that patients can still speak and change their facial expressions, even when they're way beyond any hope of resuscitation.'

'So what about the nun?'

Jim sat back in his chair. The rain had eased off now, and the sun was shining so brightly on the wet paving-stones behind him that Anna could barely see him. It was like talking to an angel, rather than a real person.

'I don't know, Anna, to be truthful. You were educated at the Ursuline Academy, weren't you? I mean, you haven't had any bad experiences with nuns in the past?'

'No, Jim. The worst they ever did was make me write out lines for wearing my skirts too short.'

243

'The nun . . . I don't know what to say. I can only think that you must be badly stressed out, which is not surprising after all the pressure you've been under in the lab and the way that David died so suddenly. Under normal circumstances, I'd tell you to take some time off. In fact, I'd insist on it. Right at this moment, though, with the Meramac School virus to cope with . . . and *this* virus, too, whatever it is . . . what I'm asking you is, do you think you can manage to keep it together? We need you right now, more than ever.'

'I could *taste* her, Jim. I could actually taste her.'

Jim said, 'I'm always here for you, Anna. You know that.' He didn't have to add that they could have been lovers, if life had turned out differently.

'Thanks, Jim. And thanks for taking care of me today. I'll be back in the lab tomorrow, I promise you.'

The sun suddenly faded, and it began to rain again.

Jim told her that she was welcome to stay at his apartment that night, no strings attached, if she wanted to. She was tempted, but she knew that she needed to return to her loft and face up to her demons, or her nuns, or whatever was triggering off all of these delusions.

She was convinced that she had heard David knocking and calling out to her in his casket, but at the same time she knew that it was impossible. She remembered her alcoholic cousin Vincent.

244

When he came off the drink he had hallucinated that firefighters were playing cards in his bedroom at night and loudly discussing how they were going to burn down his house.

Jim walked her to the door of her loft. 'Just call me if you need anything,' he told her. 'Call me if you *don't* need anything, except somebody to talk to.'

He kissed her, and for a moment they held each other tightly, although they both knew that they had to let go.

Once she was inside she switched on most of the table lamps in the living room and went into the kitchen to pour out a glass of cold sparkling mineral water. Three vodka-tonics had made her feel dehydrated.

She was still standing in the middle of the kitchen when she heard a sharp decisive click, and all of the lights in the living room went out. *Dammit,* she thought, *that's all I need.* She and David had lived there for over three years, and she still didn't know for certain where the circuit-breakers were.

She put down her tumbler and went out into the living area. There was softly suffused street light shining through the blinds, and the brighter light from the kitchen behind her, so it wasn't pitch black, but it was still crowded with shadows of all different shapes and sizes. She had a feeling that the circuit-breakers might be located in the small closet just beside the front door, so she edged her way diagonally across the room, making sure that she didn't bark her shins on the coffee table.

Oh Jesus, David, she thought. *If you only knew how much I wish you were here.*

She was halfway across the room when she realized that the shadows behind the couch were much darker than all the rest – and that there was no reason why there should be shadows there at all. She stopped and frowned into the gloom, and it was then that she realized they weren't shadows at all. They were three motionless figures, draped in black. They looked like nuns.

Oh please, God, no. Not nuns. Don't tell me I'm hallucinating again. Please.

She took two or three more steps forward, keeping her eyes fixed on the three dark figures. Maybe they really *were* shadows, and if she changed position, they would mutate into different harmless shapes or even disappear. But when she reached the end of the couch, she could see that they were real. At least, her mind was convinced that they were real, even if they were nothing more than images created by post-traumatic stress.

'I want you to disappear,' she said, as loudly as she could.

'*You . . . you are the one who must leave,*' whispered a voice. It sounded like the same coarse whisper that she had heard from the nun in the morgue. '*Time for you to go, Anna, before you and all of your kind come to serious grief.*'

'Who *are* you?' Anna demanded. She was so frightened that the word '*are*' screeched like a glass-cutter.

'*Time for you to leave, you whore,*' whispered the nun. '*You don't know what you're meddling with.*'

246

Anna's heart was drumming so hard against her ribcage that it hurt, and she felt as if the floor was tilting under her feet. She gripped the slippery back of the leather couch to steady herself and took two deep breaths. 'If you're real,' she said, 'tell me who you are and why you're here, and how you got in here, too!'

'*You want to know who we are?*' said the nun. '*We will show you who we are.*'

Anna looked around the living area, frantic. David had always said they ought to have a gun in the house, but she had always resisted the idea. She wished she had one now, though. She had never felt so defenseless in her life. What terrified her most of all was the possibility that these nuns existed only in her own mind, and that she was mentally cracking up. There was only one way in which a gun could protect her from psychosis, and that was to shoot herself in the head.

'I need you to go,' she said. 'I don't care who you are. I'm going to close my eyes and count to three, and when I open my eyes again I want you to be gone.'

'*You should know who we are,*' the nun whispered. '*If you know who we are, then you can spread the word that we have come back to take our revenge on you. You can also tell your friends that there is nothing they can do to cure the sickness that we are spreading amongst you. Nobody can cure it. You will die in your hundreds, to begin with, and then you will die in your thousands, and then you will die in your millions. The lands that you took from us will become your*

247

cemetery, and we will hunt on them again. We will hunt over your graves.'

Anna kept her eyes closed, even as the whispering continued. *Go*, she said silently, inside her head. *Go, whether you're real or not. Get out of my mind – get out of my loft – get out of my life*.

She heard a rustling, and then a creaking, and then a light, spasmodic pattering sound, like sunflower seeds being scattered on the floor. When she took another deep breath, she smelled the acrid tang of cedarwood smoke.

She opened her eyes. With a jolt of shock that made her gasp out loud, she saw that two of the nuns had grown so tall and so bulky that they almost seemed to reach the ceiling, and they no longer looked like nuns. Each of them had two curved horns on top of their heads, and they both appeared to be swathed in blankets, although their shoulders were bare. Over their shoulders, thousands of shiny beetles were swarming, and it was these beetles falling on to the polished oak floor that were making the pattering sound, not sunflower seeds.

'Oh God,' said Anna. All the strength drained out of her, and she sank to her knees. 'Oh God, tell me I'm having a nightmare.'

Eighteen

'*We know who you are and what you do,*' whispered the nun. '*This time, we will make sure that there is nothing you can do to thwart us.*'

Then – in a voice that was louder, and much more rasping – the figure on her left said, '*Your people came to believe that your medicine was greater than ours, and for many years we believed it, too, and we lost our courage and our hope of getting our revenge. But now we have discovered how we can do to you what you did to us, and this time your medicine cannot save you.*'

'Who are you?' said Anna. 'I don't understand what you're saying. What did we ever do to you? Who's "*us*"?'

'*We are the people who own this land. It was given to us, at the very beginning of time, by the Great Spirit himself.*'

'The Great Spirit? Are you telling me that you're Native Americans?'

'*You murdered us, in countless numbers. Many of us died from your infections before you even knew who we were. You murdered us, and then you stole our hunting grounds from us, and our forests, and our mountains, and our rivers. This was not only a crime but a blasphemy.*'

'But who are you?' Anna insisted. She was shivering with fear, but her mind was still working like a medical professional. To defend yourself

249

against any pathogen, first of all you have to understand how it attacks you, and how it replicates itself and mutates. Know your enemy, and above all, discover what it is that your enemy really wants from you.

'*My name is Matchitehew,*' said the huge horned figure. '*This is my brother Megedagik. We are the sons of Misquamacus – the greatest wonder-worker who ever walked on this earth. We are returned to avenge our father, and to finish what he failed to finish – to take back every last blade of grass that your people stole from us.*'

I *am* going mad, Anna thought. I can't believe I'm hearing this.

Matchitehew said, '*You, Anna – you know much about diseases. You will tell your fellow doctors that there is nothing they can do to save your people from this infection. It is a sickness bred from the Great Old Ones, from the time beyond time. There is no cure for it, not for you, just like the sickness that you brought to us.*'

Anna looked up at the two towering figures with their horns and their blankets and their shoulders shimmering with insects. She could just about see their eyes glittering, but it was impossible for her to make out the expressions on their faces, or even what their faces actually looked like.

She was just about to answer when her cellphone warbled. She reached into her pocket and took it out, almost dropping it. She could see that Jim was calling her.

'Jim,' she said.

Even as she did so, the three figures in front of her began to shudder. It was almost as if they were formed of nothing but clouds of black smoke and somebody had opened a door, so that a draft was blowing across the living area and dispersing them. They twisted and disassembled, and soon they were nothing but a few dark spirals, and then they were gone.

'Anna? You sound terrible. What's wrong?'

Anna reached out for the back of the couch again, so that she could pull herself back up on to her feet. She looked around, but there was no doubt about it. The three figures had completely vanished. In spite of that, she couldn't stop herself from shaking.

'I was hallucinating, Jim, that's all. I must have been. I thought I saw—' She paused, and then she said, 'They're gone now. It must be stress, Jim, that's all. They couldn't have been real.'

'They? Who were *they*?'

'It's nothing, Jim, really. I need some rest, that's all. I've been overdoing it in the past few weeks, and what with David going so suddenly, I think it's all been too much.'

'Listen, Anna, why don't I come around and pick you up? You can spend the night at my place, and then you'll be *sure* that you're not seeing any spooks. Not unless you count me and my cats.'

'Honestly, Jim, I'm fine. I'll have to find a way to get my head round this, that's all. I thought I saw some people, but obviously I couldn't have done because there was no way they could have gotten in, and when I challenged them they simply disappeared. They're gone now. There's no sign of them.'

'What kind of people?'

'Three nuns, to start with.'

'For Christ's sake, Anna! What's this nun thing?'

'I have no idea. Maybe you're right and something *did* happen to me at convent school, but I've suppressed it. Anyhow, two of the nuns grew bigger and bigger and ended up about seven feet tall with horns on their heads.'

'Seven feet tall? With *horns* on their heads?' Jim paused for a moment, and then he said, 'You're serious, aren't you?'

'Yes, Jim, I'm serious, whether you believe me or not. I saw them and they spoke to me. They said they were the sons of some great Native American wonder-worker, and that *they* were wonder-workers, too. They even told me their names. They said they were going to spread some disease that we wouldn't be able to cure, and that it was going to kill millions of us.'

'Anna, please. Let me come back around and collect you.'

'Jim, I'll get over it. I'll take an Ativan and have myself a good night's sleep.'

'Anna – you're seeing nuns and Native American medicine men. It would be funny if it wasn't so darned scary. What did they say their names were?'

'I can't remember. One of them was called Matchy-something. The other one was Something-lick.'

'Listen, Anna. I'm putting my shoes back on.

252

I'm driving back over there right now. Don't argue with me.'

'No, Jim. I don't think I'm in any kind of danger. It's all inside of my head.'

'Exactly. That's what I'm worried about.'

'Jim – no. I insist. You can drive around here, but you won't persuade me to come home with you. I have to deal with this on my own.'

There was a long pause. Jim knew Anna well enough to realize that she meant what she said and that nothing would induce her to change her mind.

'OK,' he said, at last. 'But you know that I'll always be here for you, no matter what you decide to do.'

'Yes, Jim, and I really appreciate it. Thank you.'

She hung up, and she was just about to resume her search for the circuit-breaker box when all of the living area lights clicked back on again, by themselves. *Now that* is *freaky*, she thought, even though she was deeply relieved. She walked into the bedroom, switched on the lights and went on through to the bathroom. She put in the plug and turned on both the hot and cold faucets. Tonight she felt like a long, warm, jasmine-scented bath. With any luck, a bath would soak away all of her stress. Maybe it would also soak away the lingering smell of charred cedarwood, which was the only evidence that those three 'nuns' had actually materialized. Even that had probably wafted in from somebody's wood-burning stove in a neighboring loft.

She undressed and switched on her sound system to play Dvorak's *Romance for Piano and*

Violin. She looked at herself in the full-length tilted mirror in the corner of the room, beside her closet. This mirror had always made her look thinner than she really was, but this evening she thought she looked almost skeletal, with her ribcage showing and her hip-bones casting triangular shadows. She hadn't eaten anything since David had died except for two slices of toast and a cereal bar.

She spent over twenty minutes in the bath, and the monotonous dripping of the faucet almost sent her to sleep. After she had toweled herself dry, she tugged on her white sleeveless nightgown and sat in front of her dressing table to brush her hair. Every now and then she stopped, with the brush held up in mid-air, because she thought she heard a noise in the living area, or in the kitchen.

But: *There's nobody there*, she told herself. *It's only the water-heater starting up, because I just ran a bath, or the air-con, or the creaking sound that all old buildings make in the evening as the temperature cools.*

She switched on the bedroom TV, but there was nothing on that she wanted to watch and so she switched it back off. She felt exhausted, both body and mind, as if she had been running a twenty-six-mile marathon, or fighting somebody for her life. She threw back the covers and climbed into bed, reaching across to her nightstand to switch off her bedside lamp.

Please, no nightmares about nuns clustering like bats on the ceiling, or sliding out from under the bed. Just let me get some deep, refreshing sleep.

Anna turned over on to her side and punched her pillow into shape. *You have nothing to be scared of,* she told herself. *It's only your imagination working overtime, trying to find some reason why David had died so suddenly.*

She was prepared to concede that Jim was right, and that the nun-figures were nothing more than a long-suppressed memory from her schooldays . . . but she couldn't think where she might have read about Native American wonder-workers. Maybe they had been mentioned in one of the textbooks she'd studied when she was cramming for her doctorate. She recalled the story of smallpox being spread amongst the Mandans and the Ankara Indians in 1837. They'd been infected by some of the European passengers on board a fur-trading steamboat called the *St Peter's* as it made its annual trip up the Missouri. Both native communities had been decimated by the disease, and it had probably spread even further, to remoter tribes who were never reached by colonists before the smallpox wiped them out, and whose existence remained unrecorded, as if their language and their way of life had never been.

Anna had also read a sensational account of how the US Army had deliberately spread disease amongst the Indians by giving them smallpox-infected blankets from the military hospital in St Louis. Several historians had said that this accusation was unproven, but it had persisted all the same. Whether it was true or not, thousands of tribespeople had died from smallpox and other European viruses, against which they had no natural resistance.

Maybe her imagination had invented two vengeful Indian wonder-workers who wanted to punish the colonists for what they had done, whether it was deliberate or accidental.

She was almost asleep when she felt a tickling sensation across her shoulder. She flicked at it, thinking that it must be a stray hair. But the tickling persisted, and she began to feel it crawling down her arm. She slapped at it, but that didn't stop it, so she slapped at it again.

The tickling continued, and then she felt more tickling around her knees, and around her thighs. She sat up in bed, switched on her bedside lamp and threw back the bedcover. To her horror, the bed was swarming with a mass of tiny brown bedbugs, thousands of them, and they were scurrying all over her legs and up inside her nightgown.

As soon as she switched on the light, they retreated into the crevices and folds of her bed, but there were still scores of them running up and down her nightgown and over her arms, and the sheets were already freckled with bedbug excrement, so that it looked as if somebody had sprinkled paprika all over them.

She jumped out of bed so fast that she caught her thigh against the corner of the nightstand and the bedside lamp toppled on to the floor, plunging the bedroom into darkness. She hopped and hobbled her way to the bathroom, lifting up her arms to wrench off her nightgown, and then brushing and smacking at her naked body to dislodge or flatten the bedbugs that she could still feel running all over her.

She switched on the bathroom light. A few bedbugs were still running up her thighs, and she flicked these off with her facecloth, which was still wet from her bath. She looked at herself in the mirror and shook her head violently to make sure that there were none in her hair. She always waxed, so they had no body hair to hide in. She felt a tickle between her shoulder-blades, and she twisted quickly around, clawing at her back, but if a bedbug had been there it must have dropped off.

Next, before she did anything else, she carefully studied her arms and her legs and her body to make sure that she hadn't been bitten. If these bedbugs were carrying the same kind of virus that had affected David and John Patrick Bridges and Mary Stephens, then she could be in serious trouble.

She switched on the main bedroom light and stood in front of the full-length mirror, but there were no red lesions on her anywhere, and she couldn't feel any itching.

She walked back over to the bed. Almost all of the bedbugs had hidden themselves now, under the cover or under the pillows or somewhere in the seams of the mattress. They had left plenty of rusty-colored specks, though, to show that they were still there, even if they were hiding, and Anna could *smell* them, too. She knew that some people likened the smell to rotten fruit, but to her it was more herby, like cilantro.

She went to her closet and took out clean underwear, as well as a silky yellow boat-sweater and jeans. She dressed very carefully, shaking her sweater and her jeans before she put them on to make sure that there were no bedbugs hiding in them. Once she was dressed she went through to the living area and picked up the phone. 'Jim? It's Anna. I'm sorry – did I wake you?'

'No, no. I was watching *The Late Show*. Well, I was watching it with my eyes closed, but I wasn't exactly asleep.'

'Do you mind if I take you up on your offer of a place to stay for the night after all? Something's happened. You need to come take a look for yourself.'

'Anna, are you OK? Anna?'

But Anna couldn't answer him. She could only stand in the middle of the room with the phone held to her ear and her hand pressed over her mouth, with tears sliding down her cheeks.

Nineteen

By the time we arrived back at Rick's place, Dazey's sister Mazey was home, and the two of them were sitting on the couch in front of the TV sharing a pepperoni pizza from an open box. Mazey was picking out the slices very carefully because she had just polished her fingernails gold, and they were still drying. In between bites she was starting to polish her toenails.

'Hi, honey,' said Dazey, without taking her eyes off Arsenio, who was interviewing some new boy band. 'How'd it go?'

'Buggy,' said Rick. 'Very, very buggy.'

Kleks the sniffer dog made a beeline for the pizza, and Mazey lifted the box up high so that it was out of his reach. 'Hey, *shoo*, Kleks! This is *our* supper!'

Mazey looked very much like her sister – pretty, but a little puffy-faced – although she was probably about five or six years younger. Her ash-blonde hair was braided into an elaborate coronet, which looked like it must have taken hours, and her eyes were shadowed with crimson. If Rick hadn't told me that she was a beautician, I would have guessed it anyhow. She was wearing a sparkly gold button-up vest that only just managed to hold her breasts in and a very short white sparkly skirt.

'Mazey, this is the Wizard, aka Harry the

259

Incredible Erskine,' said Rick, tossing his car keys on to the table. 'Wizard, this is Mazey. You guys going to be OK sharing a bedroom for a night or three?'

''S'okay with me, RB,' said Mazey, in a fluting, babyish voice. She was concentrating on painting her left big toenail, and she didn't raise her eyes even for a second to see what I looked like. ''Ceptin' if he snores.'

'I have it on good authority that I'm totally silent at night,' I told her.

She wiggled her toe, admiring her handiwork, and then she looked up at me at last and gave me a glossy red smile. 'Hey . . . not *bad*! You know who you remind me of?'

'I don't have a clue. Who do I remind you of?'

'That actor. What's his name? You know the one.'

'I'm sorry. I have no idea. Tell me one movie he was in.'

'No, he wasn't in a movie. He was in *Mad Men*. I think it was *Mad Men*. Anyhow, he's very good-looking.'

'Well, thanks.'

'He wasn't as old as you, but you sure look a whole lot like him.'

I didn't know whether to take that as a compliment or not, but Rick changed the subject by saying, 'Harry tells fortunes. He's a professional what-do-you-call-it. Voyeur.'

'Clairvoyant,' I corrected him.

'That's right. Clairvoyant. If you ask him nicely, maybe he'll get out the Tarot cards for you.'

'Oh, yes, *please*!' said Mazey, with her voice

rising to a squeak. 'I love all that fortune-telling stuff!'

Jesus, I thought, this is going to be like sharing a bedroom with Betty Boop. 'Well, OK, maybe tomorrow,' I told her. 'I'm kind of jet-lagged this evening, and I need to be fresh to hear what the cards have to say to me.' In other words: I'm too tired to make up any bullshit about who your next boyfriend's going to be, or whether you're going to get promoted at work to eyebrow-plucker-in-chief.

Rick went through to the kitchen to open a couple of cans of dog food for Bobik and Kleks. Meanwhile, I sat down next to Mazey to watch TV.

'You want a slice?' she asked me, offering me the pizza box.

'No, thanks. Seeing all of those bedbugs has kind of killed my appetite.'

'Oh, they're *gross*!' put in Dazey. 'I went out on a job with Rick just one time and one time only, and let me tell you I almost barfed. I don't know how he does it. And what's worse than bedbugs is roaches. *Urgh*! And maggots! All white and blind and wriggly!'

Mazey had just picked up a slice of pizza. She peered at it closely, and then put it back in the box.

The girls went to bed first, while Rick and I stayed up and drank a few beers and talked about the days and nights we had spent in New York.

'All seems like a long time ago now, Wizard,' said Rick.

261

'It was only five years.'

'Still seems like another lifetime. You remember those Japanese twins?'

'How could I ever forget?'

'That was the day I started to feel that age was creeping up on me. They both wanted to spend the night with *you*.'

'Believe me, Rick. Nothing happened. I was too drunk to climb the stairs to my apartment, let alone do anything when I got there.'

Kleks came into the living room and went up to Rick and started whining in the back of his throat.

'What's the matter, Kleks? *Co jest nie tak*?'

Kleks nudged Rick's knee with his nose, and then took two or three steps toward the kitchen.

'What is it? You want some more food? You've eaten a whole can each. You're not getting any more until the morning.'

Kleks came back and nudged him again.

'What?' said Rick. He was growing irritated now. 'I swear to God, Wizard, don't ever have a dog. They're like children who never grow up. I look at dogs, and I say to myself, that proves that Charles Darwin was wrong. There's no such thing as evolution. If there was any such thing as evolution, dogs would be able to speak by now, and drive automobiles, and flip burgers at McDonald's, even if they couldn't understand string theory. Mind you, I don't understand string theory myself.'

Kleks went back toward the kitchen door, but when he saw that Rick was still making no move to follow him, he barked.

'Shut up, Kleks! *Zamknij sie↓!* You'll wake up the girls!'

'Looks like he wants you to follow him,' I suggested.

Rick put down his can of beer and wearily stood up. 'You're right, of course. He needs me to let him out for a leak. I won't be a minute.'

He followed Kleks out of the room. A short time later he came back in again.

'That was quick,' I told him.

'He didn't need to go. I don't know what he wanted. He kept snuffling around Bobik, but Bobik seems to be OK. He's fast asleep in his basket, which is where Kleks should be.'

I shrugged and looked at my watch. 'That's where I should be, too, asleep in my basket. Thanks for everything, Rick – putting me up like this. Give me a couple of days to find someplace to stay and I'll be out of your hair.'

'Hey . . . don't sweat it, man. What are friends for?'

I finished my beer, and then went into the bathroom to give myself a quick lukewarm shower and wash my teeth. When I came out, Kleks was still circling around the living room whining. Rick had already disappeared for the night and closed his bedroom door.

'What's eating you, boy?' I asked Kleks. He whined again and led me into the kitchen, his claws scratching on the vinyl-tiled floor. Bobik was lying on a plaid blanket in his basket, and he appeared to be deeply asleep. Kleks sniffed at him and prodded him with his nose, but he didn't stir.

263

I knelt down and leaned over Bobik's basket. My veterinary expertise was someplace south of noplace at all, but Bobik was still breathing, and it sounded to me like his respiration was pretty regular. He hadn't emptied his bladder or his bowels, and as far as I could tell he didn't smell funny.

'Kleks, dude, I can't work out what's eating you. I'm sorry. Bobik seems fine to me. Why don't you get yourself some sleep, because that's what I'm going to do.'

Kleks stood quite still, looking up at me. I think he must have understood the gist of what I had said to him, because he didn't whine again. Instead, he appeared to be resigned, as if he had done his best to communicate something important to me, but knew that he had failed to do so and that it was probably beyond him. That in itself was very unusual. Normally, if a dog is trying to attract your attention, he will go on whining or barking ceaselessly until he does, even if he doesn't stop all night and all of the following day.

I left the kitchen and switched off the light. Kleks continued to stand beside Bobik's basket, not moving. He didn't even look around as I crossed the living room to Mazey's bedroom and very quietly opened the door. I thought: *well, he's Rick's dog, if Rick isn't worried about him, why should I be? Maybe he's just an insomniac.*

Do dogs suffer from insomnia? I asked myself. *Do dogs have nightmares?*

* * *

The red numerals on the digital clock shed just enough light for me to grope my way to my bed. Mazey had taken off all the clothes that had been heaped on it, straightened the comforter and plumped up the pillows. She was asleep now, whistling through one nostril as she breathed. So much for her asking *me* if I snored.

I took off the towel that I had wrapped around my middle and hung it over the back of the chair. Then I climbed into bed and lay there, staring up into the darkness, thinking of everything that had brought me here – of Mrs Ratzenberger's bracelet and Father Zapata's self-mutilation and the nuns who had appeared in my bedroom, but most of all of Matchitehew and Megedagik.

The night was very quiet. All I could hear were cicadas and the muffled sound of traffic and Mazey's repetitive whistling. It was hard for me to believe that the past two or three days had actually happened. In fact, I was trying to convince myself that my encounter with the nuns and Misquamacus' two sons had all been the result of my overactive imagination and too much Jameson's whiskey.

I knew, though, that it had all been real. I had seen Native American magic at work more than once before, and it was earth-shattering. You have to remember that every tree and every rock and every river from one side of the country to the other harbors a Native American manitou. This is still their land, spiritually, even if we took it away from them. It's like a haunted house. You may own the deeds, but the house itself still belongs to the ghosts.

What frightened me most of all was that Matchitehew and Megedagik wanted *me*, out of all the millions of people in the USA, to warn the whole country of what they intended to do. I couldn't – like, how could I? – but what would they do to me if I didn't? If they had found me once in Coral Gables, then there was every likelihood that they could find me again, here in Hollywood.

I was beginning to think that nuns and wonderworkers and blood-vomiting priests were going to keep on whirling around in my mind all night like some hideous fairground carousel and keep me awake until morning. After less than ten minutes, though, my exhaustion caught up with me and I fell asleep, and very deeply, too, as if I had fallen down a well.

I don't know if I dreamed or not. I don't remember any dreams. But I was suddenly aware that I could feel breathing against the right side of my face. Soft, quick breathing, like an animal panting.

Jesus! I thought. *One of the dogs has climbed into bed with me!*

I sat bolt upright and flapped my arms around and shouted out, 'Scram!' mainly because I had no idea what the Polish was for 'get the hell out of my bed, you mutt'.

Immediately, though, I felt an arm around my waist and a fluting little voice said, 'Shh! It's only me. Don't wake everybody up!'

I twisted around. It was Mazey. She was lying right next to me, and as far as I could tell in the darkness, she was completely naked. 'Mazey!' I hissed at her. 'What are you doing?'

266

'I'm giving you a cuddle, baby, that's all!'

'You're *what*? We hardly know each other!'

'That doesn't matter. You're a friend of Rick's, aren't you, and you smell nice.'

OK, I admit that I did smell nice. I had sprayed myself with Ralph Lauren Polo after my shower. But I didn't really see how being a friend of Rick's could possibly make me sexually attractive to any woman – especially a big-breasted blonde beautician who was probably fifteen years younger than me. Rick was the most unreliable scuzzball I had ever known, apart from my father, but that's another story. 'You'd best go back to your own bed,' I told her. 'I don't want to cause any ructions on my first night here. I mean, what will your sister say?'

'She won't mind. In any case, it's none of her business, and we don't have to tell her. What happens in the spare bedroom stays in the spare bedroom.'

'So far, Mazey, nothing has happened in the spare bedroom except that you have unexpectedly gotten into bed with me.'

'That's a good *start*, though, isn't it?' she said, in that squeaky little voice. She took hold of my penis, which was already half-erect, and she massaged it firmly and slowly up and down.

'Mazey—' I started to say, but I didn't try to pry off her fingers or push her away. Temptation is temptation, after all, and there's only a certain amount of temptation that any man can be expected to resist, especially with those big soft breasts squashed against me.

I lay back flat on the bed, and she continued

267

to massage me. I have to admit she really had a gift for it. Maybe it was her experience as a beautician, but whatever it was, I had never felt as hard as that in my life.

She dipped her head down and licked me, just one lick, but it was then that I started to get panicky. Irrational, I know, but I couldn't help a picture of Father Zapata flashing into my mind's eye, doubled over on my bed with his penis in his mouth – and then that crunch as he bit into it. I flinched and pressed my hand flat against Mazey's braided hair.

Mazey raised her head. 'What's wrong?' she asked me. 'I didn't hurt you, did I?'

'No, no – it's just that—' I didn't know how to explain it to her.

'Hey, you're not *shy*, are you?' she teased me.

'Shy? Me? No, of course not!'

She propped herself up on one elbow, so that her breasts tumbled to one side. 'You're not *gay*, are you? I mean, if you're gay, God, I'm so sorry!'

'Mazey—' I began, but I was interrupted by a howl from right outside the bedroom door – a hollow, agonized, self-pitying howl. It sounded exactly like one of those movies when a man turns into a werewolf. Immediately after the howl had died away, there was a heavy thump against the door panel, and then another thump and a scrabbling, scratching sound.

'Oh my God!' said Mazey, rolling off the side of the bed. 'What the hell is that?'

I bounced off the bed too, pulled open the closet and tried to find my chinos. The wire coat-hangers jangled, and some of them dropped on to the floor. '*Light*, Mazey! Turn on the goddamned light!'

She clicked on the dim little fluorescent wall-lamp over her bed. At the same time there was another howl, even longer-lasting and more agonized than the first, and more feverish scratching at the door. Then Kleks started barking, and this time he didn't stop. I heard Rick's bedroom door open and Rick say, 'What the *fuck*? Jesus!' Then he called, 'Dazey! Get your ass out of bed and get out here!' Then he knocked furiously at our bedroom door and shouted, 'Wizard! Mazey! Are you guys awake?'

Mazey had pulled on a tight white T-shirt with shocking-pink lettering on it, while I had just about managed to fasten the belt of my pants. I opened the bedroom door, and there was blood everywhere, as if it had been thrown around out of a bucket. It was splattered all the way up the walls and all the way across the floor in a twisting trail that led from the kitchen.

Lying on his side in the middle of all of this glistening red action painting, his hair soaked, his eyes glassy, one lip raised up in a snarl, was Bobik, the Labrador Retriever. Kleks was standing close to him, barking with all the monotony of a blacksmith's hammer.

'Oh my God, what's happened to Bobik?' said Dazey as she appeared in her bedroom doorway. 'Kleks hasn't gone for him, has he?'

I bent over Bobik and peered at him closely. I didn't want to kneel down because there was so much blood on the floor. I waved my hand in front of his eyes, but Bobik didn't blink, and I

269

couldn't hear him breathing, although it was hard to tell with Kleks barking so loudly. His chest didn't seem to be rising and falling, and although his tongue was hanging out he wasn't panting. I guessed those were pretty clear indications that life was extinct.

'Is he dead?' asked Rick.

I nodded. 'I think so. I don't know how many liters of blood dogs have in their circulatory system, but it looks to me like Bobik's lost most of them.'

Rick was wearing nothing but some baggy old black sweatpants and a sleeveless A-vest. He hunkered down next to Bobik and placed his hand flat against his flank. 'I think you're right, man. I can't feel him breathing.' He ran his hands all along Bobik's bloody body, and then turned him over. 'He don't seem to have no injuries noplace. No bite-marks or nothing. I just don't get it. Where'd all this blood come from?'

He stood up, shaking his head. Kleks was still barking, so he turned around and shouted, 'Shut the fuck up, Kleks, will you? *Zamknij sie!*'

Kleks kept on, so Rick took him by the collar and dragged him through to the kitchen. 'My God,' I heard him say. 'There's blood all over. It looks like a fucking massacre.'

I went into the kitchen too, to take a look. Rick had opened the door to the back yard and pushed Kleks outside. When he closed the door again, Kleks stopped barking, surprisingly, although he continued to scratch at the door and whine to be let back in.

From the state of the floor right beside Bobik's

270

basket, I could see that he had projectile-vomited blood all the way across to the base of the sink units. A haphazard pattern of paw prints suggested that he had then staggered out of his basket and made his way out of the kitchen door, vomiting blood three or four times on the way. More paw prints circled around the main trail of blood, which must have been made by Kleks as he followed his dying companion across the living room. It looked as if Bobik had been trying to find a human to help him, but by the time he reached our bedroom door he would have been beyond saving – and anyhow, what could we have done? I knew from experience that emergency veterinary clinics have blood banks for dogs and cats, because I once had a tortoiseshell cat that was partially flattened by a Humvee on 13th Street. But even if we could have found a vet at that time of night, it would have been too late for Bobik.

Dazey retreated into the bathroom, and we could hear the sound of her pepperoni pizza coming back up. Mazey clearly had a stronger stomach because she went into the kitchen and came back a minute or two later with a yellow plastic bucket filled with hot soapy water and a squeegee mop.

'Thanks, Maze, you're amazing,' said Rick. 'Wizard – I'll go find an old blanket or something. Maybe you can help me carry Bobik out to the yard.'

'What are you going to do with him, Rick? Don't you think you need to take him to a vet and find out what he died of? Supposing Kleks comes down with it? Supposing humans can catch it? I saw a priest in Coral Gables dying of a hemorrhage, and believe me it wasn't pleasant.'

'Kleks looks OK. If he was going to catch it he would have been showing some signs of it by now, wouldn't he?'

'How should I know? I mean, maybe it's *not* infectious. Maybe Bobik had an aneurysm or something like that, but I'm no expert.'

Rick looked blank.

'A weakness in one of his arteries,' I added. 'My uncle had one in his brain. Killed him in mid-sentence.'

Rick looked down at Bobik's bloodied body, and then at his own bloodied hands. 'The thing of it is, Wizard, I don't have the necessary license to operate this business. If I take Bobik to a veterinary clinic they're going to want to know what he's been exposed to. Maybe it was the cypermethrin that made him sick. Maybe he got bitten by the bedbugs and they gave him something. If it was anything related to him being a sniffer dog, then they're going to report me to the DPR and that's me finished. You know how much that goddamned van cost me, and getting it all customized like that?'

'Oh,' I said. 'So what do you intend to do?'

'What else can I do? I'm going to bury him.'

I looked down at Bobik's body, and then I looked across at Mazey, who was mopping the living-room floor now, squeezing pink water into her bucket. Mazey shrugged. If Rick had to close down his exterminating business, who was going to pay the rent and put pepperoni pizzas on the table? The lettering on the front of her T-shirt said 'This T-Shirt Was Tested On Animals But It Didn't Fit Them', but right then I wasn't in the mood for jokes.

'OK,' I said. 'I never went to a dog's funeral before, but I guess there's always a first time.'

Twenty

We carried Bobik's body out into the back yard, and Rick switched on the floodlight so that we could see to dig him a grave. Kleks stopped whining as soon as we came out of the back door, but when we laid the bloodied blanket on the patio he sat close beside it and kept his eyes on us, as if he wanted to make sure that we treated his dead companion with respect.

There was a narrow flower-bed on the right-hand side of the yard, which contained nothing much but weeds and cigarette ends. Rick found a shovel in the small storage bunker at the side of the house and started to dig. He hadn't watered the yard since he and Dazey had moved in, and the ground was cracked and dry, like broken terracotta pots. He cursed with every chunk of soil that he managed to pry up.

'Christ Almighty, Wizard! How about you taking a turn, in lieu of rent?'

'Your dog, man. Besides, my cards said I had to beware of strenuous physical exertion.'

'Oh, yeah? You watch out for Mazey, in that case.'

In spite of that, I helped him to dig, and after about an hour we had a reasonable grave about two feet deep. Between us, we lifted up Bobik's body in his makeshift shroud and lowered him in. Kleks came and stood next to us, and although

I don't believe that dogs have emotions, not the same as humans do, I swear he looked grief-stricken. His ears were flat and his tail was down, and when he looked up at me his eyes were glistening as if he was trying not to cry.

'Well,' said Rick, 'if there's a doggy heaven, let's hope that's where you are, Bobik. *Przynien' patyk.*'

'What does that mean?' I asked him.

'"Go fetch a stick." I don't know any prayers in Polish.'

He picked up the shovel and covered Bobik's body with soil, patting it down flat. Kleks looked a little bewildered by this, but he followed us obediently back into the kitchen, where Mazey had just finished mopping up the last of the blood. Kleks climbed into his basket and curled himself up.

Rick switched off the outside floodlight and said, 'I'd better make sure that Dazey's OK. Mazey, thanks for cleaning up. You're an angel. If I hadn't of met your sister before you—'

Mazey gave him the finger and said, 'Don't even think about it, Ricardo.'

We went back to our bedroom, although Mazey returned to her own bed. She didn't take off her T-shirt, and she didn't try to continue where she had left off. I was too exhausted to be disappointed. I almost felt as if I had been digging my own grave instead of Bobik's.

'What do you think was wrong with him?' Mazey asked me, in the darkness.

'I have no idea. I'm just hoping that it's not infectious. Or contagious. Or whatever.'

275

'Yeah,' said Mazey. Then, after a while, 'I think we're going to be friends, you and me.'

'Is that all?'

'You don't really want more than that, do you? You've still got somebody else on your mind.'

'How come women can always see through me? Sometimes I feel like I'm transparent.'

'You're tired, Harry. You need to get some sleep.'

'I just can't help thinking about that priest who died, back in Coral Gables. He was bringing up blood, just like Bobik.'

'Oh, come on. One was a priest, and one was a dog. And they're so far apart. I mean, like, geographically.'

It occurred to me that I had never before been lying in bed after burying a dog and heard a young big-breasted beautician use the word 'geographically'.

'Yes, you're right,' I said. 'And I do need some sleep. So, goodnight.'

I turned over and tried to empty my mind. The trouble was, my mind wouldn't stop making connections. I kept seeing those nuns standing in my bedroom and the nun who had been sitting on the plane. I kept hearing Matchitehew's rasping voice, saying, *'Your spirits know your ways. They know your magic. They know what diseases can make you sick.'*

Early next morning my shoulders had seized up from that all that grave-digging, and both Rick and Dazey looked frowzy and unfocused, with puffy bags under their eyes and their hair sticking up, as

276

if they hadn't slept at all. We sat in the kitchen looking like three worn-out zombies, although the irrepressible Mazey did her best to bring us all back to life by whipping up omelets for us and perking coffee and singing 'Mexican Wine'.

I sat on one of the kitchen bar-stools, watching her beating eggs in a bowl with her breasts bouncing underneath her T-shirt, and I thought that she was a girl with real character. I would have bet that most of the guys she went out with never appreciated how strong and funny she was, and how perceptive. I guess a lot of men would have felt angry and frustrated with her, but I really liked the way that she had teased me, but then realized that was not the way for either of us to go.

'Hey, Wizard, I have a job at eleven thirty in Van Nuys,' said Rick, with a shred of omelet dangling from his unshaven chin. 'How about it, man? You want to come along? I'd appreciate the help.'

'Urrghh . . . OK. But this afternoon I must start looking for someplace to live. And I have to start advertising for clients, too. I need to find myself some rich old widows, and quick.'

'. . . *and the sun still shines in the summertime,*' sang Mazey, her voice so high that I thought my glass of orange juice was going to shatter. '*I'll be yours if you'll be mine . . .*'

Kleks looked up from his basket. Rick forked up the last of his omelet, pushed aside his empty plate and then went across to give Kleks a toweling on the head. 'How are you doing, boy? You OK? It don't look like *you're* going to get

277

sick, thank the Lord. You want to come hunting for some bugs? That's it! Let's go get them *pluskwy*, boy!'

Rick went to smarten himself up while I helped Mazey to clear up the dishes.

'Why are you so tense?' she said. 'You're really worried about something, aren't you?'

I smiled at her and shook my head. 'You're doing that perceptive thing on me again, aren't you? I'm supposed to be the one who can read people's minds.'

'Oh, I'm no mind-reader,' she said. 'But I've known enough men to know when something's eating them, and I don't mean me.'

'Well, yes,' I admitted. 'I am kind of edgy.'

'You want to tell me why? Is it that priest thing you were talking about last night?'

'Partly. But I don't really understand *what* it is, not yet, and if the angels are looking after me I'll never have to. Let's put it this way: a few weird things happened to me in the not-too-distant past, and I'm worried there might be an action replay.'

'Weird things like what?'

I dropped the last of the knives and forks into the dishwasher, and then I looked up at Mazey and said, 'Do you believe that people can come alive again, once they're dead?'

'No, of course I don't.'

'Well, neither did I. But they do.'

Mazey looked at me sharply, as if she were making sure that I wasn't making fun of her. 'You're kidding me. Dead people come alive again? And that's what's bugging you?'

278

I nodded.

Mazey came up to me and put her arms around my waist. 'You remember what I said about us being friends? I meant it, Harry. You can rely on me, I promise. So if weird things *do* start happening, you can tell me about it. I promise I'll believe you, even if nobody else does.'

'I don't think you quite get it,' I said. 'If the same kind of weird things start happening that happened before, you won't need me to tell you about it. You'll know. You think nine/eleven was a disaster? Well, it was. But imagine a thousand nine/elevens. Imagine ten thousand nine/elevens.'

'Harry, you're scaring me.'

'I think you have good reason to feel scared. I know I am.'

'I'm not scared of all of these nine/elevens, Harry. I'm frightened for you.'

'You're frightened for me? Why?'

'I really, really like you, Harry. You know that. But I think you're losing it. In fact, I think you're nuts.'

'It's bedbugs again,' said Rick, holding up his Android tablet with his right hand while he was steering with his left.

'Looks like the bedbugs are taking over,' I told him. 'Watch out for that bus.'

The Royaltie Inn was located about three blocks east of the San Diego Freeway at the intersection of Sepulveda Boulevard and Valerio Street. It looked as if it had been designed to resemble a half-timbered Tudor mansion from merrie old England, but by an architect who had never

279

actually seen a half-timbered Tudor mansion and had only had one described to him over the phone.

Rick parked around the corner to save the owners any embarrassment. We walked into the oak-paneled reception area with Kleks following behind us. There was a fake suit of armor standing in one corner and two crossed broadswords on the wall behind the desk.

A thin woman in a pale-green suit came out of a side door. She looked nervy and underfed, as if she never had the time to sit down to a meal and when she *did* she didn't have the appetite to eat anything. Her bleached-blonde hair was stuck up with hairspray, like a yellow chrysanthemum that was starting to shed its petals.

'Rick Beamer,' said Rick, handing her his business card. 'We've come about the you-know-whats.'

'Oh, yes, oh,' she said, wringing her hands together so that her charm bracelet jingled on her skinny wrist. 'You'd better follow me.'

She led us along a paneled corridor to a suite at the back of the hotel. The bedroom was paneled too, with a Tudor-style four-poster bed, a huge tapestry couch and two huge armchairs. Diamond-leaded windows looked out over a sunlit balcony and the bright-blue hotel swimming-pool. On the wall hung portraits of Henry VIII and a plain-looking woman that must have been one of his wives before she and her head went different ways. I could smell floor polish and potpourri, but something else, too – that distinctive rasp-berry smell of bedbugs.

'My housekeeper came to me yesterday after-noon,' said the skinny woman. 'This suite hasn't

280

been occupied for the past three days, but it was booked for tonight and Saturday, and so she wanted to make sure that everything was in order. She lifted the bedcover, and – well, you can see for yourselves.'

Kleks was making that keening noise in the back of his throat, and his tail was thrashing from side to side. If Rick hadn't had his leash wrapped around his fist, he probably would have leaped on to the bed and torn the sheets to shreds.

Rick gave me a nod, and I gingerly lifted the heavy brocade bedcover. The blankets and the pillows underneath it were swarming with bedbugs, and the sheets were dotted all over with thousands of tiny brown droppings. It was like Bedbug City at rush hour.

'My housekeeper had one of the girls vacuum-clean it,' the skinny woman told us. 'I thought that would have gotten rid of them, but no. It was only three or four hours and they were back again – even more than before. I was frightened to take the mattress and the bedding out of here in case they dropped along the corridor while we were carrying them out and spread to the other suites.'

'OK,' said Rick. 'First of all we'll fumigate this room for you, and while that's taking effect we'll check out the rest of the hotel, top to bottom. If there's any more bedbugs anywhere at all, Kleks will sniff them out, won't you, boy?'

Kleks made that creaking noise in the back of his throat and thrashed his tail even harder.

'Ever had an infestation here before?' asked Rick.

'No, never. Well, not that I know of. I only took over this place three months ago. My house-keeper would know, although she didn't mention it.'

'Is she here now?'

The skinny woman shook her head. 'She didn't show up for work today. I don't know why because she hasn't called in. I tried phoning her, but I got no answer.'

'Who was the last person to occupy this room?' I put in.

'The very last people in the world who would have been carrying bedbugs, I would have thought. They were nuns.'

'*Nuns*? Where did they come from, do you know?'

'I have no idea. A man brought them in and left them here, and the next morning he came back and settled their check. I never spoke to them, and in any case their faces were covered, so you couldn't even see what they looked like.'

'Aren't you supposed to check your guests' identity?'

'They were *nuns*.'

'The man who brought them in – what did he look like?'

'Perfectly normal. Gray hair, gray suit, really quite smart.'

'Did he have a beard?'

'Yes, he did, now you mention it.'

Rick said, 'What are you getting at, man? You think he might have been carrying in bedbugs in his *beard*?'

I ignored him. 'Can you tell me the man's

name?' I asked the skinny woman. 'And any contact details, if you have them.'

'I'm sorry, I can't do that. I'm sure you understand that we have to keep guest information confidential.'

'Can you at least tell us where your housekeeper lives?'

'What? Why do you want to know that?'

'I think she may be very sick, that's why. I think these bedbugs may be carrying some kind of disease and she's caught it. You need to stay out of this room, and don't let any of your staff in here, either.'

Rick said, 'Aren't you kind of jumping to conclusions here, man? As far as we know, the lady's just pulling a sneaky Ferris Bueller.'

'If I'm wrong, Rick, I'll be the first to admit it. But why don't you start fumigating this room, while I go around and check if she's OK?'

The skinny woman looked more bewildered than alarmed, but she said, 'All right. Come with me and I'll find her address for you.'

We went back to Rick's van so that Rick could take out his bottles of Vikane bug fumigant, Nylofume bags and the door seals that would prevent the gas from escaping out of the bedroom. Then he handed me the keys and Kleks' leash and told me that if I damaged his van or lost his sniffer dog that he wouldn't complain. He would just kill me without saying a word.

The housekeeper's name was Maria Escamilla, and she lived not too far away from the Royaltie Inn in a short dead-end street called Enadia Way. I took a couple of wrong turns, and it didn't help

283

my concentration to have Kleks panting dog saliva against the back of my neck, but I found it eventually.

I climbed out of the van, and the street was hot and quiet. Maria Escamilla's house was a small single-story property painted lemon yellow, with a dusty green Equinox parked in the driveway. As I mounted the steps to the porch, I noticed that the flowery living-room drapes were closed. If Maria Escamilla was at home, it looked like she was still asleep, or maybe she had a migraine and wanted to keep out the sunlight. I pressed the doorbell and heard it chime inside the house.

No answer. I pressed it again and waited. Kleks was sitting in the driving seat of the van staring at me with his tongue hanging out. I gave him a wave, and he barked. I was almost growing to like that dog.

I tried the bell a third time and gave a sharp postman's knock, but another minute went by without an answer, and if Maria Escamilla had heard me, she obviously wasn't going to come to the door. I thought about giving up and driving back to the Royaltie, but those tightly drawn living-room drapes worried me – that, and the fact that a vehicle was still parked in the driveway.

I looked up and down the street. There was nobody in sight apart from a small boy circling around and around on a tricycle, so I stepped down from the porch and made my way around the side of the house. A narrow concrete path led to the back yard, which was mostly paved over with brick. It was crowded with purple flowering shrubs in barrels, six white plastic garden chairs and a clothes dryer with three blue Royaltie Inn aprons hanging from it, as well as a cream linen dress and two very large white brassieres.

Three concrete steps led up to the kitchen door. The door itself was half-open, so Maria Escamilla must still be at home. I went up to the door, knocked on the window and called out, 'Maria Escamilla! Maria Escamilla! Anyone at home?'

I pushed the door open a little further, and now I could hear a TV. It must have been tuned to a comedy show, because every now and then I could hear a muffled burst of laughter.

'Maria Escamilla! Are you at home? I've come from the Royaltie Inn, just to check that you're OK!'

It was then that I heard another sound, apart from the laughter. A persistent *zizz-zizz-zizz* noise, as if one of the neighbors was trimming a hedge. I opened the door as far as it would go, so that I could see through the kitchen into the corridor that led to the front door. The air was filled with a blizzard of blowflies. They were swarming in and out of the living room and crawling up the walls and clinging to the light-fitting so that it was glittering black.

I stood at that open kitchen door, and I didn't know what I should do next. I could guess what I would find if I went inside and took a look into the living room, and you can't even begin to imagine how much I didn't want to. But I knew that I had to. I had been visited by the nuns and the sons of Misquamacus and told to warn the people of America that they were going to get sick, but of course I hadn't even attempted to,

285

and now they *were* getting sick. I felt guilty and helpless, both at the same time. How can you convince people that the end of the world is coming, even when you're sure that it really, really might be?

I hesitated a few moments longer, but then I thought: *just do it.* I stepped into the kitchen and crossed over to the door that led to the corridor. As I reached it there was another burst of studio laughter from the television, but the buzzing of the blowflies was so loud that I could barely hear anything else. I had to bat them away with my hands as I approached the living room, but they kept flying into my face and into my hair and crawling down the back of my neck.

Because the drapes were drawn, the inside of the living room was gloomy and airless, and it was filled with a rotten, sweet smell that made my stomach contract. My mouth was flooded with warm orange juice and half-digested omelet.

For at least ten seconds I stood in the doorway, swallowing and swallowing and trying my best not to bring up my breakfast. On the other side of the living room a repeat of *Two And A Half Men* was flickering on the television, and I made myself stare at Charlie Sheen until my stomach had stopped heaving. Several blowflies flew right into my eyes, and two or three of them tried to land on my lips, so that I had to spit them away.

Brushing even more of them off my shirt and my pants, I finally summoned up the nerve to look around the door and see what had attracted so many of them.

Lying on the couch under the window was the

286

figure of a woman, who appeared to be made entirely of shiny green and blue blowflies. They were crawling all over her in an endless rippling motion, so that she appeared to be stirring like a dreamer in some hellish kind of sleep from which she could never wake up. At the same time, her facial expressions appeared to be constantly changing as the blowflies clustered around her eyes and her mouth. I could almost have believed as I first looked around the door that she was smiling at me, as if to say, look, death and putrescence aren't nearly so bad as I thought they were going to be . . . in fact, I'm enjoying it. But then she looked as if she was frowning and growing angry at being dead.

I went up to the couch and stood over her. I didn't have much doubt that she was Maria Escamilla, the housekeeper, but I picked up a dog-eared copy of *Fama* magazine from the coffee table, folded it up, and used it to flap away the blowflies that masked her face. A small cloud of them irritably rose into the air, and sure enough, I was looking at a plump, fortyish Hispanic woman with heavy curved eyebrows. She seemed to be looking back at me, although her open eyes were filled with scores of blowfly eggs, like grains of rice, and her lips were speckled, too.

I stopped swishing the *Fama* magazine from side to side and stepped back. As soon as I did so the blowflies immediately came back and covered her face. My stomach tightened up again, and I turned to leave the living room, but when I did I saw a leg protruding from the space between the couch and the wall under the window. A child's leg, with a small blue sneaker on its foot.

I leaned sideways so that I could see into the narrow gap behind the couch. A small boy was lying there – at least, I assumed he was a boy because his sneaker was blue. It was impossible to tell for sure because he, too, was thickly blanketed in blowflies. It looked as if Maria Escamilla had brought some of the bedbugs home with her, or maybe the sickness that they had given her was infectious.

I left the living room and went outside. Kleks was waiting for me in the driver's seat, and he barked impatiently when I reappeared around the side of the house. I had the feeling that if I had left the keys in the ignition, he would have driven off without me.

I took out my cell and punched out 911.

'Nine-one-one. What is your emergency?' the operator asked me.

If only I could have told her. *The spirits of two Native American wonder-workers are spreading a disease that could wipe out thousands, maybe even millions.* Instead, I said, 'I've found some dead people. A woman and a child. Fifteen-fifty-five Enadia Way.'

'Are you sure they're dead?'

'Oh, yes. They're dead all right.' I looked at Kleks, and he looked at me. 'Where's this going to end, Kleks?' I asked him, but he didn't answer. Didn't even whine. Then I remembered that Kleks didn't speak English.

288

Twenty-One

Anna was annoyed because Jim had allowed her to sleep until well past nine in the morning.

'I told you wanted to make an early start,' she told him as he poured her coffee in the kitchen. 'Before I do anything else, I have to arrange for an exterminator to get rid of those disgusting bedbugs.'

Jim had just taken a shower and was wearing a silky black Japanese-style bathrobe with a red dragon emblazoned on the back. 'You had a hell of a day yesterday, Anna, and your night was even worse. A couple of hours isn't going to make any difference.'

'Jim, those creatures are not just revolting. If they're carrying the same kind of pathogen that infected David, they could be highly dangerous, too.'

'Sure. I know. I'll call Sandra, my PA. She can fix it for you. We had roaches in the hospital kitchens last summer, and she found some really good pest control company.'

'Thanks,' said Anna. 'But it's not only that. I urgently need to get back into the lab. We're right on the brink of finding out why the Meramac School virus behaves the way it does, and it's critical that we isolate this bedbug virus before it starts spreading any further.'

She paused while she poured cream into her

coffee and stirred it, and then she said, 'I know you think that I've been letting my imagination run away with me, but I still think that this bedbug virus is more than just a couple of random outbreaks.'

Jim sat down next to her. 'Anna, what did I say to you yesterday? I'm not going to insist that you take any time out. I need your expertise, and I need it badly. But I don't want to see you cracking up. Nuns, Indian medicine men. I mean, you're getting very close to the edge here, sweetheart.'

'Maybe I am. But maybe it's not stress at all. Maybe it's my intuition, trying to show me something that my rational self might have been blind to.'

Jim shrugged. 'OK . . . You could be right. When I first started here in St Louis I diagnosed a patient as having multiple sclerosis. I was convinced it was MS. But the same night I had a nightmare that I was crossing a desert with this guy and we were dying of thirst.'

'Really? So what did *that* tell you?'

'Well – I'd been to a wedding-party that evening, and I could have been dehydrated from too much alcohol. But the dream made me double-check his results again the next morning. I found that he didn't have MS at all but Sjögren's syndrome, which of course gives you a really dry mouth and throat. So – yes. Maybe there are times when your subconscious knows better than you do.'

Anna sipped more of her coffee, and then she said, 'Listen – I'd better take a shower and get dressed.'

'OK,' said Jim. 'I'll give Sandra a call while you're doing that. But you're absolutely sure you don't need to give yourself a break?'

She leaned across and gave him a kiss on the cheek. In another life, she thought, if things had worked out differently, she and Jim could have been lovers, or even married. But she was living this life, and they weren't, and they probably never would be.

As Anna came out of the shower she heard the phone ring. Jim answered it, and he was still talking when she came out of her bedroom, combing back her wet hair.

'Well, OK, I'll tell her,' he was saying. 'Sure. Absolutely. I'll call you right back.'

He hung up. When he turned around to face her, his expression was so serious that she thought he must be putting it on.

'Was that your PA?' she asked. 'Has she found those exterminators for me?'

'No . . . that was Doctor Mulvaney at the Center for Disease Control. I've talked to Sandra already; she's getting in touch with those exterminators for you.'

'You mean *Ray* Mulvaney – the *director*? What did he want?'

'It's the bedbug virus, or something very much like it. He says that the CDC have been receiving notifications of similar outbreaks all across the country – including *our* report, of course, from Henry Rutgers. In almost every case the victims have been bitten by bedbugs. Unofficially, the CDC are already calling it BV-1, just to give it a name.'

'There, what did I tell you? Maybe my hallucinations weren't so bizarre after all.'

'By far the highest number of outbreaks has been in Los Angeles,' said Jim. 'Sometime yesterday afternoon people started to show up at hospitals suffering from convulsions and hemorrhage – only six or seven to begin with, but by midnight last night they had eighty or ninety, and ever since then they've been bringing them in so fast that the emergency rooms are having trouble keeping up.

'They've also had sporadic outbreaks in Chicago and Indianapolis and Kansas City, but nothing like so serious as LA. The trouble is, the media have gotten wind of it already, and it's headline news. Doctor Mulvaney's worried that it's going to start a mass panic and make things even worse.'

'So where do I come into it?'

'He's putting together a team of specialists to isolate it and come up with an antivirus before BV-1 gets beyond our control. He wants you to join them as soon as you can.'

'*Me*?'

'Come on, Anna, you're one of the leading epidemiologists in the country. You cracked that Scalping Disease almost single-handed, didn't you? Of course he wants you.'

'What about the Meramac School virus?'

'Peter and Rafik and Epiphany can follow up your work on that.'

'I'd like to take Epiphany with me, if I could. I'm going to need an assistant, and she knows exactly how I work.'

'That's OK by me. Peter and Rafik can keep

in touch with you by Skype. So what shall I tell Ray Mulvaney? That you're going to LA?'

Anna thought for a moment, and then she nodded. 'Yes. I'll go. I think it will do me some good – help me to get my mind straight. Maybe I'll stop seeing nuns and medicine men.'

While Anna finished drying her hair, Jim called Ray Mulvaney at the CDC and told him that she would be flying out later that day. At the same time he switched on the TV in the kitchen and tuned in to NBC News, and when he had finished talking on the phone he turned up the sound.

From Los Angeles, news reporter Kim Baldonado was standing outside St Vincent Medical Center, with crowds of people behind her and at least five ambulances with flashing lights. 'It's only a quarter of seven,' she said, 'and already this morning the emergency room here at St Vincent's has taken in fifty-seven patients, all of whom have been vomiting blood and suffering from uncontrollable convulsions. Every other emergency room in Los Angeles County is being overwhelmed by people with the same horrifying symptoms. So far none of the hospitals has been able to provide us with any information as to the cause of this epidemic, although the county health department have issued a statement saying that there have already been fatalities, possibly as many as a hundred.

'Unconfirmed comments from nursing staff suggest that this could be a viral infection, such as bird flu or swine flu. So far, though, the exact nature of the virus remains a mystery. Whatever it is, and whatever its origin, it is obviously highly dangerous and highly infectious. A spokesperson for the Center of Disease Control has recommended that you stay in your home for the time being unless it is absolutely necessary.'

Anna came in, all ready to go. 'I heard that,' she said. 'There was no mention of bedbugs, though, was there? So it looks like they've managed to keep *that* under wraps – for now, anyhow. But it sounds like the sooner I get out there, the better.'

Jim tore a sheet out of his notepad and handed her the address of the Department of Public Health laboratory in Downey, about twenty miles south of downtown Los Angeles, where the BV-1 team was hurriedly being assembled. 'Listen,' he said, 'be careful. I don't want you catching this thing, too.'

'Don't worry,' she told him. 'There hasn't been a single virus that's outwitted me yet.'

She went home mid afternoon to meet the exterminators from A-Z Pest Control, and to pack herself a suitcase. She would have to give the exterminators her keys so that they could fumigate her loft in her absence. She wouldn't have time herself to wrap up all of the food in her fridge and her freezer in polythene bags, as well as any jar or bottle that had already been opened, and to go around the loft opening every closet and every drawer, so that the gas would disperse once fumigation was over.

Two men in bright-red overalls were already waiting for her when she arrived – one thin and round-shouldered with a mournful moustache,

294

the other short and swarthy with a belly that made his overalls gape.

'You know something,' said the short and swarthy one as Anna led them through to her bedroom, 'I can never for the life of me think why God created bedbugs.'

'Nor termites,' added his companion sadly. 'Nor yellow-jackets neither.'

Anna pointed to the bed and said, 'There were hundreds of them. And I mean *hundreds*. By now there are probably three times as many.'

'OK, ma'am. You can leave it to us to wipe 'em out for you,' said the short and swarthy one. 'All our fumigation work guaranteed one hundred and ten percent. Fully insured, too. We'll leave you a leaflet so you'll know what we've done and any precautions you need to take when you get back.'

Anna left them in the bedroom while she went to the storage closet by the front door to take out her suitcase. When she returned, though, she found that the two exterminators had come back into the living area, and had closed the bedroom door behind them. Both of them looked pale and shocked, as if they had just witnessed some appalling accident.

'What?' she said.

'You said "*bedbugs*",' said the short and swarthy one. His voice was hoarse and he had to clear his throat before he continued. 'You said "hundreds of them".'

'That's right. What's the matter? What's wrong?'

'What you got in there, lady, that's not bedbugs. Not plural. That's bed*bug*, singular.'

'Never saw nothing like it,' added his companion, shaking his head. 'Never.'

'I don't understand,' said Anna. 'You mean there's only *one* of them? How can that be?'

The short and swarthy one put his hand on the bedroom handle, opened it two or three inches, and peeked inside. 'Looks like the coast is clear. Why don't you come check this out for yourself? I don't have any idea how we're going to deal with this baby, I swear to God.'

Anna began to feel alarmed. It had been frightening enough to find a mass of bedbugs seething all over her sheets last night, but she couldn't understand what the exterminators meant by *'bedbug, singular'* and why they both seemed so jittery.

The short and swarthy exterminator beckoned her to follow him across the bedroom. He walked on tiptoe, as if he didn't want to disturb whatever it was that they had found in the bed. She was surprised to see that they hadn't yet stripped off the bedcover and the sheets, which she would have assumed was the first thing they'd do.

She could see that the sheets and the pillow-cases were still speckled with rusty-colored bedbug droppings, but she couldn't see any bedbugs swarming over them. They had probably burrowed their way into the mattress in the hope that, sooner or later, another unsuspecting warm-blooded person would come climbing into the bed.

The short and swarthy exterminator leaned across the bed and gripped the edge of the white woven throw between finger and thumb. 'You ready for this?' he asked her. 'I don't want you to get fracashed.'

'Go on,' she told him.

He cautiously lifted the throw, tilting his head sideways so that he could see underneath it. At first it seemed as if there was nothing there at all, but as he raised it further, Anna saw two jointed legs. They were definitely insect legs, amber-colored and articulated, but they were as large as the legs of a snow crab.

'Oh my God,' she said and couldn't stop herself from giving a shiver.

The exterminator raised the throw higher still, and it was then that she realized what he had meant by 'bedbug, singular'. Frantically trying to conceal itself in the folds between the sheets was a bedbug the size of an oval casserole-dish, reddish-brown, with an armored shell in seven sections and a shield-shaped head with waving antennae. The higher the exterminator lifted the throw, the more frantically it tried to bury itself out of sight.

It *smelled*, too, like crushed cilantro, or old women's urine, even more strongly than all of those hundreds of bedbugs which had invaded her bed during the night.

The exterminator let the throw drop back. 'See what I mean?' he asked Anna. 'We can fumigate the place with sulfuryl fluroride for sure, but I don't know if that'll be strong enough to kill it. Before I saw that thing, I was going to suggest taking your mattress away with us and treating it off site, which would have cost you a whole lot less – but I don't know how we're going to be able to do that now.'

297

Anna could see the huge bedbug moving underneath the throw – a lump that struggled diagonally from one side of the bed to the other. 'I just don't get it,' she said. 'It's like all of those tiny little bedbugs have joined together to make one giant bedbug.'

'Never saw nothing like it,' repeated the exterminator with the mournful moustache. 'Never in my born days.'

'Problem is, ma'am, I won't be able to give you any kind of a guarantee that we can deal with it,' said the short and swarthy one. 'Bug that size, it's hard to know what kind of resistance it has. Roaches, they can survive an H-bomb, so they say. Don't know what we'll have to do to deep-six *this* sucker.'

'Please – if you can try, at least,' said Anna. 'I have to leave for Los Angeles in an hour. If fumigating doesn't work, call me, and then maybe we can think of some other way of dealing with it. Maybe you could trap it. You trap rats, don't you? This wouldn't be so different.'

The exterminator sucked in his breath. 'I'm not so sure, ma'am. I think I'll have to call my office and get some kind of authorization for this. It's like there are health and safety rules for every kind of extermination procedure, and I couldn't tell you what the hell *this* comes under. For all I know, the damn thing's dangerous. Your regular bedbug can give you a pretty nasty bite . . . Think what this baby could do.'

Anna couldn't take her eyes off the lump under the throw. Again, she found herself wishing that she had a gun in the house. The simplest way of

298

exterminating this bedbug would be to blow it to bits, even though she had the strangest feeling that the bits would go back to being tiny-sized bedbugs again, and simply scatter and hide, and then she would never be able to get rid of them.

'All right,' she said. 'You call your office. But tell them you can do whatever it takes, it's OK by me. I have to pack or else I'm going to miss my flight.'

Anna quickly took the clothes and the toiletries that she needed, and then they left the bedroom and closed the door. The short and swarthy exterminator called his boss on his cellphone and spent the next ten minutes pacing up and down and saying, 'Sure, but— Sure, but— Yes, but—'

Eventually, he hung up and said, 'He says we can go ahead with fumigation. If that doesn't work, then we'll have to contact the city pest control people and ask for their advice. We have to be careful we're not killing off some rare species of bug, because that could get us into a whole lot of trouble.'

Anna looked toward the bedroom door and gave another involuntary shiver when she thought of that huge amber insect crawling around in her bed. 'Here's my cell number,' she said, scribbling it down on a notepad for them. 'Let me know as soon as it's dead.'

She heard nothing from A-Z Pest Control until she and Epiphany arrived at LAX at nine that evening. As they came across the concourse, they were met by a smooth young black professor who Anna had come across at a meeting of

299

disease-control specialists two years ago in Denver, Michael Newton. He was slim and handsome with a shiny shaven head, and he was wearing a very smart cream designer suit and a splashy green-and-orange necktie.

'Professor Grey,' he said with a grin, taking their suitcases for them. 'It's a great honor to meet you again.'

'Pleasure to see you, too, Doctor Newton. Well, it would be, under any other circumstances. This is my colleague Doctor Bechet. Epiphany, this is Michael. Michael, meet Epiphany. She's been working with me on the Meramac School virus.'

'Yeah. I was reading about that. How's that progressing?'

'One really cussed bug, I can tell you. Whatever you throw at it, it mutates to become immune to it. I've even tried tyranivir on it. All *that* did was to make it even more aggressive.'

'Well, I guess human beings are much the same, if you challenge them. You know what they say – what doesn't kill you makes you stronger.'

They walked out of the terminal into the warm evening air. Anna said, 'If the Meramac School virus was a human being, it would be an out-and-out psychopath. It destroys every living thing that's different from itself, even its own cells – the ones that it replicated before it mutated.'

'So – technically – you have a disease that retrospectively cures itself?'

'Pretty much. The only problem is that we can't yet cure the disease.'

As they approached the curb, Michael Newton

300

raised his hand and a gleaming black Escalade left its parking space on the opposite side of the ramp and drew up beside them. Michael Newton opened the doors for them, and Anna and Epiphany climbed in.

'We've booked you in at the Embassy Suites,' said Michael Newton. 'It's quiet there, and it's not too far from the lab. There's an in-house restaurant, too, the Fireside Grill, so you won't have to worry about cooking.'

'I love cooking,' said Epiphany. 'You should taste my gumbo.'

How about that, thought Anna. *She's flirting with him.*

Before they had even left the airport, Anna's cell warbled, and she fished it out of her purse.

'Ms Grey? This is Bill Grearson at A-Z Pest Control. Sorry to bother you, but are my two operatives still with you?'

'I'm not at home,' said Anna. 'I had to leave for Los Angeles as soon as I let your men in.'

'They haven't called you?'

'No, I've heard nothing.'

'Well, that's real strange, because neither have we. We're thinking of sending someone around to your place to make sure that everything's OK. They said you had one whopper of a bedbug there, they weren't too sure how they were going to deal with it.'

'It was huge, yes. But they promised to call me once they'd killed it. I can only assume that they haven't managed it yet, but I'm surprised they haven't even been in touch with you.'

For all I know, the damn thing's dangerous.

Your regular bedbug can give you a pretty nasty bite . . . Think what this baby could do.

'I'm surprised, too,' said Bill Grearson. 'A single-room fumigation shouldn't take longer than four hours, tops, and so far it's taken them nearly six, and not a word. They're not answering their cells, either.'

'You have me worried now,' said Anna. 'Give me a call back, won't you, and let me know if they've had any problems.'

'Will do, Ms Grey.'

'What was that about?' asked Epiphany as Anna dropped her phone back into her purse.

'That enormous horrible bedbug I was telling you about. The two guys who came round to exterminate it were supposed to call me, but they haven't, and they haven't called their office, either.'

'That's creepy.'

'I know. It's like something out of a science-fiction movie. I hope nothing's happened to them.'

'Most likely they couldn't kill it and they simply gave up and went home.'

'Yes, but that would mean it's still crawling around my loft. It gives me the heebie-jeebies just to think about it!'

'Everything all right, professor?' asked Michael Newton, turning around from the seat in front of her.

'A little domestic problem, that's all,' said Anna. 'Leastways, I hope it is. And – please – call me Anna.'

'We're going to be making an early start

302

tomorrow,' said Michael Newton. 'We'll send a car for you at six thirty so that we can start our preliminary briefing at seven. I have a folder here for each of you with all of our test results so far. It includes ER admission figures, but people are coming in so thick and fast that all of those figures will be redundant by the morning. In fact, they're probably redundant already.'

'What's the latest count you have?' asked Anna.

Michael Newton checked his iPhone. 'Up until five this afternoon, three thousand seven hundred and twenty. Out of those, there were nine hundred eighty-three fatalities, and at that time they were dying at an average rate of seventy-six every hour. No recoveries reported so far. Not one. If you catch BV-1, that's it. You're a goner.'

They were driving through the suburb of West Athens now. Anna looked out of the window at the rows of single-story houses on either side of the highway, each looking safe and snug, with their porch lights shining and their automobiles parked outside. But she knew that in the darkness of the night, the retrovirus was spreading across the country like the tendrils of some black and poisonous creeper.

When they arrived at the Embassy Suites, Anna went directly up to her third-floor suite. She had been given a spacious living-room with leather couches and armchairs and a deep-red carpet. However, she went straight through to the bedroom, hefted her suitcase on to the bed and unzipped it. She felt exhausted and detached, as if none of what had happened to her in the past few days had been real.

While she was hanging up her clothes in the closet, her cellphone warbled. It was Bill Grearson again, calling from A-Z Pest Control.

'Ms Grey? Have the police contacted you yet?'

'The *police*? No. Why should they?'

'I'm afraid I have some bad news, Ms Grey. I sent one of my people around to check what was happening at your apartment, and find out why my operatives hadn't been in touch. Their van was still in the parking structure, so he assumed they were still on site. He went to the door, but he couldn't get a response, so he asked the super to check for him.'

Bill Grearson was silent for a moment, and Anna realized that he was finding it difficult to speak.

'Go on,' she said, gently.

At last, he managed to say, 'They found them in the bedroom. They'd brought in all of their equipment, their gas cylinders and their door seals, everything they needed to fumigate, but they never even got started.'

There was another pause, even longer this time, but Anna said nothing and waited patiently for Bill Grearson to continue.

'They're dead, both of them,' he said. 'Not just dead, but torn wide open. The guy I sent there to check up on them, he says he's going to have nightmares about it every night for the rest of his life.' Yet another pause, then, 'They were torn wide open. Their guts pulled out, and twisted around their own necks to strangle them.'

'Oh my God,' said Anna.

'The cops showed up, and one of them even

304

puked up when he saw their bodies. I can't believe this has happened. I had to call their wives and tell them. I didn't give them all the details. How could I? But they're going to find out sooner or later, aren't they? Strangled with their own guts. Who would do such a thing?'

'I have no idea,' said Anna. Then, 'What about the bedbugs?'

'The *bedbug*? What about it?'

'Well, it must have still been there somewhere, and still alive, if they hadn't yet started to fumigate.'

'I don't know. I didn't ask. It was a bedbug, that's all. I guess nobody noticed it.'

'This bedbug was huge. You've no idea how big it was. You couldn't fail to notice it.'

'Nobody mentioned it. Maybe it was hiding someplace.'

'The police need to know about it. I'll call them.'

'All right, Ms Grey, do whatever you have to. I have some more people to call. This is going to ruin my business, you know that? This is the end of the world, so far as I'm concerned. This is the end of the world.'

Twenty-Two

Anna didn't have to call the police because the police called her first. She was still trying to find their number on her laptop when her cell warbled.

'Is that Professor Grey? Professor Anna Grey? This is Detective Raymond Keiller, St Louis Metropolitan Police Department.'

'Oh, good. I was right on the verge of contacting you myself. A-Z Pest Control just called me about those two employees of theirs being killed.'

'That's right. That's what I need to talk to you about. So far as we can ascertain, you were the last person to see them alive.'

'Mr Grearson from A-Z told me what happened to them. I can barely believe it. Disemboweled. Strangled. It's horrible.'

'Let me say first of all that we're trying to keep the full details out of the media,' said Detective Keiller. 'The way they were murdered was highly unusual, and we don't want any copycats to throw us off the trail.'

'My God. Who would want to copy two murders like that?'

'Oh, you'd be surprised. There's always some nut job who wants to attract attention and can't think up his own way of doing it. Listen – I've been in touch with your CEO at the hospital. I fully appreciate that you're out there in Los Angeles doing critical research work, so I'm not

306

going to ask you to come back here to answer questions. Not yet, anyhow. One of our detectives will be flying out tomorrow to talk to you in person.'

'That's fine. I'm not going anyplace.'

'Thanks, great,' said Detective Keiller. 'In spite of that, I formally have to insist that you stay in Downey for the time being and keep us informed of your whereabouts at all times.'

'My whereabouts? I'll either be slaving away over a hot microscope at the Public Health laboratory, or else I'll be crashed out in my hotel. That's all I'll have time for.'

'Sure, I understand. All I need to ask you right now is if you noticed anything unusual at the time you let those exterminators into your apartment. Did you see anybody hanging around the corridor or the parking structure – anybody you didn't recognize, or who was acting suspicious?'

'No, I didn't see anybody else,' said Anna. 'But the reason I was going to call you was because of the bedbug that those two poor men were trying to exterminate.'

'Yes, A-Z Pest Control told me that you'd called them in to deal with bedbugs.'

'This was *one* bedbug, detective. One enormous bedbug nearly fifteen inches from head to tail and about nine inches wide.'

'Excuse me?'

'When I went to bed last night I found that my mattress was infested with hundreds of bedbugs.'

'OK . . .' said Detective Keiller. He sounded wary.

'Obviously I couldn't sleep there, so my CEO

kindly let me spend the rest of the night at his place. When I met up with the exterminators this afternoon to show them the bedbugs, the bedbugs had all disappeared. All the *normal-sized* bedbugs, anyhow. There was only this one monster bedbug.'

Detective Keiller said, 'I'm having a little trouble with this, Professor Grey. First of all there were hundreds of bedbugs, but when you came back this morning there was only one, but it was enormous?'

'Yes.'

'OK . . . so what happened to it, this enormous bedbug?'

'I don't know. That's one of the reasons I was going to call you. You must have searched my loft, didn't you?'

'Of course we searched it. We've had a five-person forensic team going over it inch by inch.'

'But you haven't found a bedbug?'

'Not a monster bedbug, no. There were traces of serious bedbug infestation, definitely, yes, on the bed linen. But no indication of anything as big as you've just described to me. Fifteen inches by nine – hey, that's bigger than some dogs.'

'I know. And I can hear by your tone of voice that you don't believe me.'

'I believe you saw something that you believed was a monster bedbug, Professor Grey. Whether it really *was* a monster bedbug . . . well, that's a matter for conjecture.'

As she talked, Anna walked out of the bedroom and across the living room to the doors that led out to the balcony. Below her, a fountain was softly splashing and a warm breeze was making the palms rustle, as if they were whispering amongst themselves. *Look up there, on the balcony. There's that mad woman who thinks she saw a giant bedbug.* Behind the trees in front of the hotel, traffic was passing to and fro on Firestone Boulevard, and the night seemed almost normal. In the distance, though, from every direction, she could hear the panicky scribbling of ambulance sirens.

As she was standing there, a glossy black Buick Verano turned into the hotel forecourt and stopped almost immediately underneath her balcony. It stayed there for almost a minute with its engine running, but its doors and windows remained closed and nobody got out of it.

'I know it sounds incredible, a bedbug that size,' she told Detective Keiller. 'But I've been making clinical studies of pathogen-carrying insects for over a decade, and there was no mistaking what it was. If you saw a lobster the size of a truck you'd still know that it was a lobster.'

She thought of telling him about BV-1, the bedbug virus, but decided that she didn't have enough information on it herself yet. As yet, there was no provable connection between BV-1 and the bedbugs that had appeared in her bed except for her own visions of nuns and Native American wonder-workers, and she didn't want to stretch his credulity any further than it was stretched already.

'Well, thank you, professor, I appreciate your cooperation,' he told her. 'Like I say, one of our detectives will be in contact with you sometime early tomorrow.'

309

Anna was about to go back inside when the Buick's doors opened and two men climbed out. The first one was wearing dark glasses, even though it was night-time, but he had gray brushed-back hair and a neatly trimmed gray beard, and she recognized him at once. At least, she thought she recognized him, but maybe he was only a lookalike, because what was he doing here, in Downey, outside the very hotel where she was staying? He was supposed to be running a funeral chapel in St Louis.

The second man had his back turned to her, and because she was looking down at him at such an acute angle it was difficult for her to see what he looked like. In spite of that he did look strangely familiar. He was wearing a dark suit and a very white shirt, and his hair was fashionably messed up.

Anna felt as if she were standing in an elevator that had suddenly dropped down ten floors without stopping

When the second man turned around and started to walk toward the hotel entrance, she could see his face clearly. It was David. Her own dead David.

After he had disappeared from view beneath her, Anna stayed on the balcony for three or four seconds, numb with shock. This couldn't be. This was impossible. She had watched David's casket disappear behind the curtains of the crematorium. His mother had even called her from Boise to say that she had received his ashes, in a green ceramic urn. How could he be here now, with

Brian Grandier, the very man who had arranged his cremation?

In the next instant, though, she threw aside her cellphone and ran for the door. She sprinted along the corridor to the elevators and jabbed frantically at the 'DOWN' button. She could hear the elevator whining, but then it stopped abruptly at the floor above her, and she could hear banging and thumping noises, and talking. It sounded as if somebody was deliberately keeping the doors open so that they could wheel their luggage in or out.

She jabbed the button again, but still the elevator didn't respond, so she ran to the end of the corridor and pushed open the door to the stairs. Her shoes clattered as she hurtled down them as fast as she could, almost twisting her ankle as she jumped down the last three stairs of the first-floor flight.

When she reached the ground floor she burst out into the lobby, turning around and around to see if she could see David anywhere. The lobby was huge and high-ceilinged, with a balcony all the way around it, a fountain and armchairs all around. But apart from an elderly couple who were sitting glumly side by side, as if they had run out of anything to say to each other about twenty years ago, there was nobody there.

She hurried across to the front desk, where a young red-haired woman was talking on the telephone. She waited impatiently until the young woman had finished and put down her receiver, and then she said, 'Two men just came in here. Can you tell me where they went?'

311

The receptionist frowned at her, as if she had spoken in a foreign language.

'Two men,' she repeated. 'One wearing a dark suit, the other with a gray beard and sunglasses.'

The receptionist shook her head. 'Sorry, ma'am, we've had nobody in here for the past half-hour. And no gentlemen who looked like that.'

'You must have seen them,' said Anna. 'They parked right outside the front entrance. They were in a black sedan, a Buick.'

The receptionist kept on shaking her head. 'Sorry, ma'am.'

Anna left the front desk and went out through the revolving door to take a look at the hotel forecourt. Behind the trees an ambulance sped past, heading north-westward, its siren silent but its red-and-white lights flashing. There were twenty or thirty vehicles parked outside the hotel, but none of them was the black Buick Verano in which David and Brian Grandier had arrived.

Or maybe they hadn't arrived at all. Maybe she had imagined seeing them.

She went back into the lobby. The elderly couple were still sitting there, side by side, staring into space. The receptionist gave her a shrug, as if to say, *Sorry, but I told you so.*

Anna took the elevator back up to the third floor. She felt as if her brain had been smashed like the mirror in her loft, and she was frightened, too. If she was so stressed and exhausted that she was continually seeing people who weren't really there, how could she trust herself to carry out the rigorous research that was required to isolate BV-1? She might even start to see imaginary cells in her microscope, or interpret her test results in a way that seemed logical to her but in reality made no scientific sense. *Anna Through The Looking-Glass.*

She knew that her expertise with viral epidemics was badly needed, but in her present state of mind her involvement in the BV-1 project could be disastrous.

She walked back along the corridor. Luckily, one of the chamber-maids was outside the door of her suite, because she hadn't taken her key-card when she had rushed out to see David.

Back in her living room, she picked up her cellphone from the floor. She had three messages already: one from Epiphany, one from Jim Waso and one from American Express. Both Epiphany and Jim were simply wishing her a good night's sleep. American Express was reminding her that her monthly account was overdue.

She sat down on one of the couches and closed her eyes. The door to the balcony was still open, and the warm night breeze made her feel more relaxed. In the distance she could still hear ambulance sirens nagging, as if they were never going to stop reminding her why she was here and how urgent it was that they needed to find an antiviral for BV-1. In spite of that, her shattered thoughts began to piece themselves together again, like a slow-motion movie of her broken mirror being run backward.

She still had her eyes closed when she felt somebody sit down on the couch next to her. She opened them at once and jolted in fright. It was David. He was much more pallid than she had

313

ever seen him, but he had an extraordinary expression on his face – triumphant, almost – as if to say: *Look what I've done! I've come back!*

Anna made a whimpering noise and tried to shift herself away from him, but he reached out and laid his hand on her shoulder.

'Anna,' he said and smiled at her. His voice sounded the same as always. A little throatier, maybe, but she would have recognized it even if she hadn't been able to see him. 'Anna, don't be frightened. It's only me.'

'David,' said Anna. 'I'm dreaming this. This is a dream. You're dead.'

'People don't have to die, Anna, not if they don't want to. I know that now. Death is a matter of choice.'

'David, you died in my arms and you were certified dead and you were cremated. This *can't* be you. David is nothing but ashes. Go away!'

'Listen to me, Anna. I was asked what I wanted to do. Did I want to die, or did I want to keep on living? Usually, at our age, that's a question that hasn't yet reared its ugly head. But what would *you* choose?'

David lifted his hand off her shoulder, and Anna stood up, keeping her eyes on him all the time. She backed across the living room toward the door.

'What's the matter, sweetheart?' David asked her. 'You're not walking out on me, are you?'

'You're dead, David! If anybody left anybody, you were the one who left me. You can't come back. It isn't possible. I'm having a nightmare. Go *away*. Go away and let me wake up!'

David stood up too, although he kept his distance. 'It *is* possible, Anna. Here, look at me. I'm the living proof. I never knew it before, but there are spirits in this world who can bring you back, even if you're dead, and give you life everlasting. This is why I need to talk to you.'

'This isn't real, David, any of it. I'm hallucinating. You're dead. I was holding you in my arms when you died.'

'I was sick, yes. I was very, very sick, and I did appear to die. I even thought myself that I was dead. OK – in a way, I *did* die. But Brian Grandier gave me the choice of coming back to life.'

'Brian Grandier was supposed to have cremated you.'

'Brian Grandier is a savior, Anna. Brian Grandier is a savior of souls – a great, great man. He's linked up with others like him, and together they're going to give this country back everything that was taken away from it.'

Now he came around the couch and slowly approached Anna, both hands held out, until he was almost near enough to reach out and touch her. She felt frightened to the point of total hysteria, and yet fascinated, too, because he *was* David, he really was. He was very pale, but the look in his blue-gray eyes was sincere, his smile was encouraging, and he was speaking just like David always used to speak to her – gently and reasonably and optimistically. David had always believed that things were going to get better. Even when she'd despaired of finding a cure for some disease, he had always promised her that she

315

would, if only she persisted and continued to believe in herself.

'David,' she said. 'Even if this really *is* you, I don't understand how it can be. How did you get in here?'

He kept on smiling and gave her a little shake of his head. 'That's the easiest question to answer. When I came up to see you, your door wasn't properly closed. I didn't walk through the wall, if that's what you're thinking. I'm not a ghost.'

'But I saw you lying dead in the morgue.'

'I spoke to you, Anna, even then.'

'Yes, but you said, "*Get it out of me!*" Whatever was happening to you, you seemed to be terrified, and you seemed to be hurting, too. Even when you were lying in your casket, at your funeral, you said, "Get it out of me!" You said that you couldn't bear it, whatever it was.'

'That's because I didn't understand myself what it was. But now I know, and I'm so grateful for it. I'm alive again, Anna, and I've come back to you, and you and I can go on living, just as we did before I got sick.'

He reached out for her, but again she stepped back. 'David . . . I don't know. I'm not sure I'm ready for this. I don't even believe it's really happening.'

'I swear to you, Anna, it *is* really happening. I'm here, in the flesh. Touch me. Feel me. I'm your David, come back to you.'

'But *how*? And what was it – this thing that you were screaming for me to get out of you? This thing that you didn't understand what it was but now you're so grateful for?'

316

Twenty-Three

David's smile faded, and he frowned in a way that she had never seen him frown before, as if he were concentrating very hard on remembering something. 'You were never religious, were you?' he asked her.

'What in God's name does religion have to do with it?'

'No, listen to me – you never really believed that there was an afterlife, did you? You never thought that there was a Heaven, or a Hell. You never believed in angels – or demons, for that matter.'

'When you're fighting a virus, David, you don't have to believe in demons. A virus doesn't have a soul, or a conscience. A virus has absolutely no pity whatsoever. A virus is a thousand times deadlier than any demon.'

'But, don't you get it? That's what viruses *are*. "Demon" was only a name given to viruses by people in medieval times who didn't understand why they got sick or why they went mad or why they acted like they were possessed.'

Anna said, 'David . . . if your coming back to life again wasn't strange enough, this is getting even stranger. I'm very, very frightened now. How do you know this? Is this what Brian Grandier told you?'

David nodded. 'Brian Grandier brought the virus to America himself.'

'*He* brought it? But why? Is he some kind of terrorist? This virus has been killing thousands of people, and it's probably going to kill thousands more before we can stop it – even if we *can* stop it!'

'That's the whole point, Anna. It has, but it hasn't. All those people who seem to have died will come back to life again, just like I have.'

'Why? Why kill people and then revive them?'

'To *change* them. To make them into better people. To stop them from ruining this country any more than they have already.'

Anna looked at David for a long time without saying anything. He smiled at her again, and he was obviously doing everything he could to win her confidence.

'It may seem like a deadly virus, Anna, but it's the opposite. After it's spread all the way across the nation, you'll see what America was supposed to be like. Idyllic.'

Anna ignored that. 'How did you know I was here?' she asked him.

'We keep our ear to the ground, that's all.'

'*We*?'

'I'm one of them now, Anna. To be truthful, I don't have any choice. Like I said, this nation is going to go back to being the paradise it was always intended to be.'

'I can't take any more of this,' said Anna. 'You're going to have to go.'

David reached out again, quickly, and this time he managed to grasp her left hand. She tried to twist it away, but he held it tight, and the terrible

318

thing was that it felt warm, and strong, and just like David's hands had always felt before.

'I thought we were lovers,' he said.

'Yes, we were. But you *died*.'

'Now I'm back. So what's changed?'

'You have. You said so yourself. And now you're all involved with Brian Grandier and this virus of his. You suffered so much pain yourself, David. You convulsed. You brought up so much blood. Do you really want millions more people to go through the same agony that you did, and for what? Some pie-in-the-sky about paradise?'

David said, 'Everything destructive and murderous that has ever been done in this world has been done in the name of God.'

'David, let go of my hand. You have to leave now. Please.'

'That so-called Scalping Virus you cured. That really made your reputation, didn't it?'

'What about it?'

'They named it the Scalping Virus because it made people's hair fall out and left their heads raw and bleeding, just like they'd been scalped.'

'So? I don't understand what you're getting at.'

'Tell me: who used to scalp their victims?'

'*What*? What does that have to do with anything? Indians, I always thought.'

'That's what most people think, but that's where you're wrong. Scalping was introduced by Europeans, as a way of killing off Native American tribes, or at least reducing their numbers so they couldn't fight back when their land was taken from them.'

'David, you're *hurting* me.'

319

'Bounty-hunting, that's what it was. Back in the eighteenth century, the governors of Pennsylvania and Massachusetts paid good money for every Indian scalp – man, woman or child over twelve, to prove that they'd been killed. Oh, yes. In the off-season, that's what kept plenty of European farm-workers in whiskey, hunting down the Lenni-Lenape and the Hurons and scalping them. They didn't even have to be warriors to get scalped. Didn't have to represent any kind of threat. So long as they were Indians.'

Anna at last managed to wrench her hand free. The two of them stood staring at each other, both of them breathing hard.

'I wasn't hallucinating, was I?' said Anna. 'Those Native American wonder-workers, or whatever they call themselves – I really saw them, didn't I?'

David said, 'Yes. And you saw the nuns, too.'

'I'm so bewildered. I don't understand any of this. Where do nuns come into it?'

'It's simple. People don't think that spirits from different religions ever encounter each other, but of course they do, just like living people from different religions. Those two wonder-workers, Matchitehew and Megedagik, they can call on any Native American spirit that you can think of, and Brian Grandier can summon up any Christian spirit. Brian Grandier summoned up Gressil, the spirit of infection, who possessed the nuns at the Ursuline convent in Loudun in the seventeenth century. Matchitehew and Megedagik summoned up Awonawilona, the Native American spirit who gives you the ability to be in more than one place at the same time. Together, those two spirits are infecting the whole country with the same virus that infected me.'

'But *why*, David? What are they trying to do?'

'What do you think? Matchitehew and Megedagik want their land back – and revenge for the way that their people were massacred when it was stolen from them. Brian Grandier wants to see religious bigots punished for all the suffering they've caused over the centuries. They have a common cause, Anna. They want justice at last for the millions and millions of innocent people who have been tortured and slaughtered in the name of God.'

Anna went back to the couch and sat down. 'This is not you talking, is it, David? What did you ever know about nuns and Native Americans? What did you ever *care* about them, for that matter?'

'This *is* me, Anna. I swear to you. But I had to make a choice, if I was going to survive. I had to agree to join Matchitehew, Megedagik and Brian Grandier and help them give this country back to the people it really belongs to.'

'David, I'm too tired to argue with you any more. I need time to think about this, really.'

David came around the couch and hunkered down in front of her. Again, his expression was deeply serious. 'I have to ask you just one thing, Anna. This is the whole reason I'm here tonight, apart from wanting to see you again. I have to ask you not to help to destroy this virus. Tell the CDC that you're backing out. Tell them that you're not well. Any excuse will do.'

'David, I can't do that! Even while we're talking about this virus, it's killing people! Can't you hear those sirens? Don't you remember what pain you went through? Don't you remember how *scared* you were? I have to find a cure for it! It's more than what I do, it's what I *am*!'

'Maybe if you think about it again in the morning, when you've had some sleep? I'm sorry. I should have realized how tired you must be.'

'No, David. I can't change my mind. I'm still in a state of shock that you're here at all, and I'm totally confused about what you and Brian Grandier and these wonder-workers think they're trying to do. You can't turn back time. This country is never going to be the same as it was before the Europeans arrived here. It's impossible. It's insane. And I can't allow millions more people to suffer, whatever the justification for it.'

David was silent for a few moments, but then he said, 'OK. I respect your decision. It's a pity, but if I really can't persuade you . . .?'

'No, David. You can't.'

'In that case there's only one more favor I need to ask. Is it OK if I spend the night here? I'll sleep on the couch, and I'll be heading out as soon as it gets light.'

Anna said, 'I'm frightened of you, David. I thought you were dead. You *were* dead. But here you are. And you're not the same as you were before you died. You're talking about Indians, and you're all mixed up with those nuns. Do you know what one of those nuns *did* to me? It still makes me sick to my stomach to think of it. And the language she used.'

322

David nodded, as if he knew who and what she was talking about. 'I understand how you feel, Anna. I'm sure I'd feel exactly the same if you died and came back to life. But I promise you I'll stay here on the couch, and I won't ask you again to quit the virus team. OK?'

Anna looked at him. She had loved him so much, and they had done so much together – talked, laughed, argued, made love. For some reason she had a mental picture of them walking hand-in-hand through Pere Marquette State Park, one golden fall, with leaves flying in the wind all around them. She had thought then that she had known him better than she had known herself. No matter what had happened to him, how could she say no?

'All right,' she said. 'But where will you go tomorrow? Am I ever going to see you again? Is Brian Grandier here, too? Are you going off with him?'

She was thinking to herself: *If Brian Grandier is still here, and he really is responsible for spreading the BV-1 virus, I ought to report him to the police or the FBI.*

'Let's just get some sleep, shall we?' said David. 'I'll be in touch, don't worry.'

Anna undressed and went to bed. She was too tired to take a shower – she could do that in the morning, before she went to the Public Health laboratory.

She had given David a blanket and said goodnight, but she hadn't kissed him. His face had looked so waxy, standing in the lamplight, and

323

he had seemed distracted. Before she'd closed her bedroom door she'd watched him take off his coat and his shoes and lie down on the couch. She'd never felt so confused in her life. It was him, it was David, and she wanted him, and felt such a strong urge to comfort him and take care of him, but at the same time his presence terrified her. She could almost understand how beaten wives must feel: I love him desperately, but why is he so unpredictable, and why does he frighten me so much?

She had closed her bedroom door and turned the key, but then she'd turned it back again. He had promised to stay on the couch, hadn't he? And supposing he came in to say goodbye in the morning and found that she had locked him out! She might just as well tell him that she didn't trust him any more and that their relationship was over.

She still wanted to find out exactly how he had managed to come back to life again, and what he was doing with Brian Grandier and those mysterious, beetle-covered wonder-workers. If she knew that, maybe it would be easier for her to understand how the BV-1 virus was spread and how it replicated itself. But one thing she did know for sure: no amount of cajoling from David was going to stop her from isolating BCV-1 and formulating an antiviral agent that would stop it in its tracks.

Exhausted as she was, she didn't think that she was going to be able to sleep, but in less than ten minutes her eyes had closed and she was breathing deeply, Her right hand was lying on the pillow next to her, and her fingers gradually opened, as if she were trying to feel if raindrops had started to fall.

She dreamed that David was lying next to her, very close, so close that she could feel his breath against her cheek. She dreamed that he kissed her hair, and then her eyelid, and her nose, and her lips.

His hand slid down under the sheet and massaged her thigh. Then he lifted her nightshirt and caressed her stomach.

'David,' she murmured. 'Don't, I'm too tired.'

He kissed her again, and now his hand made its way further up inside her nightshirt and cupped her left breast. He gently tugged and twisted her nipple until it stiffened, and then he reached across to play with her other breast.

'Don't,' she repeated, but she knew that she was dreaming and so she didn't do anything to stop him. Besides, he was making her feel aroused and warm and needed, and protected, too. She hadn't felt like that since the night he had come home from Chicago, looking so sick.

With the tip of his middle finger he lightly stroked her clitoris – so lightly that she could barely feel it, and she ached for him to stroke it more forcefully. She even lifted her hips so that he would be stroking it harder. But he kept on and on, with that light, teasing, tantalizing touch, while she became more and more slippery and started to ache for him to slide himself inside her.

At last, when she could feel the warm beginnings of an orgasm rising up between her legs, he dragged back the sheets and climbed on top of her. He opened her thighs wide and nestled the swollen glans of his penis between the lips of her vulva, but then he waited before he penetrated her, one long second after another.

'*Fuck me,*' she said, in a low, hoarse voice. Then, when he still didn't push himself into her, she reached up and grasped his buttocks, digging her long sharp fingernails into his flesh. She pulled him downward, until he was so deeply inside her that his penis touched the neck of her womb and made her jump.

It was then that she realized she wasn't asleep, and this wasn't a dream at all, and that David was really on top of her, inside her, and that she was making love with a man who had died.

'Oh my God!' she screamed. 'Oh my God get off me! David! Get off me! David! *David, get off me!*'

But instead of lifting himself off her, David forced himself into her even harder, and pinned her shoulders down against the bed. She struggled and kicked and jerked her hips up and down, trying to free herself, but he was far too heavy for her, and far too strong.

'David, get off me! David! Listen to me! David!'

He didn't answer. All Anna could hear was his thick, harsh breathing. Every muscle in his body was locked tight, and he was keeping himself inside her, as deep as he could. He was making no attempt to move himself in and out, which frightened her even more than if he had been trying to bring himself to a climax.

'David – what are you doing? David, for God's sake *get off me*!'

He still said nothing, but now he grasped her throat in both hands, with the balls of his thumbs pressed against her larynx, and started to choke her.

She gripped his wrists and tried to pull his hands away. She couldn't even budge them a fraction of an inch. The tendons in his wrists felt like taut steel wires. He kept on pressing harder and harder until she started to see prickles of light floating in front of her eyes. She was desperate to scream at him to stop, but she couldn't take any air into her lungs.

She made a last desperate effort to heave herself sideways, but it was useless. He was obviously determined to kill her, and he wasn't going to stop squeezing her throat until he had.

Although the bedroom was already dark, it seemed to Anna to grow even darker. She was gradually losing her sight, and she knew that it would take only a few seconds now before she lost consciousness.

She let go of his wrists and allowed her arms to flop down. Even though every instinct was urging her to fight for her survival, she said to herself, *relax*. Her brain felt as if it were bursting from lack of oxygen, but her medical discipline was telling her that if she wanted to stay alive she had to appear to be dead.

She lay there, unmoving. The last few seconds were the worst, as David kept squeezing her neck and crushing her larynx even harder with his thumbs. Her lungs were aching, and she was not only going blind but deaf, so that she could no longer hear David panting, or the creaking of the mattress underneath her.

Then, quite abruptly, he took his hands away. She needed every ounce of her willpower not to take in a huge, screaming gasp of air, but she managed to control herself enough to breathe in thin and steady through her nostrils. David sat up straighter and stayed like that for a moment, with his penis still inside her, and his chest was rising and falling so hard that he obviously couldn't detect that she was still breathing, too. She faintly heard him say something, but her hearing was so blurry that she couldn't make out what it was. He slowly withdrew himself, and she suddenly felt the wetness between her legs. He rolled off the bed and stood up. She kept her eyes closed, but she could sense that he was standing close to the bed, staring down at her.

'You wouldn't listen, would you?' he said, as loudly and clearly as if he thought that she was still alive. 'I asked you nicely, but you wouldn't freaking listen. Well, what could I expect? You always were a stubborn bitch.'

She stayed where she was, motionless, breathing as imperceptibly as she could. Her neck felt horribly bruised, and she hoped that he hadn't damaged her larynx. She had known several patients whose larynges had been crushed in car accidents and who hadn't been able to speak above a whisper for the rest of their lives, if at all.

After what seemed like hours, but was probably less than a minute, she heard David walk out of the bedroom. She took six or seven really deep breaths, which clawed at her throat, but they gradually stopped her heart from palpitating and made her feel calmer. From the sound of it, David was dressing. She heard him sit down on the couch, presumably to lace up his shoes. After that there was silence from the next room, and she wondered if he had gone, although she hadn't heard the door.

You wouldn't listen, he'd said. *I asked you nicely, but you wouldn't freaking listen.* It seemed as if he'd come here with the express purpose of stopping her working on the BV-1 virus. But a dead man, sent by a mortician and by two Native American spirits? It all seemed like complete madness. On the other hand, she knew from her long experience with epidemics that viruses were exactly how David had described them – *demons* – and when demons appear, real or imaginary, they always bring madness in their wake. Illusions, or delusions, or psychosis, or utter insanity.

She carefully lifted herself off the bed and tiptoed over to the bedroom door. She couldn't see David in the living room, so he must have gone. Thank God – not that she believed in God. She didn't think that God would have allowed her dead lover to come back to life and try to strangle her. Or maybe he would. Maybe that was why God had created us: to fight his demons for him.

She needed to find an emergency room and have her larynx checked out. If David had damaged her vocal cords, she was in serious trouble. She crossed the living room to pick up her purse from where she had left it last night, beside the coffee table.

She was halfway across the room when she froze. The doors to the balcony were open, and there was a cool early-morning breeze blowing in. Standing on the balcony in his dark suit was David, watching the sky gradually becoming lighter as sunrise approached. He had his back to her, so he hadn't seen her, and even at this time of the morning there was traffic noise outside, so she was fairly sure that he hadn't heard her, either.

Very carefully, she picked up her purse and then began to tiptoe back toward the bedroom. She had only taken two or three steps, however, before David said, 'Anna?'

She stopped still. She waited. Maybe he had spoken her name simply because he was thinking about her. But when she took another step, he turned around and smiled at her and said, 'Anna? You're supposed to be dead.'

So are you, she thought, although couldn't say it out loud. All she could do was cough, and that was so painful that it brought tears to her eyes.

'I can't let you spoil everything, Anna. There's too much at stake here. I'm sorry.'

She glanced to her left, back toward the bedroom door. She wondered if she could reach it and slam it shut before David could catch up with her. Probably not, she thought. There was a large red armchair between her and the bedroom, and he would be able to cut her off before she had made her way around it.

She quickly turned and looked behind her. She

doubted if she could reach the front door, either. It was heavy, and the security chain was fastened, and it would take too many precious seconds to open it. He could easily seize her before she had managed to get away.

David was leaning back against the balcony rail, almost casually, still smiling at her. 'I'm giving you a choice, Anna, the same way *I* was given a choice. Life or death, that's what they offered me, and I chose life. You can do the same.'

Anna opened and closed her mouth, but she couldn't answer him. What could she have said to him, in any event? *I thought you loved me, but you tried to strangle me? Look at you standing there, so calm and confident and sure of yourself. You know that I can't escape you. You're not David. You may look like him on the outside, but there's somebody else inside you.*

Get it out of me, you begged me, in the mortuary. Even in your casket you were pleading with me to get it out of you. But I couldn't, and now it's taken you over. And whoever you are, or whatever you are, you're not the David I was in love with.

'What's it to be, then, sweetheart?' said David.

Anna took a step toward him, and then another. She lifted both her arms as if she were going to embrace him. He smiled even more broadly and lifted up his arms, too.

'There,' he said. 'I knew you'd see sense.'

A car horn beeped below him in the hotel forecourt, and he turned his head to see who it was. Maybe he was expecting Brian Grandier to show up.

Whatever it was that had distracted him, Anna took her chance and started to run toward him as fast as she could, as fast as she used to get off the starting-blocks for her high school athletics team. David turned back again as he realized what she was doing, but he was too late. She collided with him at full pelt and pitched him backward over the balcony rail.

He frantically scrabbled at the air, but there was nothing to hold on to, nothing to stop him from dropping three stories down to the marble steps in front of the hotel. He hit them with a dull thud, like a sack of flour, and when Anna looked down she saw to her astonishment that he had burst apart. His dark suit was lying spread-eagled on the steps, but it appeared to be flat and almost empty, while out of the collar of his white shirt, a fine gray powder had fanned out into a star shape.

She saw two of the hotel receptionists come out on to the steps and look down at David's remains in horror. Then they looked up, toward her balcony. She knew that they had seen her, but she stepped backward into the living room, her heart beating hard, her hand held up to her aching throat.

She had been right. That might have looked like David, but it was no more than David's ashes brought back to life, by some incredible trickery, and the soul that had spoken out of his mouth had not been David's soul.

There was frantic knocking at her door. 'Professor Grey! Professor Grey! Are you all right in there? Open the door, please, professor!'

Anna turned around and went to the door. She managed to squeak, 'I'm coming,' although she doubted that they could hear her. She slid off the security chain and let them in.

Twenty-Four

The traffic on Sunset crawled along unbearably slowly. We didn't get back to Rick's house until early in the evening, and the sky had already turned that orangey-purple color. We were both tired and sweaty and out of sorts, and the first thing that Rick did was go to the fridge and take out two cans of Coors.

We stood in the kitchen drinking them and saying nothing. Dazey came out of the bathroom and found us standing there and said, 'What?'

'You don't want to know,' said Rick.

'Of course I want to know! What's happened? You both look like somebody died!'

'Somebody did,' I told her. 'Two people, in fact. The housekeeper from the Royaltie Hotel and her five-year-old son. They both contracted this infection that's going around. We've spent most of the afternoon waiting around for the cops to talk to us, to make sure that we weren't responsible, and then we had to go to the hospital to have a blood test, just to make sure that we hadn't caught it.'

'But you haven't?'

'Haven't what?' asked Rick, burping and punching his solar plexus with his fist.

'Haven't *caught* it! It's terrible. Have you seen the news? People are falling down in the streets, and they're barfing up blood all over the

334

sidewalks. The last I heard, more than seven thousand people have gone down with it. Seven *thousand*! I mean, they're dying like – I don't know, what do you call those flies that die?'

'Flies, Daze, that's what you call them,' said Rick. And then, wearily, 'Me and the Wizard, we were at the Valley Presbyterian Hospital. They was bringing in so many of those people, they had to lay them down on the floor, along the corridors. The nurse who took our blood samples said she didn't know why she was bothering. That they wouldn't be able to test them for weeks, and if we *had* caught it, we'd be dead by the time we found out the results.'

'Maybe we should get out of town for a while,' Dazey suggested. 'You know, until it's all over.'

'It's happening everywhere, Daze, from what the cops was saying to us. They got it in Portland, and Denver, and New Orleans, and St Louis. It's sweeping through the whole goddamned nation. The way I see it, there's no fucking point in getting out of town.'

'So how do we keep ourselves from catching it? Did they say?'

'I think the best thing you can do is stay here at home and sleep in your own bed,' I told her. 'I'm ninety-nine percent sure this disease is being spread by bedbugs.'

'I'm pretty sure of that, too,' said Rick. 'I told you, didn't I, that eight or nine years ago they was almost extinct. Now there's billions of them. They didn't used to give you nothing more than a whole lot of itchy bites, but now it looks like they're carrying this infection.'

335

I didn't say anything about the nuns, or Matchitehew and Megedagik, and I very much doubt that Dazey would have understood me if I had. I didn't really understand it myself, except that it was a way for the sons of Misquamacus to pay us palefaces back for killing their people and taking their land. Understandable, but you know the old saying about people who go looking for revenge? They need to dig two graves: one for their enemy, and one for themselves.

'So maybe that was what killed Bobik?' said Dazey. 'That hotel you went to yesterday – that was crawling with bedbugs, wasn't it? And Bobik was barfing up blood. Maybe he was bitten by bedbugs, but we couldn't see the bites because of his hair.'

'I don't know, Daze,' said Rick. 'It could have been. Meantime, what have we got to eat? I'm starving.'

'Nothing. We'll have to have something delivered. How about Thai?'

'Anything.'

We collapsed in front of the TV, with Kleks sitting between us and noisily panting. We watched the news for a while, but it was all about the sickness that was causing people to hemorrhage and throw fits, and then die. A grim-faced spokesman for the Center for Disease Control said that nearly a quarter of a million Americans had already succumbed to it, and he expected to see thousands more deaths before they could bring it under control.

'We have a highly qualified team of

336

epidemiologists working on it right now, at our research laboratory in Downey, California. I can tell you that individual experts in public disease control have already made considerable progress toward understanding how this infection spreads, and how we can prevent it from spreading any further. We are confident that this team can soon come up with a cure.'

Just then, Mazey came home, slamming the front door and walking into the living room blinking. 'Hi, everybody! I'm back!'

She was wearing a tight yellow sleeveless T-shirt with a picture of a tiger on it and a short white denim skirt that had creased to make it even shorter. She smelled of perfume and pot, and she was carrying her platform sandals over her shoulder, with her finger hooked into the straps. She dropped down next to me on the couch and wrapped her arm around my neck and breathed alcohol into my face – mojitos, at a guess. 'Oh, Wizard, you're so *wizardly*, did you know that?'

'So where have you been, Maze?' asked Rick, although he didn't sound particularly interested in hearing the answer.

'Sancho's, on Santa Monica. But it was like a goddamn *morgue* in there. There was only about six customers in the whole place, and everybody was glued to the TV news. And it's crazy out there! Ambulances speeding every which way. Olly didn't show, like he'd promised, and Sylvia didn't show either, and there was only this one guitarist singing all these miserable Mexican songs, so I called it a night.'

'You want Thai food?' asked Dazey. 'I'm phoning our order right now.'

'Urrgh, nothing, thanks. I'm feeling too pukish. I think I'll just hit the sack for now.' She leaned over, pressing her breast against my arm and giving me a sticky crimson kiss. 'See you later, Wizard,' she said, and then she pulled herself upright and walked across to our bedroom as if she were trying to keep her balance on a speeding train. She slammed that door behind her, too.

'How about another brewski?' asked Rick.

'No – no thanks,' I told him, nodding toward the bedroom door. 'Tonight, I think it might be wise to stay reasonably sober.'

'Hey, Daze! Didn't you get through to the restaurant yet?' Rick asked her. 'Who you been calling?'

Dazey was frowning at her phone. 'Pink Pepper. That's twice I've called them now, but nobody's answering.'

'How that can be?' said Rick. 'Are you sure you got the right number? Pink Pepper are usually so goddamned fast, they're ringing the doorbell with your food before you've decided what you want to eat.'

'No, no answer,' said Dazey. 'We'll have to have Chinese instead.'

She tried Kung Pao and Asakuma Rice and Sushiya, but again nobody picked up. Then she tried California Wings, but it was the same. It was like every delivery restaurant in Hollywood had gone dead.

'This is like some end-of-the-world movie,'

338

said Rick. 'Next thing we know, there's going to be zombies dragging their feet through the streets.'

It was dark now, and the feeling that the apocalypse had arrived was heightened by the endless shrieking of ambulance and police car sirens, and these were soon joined by the honking of fire trucks, too. It sounded like the whole city was in a panic.

'I have pepperoni pizzas in the freezer,' said Dazey.

'OK,' Rick told her.

Dazey went through to the kitchen. She hadn't seen his expression, but I could, and he was frowning. I don't think I had ever seen him look so worried before, not about anything. Not even when some shaven-headed debt-collector twice his size had threatened to punch his teeth down his throat.

He pushed Kleks off the couch so that he could lean over and talk to me *sotto voce*. 'The fuck's going on, man? This is getting scary. When you found that housekeeper and her kid, I thought, *whoa*, if she *did* get this from bedbugs, I'm going to do great business. Like, everybody's going to want their home fumigated, aren't they? But when we went to the hospital and saw all those scores of people jerking around like Mexican jumping-beans and bringing up all of that blood, and nobody knowing what the fuck to do to save them – I thought, man, this isn't funny. If that's what happens to you when you get bit by those bedbugs, I don't want to be going anywhere near them.'

339

He paused for a moment, shaking his head, and then he said, 'Dazey could be right, and that's what happened to Bobik. I think I'm going to go through Kleks's hair with a flea comb, just to make sure that he didn't pick any up.'

'How about waiting until we've eaten our pizzas?' I asked him.

That night, Mazey snored even more loudly than she had before. Not only that, she kept twisting herself up in her sheets and muttering to herself. I didn't go to sleep right away. I was too stressed after my discovery that morning of Maria Escamilla's body, crawling with blowflies, and I couldn't erase the picture from my mind of her young son's blue sneaker protruding from behind the couch. His name, it had turned out, was Feliciano, which means 'lucky'.

I sat up in bed for an hour with Rick's laptop, trying to find out more about Matchitehew and Megedagik and all of that stuff that Father Zapata had told me about the nuns of Loudun being possessed by demons.

According to the legends, Matchitehew was a young hunter who shared some of his meager bag of deer meat with a hungry stranger he met in the forest. The stranger was actually Wisakachek, a shape-shifting spirit who could transform himself into a wolf. In return for Matchitehew's generosity, Wisakachek endowed him with the same shape-shifting power that he had, so that on his hunting expeditions Matchitehew could become a wolf and catch many more deer than he could with his bow and arrows. The only condition was that in his wolf-like form he was not allowed to harm any humans.

It was the same old story, however. One day Matchitehew lost his temper with a friend, turned himself into a wolf and tore his friend apart. Wisakachek was furious and not only banished Matchitehew into the forest, but also took away his shape-shifting powers, so that he was an ordinary man by day and a mindless wolf by night. Some Native American tribes call Matchitehew the Father of Wolves – in fact, the very first werewolf.

I found out, too, that the name Matchitehew means 'evil-hearted', which didn't surprise me – what with the b.s. he had told me about his father, Misquamacus, not being such a vengeful old wonder-worker after all.

I couldn't discover too much in the way of mythology about his brother Megedagik, except that he never gave his enemies any mercy and slaughtered them as painfully and viciously as he could. In Algonquin, his name simply means 'kills many'. One of his specialties was chopping off his victims' genitals and stuffing them down their throats until they choked. Now I began to understand what had happened to Father Zapata.

Whatever the legends said about them, both Matchitehew and Megedagik were the sons of Misquamacus, and whatever shamanistic powers they had, they had inherited them from him. Misquamacus had been in direct touch with the Great Old Ones, who had ruled the world in the time before time, and it was those ancient gods who had made him the most fearsome wonder-worker ever.

What I found ironic was that both Matchitehew's and Megedagik's names had been borrowed for heroes in sword-and-sorcery type video games. If only the geeky designers of those games had known how malevolent those two brothers really were, and how many real people they would massacre, all across America.

It was when I came to check up on the Loudun possessions, though, that everything really began to click into place. Father Zapata had told me that a nearby parish priest had been accused of being responsible for the nuns at the Ursuline convent becoming possessed by demons – but I soon realized that this dude had been much more than your garden-variety parish priest. He was wealthy, well-educated and very good-looking, apparently. After he'd been appointed to St-Pierre du Marché, he had affairs with several of the prettiest local girls and even made one of them pregnant.

In September of 1632, however, an apparition appeared in the corridors of the Ursuline convent in Loudun, and after it had appeared several more times, it was identified by the nuns as him. Soon afterward, the nuns started to show signs that they were possessed by demons – cursing God, screaming, barking and running around naked.

Even when prayers were said to prevent the parish priest's living spirit from entering the convent, he was alleged to have introduced more demons by throwing a bouquet of pink roses over the wall. That could explain the bunch of dead pink roses that Father Zapata had found under my bed.

The nuns picked up the roses and handed them around to each other, and they were immediately infected with evil. They began contorting their bodies, lifting up their habits to flaunt themselves to priests and masturbating in front of the altar with all kinds of objects, from bottles of holy water to pastry-rolling pins.

To cut a long seventeenth-century story short, the parish priest was charged by the church authorities with being a sorcerer and having sent demons to possess the nuns so that he could take advantage of them for his own sexual pleasure. He was locked up in prison, his body was shaved all over to see if the Devil had left any marks on him, and then he was tortured by having both of his legs slowly broken with wooden wedges. In spite of that, he refused to confess.

Finally, he was sentenced to death by being taken out to the public square in St Croix, hoisted up on to a scaffold and burned alive. Through the smoke and flames, however, he was seen to be praying, with what appeared to be a smile on his face, as if he had somehow outwitted all of his persecutors.

At the end of the article about the Loudun possessions there was a contemporary engraving of this parish priest. As soon as I saw it, I felt that same cold creepy sensation that I'd felt when that faceless nun had first appeared in my bedroom. He looked identical to the gray-bearded man in the gray suit that I'd seen with the nuns

343

at LAX. There was no question about it. It was him.

Now it all started to fit together, or at least I thought it did. Misquamacus had deliberately burned himself alive so that he could be reborn in the future. This parish priest had also been burned alive – and if there were any Roman Catholic rituals that were similar to the one Misquamacus had used, and the parish priest had recited them as he burned, then he, too, could have been reborn. That would have accounted for the smile on his face as he was consumed by the flames. *He knew that he was coming back.*

He could well have been reborn as the child that Sister Marysia was carrying on her back. Misquamacus had been reborn in almost exactly the same way, on Karen Tandy's neck. Those two births had been too damned similar to be a co-incidence. So what if Misquamacus and the parish priest subscribed to two totally different belief systems? God is the same, whatever you call him. Water is made up of the same elements, all over the world, whether it's *aqua* or *woda* or *nibi*. Death is the same, in any religion, and so is reincarnation.

I stared at the picture of the parish priest for a long time, listening to Mazey mumbling and snorting. *I know you*, I thought. *I know who you are now.* The caption beneath the picture said that his name was Father Urbain Grandier.

I closed the laptop and laid it carefully down on the floor beside my bed. I sat there in darkness, listening to the echo of sirens outside and thinking about what I had just found out. What

344

had Matchitehew said to me? *Now we have* your *spirits on our side.* Father Grandier was here, or his direct descendant, at the very least, and if Father Grandier had been the child of Sister Marysia, and was still possessed by Gressil, the demon of infection, then everything that Matchitehew had warned me about made sense.

Unbelievable sense, maybe. Insane sense. But sense. If there was one thing I had learned from my encounters with Misquamacus, it was that extreme acts of evil are always committed for a reason, no matter how deluded that reason may be, and when you start bringing religion into the mix, the delusion index goes sky-high.

It made sense to me that Matchitehew and Megedagik had enlisted Father Grandier to help them to take their revenge on the colonists who had taken their country from them and murdered their people. From the Pilgrim Fathers onward, so much of the invasion of America had been done in the name of religion, and Father Grandier wanted his revenge on that religion, too. They both had a score to settle with Christianity.

By now I was so bushed that I wasn't thinking straight. I lay down and dragged the sheet over my shoulder and closed my eyes. Exhausted as I was, though, it took me a long time to fall asleep. I kept seeing nuns who bubbled up to the ceiling like thick black oil gushers, grew horns, and stared at me with smoldering red eyes. I kept hearing whispering and prayers and the shuffling of sandals on a cold convent floor. I smelled smoke and burning firewood and incense.

* * *

345

I had been asleep for less than twenty minutes when I was woken by a loud thumping sound, and then a furious scratching. This was followed by another thump, and then another, and more scratching. Then I heard a weird, distorted howling, like the wind that blows down a subway tunnel long before a train arrives.

I sat up and switched on the bedside lamp. Mazey was still tangled up in her sheets, and she hadn't stirred. I climbed out of bed and went to the bedroom door, just in time to see Rick coming out of his bedroom, wearing nothing but a droopy gray pair of shorts. He switched on the living-room light.

The howling noise was going on and on, and every few seconds there was another thump and even more scratching.

Rick squinted at me, bleary-eyed. 'The *fuck* is that? Sounds like a fucking coyote!'

We could hear now that the noise was coming from the back door.

Rick returned to his bedroom, and I could hear him say something to Dazey. A few seconds later he reappeared carrying a black Smith & Wesson Governor revolver. 'OK, Wizard? Now you're going to see an *ex*-coyote!'

'Just be careful, will you?' I told him. 'The last time I saw you fire a gun was in my apartment, that time you blasted my coffee machine to pieces!'

'I was drunk then. Now I'm sober. Pretty much, anyhow!'

I followed him into the kitchen. He might have had a gun, but there was another almighty thump

346

and a scrabbling noise against the back door that sounded like claws, followed by a howl that made the back of my neck prickle, and we both stopped right where we were. I suddenly thought: *Matchitehew, the father of wolves. A man by day, but a wolf by night. Jesus Christ, what if it's him, and he's tracked me down because I didn't do what he ordered me to do and warn everybody that the sickness was coming?*

Another thump, and another, and more scrabbling, and the howling grew higher and even more eerie.

'Switch on the light,' said Rick. 'If it sees us, it'll probably get scared and run off.'

'I didn't think coyotes were afraid of humans.'

'Well, how the fuck should I know? I never had one scratching at my door before, trying to get in. I was brought up in the city, just like you.'

Thump – thump – thump! It was the sound of an animal's body hurling itself repeatedly against the door. I guessed that the door was probably strong enough to keep it out, but all the same the plaster around the frame was cracking, and one of the door panels had split.

Rick raised his revolver and cocked it. He edged toward the door, his knees slightly bent, his left hand held up as if he half-expected the animal to come bursting in.

I don't know what unnerved me the most: the repeated thumping, or the scrabbling of claws, or that endless, hollow howling.

Rick had almost reached the door when, without any warning, the animal reared up on its hind legs and glared in through the window. Its pointed ears were sticking up erect, and its eyes gleamed yellow. When it saw us, its lips peeled back and it snarled at us, baring its teeth.

My God, I thought. *It is a wolf. It must be Matchitehew.* But Rick said, 'Holy shit, Wizard, it's Bobik!'

I tried to see through the window, but there was too much reflected glare from the living-room light behind us, and the animal dropped out of sight. Rick turned to me and said, 'I can't believe it! It's Bobik!'

'It can't be Bobik! Bobik's dead. We buried him ourselves.'

'Maybe he wasn't quite dead and he managed to dig himself up.'

'He was *dead*, Rick, for Christ's sake! He suffered from a massive loss of blood.'

Rick stood still for a moment, thinking. The thumping and the scratching and the howling had stopped, and now the night was quiet again, except for the cicadas chirruping and the wailing of sirens. 'I'm sure it's Bobik. Maybe he didn't lose as much blood as we thought he did. I mean, how much blood does your average German Shepherd have in him? Do you know? I'm damned if I do!'

We waited. Whether it was Bobik or not, the animal had stopped flinging itself at the door and howling.

Rick said, 'If it's Bobik, we can't just leave him out there. He'll be hungry and thirsty, and maybe he needs some medical attention, too.'

'If he's survived being buried alive, Rick, I'm sure he'll survive until morning.'

'I'll switch on the yard light. Maybe we can see him.'

'Rick—' I didn't think that switching on the outside light was a very good idea, especially if it wasn't Bobik out there, but Matchitehew in the guise of a wolf, or even a mangy old coyote. The trouble was, I couldn't really think of a reason to stop him. I had to agree. If it was Bobik, then leaving him out there would be heartless.

Rick switched on the light and peered out of the window into the back yard, shading his eyes with his hand to cut out the reflection.

'Is he out there?' I asked him.

'Mmm . . . not that I can see. Maybe he's decided to call it a night.' He turned the key in the door and bent down to shoot back the bolt.

'Rick . . . be careful.'

Rick held up his revolver. 'This baby can stop anything, Wizard. It's loaded with point four ten shotshell, muzzle velocity eight hundred fifty feet per second.'

'All the same, be careful.'

Rick eased the door open and peered out into the yard. I stayed well behind him. Quite apart from the fact that I wasn't at all sure that the animal that had been thumping and scratching and howling at the door *was* Bobik, I didn't want to risk getting between Rick and some maddened coyote if he was firing shotgun shells with his usual wild abandon. He hadn't only blasted my coffee machine in New York, he had shot three large holes in my ceiling and narrowly missed killing Mrs Greenbaum, my *opstairsikeh*.

Apart from the usual noises of the night, there

349

was nothing. No howling, no growling, no snuffling. Rick stepped outside and circled around the yard, ducking down now and again to check beneath the shrubbery.

'Nah,' he announced. 'I'm pretty sure it's taken a powder.'

He was still crouched down, trying to see beneath the shadows of a boxwood bush, when there was a screeching howl like every werewolf movie you ever saw, and the animal came bursting out of the bushes and ran straight across the yard toward the open kitchen door.

It bounded up the steps and leaped toward me before I had time to dodge aside. It was Bobik, his hair thickly matted with blood and mud, but this wasn't the gentle, obedient Bobik that he had been before he had died, or supposedly died. His yellow eyes were staring, and his teeth were bared, and he hit me as hard as a sack of wet cement. I fell backward and sideways, jarring my shoulder against the kitchen table and knocking over one of the kitchen chairs.

Bobik was on top of me immediately, his claws digging into my chest, his spit spraying into my face. He was cold and filthy and incredibly heavy, and when I tried to lift myself up he went for me, sinking his teeth into my upraised arm and shaking it furiously from side to side. The pain was unbearable, and I shouted out, *'Gaaaahhh!'* and wrenched my arm out of his jaws, but I was immediately spattered in my own blood.

Next he went for my neck. I tried to beat him off, punching the top of his head again and again and pulling at his ears, but he seemed determined

350

to rip out my throat. I felt his hard, chilly nose against the side of my face, and his teeth tore into my ear lobe. At the same time he continued to claw at my chest and my thighs, and he stepped between my legs, which made me shout out again.

I couldn't hold him off much longer. His wet muzzle was lungeing at my neck again and again, and twice I felt his teeth tearing at my skin. I thought: *Jesus, he's determined to kill me, and he's going to succeed.* I had read somewhere that you could stop a mad dog by grasping both of its front legs and yanking them outward in opposite directions at ninety degrees, which would burst its heart, but I was too busy struggling to keep Bobik away from my neck to try anything like that – apart from which, he was much too aggressive and much too heavy. It was like he was possessed.

Suddenly, I became aware that Rick was kneeling down close beside me. *'Hold still!'* he was shouting, although Bobik was snarling so loudly that I could hardly hear him.

He seized one of Bobik's ears and pressed his black revolver against the side of his head. Bobik twisted his head around and tried to snap at his fingers, but Rick squeezed the trigger and the gun went off with a mind-stunning bang. Bobik's head exploded, with fragments of skull and hairy skin and brain spraying everywhere like warm gray custard – mostly into my face, by the feel of it.

Incredibly, with half of his head missing, Bobik still didn't stop blindly attacking me. He had lost his eyes and his nose and his upper jaw, and his lower jaw was dangling, but he kept on jerking his neck up and down, trying to snag my neck with his remaining teeth, and he continued to rip at my chest and my legs just as viciously hard with his claws.

'Get him off me!' I wheezed. I was so winded by Bobik's weight that I could hardly get the words out. 'Sharky, for Christ's sake, *get him off me!*'

Rick fired again, into the side of Bobik's body this time. I felt the dog shudder with the impact as the shotgun pellets blew out his insides. But still he kept clawing at me, even if his leg movements were feebler, and spasmodic, and no longer seemed to be voluntary. Rick fired a third time, although I didn't hear the shot because I was totally deafened by now. This shot blasted off Bobik's pelvis with both of his back legs attached, and he finally dropped sideways on to the kitchen floor.

Rick gave me his hand and helped me on to my feet. I was plastered in blood and glutinous brain matter and tiny chips of bone.

'That was *crazy,* man,' said Rick, looking down at Bobik's body. 'One shot should have finished him off, easy.'

'Rick,' I said, 'he shouldn't have been alive at all.'

Dazey had come out the bedroom and was standing in the living room in her Minnie Mouse T-shirt, her hair all tangled. 'Rick – what's happened? Oh my God! What's happened? Is that *Bobik*?'

'What's left of him,' said Rick. He opened the

chamber of his revolver and shook out the empty shell casings. 'Don't know how in God's name he done it, but he dug himself out of the ground and came for the Wizard like a bat out of hell. To quote Meatloaf.'

Dazey looked around. 'Where's Kleks? He's not in his basket.'

'I don't know,' I told her. 'I don't remember seeing him when we first came in here.'

At that moment, Kleks appeared from behind the couch in the living room. He came to the kitchen door and looked at the bloody remains of his companion and let out a thin, sorrowful whine. I guessed he must have been frightened when he first heard Bobik thumping and scratching and howling, and he had slunk off into the living room to hide. I didn't say anything to Rick, but that reinforced my opinion that Bobik had been possessed by some spirit or other, maybe Matchitehew, the father of wolves. After all, he had ignored Rick and rushed straight at me. That made me suspect that Matchitehew and Megedagik were out to punish me now, for not having done what they wanted. Like they had told me, their tribal code of honor prevented them from personally harming anybody who had defeated their father Misquamacus, but that obviously didn't stop them from setting a dog on me, even a dead and resurrected dog.

'You're a mess,' Dazey told me. 'You'd better get yourself washed up. Rick – I'll help you clear up the kitchen.'

I think all of us were still in shock. Without another word between us I went to the bathroom

353

to take a shower, while Rick took out a khaki plastic trash bag and started to drop Bobik's body parts into it. Dazey filled up the kitchen sink with hot water and Astonish floor cleaner.

Kleks stayed by the door, his head cocked to one side, as if he couldn't understand what was happening. He wasn't the only one, I can tell you.

Twenty-Five

None of us really felt like going back to bed, but we were all exhausted and even if we couldn't sleep we decided that we needed the rest. It was still only 3:35 a.m., and we had no idea what kind of a situation we'd be facing tomorrow. Even Kleks crept back into his basket, although he hung his head over the side like a seasick sailor in a coracle, and it didn't look as if he was going to sleep either.

Because of the shots, we thought maybe that the cops would come knocking, but either our neighbors were unfazed by a little explosive night music, or the cops had their hands full with hundreds of people falling down sick on the city's sidewalks.

In spite of all of the noise and commotion, Mazey still hadn't woken up. Before I switched off the bedside lamp I leaned over to make sure that she was OK. She was perspiring so much that her hair was damp, and she was breathing quite quickly, as if she had been jogging. It was a hot night, though, and who could tell how many mojitos she was sleeping off?

I climbed back into bed and switched off the lamp. I could faintly hear Rick and Dazey talking for a while, and then there was silence. I took me a minute or two to realize that there was *silence*. No cicadas flexing their abdomens, no ambulance sirens, no traffic. Nothing.

355

At first I thought I must still be deaf from Rick's gun going off about two inches from my ear, but then I realized that I could clearly hear Mazey breathing and the rustling of her sheets as she kept turning over.

'*Mishkway*,' she murmured. At least that's what it sounded like.

I lay there listening. Her breathing had a slight catch in it, but I didn't think it was anything to worry about.

'*Mishkway*,' she repeated. Then, '*Soggy mass.*'

Oh well, I thought, *I've probably said stupider things in my sleep.* In fact I knew I had. Sandy had once told me that I recited some Walt Whitman poem about the stars but got it all wrong. '*Look'd up . . . in puffing silence . . . at the stars.*'

I closed my eyes, and I was right on the brink of falling down the rabbit hole when I heard Mazey wrestling with her sheets, and then her heels bumping on the floor. I opened my eyes again. There was a very long silence while I lay there listening, and she sat upright on the side of her bed, breathing very loudly through her nostrils.

After a while I said, 'Mazey? Are you OK?'

She didn't answer.

'Mazey?'

Still no answer, but now she stood up, lurched across to my bed and started to climb in beside me, all knees and elbows. She smelled strongly of alcohol and some musky Oriental-type perfume she always wore, and although she was so sweaty she felt freezing cold. Her T-shirt was soaked, and it had ridden right up under her breasts.

'*Mazey*,' I said, but she collapsed on top of me, and her forehead hit me right on the bridge of my nose. I saw stars for a moment, just like Walt Whitman, but then I managed to heave her over me and lay her down beside me.

I was reaching out for the bedside lamp when she convulsed, her back arching and her thigh-muscles shuddering and her fingers clenching and unclenching.

'*Get – get it—*' she began, through teeth that were tightly clamped together, but then she retched and a warm torrent poured out of her mouth, all over me.

I switched on the lamp and saw that I was covered in blood and the sheets were drenched in blood, too. Mazey was staring at me, white-faced, her mouth smothered in red like a zombie who has just looked up from eating somebody alive.

'Get it out of me, Wizard!' she gasped, and bubbles of blood popped between her lips. 'Please – *get it out of me!*'

I said, 'Mazey, I need to get you to a hospital, and fast!' even though I knew that all of the emergency rooms were overwhelmed with patients and there was probably nothing that any of them could do for Mazey, even if one of them would take her in. But what else could I do? Just watch her convulsing and vomiting up blood until she died, the same way that Father Zapata had died?

The bedroom door was flung open, and it was Rick, looking even more disheveled than he had before. 'Holy shit, Wizard!'

I don't know if his first impression was that he had surprised me right in the middle of murdering Mazey, but any doubts he might have had were quickly dispelled when she convulsed again and brought up another flood of blood.

'Holy *shit*, what's wrong with her?'

'I think it's the same sickness that killed Bobik,' I said. 'In fact, the same sickness that everybody's catching.'

'Harry, get it out of me! Get it out!' shrieked Mazey.

'What does she mean?' asked Rick. 'Get *what* out?'

It was then that Dazey came into the bedroom. 'Mazey! Oh my God! Harry, what's wrong with her?'

'It's this epidemic,' I told her. 'I don't know where she caught it from, but we need to get her some help, and quick. Where's the nearest ER?'

'Just call nine-one-one!' said Dazey breathlessly. 'Get her an ambulance!' She knelt down on the floor beside her sister and held her hands, in spite of all the blood. 'Hold on, Mazey! Hold on, darling! We're going to get you to a hospital, right now!'

I picked up my blood-smeared cellphone and punched out 911, although I didn't expect an answer and I didn't get one. After thirty seconds of listening to the ring tone, I looked across at Rick and shook my head.

Rick said, 'There won't be any ambulances free, Daze. You saw the news. Thousands of people are getting sick. I don't even know if we'll be able to get her into a hospital.'

'We can't let her die!' said Dazey. 'She's my kid sister! I always promised to take care of her. I promised mom!'

Mazey quaked yet again and brought up even more blood. 'Please,' she said, although she was so weak now that she could barely move her lips. 'Please get it *out*.'

Meanwhile, I had been tapping away at my cellphone, looking for the nearest ER. The Valley Presbyterian Hospital where Rick and I had spent the previous afternoon was probably the closest, but even then it had already been massively over-crowded. I guessed that Mazey might have more of a chance of being treated at Cedars-Sinai, on Beverly Boulevard, because it was so much larger.

'Get some clothes on, Sharky,' I told Rick. 'We'll take her to the hospital ourselves.'

I went into the bathroom, filled the basin with warm water and plunged a hand-towel into it, so that I could wipe off most of Mazey's blood. Then I roughly dried myself and went back into the bedroom to pull on a pair of jeans and a blue checkered shirt. Dazey was hugging Mazey, and it didn't look as if she had brought up any more blood. Rick appeared a few seconds later, all dressed in black, as usual.

'I'm coming too,' said Dazey. 'If you take her out to the van, I won't be two seconds.'

I pulled one of the blankets off Mazey's bed, and we wrapped her up in it.

She lifted one arm feebly and said, 'Wizard . . . *please* . . .'

'It's OK, Mazey,' I said, speaking close to her

359

ear. 'Everything's going to be fine. Just hang on in there, OK? Just hang on in there.'

Her eyes rolled up so that only the whites were showing, and she let out a terrible creaking groan. 'Please, Wizard . . . *get it out of me*. Please. It's killing me.'

There was nothing else that I could say to her. Together, Rick and I carried her out to his van, with me holding her under her arms and Rick holding her legs. We laid her down in the back, amongst all of Rick's bug-spraying equipment, and we tucked door-sealant strips either side of her so that she wouldn't get flung around too much when we were driving to the hospital.

A few seconds later, Dazey came hurrying out of the house, wearing a white T-shirt and denim shorts and carrying a bath towel. She climbed into the van and sat down next to her sister. 'Mazey?' she said. 'I'm here now, baby. We're going to take you to the ER and get you fixed up.' Then she turned to Rick and said, 'Let's get going, Rick. I'm not going to lose her, I mean that.'

We backed out of the driveway with smoke coming out from our tires, speeding south-west and then due south.

No wonder I had heard nothing but silence when I was lying in my bed. The streets were almost completely deserted, with only six or seven stray vehicles driving around, and they all appeared to be driving pretty aimlessly, as if they had no idea where they were going. As we turned into Santa Monica Boulevard and headed west, I saw three people lying on the sidewalk outside

360

Michelle's Donut House, a man and two women. Blood was glistening on the concrete all around them, and the man was convulsing and bending his spine like a caterpillar.

Rick slowed down, but I heard Mazey retching again in the back of the van.

'We can't, Rick,' I told him. 'I don't even think that we can save Mazey, let alone anybody else.'

One of the women lying on the sidewalk must have seen us, because she raised one hand and attempted to wave. Rick looked at me, and I looked back at him, and then he put his foot down on the gas and we sped off along Santa Monica at more than sixty miles an hour. There was no other traffic around, so we drove through one red light after another.

It took us no more than ten minutes to reach Cedars-Sinai. On a normal day, I guess it would have taken us more than twice as long. But as we drew up at the hospital, we could see that the parking lot was jammed up with scores of vehicles, most of them parked every which way, as if their owners had arrived in a hurry. Outside the entrance to the emergency room, there must have been twenty or thirty ambulances, all with their lights flashing.

'Look at all those busses,' said Rick as he pulled into the side of the road. He managed to find a tight space behind a Winnebago with blood smears across it and park with two wheels on the sidewalk. 'Why aren't they out there, picking up more people?'

'Maybe the ER has run out of room,' I suggested.

'Yeah, well, let's see.'

He opened the back of the van and together we lifted Mazey out. The bath towel that Dazey had brought with her was half-soaked in blood, and there were spatters of blood all over Dazey's T-shirt.

'Oh God, I think she's dying,' said Dazey as she awkwardly climbed down. 'She keeps saying, "Get it out, get it out," but I don't understand what she means.'

'Let's just get her inside,' said Rick. 'What she needs is a blood transfusion, and fast.'

Even as we carried her across the parking lot, Mazey started to convulse again, twisting and jerking and kicking her legs, and it was all that we could do not to drop her. As we approached the entrance to the emergency room, we found that the sidewalk outside was scarlet and sticky and criss-crossed with hundreds of footprints.

Two weary-looking security guards were standing outside, and one of them raised his hand to stop us. 'ER's full to capacity, sir, I'm real sorry.'

'Oh, really?' I retorted. 'So what are we supposed to do? She's dying.'

'Hundreds of people are dying, sir. Our medical staff are doing everything they can, but they just can't cope with any more patients.'

'So what do you suggest we do? Take her straight to the nearest mortician?'

'I'm sorry, sir. I honestly wish I could help you. You could try the Olympia Medical Center on West Olympic, or maybe St Vincent's on West Third Street.'

'I saw both of those hospitals on the news,' put

in Dazey. 'They were turning people away as early as yesterday evening.'

'I'm afraid that we're having to do the same,' said the security guard. He was young and Hispanic with a fuzzy black moustache, and apart from sounding tired he also sounded genuinely upset that he wasn't allowed to let us in. He reminded me of Marcos Hernandez' son Felipe, and I felt really sorry for him.

Rick, however, was not in a sympathetic mood. He drew back the left-hand side of his black denim jacket and said, 'You see this, pal? This is a special pass that lets us in anyplace we want to go. Right now we want to bring my girlfriend's sister into the emergency room and see if we can't manage to get her some life-saving treatment. This special pass says we can. *Capiche*?'

The young security guard looked down at the black patterned grip of Rick's Smith & Wesson Governor, which was protruding from his studded black biker's belt. Then he turned to his fellow security guard, who was middle-aged and gray-haired. The older man shrugged, as if to say, *What the hell?* There were no police around, and there was little chance of finding any in the middle of this crisis. In any case, the chances of Mazey surviving were practically zero, so what difference was it going to make *where* she died? Under these circumstances, why argue with a sour-looking man with a powerful handgun?

The young security guard opened one of the side doors for us, and we carried Mazey inside. As we crossed the reception area our shoes made Scotch-tape noises on the bloodstained floor.

There was nobody behind the reception desk, and so we followed the sign saying 'Emergency Room' and continued to carry Mazey along the corridor.

Even before we reached the Emergency Room I felt that we were wading our way through the aftermath of a Civil War battle, with people lying on both sides of the corridor on bloodstained blankets. Some of them were clearly dead already, because their eyes were staring blindly at the ceiling and the blood was drying on their chins. What was really scary was the expression on their faces, these dead people. Their mouths were stretched open, as if they had died in mid-scream. You would have thought that they had died of sheer terror instead of disease.

We carried Mazey into the center of the room, and now we had to be careful not to step on anyone. The screaming and retching was deafening, and there was a constant irregular drumbeat as people in convulsions thumped against the floor. There must have been over three hundred patients crowded in that room, and the smell of blood and vomit was almost unbreathable.

A Korean nurse in a bloodstained uniform approached us, shaking her head.

'I can't do anything for her, I'm sorry. You can see the situation.'

'Aren't there any doctors around?' Rick demanded.

'Every doctor is tied up with other patients. It was first come, first served. The kindest thing you can do is take her home.'

'She's dying,' said Dazey. 'Can't you do anything?'

The nurse continued to shake her head. 'I will be truthful with you, ma'am. We don't even know what this sickness is yet, let alone how we can treat it.'

I said to Rick, 'I'm going to have to put her down for a while, Sharks. My back is killing me.'

We lowered Mazey on to the floor. She had stopped convulsing for a while, and her eyes were closed. But when I looked around the emergency room I could see plenty of people like that, so it obviously didn't mean that she was getting any better.

I did, however, catch a glimpse of something else. Over on the far side of the room, half-hidden by the curtain that had been drawn across a cubicle, I saw a nun.

'What's wrong, Wizard?' asked Rick. 'You look like you just seen a ghost.'

'There's a nun over there,' I told him.

'A *nun*? So what? People are dying in here. She's probably giving them the last rites or hearing their confessions or somesuch.'

I took a few steps to the left, making sure that I didn't tread on any of the people lying all around me. Only six feet away, a woman vomited a fountain of blood that splashed all over herself and everybody lying around her, but they were all too weak to wipe it away. Now, however, I could see the nun more clearly. In fact, there were two nuns, and both of them wore black, with black scarves draped over their heads so that their faces were concealed.

I went back to Rick and said, 'There's two of them.'

'So there's two of them.'

'But it's *them*. They're the ones who are spreading it, this disease. Who were the last guests at the Elite Suites, before they got infested with bedbugs? Nuns. Who were the last guests at the Royaltie Inn, before they got infested? Nuns. What happened to the housekeeper and her son? What happened to Bobik? Now Mazey's caught it. It all ties up, Rick.'

Again, I was tempted to tell him all about the nuns who had appeared in my cottage in Coral Gables, and all about Matchitehew and Megedagik, but Rick was a natural skeptic, and I reckoned that I had told him enough to prove my point.

'I think we should take Mazey home,' said Dazey. Her cheeks were streaked with tears. 'If she's going to die anyhow, I don't want her dying in a hellhole like this.'

'OK,' said Rick. 'It looks like we don't have much of a choice, do we?'

We were about to pick Mazey up when I saw a tall ash-blonde woman in a white lab coat appear through the double doors at the end of the room. She was wearing spectacles and carrying a clipboard, and she had a businesslike air about her, as if she might be in charge. I said to Rick, 'Wait up just a moment. That babe looks like she's a doctor.'

I hip-hopped my way over the patients lying on the floor until I reached her. She was talking to two of the nurses about taking blood samples,

366

and I waited patiently beside her until she had finished.

She was already turning to walk away when I said, 'Doctor?'

She took off her glasses and frowned at me. 'I'm not a doctor, I'm afraid. I'm only here to carry out research.'

'Oh. Pardon me. It's just that my friend's girl-friend's sister, she's caught this disease, whatever it is.'

'I'm very sorry to hear that. We're working on it intensively, I can assure you, but so far we haven't come up with a cure. We don't really know how it's spreading, either, although we have some ideas.'

'Bedbugs,' I said.

She looked at me narrowly. '*Bedbugs?* What makes you think that?'

'I don't think you'd believe me if I told you.'

'No, go on. Why do you think it's bedbugs?'

'Because my friend runs this exterminating business, and twice now we've been called out to bedbug infestations – I mean really major infestations, thousands of them. And after we went out to treat the second infestation, one of my friend's sniffer dogs got sick and died the same way these people are dying, bringing up blood and having fits and everything. The hotel's housekeeper and her son, they both got sick, and they died, too. Now my friend's girlfriend's sister has it, and we don't know what the hell to do to save her.'

'Just a minute,' the woman said. 'Why are you so sure that it was the *bedbugs* that made them sick?'

367

'Because of the nuns.'

'*What?*' she said, and I never saw anybody turn so white.

'Both times, the guests who stayed in those hotels before they got infested were nuns.'

The woman grasped my upper arm, so tightly that it was almost painful. 'Let's find a room where we can talk,' she said.

I turned back to Rick and Dazey and lifted my hand with my fingers spread out, to indicate that I was going to be away for five minutes. Rick gave me a thumb's-up in acknowledgement, and then the woman in the lab coat led me through the double doors and into a corridor, still gripping my arm.

She opened two doors before she found a small unoccupied office with a desk and two chairs and heaps of medical reports. She switched on the light and said, '*Nuns.*'

'That's right,' I said cautiously. 'Nuns.'

'You don't have any actual proof, though, that it was nuns who were carrying the bedbugs?'

I hesitated for a moment. Then I said, 'Listen, doctor—'

'I'm not a doctor. I'm a professor of epidemiology. My name's Anna Grey, and I'm working with a team who are trying to isolate this virus and find a way to inoculate people against it. I came to Cedars-Sinai this morning to take some fresh blood samples.'

I looked up at the clock on the wall. It was two minutes shy of ten after five. She saw me looking and said, 'I couldn't sleep. Besides, this is very, very urgent. I don't have to tell *you* that, do I?'

I said, 'What I'm going to tell you, you're not going to believe a single word of it, but I have to tell you anyhow, because I'm sure that it's the cause of this sickness. My name's Erskine, by the way. Harry Erskine. I'm a kind of a therapist.'

'Which particular field?'

'Personal growth, I guess you'd call it. But that's neither here nor there. The most important thing I need to tell you about is these nuns.'

I told her everything. I told her all about the nuns, and the roses that had been pushed through my window, and Father Zapata biting off his manhood, and Loudun Syndrome. I told her all about Misquamacus and my struggles with him in the past. I told her about Matchitehew and Megedagik.

To my growing amazement, she sat there and listened to all of this without saying a word. In fact, she nodded now and again, as if she actually understood what I was talking about. Like, this was a leading medical expert, in the middle of trying to deal with one of the most disastrous epidemics to sweep across America since Spanish flu, and yet she was prepared to take the time out to hear me give her one of the most bizarre stories that anybody could have invented.

'You know what finally convinced me?' I told her. 'Misquamacus and this parish priest were both reincarnated in almost exactly the same way. They were both burned alive. They were both reborn on the back of some innocent woman's neck.'

Anna said slowly, 'What was his name? This parish priest.'

'Does it matter? I'm not sure that I remember.'

'Please, try.'

I stared at her hard. 'Do you *believe* what I just told you?'

'Try and remember his name, if you can. Otherwise we can always Google it.'

I closed my eyes for a moment, and then I opened them again and said, 'Gander. That's it. Something like that, anyhow.'

'It couldn't have been "Grandier"?'

'That's it, Grandier. How did you know that?'

'Because he's here. He's here *now*. You're absolutely right. He's come back, just like your Native American wonder-worker came back. And, yes, I *do* believe you, Mr Erskine. I believe every word. The nuns have appeared to me too, and Misquamacus' sons.'

'*You've* seen them?' I have to admit that I was stupefied. 'You're actually telling me that you've seen them?'

She nodded again. 'They warned me, just like they warned you. Only, they didn't tell me to spread the word about this sickness. They told me that I mustn't try to find a cure for it.'

Now it was my turn to sit and listen while Anna explained how her partner David had died and how he had spoken to her after he was supposed to be dead. She explained how the nun had appeared in the morgue, and cursed her, and assaulted her. She told me about the bedbugs that had infested her bed, and how they had turned into one monster bedbug, and how the two exterminators who had come to her apartment had been killed. She told me how David had

370

reappeared, and how she had pushed him off her balcony. She was supposed to be talking to the police about that later, but there had been no body in his suit, only ash, and the police had more important things to worry about, right at the moment, than ash.

When she had finished, we just sat there and looked at each other.

'Why *us*?' said Anna. 'Why have they appeared to you and me, and nobody else? Not so far as we know, anyhow.'

'Well, I know why they appeared to *me*, because they told me,' I said. 'They want to drive us out of their land, us palefaces, the same way that we drove *them* out, with diseases that they had no immunity to. But they want us to know *why* we're being driven out. What's the point of getting your revenge on somebody if they don't realize it's you who's doing it and what you're doing it for?'

'But you said they tried to kill you, with that dog?'

'It could be that they were just trying to scare me into getting on with it and doing what they wanted. Giving me a kick up the rear end, so to speak.'

Anna said, 'You don't know what a relief it is, Mr Erskine, talking to you. I was sure that I was going mad.'

'Call me Harry, please. If we're *both* being haunted by nuns and Native American spirits, we might as well be on first-name terms. But what about this Grandier character?'

'I think what your poor priest Father Zapata said about him was probably right. Father Surin

371

passed the demon Gressil on to him, after he was reborn, and Gressil is the demon of infection. David said that "demon" is simply another name for "virus", which of course is true. If somebody got sick in the Middle Ages, people blamed possession by Satan, or one of Satan's minions. Misquamacus' sons have somehow gotten together with Grandier, in whatever dimension it is that spirits exist in, and between them they're looking for their revenge.'

'Me – I've run into this kind of supernatural stuff before,' I said. 'But did you ever think that *you* would? Like, you're a scientist, and science is logical, isn't it? Some of it strains the brain – well, it strains *my* brain, anyhow, especially that God-particle stuff – but at least it generally makes sense.'

'Viruses are very far from logical, Harry. Viruses are very perverse, and sometimes you can almost believe they have a mind of their own.'

'But why do you think they picked *you* to appear to, these nuns? Why are they warning *you* off, instead of some other eppy-deema-lollogist?'

'I don't know for sure, but since you've been talking about those two sons of Misquamacus, I've been wondering about the Scalping Virus.'

'I heard about that. That was some kind of sickness when some people in the Midwest went bald, wasn't it, like they'd been scalped?'

'Exactly that. And it was mainly me who devised an antiviral drug that stopped it in its boots.'

I didn't like to correct her and say 'tracks', and

372

so I just said, 'You think that might have something to do with your being warned off from trying to cure *this* virus?'

'It could well have. The Scalping Virus wasn't difficult to kill off. It was quite an old-fashioned virus, if you understand what I mean. It didn't seem to have ever been exposed to any of the latest antivirals, not even tamiflu, so it hadn't mutated to have any resistance to them.'

'I see what you're driving at,' I told her. 'It could have been the brothers' first shot at spreading an epidemic among the palefaces, but it all came to nothing because you knocked it on the head. That's why they went to Grandier to find a disease that wouldn't be so easy for us to cure, and that's why they warned you not to try.'

'So why didn't they simply kill me? Why didn't they give *me* the disease, like they gave it to David?'

'If you defeat them fair and square, Anna, they *won't* kill you, just like they won't kill me. It's part of their tribal lore. And I'm guessing now that you *did* defeat them, by curing their scalping disease, so you're untouchable. By them, at least. It sounds like they could still send your David to do their dirty work for them.'

Anna said, 'This is like a nightmare, isn't it? It's so crazy that it must be true. And all of those people are dying out there. That's no nightmare. That's reality.'

'I saw two nuns out there. You need to get your security after them.'

'You're sure they weren't bona fide nuns?'

'Short of lifting up their habits to see if they

373

have bedbugs crawling up and down their legs, I have no way of telling.'

'All right,' said Anna. 'I'll have a word with security.'

I stood up. 'I'd better go see how Mazey's doing.'

'I'm afraid to tell you that she's probably going to die,' said Anna.

'Yes,' I said. 'I know.'

'Can you come down to the Public Health laboratory in Downey later today? It's a lot to ask, under the circumstances, but I think we need to talk more about this, and I'd very much like you to meet my colleague Epiphany and tell her what you just told me.'

'You think it will help?'

'I'm sure it will. It's difficult enough understanding how a virus attacks the human body. It's even more difficult understanding why.'

We shook hands. I have to say it was one of the strangest meetings that I'd ever had in my life, and one of the most coincidental, but maybe it wasn't really a coincidence after all. We were both being controlled by influences that were very much stronger than we were. If my cards hadn't all turned black, I would have told my own fortune, but maybe that had happened because I wasn't supposed to know what it was.

Twenty-Six

We carried Mazey out of the hospital and drove her back home. What else could we do? She was dying, and at least she would die with people around her to keep her as comfortable as possible and tell her that they loved her.

She was so weak when we lifted her on to her bed that she couldn't lift up her head, although now and again she twitched and retched and brought up a tablespoonful of blood. Dazey sat beside her stroking her forehead and wiping her mouth with a damp towel whenever she needed it.

Kleks came into the bedroom and sat at the end of the bed looking sorrowful, in the way that only dogs can look sorrowful.

I went into the living room and said to Rick, 'Is it OK if I borrow your van?'

'What for?'

'That doctor woman wants me to go down to her research laboratory in Downey. She thinks I might be able to help her out.'

'What, today?'

'Yes, today. It's urgent, Rick. The sooner she finds out how to kill this virus, the more lives she's going to save.'

'I'll drive you there,' said Rick. He looked into the bedroom. 'I don't want to watch Mazey die.'

'What about Dazey?'

375

'She'll manage. She's tough. Besides, she has a good friend next door if it all gets too much, Veronica.'

Rick went into the bedroom and talked to Dazey. I couldn't hear what they were saying, but I saw Dazey nodding and laying a hand on his arm as if to reassure him that she was going to be all right. He may have been her friend and her lover, but she and Mazey had grown up together, and this was a time when they really needed to be close.

We climbed into the van and backed out of the sloping driveway with smoke coming out from under the tires.

It was a hot, clear day and very quiet. In fact, the only indication there was a deadly virus sweeping across the city was that it *was* so quiet. There was scarcely any traffic, apart from a few stray cars that didn't look as if their drivers had much idea of where they were going and occasional ambulances and squad cars screaming past us. The streets were almost deserted, with hardly any pedestrians, even on Hollywood Boulevard, and the sidewalks were covered with dried blood, like maroon varnish, from people who had collapsed before they'd managed to make it home.

'This disease scares the shit out of me,' said Rick. 'What am I going to do if Dazey gets it?'

'Let's just take it one step at a time,' I told him. 'If fate throws a knife at you, you can either seize it by the blade or by the handle.'

Rick nodded, but after he'd been driving for a few minutes longer, he said, 'What the fuck does that mean?'

'I don't know. But it always makes my old ladies happy.'

It took us about a half-hour to reach Downey. The Public Health laboratory was located on Erickson Avenue, a dull-looking single-story red-brick building with a gray shingled roof. As Rick parked his shiny bug-covered van outside the entrance, I could see people in lab coats staring at us out of the windows. We had only started to climb the steps to the entrance when a uniformed security guard came out and held up his hand to stop us.

'Help you, gentlemen?'

'We've been asked to come here by Professor Grey. Well, I have. My name's Harry Erskine, and this is my friend Rick Beamer.'

The security guard clicked on his r/t and said, 'Security here. Two guys here say that Professor Grey invited them here. Name of—?'

'Erskine,' I repeated. 'Harry Erskine.'

The security guard listened and nodded, and then he said, 'Follow me. I'll fix you up with identity badges.' He sounded genuinely put out that he hadn't been told to throw us off the premises.

Once we had pinned on our badges, he led us with squelchy rubber-soled shoes along a shiny waxed corridor. Through successive windows, I could see people in glasses and lab coats staring at microscope monitors and holding up test tubes. It was almost like a movie set for a film about a research laboratory.

When we reached the very end door, he knocked and opened it for us. 'Professor Grey? Your visitors.'

377

It was gloomy inside the laboratory because the blinds were drawn down, and the only light came from three computer screens. Anna was sitting on the opposite side of the room, frowning at what I assumed was a microscope, although it was completely unlike the microscopes we used to have in science lessons at high school. Beside her, a tall black woman was taking a tray of test tubes out of a refrigerator.

'Harry,' said Anna, standing up and coming across to greet us. 'I'm so pleased you've come.'

'This is Rick,' I told her. 'It's Rick's partner's sister who's sick, so he knows what this is all about.'

'I'm so sorry,' said Anna. 'How is she?'

'Just about as sick as it's possible to be,' said Rick. 'I don't think she's going to be with us much longer. That's if she hasn't left us already.'

Anna beckoned the black girl to come over and join us. 'Harry, this is Epiphany. She's been working with me on the Meramac School virus and this bedbug virus, too. I want you to tell her everything that you told me – about the nuns, about the Native American wonder-workers, everything.'

'Anna's told me most of it,' said Epiphany. 'All the same, I'd really like to hear it from you.'

She was taller than I was, Epiphany, but she was very pretty, with feline eyes and glossy crimson lips and her hair braided with multi-coloured beads. I don't suppose I should have been taking any notice, under the circumstances, but she was so full-breasted that the top three buttons of her lab coat were straining.

378

'Have you had any breakfast?' asked Anna. 'How about some coffee?'

'I could murder a cup of coffee,' said Rick. 'Black, with six sugars. No, make it eight. My energy level's at an all-time low.'

Anna went back to her microscope, while Epiphany started to prepare slides from the test tubes that she had taken out of the fridge. I stood beside her at her workbench and told her all about the sons of Misquamacus and the nuns. It wasn't easy, because we both had to wear surgical masks and my voice was muffled, which meant that I had to stand very close to her. She smelled of some very arousing perfume.

'It's almost incredible,' said Epiphany, when I had finished. 'If Anna hadn't had the same experience as you, I never would have believed it.'

A young girl assistant brought us a tray of coffee and a plate of cookies. Anna raised the blinds, and we sat down together and talked.

'I've been thinking,' I said. 'I'm beginning to wonder if there isn't some kind of a parallel between the way I first beat Misquamacus and the way you cured the Scalping Virus.'

'I don't follow you,' said Anna.

'Well, Misquamacus called on Native American spirits to get his revenge on the white man. I had a friend who was an Indian shaman, Singing Rock, and he explained to me that every rock and tree and animal and body of water has its own spirit, which is called a manitou. Misquamacus concentrated the energy of those manitous against us and used them to summon up the forces who created the Native Americans in the first place,

379

the Great Old Ones. But what *we* did was call on the spirits that exist in computer servers and motor vehicle engines and airplanes and all kinds of modern technology – and those modern manitous were a hundred times more powerful than the manitous you can call up from rocks and trees and muskrats. In fact, there's more spiritual energy in a *cellphone* than there is in a muskrat.

'Every time we create something, we put part of our soul and our intellect in it, and we give it a manitou. Misquamacus was trying to beat us with manitous that were nearly four hundred years out of date. You can't beat a guided missile with a bow and arrow.'

'I still don't see what you're getting at,' said Anna.

'Matchitehew and Megedagik tried to wipe us out by using the Scalping Virus. But you said yourself that the Scalping Virus was behind the times, biologically speaking. It hadn't mutated to resist modern drugs, so it wasn't too hard for you to find a cure for it.'

'It wasn't *easy*,' said Anna. 'It was so unlike most of the viruses we have to deal with today. It was like trying to cure the Black Death. But once I'd realized how archaic it was, I was able to devise an antiviral for it comparatively quickly.'

'OK – so that's why Matchitehew and Megedagik went to Grandier to help them. Grandier's possessed by Gressil, and Gressil is the demon of infection. Gressil was able to give them a virus which could shrug off any antiviral drug, ancient or modern. Maybe Gressil *is* the virus, from what you've told me.'

'I still don't see how this helps us. We've made a start on isolating the bedbug virus, but its structure and the way it replicates is absolutely baffling. I've never come across anything like it.'

'Maybe you can't find a state-of-the-art drug to beat it,' I said. 'But how about a state-of-the-art virus?'

'You're talking about the *Meramac School* virus?' said Epiphany. 'Are you seriously suggesting we use it as a *cure*?'

'It makes some kind of sense,' said Anna. 'The Meramac School virus makes its sufferers seriously ill, but the bedbug virus is one hundred percent fatal. We've seen already that the Meramac School virus attacks and destroys every other virus it comes into contact with, including type-A flu and avian flu, and even previous mutations of itself. If we can get it to destroy the bedbug virus, all we need to do is carry on trying to find an antiviral that will persuade it to destroy itself – to commit suicide, so to speak – and I think we're getting very close to it.'

'So – we use a virus to kill a virus,' said Epiphany. 'Dog eat dog. Or at least, new dog eats old dog.'

'It's very risky,' said Anna. 'There's no doubt that if we inject BV-1 sufferers with the Meramac School virus, a high proportion of them will die anyway, and *we* will have killed them.'

Rick sniffed and said, 'Me, personally – if I was faced with the choice of having some chance of living, or no damn chance at all, then I know which I'd choose.'

As we sat there talking and drinking coffee, we heard a rumble of thunder in the distance. Epiphany looked toward the windows and said, 'Sounds like a storm's brewing, doesn't it?'

Rick's cell rang, and he answered it. 'Dazey? Hi, sweetheart. How is she? OK. Yes. OK. I won't be more than a half-hour, I promise you.' He dropped his cell back in his pocket and said, 'Mazey's gotten much worse, and Dazey wants me home again.'

'I'll come with you,' I said. 'I don't think there's much more that I can do here.'

'Well, I have to thank you for coming, Harry,' said Anna. 'I really thought I was going mad until I met you at the hospital. You've been wonderful.' At that moment, her own cell buzzed. She picked it up from the table and said, 'Professor Grey.' She listened for a moment and then she said, 'What?' She looked at me, and her expression was shocked. 'Don't let him in,' she said. 'Tell security to get rid of him. Yes. You don't have to give him any excuses.'

She put the phone down, and I said, 'Who was that?'

'It's Brian Grandier. He's in reception, asking to see me.'

'*Grandier*? You're kidding me! How did he know you were here?'

'I have no idea. But you heard what I said.'

'I think we should see him,' I said. 'At least, I should. Come on, Anna, he's the key to this whole epidemic. We can't just turn him away.'

'I'm frightened,' said Anna. 'Why do you think he's come here?'

I stood up. 'Rick and me, we'll go and find out. You just wait here.'

I went to the door, and Rick got up to follow me. As I reached the door, however, I saw Brian Grandier's face in the circular window. He was right outside, staring in at me. His gray hair was brushed back, and his gray beard was neatly trimmed, and his eyes were as hard and gray as two stones.

I opened the door, and he took a step inside, so that I couldn't close it again without pushing him back into the corridor.

'Well, well,' he said. 'Mr Erskine and Professor Grey, both together. Ill met by daylight, as Shakespeare didn't say.'

'Brian Grandier,' I said. 'Or should I say *Urbain* Grandier? Because it is you, isn't it? Burned alive, and then reborn?'

The muscles in Grandier's face knotted with suppressed anger. 'I have no idea what you're talking about,' he said. 'Burned alive? Reborn? Are you mad?'

'You were reborn in exactly the same way that Misquamacus was reborn,' I persisted, trying to stay calm. 'You infected Father Zapata, didn't you, so that he couldn't tell me who you were – or rather *what* you are? But he didn't die before he told me all about you.'

'What are you doing here, Mr Grandier?' Anna demanded. 'What do you want? I'm calling security!'

'Security? I wouldn't bother to do that, if I were you,' said Urbain Grandier. 'As for what I want . . . it's very simple indeed. I want *you* to

383

stop your research on this virus, Professor Grey. And you, Mr Erskine, I thought you were going to advise your compatriots that if they didn't quit this land as soon as possible, they would die. And now they *are* dying, which makes you personally responsible for every one of their deaths.'

There was another rumble of thunder, so much closer this time that the windows rattled.

'You don't *get* it, do you?' I said. 'You're *history*, Grandier! This country has changed beyond any recognition in four hundred years, and you can't expect it to change back again. It doesn't matter any more who murdered who and who stole what. You can't turn back time. Haven't you seen the cities and the highways and the planes and the tunnels and the bridges? And as for you – those bishops who persecuted you and tortured you and burned you at the stake, they've been dead and buried for centuries, along with all of their beliefs and all of their superstitions.'

'There is still revenge,' said Urbain Grandier. 'I want my revenge, and my Indian friends want their revenge. Your ancestors didn't just steal land, they destroyed whole nations, whole cultures, whole languages – wiped them out for ever, as if they had never been. And in Europe they did the same, all in the name of Christ. Revenge is the very least that is owing to us. You have been warned not to stand in our way, both of you. This is your very last chance.'

'You can't touch us, either of us. You know that.'

384

Right in front of me, Urbain Grandier's face began to alter. His eyes became wolfish and bloodshot; his nose became longer and sharper. His skin darkened until it was almost maroon, and his lips turned black. He opened his mouth, and his teeth were sharp and amber and crowded together like a shark's.

With a chilly sense of dread, I realized what was happening. He was showing us the demon that had possessed him ever since Father Surin had exorcized his mother, Sister Marysia. This was Gressil, the demon, or the virus. He was real. He looked just like one of the demons that you see in medieval paintings and engravings, and the reason for this was that in the Middle Ages demons were openly walking abroad, and the artists had seen them and knew what they looked like.

'Of course, we cannot harm *you*,' said Grandier-Gressil, in a voice that sounded as if he had grit between his teeth. 'We have codes of honor, just like you do. But that doesn't mean that we can't punish your friends, and all those around you. We will rip them open and strangle them with their own intestines. We will blind them and make them mad. By the time we have finished, you will be pleading for mercy on their behalf.'

Another detonation of thunder sounded as if the storm was right on top of us now. The whole building shuddered, as if it had been shaken by an earthquake, and three glass retorts fell out of their stands and shattered on the floor.

We heard a man shouting and a woman scream. Then there was a splintering, crashing noise and a strong wind came whistling down the corridor, carrying with it a blizzard of paper. It sounded and felt as if the main entrance to the laboratory had been blown in. A fire alarm started to ring, and we could hear more shouting.

Rain started to patter against the window, and I glanced quickly behind me. It was almost as dark as night outside, although I could see the trees on the opposite side of the parking lot thrashing their branches like drowning bathers.

I saw something else, too. *Figures.* There were scores of dark, hunched figures making their way toward the laboratory. All of them were dressed in black, with black veils over their heads, and as they came nearer I could see that they were swaying as if they were walking in a religious procession. Nuns.

Epiphany stepped forward and confronted Grandier-Gressil. 'You're nothing but a monster,' she said, although her voice was shaking. 'You just *dare* to touch us. We're getting out of here now, and there's not a damn thing you can do about it.'

'Oh, but I can, and I will,' grated Grandier-Gressil. 'Whatever you try and do, you bitch, I can lick you.' With that he drew back his lips and waggled his tongue in a lewd simulation of cunnilingus.

But now Rick came up, took hold of Epiphany and moved her aside. He levered his revolver out of his belt and pointed it directly at Grandier-Gressil's face, only six inches from the tip of his nose. 'I think that's where you're wrong, shitface, and if you try to stop us, I swear to God that I'm going to do you an injury – like, blow your fucking head off.'

Grandier-Gressil stared at the muzzle of Rick's revolver, as if it amused him. I could swear that he was actually smiling. Three or four seconds passed, and then he suddenly made a grab for Rick's wrist.

Rick was too quick for him: he fired and hit Grandier-Gressil point-blank in the face. I was expecting him to drop dead on the spot, but I couldn't believe my eyes. His head snapped back a little, as if he had been slapped, but he stayed where he was. Not only that, the pellets from the shotshell should have blasted all the flesh from his cheekbones and blinded him, at the very least, but instead they left nothing but tiny black lumps all over his forehead and the bridge of his nose.

Rick didn't have the chance to fire a second time. Grandier-Gressil seized his wrist, wrenched the revolver out of his grasp and slung it across the laboratory, so hard that it smashed one of the windows. Then he grabbed hold of Rick's jacket and forced him face-first into one of the laboratory cabinets, cracking the windows and breaking most of the beakers and retorts inside it. Rick toppled sideways on to the floor, his face and his hands smothered in blood.

I tried to snatch Grandier-Gressil's sleeve, but he swung his arm and hit me in the ribs. It was like being hit by a scaffolding pole. Winded and bruised, I stumbled back against the wall, and before I could regain my balance, Grandier-Gressil had caught hold of Epiphany and wrapped his arm around her neck. She flailed her fists against him, trying to break free, but he yanked his elbow up even higher, almost choking her.

Outside in the corridor I could hear more screaming, and then a man shouted, 'No! No! Help me! No!' This was followed by a succession of squeaking, tearing sounds, like doors being twisted off their hinges.

'Now we are going outside,' said Grandier-Gressil. 'Now you can face the people you have wronged and tell them how sorry you are and that you beg their forgiveness.'

He tightened his stranglehold around Epiphany's throat even more. She was desperately tugging at his sleeve, but he was much too strong for her. Her eyes were bulging, and she was whining for breath.

I looked across at Anna, and all Anna could do was shake her head. We didn't have a choice. I had no doubt at all that if we didn't do what Grandier-Gressil wanted us to do, he would break Epiphany's neck right in front of us.

Twenty-Seven

Outside in the corridor, the scene was chaos, with bodies heaped everywhere. The wind was still blustering through the building, and sheets of paper were still whirling around. The doors to every one of the laboratories had been smashed open and the lab technicians dragged out into the corridor and killed. They were lying on top of each other in their bloodstained lab coats, and we could have been walking through a slaughter-house. There was blood on the floor and blood up the walls and even blood spatters on the ceiling.

Every one of the technicians had been ripped open from crotch to breastbone, and their intestines dragged out of them, wound around their necks and used to strangle them. Whoever had killed them had made no distinction: there were women lying there, as well as men. The sight of all those glistening beige ropes made me gag, and the stench of feces and bile and half-digested food was overwhelming.

Grandier-Gressil forced Epiphany along the corridor toward the main entrance, and Anna and I reluctantly followed him. We had to high-step over the bodies, as if we were performing horses. I had left Rick sitting on the floor of the laboratory, half-concussed. His chin was badly cut and his left eye was closing up, but I didn't think that he was too badly injured.

The reception area was strewn with shattered glass and broken furniture and potted palms that had been knocked over and smashed. The stuffing had been torn out of a brown leather couch, so that it looked like a disemboweled cow.

The storm was even more furious now. The sky was black, and lightning was crackling all around us. Every now and then there was a deafening bellow of thunder and the rain would lash across the parking lot even harder, flooding the gutters and filling the drains. The wind was so strong that we had to keep our heads down and lean against it.

Yet – they were there, waiting for us. There were more nuns than I could count, maybe fifty, maybe a hundred. They were standing in a semi-circle, their rain-sodden habits flapping with a sound like muted applause. Right in the middle of this semicircle stood Matchitehew and Megedagik. Although it was so dark, they were lit up intermittently by flashes of lightning, so that I could see at last what they really looked like – the sons of Misquamacus, the greatest wonder-worker who had ever lived, and lived again, and then again.

They were both nearly seven feet tall, and they both wore elaborate headdresses with buffalo horns on them and patterned blankets over their shoulders, although one of them was in black and the other red. They both wore necklaces, too, of teeth and beads and bones, and both of them had rattles hanging from their waistbands, with eagle feathers and beads and tufts of hair attached to them.

As before, they had beetles crawling all over them, hard-shelled and shiny. Some of the beetles dropped to the ground, but they immediately crawled back on to the brothers' bare feet and up their legs.

Their faces were extraordinary. I didn't know which one was Matchitehew and which was Megedagik, but they both had deep-set eyes, sharply-sculptured cheekbones and hooked noses. Their cheeks were painted with white stripes.

Grandier-Gressil forced Epiphany down the steps and across the parking lot to stand right in front of them. Then he twisted around and pointed with his free hand toward me and Anna. 'They have come to ask for your mercy!' he shouted at the wonder-workers. 'They have come to tell you that they will do everything they can to help you claim back your land!'

The wonder-worker with the red blanket said, '*Is this true?*'

I tried to hold Anna back by catching at her hand, but she shook herself free from me and stepped forward until she was standing right beside Grandier-Gressil and Epiphany.

There was another rumble of thunder, but it seemed to be further away now, and quite suddenly the wind began to subside and the rain ease off. I saw a last flicker of lightning off to the west, and then the storm appeared to be passing, although the sky remained dark. It was so quiet now that I could hear Anna speaking quite clearly.

'I can't do what you ask,' she said. 'You have your beliefs, but I have mine. I swore when I started my career to save as many lives as I could, and that is what I have to do. I am sad for all of your people who were killed and had their land taken away from them, but killing more innocent people will never bring them back – either your people or your land.'

'*You do not belong here,*' said the wonder-worker in the red blanket. I assumed he was Matchitehew, because his brother, Megedagik, had hardly spoken before. '*All we are doing is reclaiming the country that is rightfully ours. You must go, and if you will not go, then we will make you go.*'

'Do you know how many thousands of people have already died because of this sickness you've been spreading?' said Anna. 'Do you know many *millions* are going to die, if I don't find a way to stop you? Far more people than *we* ever killed!'

She was clenching her fists in righteous anger, and I have to admit that I was deeply impressed by how brave she was, standing alone in front of these two looming figures, with their head-dresses and their rattles, and all of these silent, creepy nuns.

'*An eye for an eye!*' said a sharp, female voice.

Out of the crowd of nuns standing behind Matchitehew and Megedagik, a taller nun appeared with her face uncovered. Her face was long and oval, and it was so pale that it could have been carved out of ivory. Her eyes, however, were coal-black, with charcoal circles around them, as if she hadn't slept for centuries.

'So your people have multiplied, since you

settled here?' she said. 'They have fornicated, like you, you slut! There are millions of you now, are there? Well, there would have been millions of *these* people, if they had been given the chance to live in their own land and prosper. It is just as much of a sin to have denied a people what they might have been, as to have denied them what they once were.'

'It was you who threatened me before, wasn't it?' Anna challenged her. 'It was you who assaulted me. I didn't give in to you then, and I won't give in to you now, no matter what you do.'

'Do you know who I am?' said the nun, coming even closer to Anna and staring into her face, unblinking. 'I am Jeanne des Anges, Mother Superior of the Ursuline Convent of Loudun. Do you know who brought me back to life and brought me here? Gressil, the Lord of Infection, in the shape of Father Grandier, aided by the power of Matchitehew and Megedagik, the wonder-workers. We five together are justice. We are revenge. We are a spiritual league to bring hypocrites and thieves and murderers to account, no matter how long ago they committed their sins!'

Anna tried to hold her ground, but the nun took another step closer to her, and she was so intimidating that Anna stepped back two paces. I could see that Grandier-Gressil was watching this confrontation with the same sardonic smile as before, although he still kept his choke-hold around Epiphany's neck.

Matchitehew and Megedagik were watching,

393

too, their feathers hanging damply now the wind had dropped, but their shoulders still alive with glittering beetles. It was still very dark, but up above us the clouds were gradually beginning to tear apart, like damp gray tissue-paper.

'We are the carriers of this infection, me and my sisters,' said Jeanne des Anges. She spoke in a triumphant croak, and as she did she stooped down and began to gather up the heavy wet hem of her habit. Slowly, she lifted it up, higher and higher, first of all revealing her thin white legs, and then higher still, right up under her breasts. What appeared at first sight to be a triangle of brown hair between her legs was not hair at all, but brown bedbugs, hundreds of them, swarming in and out of the moist white lips of her vulva and down her thighs.

She held her habit up like that for almost five seconds, and then she let it drop down to the ground again.

'There is no stopping us,' she said. 'And you, Professor Grey, must agree not to try.'

As if to emphasize her point, she turned to Grandier-Gressil, and Grandier-Gressil jerked Epiphany's head sideways, so that she let out a stifled gasp of pain.

I stepped forward until I was standing beside Anna. My heart was thumping, but Jeanne des Anges didn't even look at me. She kept her eyes on Anna, as if she were trying to hypnotize her.

'Anna,' I said, out of the corner of my mouth. 'For Christ's sake, Anna, just say yes, you'll do whatever they want. Let's *both* say yes. Tell them you'll stop your research, and I'll agree to spread the word. Maybe it will save some lives if I do.'

'I don't think we have to,' she said, quite calmly.

'What?'

'There's another way. I *hope* there's another way, anyhow. I can't be sure of it, but if you were right about the manitous—'

'Manitous exist. I know they do. I've seen the proof of it.'

'I meant what you said about modern manitous being more powerful than ancient manitous.'

We were interrupted by Jeanne Saint Anges. 'So do you *agree*, professor?' she asked, in her harsh, penetrating voice. A watery sun was beginning to appear behind the clouds. At the moment it looked more like the moon than the sun, because it was silver, but the wet asphalt was glistening, and the scores of nuns standing silently around us appeared more sinister than ever, because they could no longer be mistaken for shadows. They were real.

Anna took a breath, but she didn't get the chance to answer, because at that moment the silence in the parking lot was shattered by a loud, echoing gunshot. Shreds of black cloth were blown from the habit of one of the nuns who was standing close to Grandier-Gressil, and she flinched and staggered a few paces, but she didn't fall over.

Rick came stalking unsteadily down the laboratory steps. He was still wearing a beard of dried blood, and he was holding his revolver in both hands and pointing it directly at Grandier-Gressil.

Anna gripped my arm and said, 'Oh God, Harry! Don't let him do it! He's going to spoil everything!'

'Rick!' I shouted. 'Rick, put it *down!*'

But Rick ignored me. He walked up to Grandier-Gressil, stuck the muzzle of his gun into his side and said, 'Let her go, you freak, or I'll blow you outside in!'

To my surprise, Grandier-Gressil let go of Epiphany and stood back, with both of his hands in the air. They were actually more like claws than hands, with mottled gray skin and long, curved fingernails.

Rick reached out for Epiphany and said, 'Go on, darling, you go over there and get yourself into my van. You too, Wizard! Anna! We've all decided that we've had enough of this shit, and we're leaving!'

We had hardly had time to turn around, though, before we heard an ear-splitting howl that made me go cold all over. It went on and on, and it sounded like every coyote that ever existed howling all at once. A second later, a loud tapping noise started up, arrhythmic but insistent, and that made me go even colder, because I knew exactly what it was. It was the tapping of medicine sticks, which meant that Matchitehew and Megedagik were calling on something from Native American magic to stop us.

Not only that, but the nuns were circling themselves around so that they were blocking our way toward Rick's van. They had moved slowly before, when I had first seen them approaching the laboratory, but now they seemed to multiply in front of my eyes. We had managed to run less than thirty feet before we realized that escaping was out of the question. Even if we forgot about Rick's van and tried to make it to the main laboratory gates, those nuns would surround us before we were even halfway there.

We all stopped and turned around again. Grandier-Gressil and Jeanne des Anges were standing side by side with pitying smiles on their faces, two beings resurrected from a time when people truly believed in demons. Right behind them towered Matchitehew and Megedagik. It was Megedagik who was howling, with his eyes closed and his head thrown back, while Matchitehew was beating out that complicated clatter with his medicine sticks.

I felt exhausted and beaten, and most of all I felt a cold sense of utter dread. I had thought that I would never again hear those medicine sticks tapping, and see spirits rising out of nowhere, and have to fight against the bitter resentment that still festers beneath our feet, in the very ground we walk on, because that ground isn't ours.

But Rick wasn't going to give in so easy. He never had given in to anyone or anything, ever since I'd known him. He walked back toward Grandier-Gressil and fired his revolver again, and then again. The shots tore at Grandier-Gressil's coat and vest, but they had no more impact than if Rick had gone up to him and simply punched him with his fist.

Megedagik's howling reached a crescendo, and

Matchitehew was tapping the medicine sticks so fast that they were a blur.

Rick strode even nearer to Grandier-Gressil and Jeanne des Anges, still leveling his gun at him. Before he could reach them, though, three or four of the nuns appeared from behind them and barred his way. They moved so quickly that I could hardly believe what I was seeing. They *scuttled*, like characters in a speeded-up movie.

'Oh please God,' Anna panted, right beside me. 'Don't let these be what I think they are.'

Megedagik was screeching now, and as he did so the nuns lifted their habits like Jeanne des Anges had lifted hers. To my horror, though, I could see that they weren't pulling up their habits with human hands, but with sharp insect-like legs. They clawed their habits right back over their heads, tearing off their veils as well, and it was then that they revealed what they really were. Not nuns, not even women, but huge amber-colored bedbugs, with hard articulated shells and waving antennae.

Even Rick stopped in his tracks. He looked back at me and his eyes were wide with sheer terror.

'*Wizard*!' he shouted.

He turned back to face the bedbugs, but even before he could raise his revolver, three of them had run toward him on their six legs and sprung on him. They weren't as tall as he was, but each of them must have weighed twice as much, because they knocked him on to his back and clambered all over him.

'*Wizard!*' he screamed. '*Wizard!*'

I went up to him, as near as I could. He was

398

staring wildly up at me from underneath the carapace of one of the bedbugs. The three of them were all over him, and his face was almost all I could see of him.

I clenched my fist and thumped one of them on the back of the head, three times as hard as I could, but it had no effect at all. It was like hitting a copper water-tank. The stench of rotten fruit was so strong that I was close to bringing up my coffee. Next I tried to get my fingers underneath the edge of one of their shells, but it was much too heavy for me to lift it.

Rick let out a thick, prolonged gargle, and I stepped away because I realized then that there was nothing I could do to save him. One of the bedbugs had torn open his black denim shirt and then torn open his stomach. I could already see his intestines bulging out, and I didn't want to see any more.

I looked over at Grandier-Gressil, and his demonic red eyes were alight with pleasure. Beside him, Jeanne des Anges had her hand pressed into the front of her habit, deep between her legs. Her lips were parted, and her eyes were half-closed.

Behind them, Matchitehew and Megedagik were swaying and stamping their feet. The rattle of medicine sticks was as loud as sporadic machine-gun fire.

I felt a hand on my shoulder, and I jumped. It was Anna.

'We'll have to do it now,' she said. Her mascara had run, so it looked as if she was crying black tears.

'Do what?'

'I was going to do this before Rick came out . . . go up to Grandier as if I was going to agree to stop my research . . .'

'And?'

She reached into the pocket of her lab coat and took out a hypodermic syringe with a yellow plastic cap on it. She pressed it into my hand, making sure that Grandier-Gressil didn't see her doing it.

'I'll approach him now. If I don't, he's going to have those creatures kill Epiphany next. You come with me. Move behind him, and when I've got his full attention, stab him in the neck with this. Make sure you press the plunger right down.'

'What is it?' My voice was shaky because right behind me, I could indistinctly hear a treacly, stretching sound, and several desperate grunts. That was Rick, in the last stages of being strangled with his own bowels.

Anna and I went over to Grandier-Gressil. I couldn't help myself from looking at Rick as we walked around him, but all I could see was those gigantic bedbugs climbing all over each other, with loops and smears of blood on their shells.

'Don't tell me that we've convinced you,' said Grandier-Gressil, raising his voice so that we could hear him over the howling and the tapping of medicine sticks. Jeanne des Anges was standing very close to him, with her eyes closed as if she was dreaming, although I had the feeling that she was listening to us intently.

'I can't see you murder any more of us like this,' said Anna. She lifted her hand toward the shattered entrance to the laboratory building. 'All of those lab technicians . . . they didn't deserve to die like that. Neither did this man. He was only trying to protect us and help us to get away.'

'All you had to say was yes,' Grandier-Gressil said, grinning. He nodded toward Epiphany, who was standing on her own with her back turned, so that she wouldn't have to look at Rick and the bedbugs jolting and jostling against each other as they climbed all over him. 'I assume you *are* going to say yes? You don't want to see that lovely young Nubian die in the same way, do you?'

'I don't think I have much alternative, do I?' said Anna. Her integrity amazed me. Even now she wasn't going to say yes to him. Personally, I would have told him anything he wanted to hear, so long as he didn't send those monstrous bedbugs to tear anybody else apart, especially Epiphany.

'You must give me your solemn promise,' said Grandier-Gressil. 'And don't even *think* of breaking it. If you do, my darling black sisters will go hunting for your nearest and dearest. Your mother, Caroline. Your father, Daniel. Your brother, Luke.'

'You know my family?' asked Anna. 'You know all their *names*?' At the same time, she nudged me, hard, and I knew that the moment had come for me to strike. While Grandier-Gressil gloatingly told Anna that he knew *everything* about his enemies, all of them, I sidled around to the left, until I was standing close behind his right shoulder. Jeanne des Anges was now leaning against his *left* shoulder, her fingers stroking the side of his neck and playing with his wiry gray hair. If her eyes had been open, she would have been looking straight at me. For the moment, however, she seemed to be lost in a world of her own. All of that howling and tapping and grisly killing had obviously aroused her.

Ann was saying, 'You realize how much this promise conflicts with my professional principles and my religious beliefs—?' She didn't look at me, but I realized that she was trying to hold Grandier-Gressil's attention so that he wouldn't suddenly become aware that I'd moved around behind him.

My own attention was caught for a split-second by the giant bedbugs that were crawling over Rick's bloody and half-dismembered body. It looked as if they had finished with him now, and they were turning toward Epiphany, with their antennae twitching.

This had to be the moment. I was holding the hypodermic in my left-hand coat pocket, and I pushed the plastic cap off it with my thumb. Then, as fast as I could, I whipped it out and stabbed it into Grandier-Gressil's neck. It felt like stabbing a needle into thick papier-mâché and made the same kind of *chut!* sound.

He jolted with shock, jerking his arm up to feel what had pricked him and twisting his head around. He hit me hard in the ribs with his elbow, trying to knock me away, but I pressed the hypodermic's plunger all the way down, and then left it dangling in his neck.

'*Qu'est-ce que tu as fait pour moi, salaud!*' he

402

screamed. '*Qu'est-ce que tu as fait pour moi, tu diable!*'

He came after me, his eyes red, his yellow shark's teeth bared in rage. Jeanne des Anges opened her eyes and stood rigid, her arms by her sides with her hands looking as if they were fixed on backward, her ivory-white face even more elongated and unearthly.

'*You cunts*!' she shrieked. 'You *miserable* shit-swallowers! What have you *done*!'

I backed away from Grandier-Gressil, but there wasn't any place for me to go. I was surrounded by nuns, and I collided with three or four of them. I could feel their hard-shelled bodies and their insect legs beneath their habits. They jostled me and pushed me, and the next thing I knew Grandier-Gressil had seized my sleeve.

Instead of hitting me, though, he stood still, although he didn't release his grip. He stared at me with that gray demon's face, and I could see that he was beginning to find difficulty in breathing. His chest rose and fell like an old-fashioned leather bellows, and I could hear the air rasping in and out of his throat.

'*Tu es fou,*' he said. '*Vous n'avez pas compris, vous avez fait? Vous m'avez parlé de l'histoire. Qu'est-ce dio vous connaissez l'histoire, vous la fraude, vous faux, vous diseuse de bonne aventure.*'

I stared back at him – it – or whatever he was.

'Do you know something?' I told him. 'I don't understand a single fucking word you're saying.'

He almost smiled. His black upper lip curled upward, and he nodded. 'This was meant to be, wasn't it?' he said. 'This was always meant to

403

happen this way. That's why we couldn't touch you two. You were our nemeses.'

With that, he let go of my sleeve and dropped to the ground at my feet. Jeanne des Anges took two or three stiff-legged steps toward us, but then she stopped and looked at me, aghast.

Grandier-Gressil shriveled. He literally shriveled up, his head collapsing into the collar of his shirt, his sleeves flattening out, his coat folding up. Within a few seconds he was nothing but ash, and the light damp breeze that was blowing across the parking lot began to whirl him away.

All around us, the nuns began to fade and disappear. The monstrous bedbugs, too, because that was what they were. One moment they were translucent, and I could still see their shadowy outlines, but the next they were gone altogether, as if they had never been there.

Jeanne des Anges was the last to fade away. She spoke some obscenity, which echoed like somebody calling out to us from a crypt, and then she was gone.

Only Matchitehew and Megedagik remained, their feathers and horsehair decorations fluffing in the wind, but even they seemed blurry and unfocused. Either that, or I was tired out and suffering from eye strain.

They looked as weary as I felt, but they stood there upright and dignified, and even though I couldn't forgive them for what they had done, and all of the innocent people they had caused to die, I could understand why they'd done it.

'I think our father knew that the story of our people had to end like this,' said Matchitehew.

'We will never forget how you murdered our women and children, and how you destroyed our crops and burned our homes, and even washed away the memory of what we were. And after you had done that, what did you do? You went into your churches, and you thanked your God for what he had given you.'

He paused, and then he said, 'We spit on you.'

I was about to say something to him and his brother when there were two thunderous bangs, like two bombs exploding. A shock wave almost knocked me off my feet, and it made Anna and Epiphany both stagger too.

Two clouds of gray smoke rolled up into the air, although they were quickly snatched away by the wind and vanished. All we saw were two ravens, flying high above the trees, and then they were gone, too.

I leaned down and picked up the hypodermic. Anna had gone over to Epiphany, and they were holding each other tight, too stunned and shaken even to cry.

I held up the hypodermic and said, 'It was that Meramac School virus, wasn't it?'

Anna nodded. 'You said that everything has its manitou, didn't you? You were right.'

I looked around at the wreckage of the health laboratory, and Rick's ripped-open body, and Grandier-Gressil's empty gray suit, and I thought of Misquamacus. Mostly, though, I thought of Singing Rock. I could almost hear him saying, 'Even the wind has its manitou, Harry, and the wind blows every day, and the wind never forgets where it blew the day before.'

Twenty-Eight

As I don't have to tell you, the BV-1 retrovirus disappeared overnight, and everybody who was showing symptoms of it slowly recovered. The CDC were at a loss to explain why, so I thought I'd set the record straight, even if you don't believe me. I don't know what the final death-toll was, and I don't suppose that we'll ever know for sure, although it ran into several thousands. The only lasting effect among the million or so survivors appeared to be persistent nightmares about insects crawling all over them.

Mazey survived, but only just, and it took her weeks to fully recover. She was only just well enough to come with Dazey and me to Rick's funeral. It was a hot day, too hot to wear black, and I stayed out of earshot of the priest's valedictory prayers. Dazey cried all the way through it, a thin howl that reminded me uncomfortably of Megedagik's howling.

After two weeks I flew back to New York. I would have preferred to go back to Florida, where the rich old ladies lived, but I guessed that Detective Blezard still had my card marked. As for my own cards, they stayed black, and the pictures never returned, so I had to buy a new deck. I put it down as business expenses.

On the way back to New York I stopped off in St Louis and went to see Anna at her laboratory at SLU. Epiphany was there, too, and we all went out to lunch together at an Italian restaurant called Joseph's, on North Sixth Street. None of us were very hungry, because we still had a strange and sickening experience to talk about, but the place was bustling and cheerful, which was what we needed.

I was pleased to see Epiphany again, too. You know when you sometimes meet people and immediately get along with them, as if you had known them practically all your life? She and me were like that. By the time we had finished our meal I was sorely tempted to stay in St Louis so that I could get to know her better. After all, I thought, all I ever need to set up shop is a deck of cards and a steady supply of wealthy old biddies who needed to hear if they were ever going to find themselves a gigolo.

Anna said, 'We're making very good progress with the Meramac School virus. I'll almost be sorry when we find a way to make it destroy itself. God knows what would have happened if we hadn't been able to kill BV-1.'

'So how about BV-1?' I asked her. 'Have you found out any more about that?'

She nodded. 'We've done hundreds of tests on those samples I took from Cedars-Sinai, and we have some theories, although I have to admit that they're only theories. BV-1 is a very old-fashioned virus, even when you compare it with the virus that caused the Spanish flu pandemic in 1918. We believe it was Grandier's influence that made it so deadly – or should I say Gressil's? I don't know. Maybe I should say Satan's.'

'Gressil himself was the virus,' said Epiphany. 'We think that he impregnated Jeanne des Anges with those infected bedbugs, and that when she had given birth to them they somehow combined together to form those giant bedbugs. There are plenty of other creatures in nature which combine together to form one larger creature, just like amoebas splitting, but in reverse.'

'You were so right about Urbain Grandier and those two wonder-workers being behind the times, though,' said Anna. 'Only certain people caught the BV-1 virus, and at first we couldn't understand why. I did some genealogical research on them, though. We're still not one hundred percent sure of it, but it seems as if they were the direct descendants of the colonists who landed in America in the 1600s, when those three were first alive.'

'But the virus itself,' I said. 'How did it make people have fits like that and bring up so much blood?'

'Again, we can't be completely sure. But what Gressil seemed to do was invade your body and your mind with his own personality. He made you vomit out all of your blood, which contained any antibodies that might have prevented him from taking you over, and then he pushed your own personality out of your brain, which made you convulse. That was why its victims kept saying, "*Get it out of me!*" And that's why they appeared to come alive again, after they had died.'

She toyed with the wild mushroom risotto that she had ordered, and then laid her fork down. 'I'm sorry, I can't eat this. I keep thinking of

David and what he must have suffered. And your friend Rick. And all of those other poor people who died.'

Her eyes filled with tears, and she wiped them with her napkin. Epiphany reached across the table and held her hand.

'Hey – it's going to take all three of us a long time to get over this,' I told them. 'Apart from that, nobody will *ever* understand what we did, although it's probably better that they don't. Knowing what's *really* out there, you know – knowing what they really need to be afraid of – that's more than most people could take without going doolally.'

It started to rain as I left Anna and Epiphany at the entrance to SLU. An ambulance was turning in, with its siren shrieking, and I didn't hear what it was that Epiphany said to me. I kissed them both, and then I hailed a cab and asked the driver to take me to Lambert. I could still taste Epiphany's perfume on my lips.

When we were halfway to the airport, my cell buzzed, and I saw that I had received a text message. It said simply: *One day can you tell my fortune? E.*